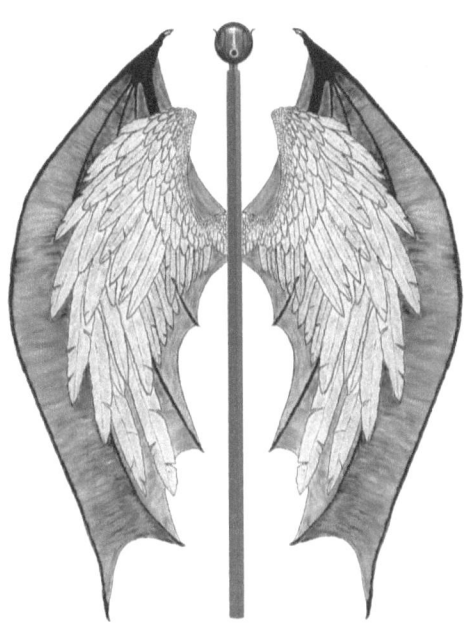

Destiny's Flame

(A Land of Destiny Novel)

By D.S. Schmeckpeper

Printed in the United States of America

First Printing: April 2015

Published by Seraph Wing Publishing

ISBN-13 978-0-9907111-2-4 (ebook)
ISBN-13 978-0-9907111-3-1 (print)

Acknowledgements:

A huge thank you to my wonderful husband, Steve. Your love, support and encouragement mean so much to me. Without you, there would be no Altierra, and I am honored to be able to name you as my co-author. Another special thank you for the world map, gorgeous cover and all the other art you contribute on a regular basis.

I'd like to thank my editor, Ella Medler, for your extreme patience and willingness to help me with this manuscript, despite my insane scheduling issues. You'll never know how much I appreciate all of your advice and encouragement. You have been my rock as I've embarked down this path once again. I would be lost without you, and am so glad to call you my friend.

To my editor, Matt Schiariti, you are always honest with me, even when it would be easier not to be. I have so much respect for you and can't thank you enough for all your hard work. I am lucky to know you and am a better person for it. I hope you haven't been too traumatized and will continue to edit for me in the future. You'd better ... I'd miss your wit and "epic notes."

Judith Lauren Frazee, your continued support and encouragement has meant the world to me. You work tirelessly to promote so many Indie authors, and it is often a thankless job. I'm so glad we met and that you accepted me as one of your platypires. Look forward to *maybe* seeing a real platypire in the next book! Platypire World Domination!

Colleen Treep, you're the most awesome boss in the world! Thanks for listening to me go on and on about anything and everything to do with this book and for being so understanding.

To my Beta Readers–Laura Ice, Katie Harder-Schauer, Victoria Clemente, Laurie Bianchi, Jacinta Brown, Jessica Tarrats, Lacia Carabas, Toni Michelle, Riley Wiederhold and Kelly Clevinger– thank you for everything you have done. Each and every one of you has touched this book in some way, and helped to make it better.

Leslie Cox, every writer should have a fan like you. Your positive, upbeat attitude is an inspiration to us all. You're always there to help out however you can, and words cannot express the gratitude I feel for you. You are truly an angel in my eyes!

A special note of thanks to Katie Harder-Schauer for helping with chapter titles.

Last, but not least, a huge thanks to you, the reader. Without readers, there would be no reason for writers to write. I hope you enjoy Destiny's Flame.

This book is dedicated to Steve.
You are the calm to my storm.
I love you.

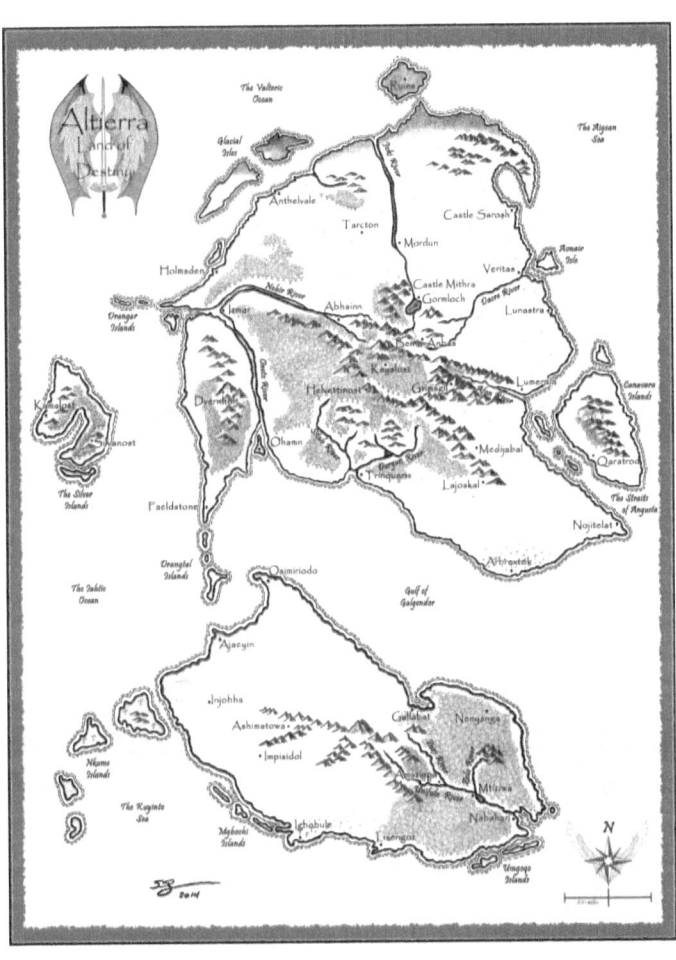

Chapter One
Accountability

P*op.*

Izmar, where it all began. Had it really only been a year since he had last set foot here? Arcus released his beautiful wife, Siobhan, to stand on her own. The two parrots on his left shoulder squawked and took flight. After circling around, the birds shifted into his friends, Celeste and Tarnelius, as they landed. Siobhan handed him the staff she had been holding for him.

Arcus looked around and tried to get his bearings. They had teleported outside, to an alley only a block away from the Dragonfire Tavern, a bar he and Joseph used to frequent. Arcus furrowed his brow as he thought about the last time he was here.

"What's wrong, Arcus?" Siobhan asked.

"Nothing, Shiv. It's just been a while. Come on, let's get out of this alleyway before some idiot thinks it would be a good idea to try and mug us."

Tarnelius smirked. "Are you actually worried about being mugged, Arcus?" The elf adjusted his hooded cloak, attempting to hide his ears.

"Not at all. I just don't want Siobhan to have cause to be mad at me for using 'unnecessary force'."

They walked out of the grimy alley toward the docks. The stale air of the city was replaced by the fresher smell of the salt air. All around them, sailors and merchants bustled about. People carried cargo on and off the ships, while drunks and vagabonds shouted and begged.

"Let's split up," Celeste said, eying the chaos all around them. "Why don't the two of you check out the south wharf, and Siobhan and I will take the north."

Arcus nodded. Breaking off toward the south wharf, he and Tarnelius approached a man barking out orders in front of a large carrack. The man stood about as tall as Tarnelius, but was very bulky and muscular. Tattoos covered his shaven head and exposed, muscular arms.

The carrack bore the name "*The Southern Hope*".

"Are you the captain of this vessel, sir?" Tarnelius asked.

"Aye. Who wants to know?"

"My name is Tarnelius, and this is Arcus. We are trying to book passage to the southern continent, on the kedistam side. There are four of us altogether, including ourselves and our wives."

The man paused and looked them over from head to foot. "I don't transport passengers. This is a trading vessel. The seas get choppy out there, and I don't need any lubbers puking their guts out on my ship. Besides, it's bad luck to have a woman on board. Two would be twice as bad."

"What if one of those women were able to control the weather and guarantee smooth sailing?"

The captain cocked his head to the side as he seemed to consider this. "Seventy-five gold pieces each, to be paid when you board. Also, I want this woman to prove this claim before we leave."

Arcus' gray eyes narrowed. "That's insane. I happen to know that the normal passage to the southlands is never more than thirty gold."

"If you want aboard my ship, you have to play by my rules. Feel free to see if anyone else will sail you to Gallabat; it makes no difference to me. Just make sure you are here before high tide tomorrow morning, if you are coming along. Good day, gentlemen."

"Wait, you never told us your name. How will we look for you?" Tarnelius asked.

The man yelled back over his shoulder as he strode up the gangplank. "It's Stone."

The pair continued down the wharf, to see if they would have better luck elsewhere.

"I'll check in with Celeste and Siobhan, see what kind of luck they've had," said Tarnelius.

The two elves, Tarnelius and Celeste, had married almost eleven months prior. The bonding ritual split their souls so that they each carried half of the other's. Among other things, this allowed them to communicate even when they weren't together.

"Celeste says they've been shot down by six captains because few travel that way. They were told to meet the captain of a ship that does sail to Gallabat in some tavern. She wants us to meet them there after we finish up."

Tarnelius and Arcus approached several other vessels without success, trying to book passage to the southern continent. They had been hoping to find the family of their fallen friend, Therinsalla. However, none of the other captains they were able to speak to crossed the Gulf of Galgendor. Most of them commanded Galley ships, intended for river travel or following the coastline. *The Southern Hope* was, by far, the largest ship in the port. Discouraged, the pair turned to go find their women.

Izmar was a sprawling city that had started as a small port town. Near the docks, there were several bars and inns. From there, the buildings spread out more haphazardly. In the northern part of town there was a large manor house where the Lord of Izmar lived. A sorcerer school lay to the east. In between were many residences, other businesses and even more bars. Though the city was a bustling port of trade, it contained a dark and chaotic underworld. The law always favored whomever offered the biggest bribe.

Leaving the docks behind, Arcus and Tarnelius entered the tavern district. "Celeste said they were in a bar called the Dragonfire Tavern," said Tarnelius.

Arcus' eyes widened, "The Dra–"

"Arcus, is that you?" came a feminine voice from behind them.

Arcus spun around. Standing a few feet away, with a look of surprise on her face, was a short young woman with curly brown hair and chocolate colored eyes. A dark blue dress with silver embroidery on the neckline and sleeves clung to her slender frame.

"Victoria?" he asked, astonished.

She flung her arms around his neck. "Arcus! It *is* you. I've missed you so much."

Arcus stiffened and tried to disentangle himself.

Tarnelius smirked. "I'll just be waiting in there with *our* wives. See you soon." He strode away.

"Tarnelius, wait!" Arcus begged, but the elf ignored him.

"So, this is awkward," said Victoria.

"What is?" Arcus snapped as he ran his hands through his unruly black hair.

"You're married now? You? I was sure you'd be single forever. You certainly never gave me or any of the other girls a second glance in school. Is she a sorcerer, too?"

"No, she isn't. She's a paladin."

"Huh. So that's what you're into. Don't you find the warrior type to be emasculating?"

"Not that it's any of your business, but no, I don't."

"You still friends with that loser, Joseph?"

"I haven't seen him since we left. Listen, I really need to go. My wife and friends are waiting for me in there. It was good seeing you." Arcus turned away, pretending not to notice her pout. He walked toward the Dragonfire Tavern, feeling nervous. The last time he had been inside this bar, he had gotten into a fight and "accidentally" killed his opponent. He didn't want to go in there, but he had no way to get his friends out if he didn't. He could wait, but then he'd be stuck out here with Victoria. He sighed. Maybe, if he kept his head down, the bartender wouldn't recognize him.

Inside, Arcus located the rest of his group seated in the corner farthest away from the bar. That was something, at least. Trying to not draw attention to himself, he walked straight to their table and sat in a chair with his back to the bar.

Arcus glowered at Tarnelius. "I was trying to get you to wait."

"I figured you'd have an easier time escaping your little friend if she knew we were waiting."

"'She?' Who is this 'she,' Arcus?" Siobhan asked, smirking.

"Someone Joseph used to have a crush on. She was in the sorcerer school with us. That's not important right now. What *is* important is that we need to get out of this bar."

"We can't leave now." Celeste slid her chair closer to the table and leaned forward. "We're waiting for Captain Zane to come back. He said he would speak with us, but that he had a meeting to take care of on his ship first. I think he may be willing to negotiate."

"Then we'll wait for him outside. We need to leave."

"Arcus! There you are." Victoria's shrill voice cut through him like a knife. "Why don't you introduce me to your … friends?"

Arcus flinched, then sighed. "Everyone, this is Victoria. She and I went to school here together. Victoria, meet Tarnelius, Celeste and my wife, Siobhan."

Victoria smirked at Arcus, a predator's grin gracing her lips. Her eyes seemed to undress him as she stared for far too long before moving on to the rest of the group. He uneasily remembered the way she used to always watch him. She would follow him around and chatter about all sorts of inane things. He had never understood why Joseph had been so enamored with Victoria. Arcus glanced at Siobhan and smiled weakly. He hoped she understood Victoria wasn't a threat.

Victoria moved on to Tarnelius, who wore brown pants and a tan shirt, with a hunter-green cloak. His hood was lowered, exposing golden blond hair that hung down past his shoulders. His pointed ears poked through his hair. He had huge green eyes that almost glowed. Victoria wrinkled her brow as if confused about something. She looked to Celeste, who had the same eyes. Jet black hair framed her face and cascaded down the back of her deep green dress. As was normal for her, her huge white feathery angel wings were magically tucked away so that no one could see them. Arcus knew she hated to draw attention to herself in public. Victoria snapped her fingers, grinning. "You two are elves! I've never met any elves before."

Tarnelius nodded to her in acknowledgment.

Siobhan rose to her feet and looked down at Victoria, her hand extended in greeting. She wore tan riding breeches and a blue blouse. She was tall, only a couple of inches shy of six feet, and had hazel eyes and shoulder-length coppery red hair. Victoria winced at the strength of the paladin's grip as they shook hands.

Siobhan returned to her seat. With a forced smile, she leaned toward Arcus and took his hand possessively. He gave her hand a reassuring squeeze and lightly kissed her on the cheek. Siobhan met his gaze, her eyes conflicted. Great. She *was* jealous and worried. Arcus wished he could have kept them apart. In fact, he wished he could have kept them all out of this gods-forsaken bar.

Victoria hesitated for a moment, then turned to a neighboring table to grab one of their chairs. Dragging it over, she sat down with a smirk.

"I'm sorry, Victoria, but we were just leaving," Arcus said.

"Why? Outside you told me that you were coming inside to join them. Are you avoiding me?"

"We aren't leaving, Arcus," said Siobhan. We are waiting for Zane to come back."

Arcus sighed and shook his head, resigned to his fate. He decided not to speak another word of argument, and held his tongue. Victoria relaxed and started chattering animatedly. She seemed determined to tell Siobhan embarrassing stories about him, but Arcus couldn't care less. He didn't even focus on what they were talking about, because his mind insisted on traveling in ten directions at once. A barmaid brought them all mugs of ale. Arcus picked up his and Siobhan's, his hands flashing green from a purification spell. It had become a reflex to him, back when he often came here. The pewter mugs were never cleaned well and he soon learned the spell out of necessity. To forget the simple act would be to regret it later. He hoped that Siobhan hadn't had much to drink before he got there.

After several long minutes, the door opened and Arcus heard the unmistakable sound of someone wearing heavy armor walk in. The bartender, Jack, hurried to meet him.

"Oh, Constable Bennett, I'm so glad you stopped in. There is a little matter I needed to speak to you about. Come in, I'll get you a drink." Jack lowered his voice as he led the armored man over toward the bar.

Arcus pulled his cowl lower over his head and slouched down, but all too soon, the pair of them walked over to Arcus' table.

Arcus set his mug down and rubbed his temples. He looked up at the bartender, a resigned expression on his face. "Hi, Jack. It's been a while, hasn't it?"

"Not anywhere near long enough. You never did pay for the damages you and your delinquent friend caused here. I can't believe you were so arrogant as to think I wouldn't recognize you."

Constable Bennett placed his hand on Arcus' shoulder. "You are under arrest for the charge of second degree murder, as well as destruction of property and disruption of the peace."

"I think you need to take your hand off me," Arcus snarled. He gripped his staff and stood up to face the constable, who dropped his hand.

"Arcus, calm down," Siobhan said in a warning tone.

The constable placed an armored hand on the hilt of his gleaming broadsword. "Will you come peacefully?"

"No, I don't think so. Look, what happened that night was a mistake, and those other guys started it. If anyone should be charged for anything, it's them."

"Did you, or did you not, kill that man?" Bennett glared at him.

"I don't think I should answer that question."

"That means yes." Bennett lunged and grabbed Arcus by the arm.

Arcus' forearms burst into waves of searing flame. The constable yelped and let go, shaking his burnt hands wildly. The smell of burning flesh weighed heavily on the air. Before anyone could react, Arcus bolted for the door, flinging it open and storming through.

"Wait here!" Siobhan said to the others. She jumped up and followed after him through the still-open door. "Arcus, stop. That is enough!"

He froze, regarding her sadly. "I told you we needed to leave."

"You need to turn yourself in."

"You know what? I think the heat from being encased in metal most of the time might have gone to your head. Why on earth would I turn myself in? We are supposed to be leaving to head south, or have you forgotten?"

The door burst open and the constable stormed toward them, his blistered hands held out in front of him, useless. "You'll pay for that! Stop right there!"

"You know what you did was wrong," Siobhan continued, ignoring the interruption. "But it was an accident. Truth and justice always prevail."

"Not here, they don't. You don't understand. You are from a whole different world. Truth and justice are foreign concepts in this city."

"Arcus, you need to do what is right."

The flames once more licked up and down Arcus' hands and arms. Bennett stopped his approach. "What is right would be for me to burn down this entire wretched place and call it a tender mercy."

"I'll take care of it. I'll make sure you are treated fairly. I'm positive I can get this whole thing smoothed over. Burning the city down is not the right course of action."

"It sure would make *me* feel better," Arcus grumbled.

"Give us just a minute, guard." Siobhan stepped close to Arcus and placed her hand on his jaw. She stared deeply into his eyes, then rested her forehead against his. "Do this because it's right. Do this because I want you to and it would mean a lot to me. Do this because you promised on our wedding day to be what I need you to be, and right now I need you to be a good and honest, law-abiding man. I swear to you, I will take care of this."

The flame on Arcus' arms extinguished, then he pulled Siobhan to him and kissed her deeply. When they broke apart, he removed his satchel and handed it to her, along with his staff.

"I'll need to take that stuff as evidence," said Constable Bennett.

Arcus spoke a word of magic and flicked his hand upward in a throwing motion. A tiny, fiery bead flew up in the sky above their heads. He glared at the constable. "That's not how this works. I will go peacefully, but she takes my belongings.

Believe me, nothing I carry will be evidence anyway. I don't need possessions to be dangerous."

"No, I said, I–"

Arcus snapped his fingers and a massive fireball exploded one hundred feet above them. People on the street screamed and pointed. "Do you want me to come peacefully, or do you want me to burn the place down?" He offered his hands in submission.

The constable nodded once, and moved to bind Arcus' hands. Arcus watched Siobhan until he was led away. He hoped she knew what she was doing. Had it been anyone else, he would never have allowed this to happen.

"I love you, Arcus," she called.

"I love you, too," he yelled back.

Chapter Two
One Last Chance

Siobhan watched Arcus be taken away, her heart heavy in her chest. When she could no longer see him, she turned to march back to the tavern. She was startled to find her friends standing right behind her with the bartender and that girl in the blue dress nearby. Tarnelius had once more pulled his hood over his head.

"Good job, girl. About time that monster was apprehended," said the bartender.

Something inside Siobhan snapped. Dropping Arcus' staff, she grabbed the bartender by the shirt and yanked him close. His eyes widened and he whimpered.

"What was your intent in calling the guard on my husband? He was doing nothing wrong."

"Y–your husband? You married that delinquent? Did he tell you that he murdered someone in cold blood right in front of me?"

"You lie! He did tell me that story, only his version involved him defending his friend from three men who came into your bar looking for a fight. What are you hiding? Did you press charges on the others?"

The old bartender refused to meet her gaze, which further incensed her. He shook his head.

"Why not? Did they, or did they not, come here with the intent of causing a fight? An unfair and dishonorable fight; the three of them on just one–Arcus' friend."

Celeste stepped closer and placed a warning hand on the paladin's arm. "Siobhan, he's not worth it. You need to stay calm. We'll get Arcus out. Let this filth go."

Siobhan shoved the bartender away. He crashed into the door and fell to the ground, a stunned look on his face. "Get out of my sight," she snarled. Then she picked up the staff and turned on her heel to stomp away, walking with no clear destination in mind. Celeste, Tarnelius and Victoria hurried to keep up with her.

"Siobhan, wait!" Celeste called. "Where are you going?"

Siobhan paused a moment, waiting for the others to catch up. "I–I'm not sure. I had to get away from that bar, though. I need to find out whom to talk to so that I can get this sorted out."

"First things first," said Tarnelius. "We will need to figure out a place to stay. I doubt this will be a quick process."

Siobhan frowned as she noticed Victoria still following them around. "What are you doing here? This doesn't concern you."

"I want to help. I don't want Arcus to be locked away in prison any more than you do."

Celeste gave Victoria a warm smile, which contrasted sharply with the angry glower from Siobhan. "Don't mind Siobhan. She's having a rough day. She clearly isn't thinking straight, because if she were, she would realize that the only one of us who knew anything about this city was just led away. Therefore, we are in need of a guide. Any chance you know of an inn that would take us in for an undetermined amount of time? Or whom we need to talk to regarding Arcus' freedom?"

"I don't know of an inn, but I do know that Damon has unoccupied rooms in his dorm right now. I'm sure he will help us. He was always fond of Arcus."

"Lead the way," said Celeste.

Victoria led the way east, the setting sun at their backs. As they walked through a network of filthy winding roads, Celeste held out her hand to take the staff from Siobhan and stuffed it into her small magic bag–which was capable of storing an unbelievable number of items.

"Since when does Arcus use a staff?" inquired Victoria. "I never saw him use any magical props when we attended school together."

"This staff is special," said Celeste. "For what it's worth, Arcus hasn't ever used it. He is still studying it."

When they arrived at the dorms, Victoria walked with purpose over to one of the doors and knocked. A moment later the door was pulled open, and a man wearing dark blue pants and a matching vest stared down at Victoria in mild surprise. The man's dark hair was graying at the temples, and he looked to be in his mid-forties. His gray eyes widened when he noticed the other three standing behind Victoria.

"What is going on, Victoria?"

"Damon, these are friends of Arcus'. He's back in town, but he's been arrested. I was hoping they would be able to stay here. They have nowhere else to go."

"What do you mean 'Arcus is in town, but has been arrested'?" came another voice from inside. A tall, thin man dressed in a red tunic with black pants pushed past Damon to walk outside onto the breezeway. Sandy brown hair curled slightly at the ends, and he had light brown eyes that crinkled in the corners when he smiled.

"Joseph!" Victoria gasped. "What are you doing back here?"

Joseph ignored her, hurrying to greet the two elves. "I remember the two of you. Tarnelius, right? Only, I don't remember your name, beautiful," he said turning to Celeste. I just recall that you were the first girl I had seen Arcus look at in years. Tell me what happened."

Celeste glanced at Siobhan. "My name is Celeste, and I have no idea what you are talking about. What are you doing here? Last I heard, you were in Abhainn with your parents. We went there looking for you, but you had already moved on."

Joseph looked grim. "I'll explain everything, and I'll need you to explain your side. Come inside, away from prying eyes."

They walked into Damon's home. Being the master's residence, this one was really two dorms with one of the walls knocked out to increase living space. The first room was the living area, and the second was Damon's bedroom. Joseph stared at Victoria as they sat down, his expression unreadable.

Tarnelius spoke first. "So, in a nutshell, we travelled to the Sacred Tombs around ten months ago. There, Celeste, Siobhan, Arcus and I helped to defeat Kuunkierto, the ultimate evil. We witnessed the death of the onyx dragon, Tarextros, and the ascension of Aanhextrlos, who became the moon."

Joseph stared at him. "Wait. Question time. First of all, who is Aanhextrios?"

"Aanhextrios was the golden dragon," answered Celeste. "Now he is the moon god."

"Okay, and who is Siobhan?"

"Oh!" said Tarnelius. "I'm sorry, I forgot you two haven't met. Joseph, this is Siobhan, Arcus' wife. Siobhan, this is Arcus' friend, Joseph."

"Back the carriage up! Stop everything. Arcus' what, now? Did you just tell me that she is his *wife?*"

"Why is that so hard for everyone to believe?" Siobhan huffed.

"Forgive Joseph's rudeness, please, milady. I'm sure he meant no offense," said Damon as he brought a bottle of wine and six glasses over to them. "We just remember him from when he lived here. Arcus was a quiet man who kept mostly to himself, at least when he wasn't trying to keep Joseph, here, out of trouble."

"Exactly." Joseph smirked. "He never showed any real interest in the fairer sex at all."

Victoria sighed and took a big sip of her wine.

"So, now for the real question," continued Joseph. "How did the guard catch up with him? Arcus is smart and strong. I'm amazed they managed to take him down."

"He's even stronger now than he used to be," said Celeste. "He has learned so much in the last year. This one," she nodded toward Siobhan with a frown, "talked him into allowing himself to be arrested."

"It was the right thing to do! Fighting with the guard would have only made things worse. This way, he will get his name cleared and truly be free."

"Well," added Tarnelius. "We'd better hurry up and figure out how to get him out, before he loses patience and blows the whole place up."

"True enough. Joseph, how did you come to be here now? We looked for you in Abhainn."

"Right after the moon turned to gold, I decided to travel to Lumernia to try to find Arcus. My parents were making me crazy, and I felt guilty about abandoning him. I found a mage in Abhainn who was willing to let me pay him to teleport me to Lumernia. I looked everywhere, but had no luck. Lumernia was in a state of chaos. It seemed the king and almost everyone in any position of power there had died during some excavation mission. Some of the paladins were trying to grab power, others were campaigning for democracy." He paused to take a sip of wine. "Then the orcs came. They swept in, and with the city in such a state, it was easy pickings. Lumernia is now an occupied, orc-controlled city. People were slaughtered in the streets and in their own homes. For a while, I joined an underground resistance, but eventually decided I would be of more use trying to find others who could come in from outside the city and help. I escaped during the night, and ran until I was clear of the enemy territory. I've travelled for months to get here."

News of Lumernia's fall shocked the group into silence.

Celeste was the first to recover. "I can't believe it never occurred to us that Lumernia would be left leaderless. We were so wrapped up in stopping King Liam, we didn't consider the possibility that they would not have a succession plan in place. Why would they bring *everyone* in a position of power to the north? Who does that?"

"We have to go back," said Siobhan. "We did this, we have to fix it. Just as soon as we get Arcus out, we need to go back."

Tarnelius cleared his throat. "I hate to be the one to ruin your big plan, but it may be time to break him out. Lumernia under occupation is a big problem."

"Give me a chance; one chance to clear his name. Just forty-eight hours. It will be much better for him in the long run.

If I fail, we'll break him out. We can get to Lumernia quickly with magic, anyway."

Celeste exchanged a glance with Tarnelius. She nodded. "One chance. Twenty-four hours, not forty-eight. Then we must focus on freeing an entire city. Damon, do you have extra rooms we can use for tonight? Please? We can pay you."

Damon waved his hand dismissively. "Nonsense. I would never charge you. Arcus became like a son to me in the years he was my student. Anything I can do to help him, I will do."

"We appreciate it. We won't be in your way more than just one night." Celeste sighed. "Looks like traveling to the south to find Theri's family will just have to wait for another time."

"Theri was the kedistam, right? Where is she?" asked Joseph.

"She died in battle. Never made it to the northern tombs," Celeste murmured.

"Oh. I'm so sorry." Joseph frowned, averting his eyes to the floor. Awkward, painful silence filled the room and seemed to become a physical thing. "Well, anyway, count me in. I know how to find the underground resistance. You'll need me. I'm ready."

"I will help as well," offered Damon, "and I have a couple of students who might be up to the trip. I will talk to them."

"Me, too," said Victoria.

"No," snapped Joseph.

"What do you mean, no?"

"You should stay here, where it's safe. An occupied city is not the place for you."

"You listen to me, Joseph Hale. You are not in charge. You will never be in charge. I'm far superior with magic than you could ever hope to be. 'Safe.' Ha! If anyone should stay where it's safe, it's you. Stay here with your taverns and your bimbos."

Joseph looked like he'd been slapped. He stared down at Victoria, at a loss for words. He was almost a foot taller than her, but what she lacked in stature, she made up for in attitude. It was clear that when she got riled up, she knew how to strike.

"That's enough, you two," Siobhan interrupted. "Joseph, if I'm going to get Arcus out of prison, I'm going to need you to tell me *exactly* what happened that day. I'll also need help finding out whom to talk to about getting him released."

Joseph stared off into the distance, focusing on nothing. "I wanted to go to the bar, wanted to find some new company. Victoria had, um, well, she had shot me down again and had cursed me with tentacles all over my face. When I tried to figure out the counter-curse I only succeeded in making them worse." Victoria chuckled under her breath at the memory. "My pride was injured and I wanted to feel good about myself again. Arcus seemed homesick for Kayalost, so I figured it would do us both some good. The evening started off well. There were two women at the Dragonfire Tavern I had never seen before, and they were definitely interested."

He paused a moment and glanced at Victoria. "Before the evening could lead anywhere, the door flew open and these three men burst in. It seemed I had chosen poorly with a recent dalliance and ended up with the girlfriend of one of the sailors. They came that night looking for my blood. Said they were going to kill me. Arcus stepped forward and took on two of them by himself. I dodged the attacks of the leader, but he eventually caught me. Arcus saw what was happening and took action to draw the battle to a close before the man could kill me. Yes, he did kill that man, but I know he didn't mean to. Plus, in the grand scheme of things, it was either me or that thug. Honestly, I'm much more comfortable with it having been him.

"Anyway, the bartender, Jack, was screaming at us and demanding we pay for damages. Arcus took charge, steering me out of there and straight here to pack. We left town as quickly as possible, but were nearly too late. The guards almost found us here."

Damon scoffed. "I only let them in your rooms because I knew you were gone. As soon as they came inside, I cast an enchantment on them that made them completely forget why they had come. You two were never in any danger from the likes of them."

"And how would we have known that?"

"You two should have just had a little more faith in your master. Arcus wanted to take charge. I understood that. He was doing what he thought was right by getting you both out. There was nothing I could have possibly said to convince him otherwise."

"So nothing more came of it? They never came looking for them again?" Siobhan asked.

"Oh, they did," answered Damon. "I'm sure those guards had an entertaining conversation with whomever sent them out here in the first place. By that time, Arcus and Joseph were long gone. I no longer worried about them being caught. I simply told the guards they had packed their things and left, and that I had no idea why."

"Do any of you know whom I need to speak to regarding Arcus' trial?"

Joseph and Damon looked a little uncomfortable. Victoria spoke up. "You'd need to speak to Lord Simon. His manor is in the northern part of the city."

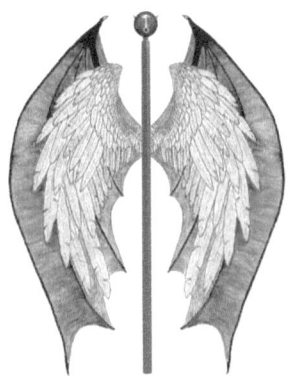

Chapter Three
Creating Order From Chaos

"**Y**ou were a fool to think you could come back here," snarled the guard as he shoved Arcus into the jail cell.

"I'm starting to think so, yes."

The guard turned the key in the lock and gave Arcus a cruel smile. "You think you're funny. Well, you aren't. I can't wait to find out what they decide to do with you."

"It doesn't matter. I won't be staying long."

"We'll see about that. I wonder if you'll get a trial. It's been so long since we've had a good show. If you get one, I hope it's a trial by combat. The trials by ordeal are so quick and boring. Maybe they'll just hang you instead. I do love a good hanging."

"What could I have possibly done to make you hate me so?"

"It's my job to keep scum like you off the street."

Flames licked up and down Arcus' forearms, burning away his bindings. He pointed at the guard. "Never misunderstand why I am here. I am here because I *choose* to be. You didn't catch me; I gave myself up. If I hadn't chosen to be here, you would be dead now. It really would be easy." Arcus cocked his head to the side. "In fact, I'll bet I could magically convince you to kill yourself, and save me the trouble. I've never tried anything like that before. It could be an interesting experiment."

The guard's eyes widened and he took a step back.

Arcus grabbed hold of the cell bars, extinguishing the flames. "Relax. You're safe … for the moment. Luckily for you, my wife is a paladin and I suspect she would frown on me taking petty revenge against pseudo-guards in this pathetic excuse for a city. I just wanted to make a point. Now, leave me be."

The guard backed out of the room, leaving Arcus alone. He walked to the far corner and slid into a sitting position on the hard floor. Resting his head against the wall, Arcus sighed. *Siobhan, I really hope you know what you are doing,* he thought.

Arcus silently contemplated his options. He wasn't concerned about being stuck in jail. What he was concerned about, however, was what Siobhan thought she was going to accomplish. His time with the Mithran paladins had taught him they valued order above all else, but he wondered what sort of law she expected to find in a city built on chaos. Lord Simon ran things as he saw fit. Thieves and murderers were often allowed to walk free as long as they properly greased the palm of the city's overlord. Izmar was one of the few cities where the largest tradesmen's guild was actually the thieves' guild. It had long been rumored that Simon himself was a member of the thieves' guild, but no one was brazen enough to openly accuse him.

Arcus must have dozed off, because all too soon he was jolted awake by the sound of more guards stomping into the room. He raised his head. The sun had barely begun streaming through the barred window of his cell.

Two guards dragged between them the unconscious form of the biggest orc Arcus had ever seen. The orc had ebony skin and was bald. His nose was large and snout-like. Judging by his physique, the orc was clearly a warrior, but Arcus could sense the magic on him; this orc was an arcane master, like himself. The two guards threw their prisoner into the adjacent cell and slammed the door, locking it with a clicking sound. A moment later, another mage entered through the front door. He scowled at the orc lying in a heap on the floor and cast a spell. Arcus recognized the words as being a sleep incantation.

"Why bother casting a sleep spell on an unconscious orc who is chained up?" Arcus asked.

"Not that it's any of your business, but we found this one on the southern edges of our border. He and his raiding party had apparently gotten it into their heads that we wouldn't notice if they raided the southern farming community. I'm keeping him asleep until we decide what to do with him."

Arcus stood and approached the door to his cell, examining the other mage and the orc. Arcus raised his hand, which glowed a light green for a moment. He smirked. "You are no match for him. Make sure you keep your spell updated. We wouldn't want there to be an accident."

"No one asked for your opinion. Mind your own business." The mage turned and stomped from the room.

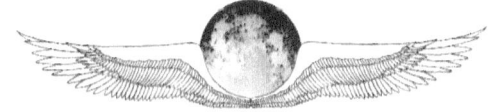

"Simon's manor house is in the north part of town," explained Victoria. "You can't miss it."

"Then let's go," said Siobhan. After spending a restless night in the dorms, she had stepped outside to try to clear her head and think her next step through. Victoria had followed her.

"It's not that simple."

"What's not simple about it? The city's legal system will bring the truth to light. I just need to convince Lord Simon to move the proceedings forward so that we can be on our way."

"I mean, it's not that simple. Whether Arcus is innocent or not is irrelevant. It doesn't matter if there are extenuating circumstances. All that does matter is whether Simon has anything to gain by either keeping him or letting him go. Plus, he's dishonest. He–I mean–" Victoria sighed. "Look, there's no easy way to say this, so I'll just come out and say it. Simon is a thief. He has gained every bit of the power he has by stealing it from others. He uses intimidation and, more than anything else, he is a bully. If you want Arcus out, you'll have to give Simon something he wants instead."

"Are you suggesting I bribe him?"

"To put it bluntly, yes."

"That isn't justice," Siobhan huffed.

"Nothing in Izmar ever is. Where did you think you were?"

"How do you know all of this, anyway?"

Victoria wouldn't meet her eyes. "I'm no stranger to Izmar's legal system."

"What does that mean?"

"It means I'm a thief. Or I was, anyway. I grew up here, on the streets. I was homeless. My family lived anywhere we could find shelter and we took what we needed to survive. The first time I ever had a real place to call home was when I came into my magic and Damon took me in. That's when I turned my life around."

"And your family?"

"I can't help them if they won't help themselves."

"So if you are no stranger to Izmar's legal system, how did you get yourself out? Was there a trial?"

"I gave Simon something he wanted."

"Which was?"

Victoria's cheeks flushed. "It doesn't matter. So, like I was saying, the road is there. You can't miss it."

"Oh no. You're coming with me. I might need you. Come on."

"No, you really d–"

Siobhan grabbed Victoria's arm and dragged her up the north road. Victoria struggled and tried to shake her off, but soon gave up.

"If this were for anyone but Arcus, you'd have a knife to your throat for not letting me go. I can't see how this will help, but I'm willing to give it a try. You're strong. If anyone can get Simon to do what they want, it's you."

Siobhan nodded. A twinge of jealousy tore through her, though she tried to suppress it. Victoria's words reminded her that she really should be keeping this girl as far away from her husband as she could. The fact remained the former thief could prove useful, though, and Siobhan trusted her husband above all else.

The pair weaved their way up the streets, having to switch roads often when they dead-ended into various buildings. They continued north until they arrived at the door to Simon's home. The large manor house was an elaborate homage to Simon's wealth. It was several stories high and probably had enough room to comfortably house fifty people.

Siobhan rapped on the door, then stood in stoic silence as they waited. After a few moments, the door swung open. A man with blond hair and pale green eyes stood before them, wearing the garb of a servant.

"May I help you, ladies?"

"We've come to speak to Simon," answered Siobhan.

"Of course you have. I didn't presume either of you wanted to speak to me." The man rolled his eyes. "Do you have an appointment?"

"No."

"Pity, that. His Lordship is busy. Why don't I just schedule you for three months from now? I think there is a day that week he is available."

"No. We need to speak to him now. My husband has been arrested and–"

"His Lordship is busy."

"But–"

"I'm sorry, young woman, the answer is no." The servant moved to shut the door, but Victoria stepped in.

"Shadow-finch," she hissed.

The man stopped as if she had stung him. He turned to face her head-on, eyebrows arched. "Are you sure this is what you want?"

Victoria nodded, her eyes downcast.

He glowered at her, then shoved the door open. "As you wish, mistress. Come in."

Without a word, Victoria walked into the manor and continued down the hall, gesturing only once for Siobhan to follow.

"What was that all about?"

Victoria shook her head in response. When she reached the third door on the left, she stopped and grasped the handle. She took a deep breath and threw open the door, gesturing for Siobhan to enter ahead of her.

Siobhan stepped into the room and gasped. The area was covered in expensive silk draperies and exotic-looking cushions of bright red, blue, green, purple and gold. Dominating the chamber was a huge four-poster bed, adorned with equally colorful curtains and covers.

Siobhan whirled around to face Victoria. "What is the meaning of this?"

Victoria stared at the bed, her features expressionless. "What does it look like?"

"It looks like you are a common whore and I have no idea why you–"

Siobhan stopped short as a dagger hit the floor a mere hairsbreadth from her booted foot. She looked up to see Victoria glaring at her, a second dagger clenched in her right hand.

"You should be thankful I do not have my sword or armor right now."

"No. *You* should be thankful that I have excellent aim."

Time seemed to stand still as the two stared at each other. After a while, the door eased open and Victoria leapt at Siobhan, kneeling at her feet to grab up her dagger, concealing it once more beneath her sleeves.

"Ah, Victoria. This is an unexpected but pleasant surprise. I must admit, after our last encounter, I had not expected to see you again. On top of that, it looks like you brought a playmate. I never thought that day would come. Rise, my dear. You know the rules. Although I enjoy seeing you kneel before me, I like it more when I know your huge collection of knives is safely stowed in the urn over there. Go on, get on with it."

The man in the doorway was tall, with short black hair and a goatee. He stood in a confident manner, with his shoulders back. The top several buttons of his off-white shirt were unbuttoned, showing off his tan chest. He leered at Victoria, who rose from the floor and obediently walked to the urn, where she began removing daggers.

"How dare you?"

"How dare I what, my beautiful redhead? You have come into my home, into my private space. What did you expect of me?"

"I expected you to listen to what I had to say, not to be a hopeless cad!"

Simon cocked his head as he considered her words, the silence only broken by the sound of Victoria dropping her knives into the large urn one at a time. A lengthy process, considering she had all manner of small blades strapped to her arms and legs, concealed beneath her flowing dress. Simon and Siobhan stared each other down, completely ignoring her.

Simon shut the door and prowled toward Siobhan, his gait that of a predator. He stood over six feet tall, a couple of inches taller than Siobhan herself.

"My apologies," he breathed. "My name is Simon de Vaux, and I am master of this house and all of Izmar. I am unaccustomed to having women enter this room for any purpose other than the obvious. Tell me, who are you, and why are you here?"

Siobhan was uncomfortable with how close he stood, though she held her ground. "My name is Siobhan, paladin of Mithra, and I–"

"Beautiful Siobhan, I am pleased to make your acquaintance. How may I be of service to you?" He took her hand and kissed her knuckles.

Siobhan took a small step back. "I have come to ask for the release of my husband, Arcus. He was arrested today for charges that were not his fault."

"I see." Simon's eyes darkened as he took another step toward her. "And what are you willing to do in exchange for his freedom?"

Siobhan stiffened. "My husband is an innocent man. You have no cause to keep him locked up."

"This is my town, my rules. If he is innocent of whatever he did, as you say, I can free him like *that*–" Simon snapped his fingers, "–but what is in it for *me*?" He caressed her hair.

Simon jerked back as Siobhan slapped him hard across the face. Fury burned in her hazel eyes.

"Perhaps you did not hear me. I am a paladin of Mithra. I am not one of your whores that you can so easily seduce. I *demand* justice for my husband and nothing further. Release him at once, or grant him a fair trial."

Simon turned to Victoria, who stood in silence near the urn. "Victoria, I am displ–"

His words were cut off by frantic knocking on the door. With a sigh, Simon yanked it open. A nervous-looking man in mage robes stood outside the door.

"My apologies for interrupting you, sir. We have a complication involving the orc prisoner."

"You know I'm never to be bothered when I am entertaining guests in this room."

"It is important, sir."

"Then stop wasting my time and spill it."

"The prisoner is very powerful. I doubt we have the resources to keep him contained, much less to make him talk."

"So your emergency is to let me know that you are incompetent?"

The mage shifted from foot to foot. "The other prisoner is also very powerful. I'm not actually sure why he is even still in our jail. Our bars are certainly not restraining him. Together, the two of them could be trouble. If we're being honest, we only captured this orc at all because we caught him and his two cohorts unawares inside the farmhouse. My Lord, I know you wanted to interrogate him, but my council would be to eliminate him while we still have the chance."

Simon jerked his hand in annoyance. "What other prisoner?"

"The mage being held in the jail. I could sense his power when I wasn't even looking at him. He advised me to detect the orc's magic, and he was right to do so."

Simon whirled around and glared at Siobhan. "Your husband isn't really a paladin, is he?"

"I never said he was. He is a mage and druid."

Simon stroked his goatee. After a moment, he turned back to the mage. "Both of you get your wish. Mistress Siobhan's husband is to get a fair trial–a trial by combat. Let him kill your orc for you. If he succeeds he can have his freedom. If the mage dies, at least he will weaken the orc enough so your men will be able to finish the job. In either case, make sure the townspeople are aware. The battle will be at midday tomorrow in the south fields. Charge everyone admission. I'll have some benefit from this fiasco."

The mage paled. "As you wish, my lord, but–"

"But what?"

"I am unsure if I'll be able to keep the orc contained that long. It would be easier to kill him now, while he's unconscious."

Simon glared. "No. That doesn't benefit anyone. Move the trial up to this evening, then. Use all your resources to let the Izmarians know of the battle. No more complaints! You are dismissed."

"As you–"

"Go!"

The mage turned and ran back down the hall, out of sight.

"I hope this completes our negotiations to your satisfaction, Siobhan. You may go. I no longer have the time or inclination to deal with either one of you. Victoria, we will discuss this at a later date." Simon snarled his words without even turning to look at them, then he strode down the hall and into another room.

Victoria gathered up her daggers out of the urn and began restrapping them as fast as she could. With several still loose from their scabbards and belts, she grabbed Siobhan's forearm and pulled her from the room and out the door.

Once they were a safe distance away, Victoria ducked into an alley and carefully finished strapping her daggers back where they belonged. Siobhan watched in bemusement.

"I had no idea you kept so many of those concealed on you," she said.

"That's why my dress is so long and my sleeves so full. You weren't meant to know about them. I may have learned magic, but it never hurts to be prepared."

"I suppose that is true, but you seem to trust your daggers first and your magic second, if our argument was any indication."

"Not all of us were blessed with the magic of fire and lightning. I am a conjurer. I can summon creatures or things to serve me, but when it comes down to it, I learned from an early age to protect myself, and that is still my base instinct."

"Creatures?"

"Every child has imaginary friends. Mine became real. Come on, we have to hurry. You need to bring back those sweet-talking abilities for the jail guard to let you talk to Arcus so you can warn him of what is coming." Victoria looked to the sky and sighed. "He'll need to prepare and focus. It is already midday, so we don't have long. I'll take you there so you don't get lost, then I'll go get Damon and the others."

"No, I must see Celeste. I need to get my armor and sword from her. We'll head back to the dorms, then you can give me directions."

Chapter Four
Guilty Until Proven Dead

Siobhan summoned Apollo with a thought, and the handsome palomino stallion stood before her. Reciting the directions over and over in her mind, Siobhan rode off in the direction of the jail. Heads turned to stare as they passed. Siobhan supposed she made quite a sight in such a chaotic place as this. Celeste had helped her into her paladin armor, which gleamed in the sun. Before long, she arrived at what could only be Izmar's jail. It was small and unkempt, with bars on the windows. The paint on the outer walls was peeling. Dismounting, she dismissed Apollo–who vanished–and strode up to the door. A guard leaned lazily against the doorway, but he straightened up in a hurry when it became obvious she was headed his way.

He stepped into her path, blocking the door. "How may I help you, milady? Are you lost?"

"No. I am here to see the prisoner, Arcus, before his trial."

"Impossible. No trial has been set, and he is not to be allowed visitors anyway. One such as yourself should not associate with him. He is a murderer. Unless ..." He lifted his hand, rubbing his thumb against his fingers, clearly asking for a bribe. Siobhan narrowed her eyes.

"Who are you to pass judgment on him before his trial has even taken place? I have just left Simon's and he is to be allowed a trial this very day. Now, you will let me pass." Her hands began to glow a bright gold.

The guard seemed conflicted. "I will need to speak to the other guard. Wait out here."

"Unacceptable. I will go with you to speak with him. I have had quite enough of this city's corruption. Corruption is nearly the same as lawlessness, and I will not stand for it."

She shoved her way through the door, quickly passing the desk and marching down the hall to the room where Arcus sat in his cell. The guard from outside ran in after her, yelling for her to stop. Another guard, who had been sitting inside behind the desk, jumped to his feet and grabbed her by the shoulder as she passed.

"Stop moving, both of you," Arcus snarled in a hypnotic voice. The two men froze in place. The one nearest Siobhan found himself trapped in an awkward position, his hand still outstretched.

Arcus turned to his wife and stared at her as if he hadn't seen her in days. He devoured her with his eyes and she blushed as she approached his cell, her face burning hot.

"Siobhan, what is happening? Have you come to admit that this city is too corrupt for even you, and to tell me that I can come out now?"

Siobhan sighed. "It is all that and more. Despite knowing that you are my husband, Simon would have traded your freedom for a dalliance with me … and Victoria." Siobhan's eyes darkened at the name.

Arcus shook with rage. "He didn't touch you, did he? I'll kill him."

"Don't you think maybe that is what got you into this mess in the first place? No, he didn't touch me. He made some rude comments and I slapped him. Calm down. We have bigger problems to deal with than Simon. You're to have a trial by combat today, this very evening."

Arcus' eyes widened. "A trial by combat? Who is to be my opponent? Not Damon or one of his students, is it? I won't fight them."

"Relax. It's him, apparently." Siobhan pointed at the dark-skinned orc, who was still out cold in the neighboring cell.

"Ah. They realized they can't control him, so they want me to do their dirty work."

"Exactly. Apparently the mage who brought him in is afraid of him. If you win, you gain your freedom and are declared innocent. If you lose, they are hoping you weaken him enough that they can finish him off. Either way, it will be in front of the whole city."

"I suspect Simon will be selling admission tickets, too."

"You're right about that. One other thing. Joseph is here."

Arcus' eyebrows shot up. "You're kidding! All these long months I've been searching for him, and he was here the whole time? How did he avoid capture?"

"He hasn't been here the whole time. He's just arrived, same as us. He was in–actually, I'll tell you when you are free. You need to focus on your fight for now. I'll tell you later, or he can."

Arcus reached between the bars for her, and she gladly walked into his embrace. "Is he going to be a problem?" she asked, gesturing to the orc.

Arcus paused. "No."

Siobhan gave him a worried look. "Are you sure? You hesitated. I'm worried for you."

"I'm sure. Look, I'm so glad to see you, truly, but you were right–I need to plan my attack." He gave her a long, lingering kiss. "Don't worry, everything will be fine. I'll see you soon."

Siobhan caressed his face and stared into his eyes, uncertain. Then she nodded briefly and marched past the still-frozen guards and out of the room.

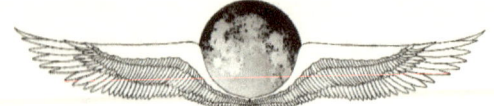

Celeste walked silently alongside her friends. They had come with Siobhan to see the trial, even Joseph, though he kept his cloak on and his head down. Celeste saw that the paladin was making every effort to appear unworried, but every so often, when she thought no one was looking, the elf caught Siobhan biting her lip, frown lines marring her forehead as she gazed off into the distance. It had to be hard on her, knowing they were about to see Arcus in a fight to the death ... and there was nothing that could be done to help him. Celeste worried that Siobhan would not be able to handle it if the unthinkable happened.

Tarnelius placed a gentle hand on Siobhan's shoulder. "Stop worrying about Arcus, Siobhan. I've known him since he was a child. He's smart and strong. He'll be okay."

Siobhan nodded but didn't utter a single word.

The group walked along, following the crowd on their southward march. The city officials had done an excellent job spreading the news in the last few hours, and it appeared most of the city was turning up to watch the trial. Celeste mentally shook her head. She would never understand why humans were so fascinated by watching people kill each other. At the end of the road, they were stopped by the city guards to pay their admission. Then they found space toward the left side of the field, a short distance from where everyone else had gathered. Nearby, several mages chanted nervously in unison as they tried to maintain their hold on the magical bindings that held the now-irate dark orc.

Celeste approached them. "Need a hand?"

The mages didn't dare stop their chanting, but several nodded.

Celeste stretched out her hands, palms down, as she too began to chant. Vines sprouted from the earth at the orc's feet and quickly grew, twisting around him until he was encased in a leafy cage.

"Keep chanting," she said. "The vines are only stopping him from moving, not from casting. I'll drop them when it is time."

On the other end of the field, Arcus was being shoved into place by the guards. He didn't react to his aggressors at all, and merely stared at the ground in silence.

Once most of the crowd had arrived, Simon strode to the center of the field, a robed mage hot on his heels. The mage cast a spell on Simon, touching his throat, and Simon began to speak, his voice magically amplified.

"Thank you all for joining us on such short notice. This, as I am sure you already know, is a trial by combat. On trial this evening is one known to us as 'Arcus,' charged with murder. How do you plead, Arcus?"

Arcus glared at Simon, then touched his own throat and responded with equal volume. "Not guilty."

"That's up for the gods to decide. If you are innocent, you will have no trouble defeating your opponent. Failure brings a verdict of guilt, and with it ... death!" Simon surveyed the crowd, a serious expression on his face. "Remember, none must assist either combatant. If any are caught helping them in any way, the trial will be immediately ended and not only will the one who was helped be declared guilty, but the one helping him will share his fate. Now, begin!"

The guards released Arcus at the same time Celeste dropped the entanglement spell on the imprisoned orc.

Arcus and his opponent stalked toward each other, neither anxious to make the first move, both feeling the other out. The orc's eyes narrowed in cunning anticipation. Arcus tried to focus his strength and the anger that he felt toward the creature's entire race to act in his favor. He knew this one would be different. He had heard of dark orcs, but had never seen one. The specimen standing before him bore very little resemblance to the orcs Arcus had seen so many times, both in reality and in his nightmares. He was tall and muscular, his ebony skin glistening in the fading light.

The dark orc lifted his arms and threw a massive fireball at Arcus, who dropped to the ground and rolled to the side. Arcus pointed at the fire that burned where he had just stood, and with a word of magic, the fire flickered and exploded in a brilliant display of color. Several in the crowd screamed and rubbed at their eyes. The orc jeered at the blinded people. Arcus turned just in time to see his nemesis lunge at him. With a yell, Arcus vanished and reappeared in a standing position behind the orc, who skidded across the ground.

"Stop moving," Arcus hissed. The creature froze in place. Arcus prowled over to him, wanting to look him in the eye when he took his life. He circled around and stared into his enemy's crimson eyes. He thrust his hands forward to use the same lightning spell that had landed him in a prison cell, when he saw the orc blink and sneer. Arcus quickly backed up but was too late. The orc punched him in the face, knocking him to the ground. Blood poured from his nose and the crowd roared.

Snarling out words in his guttural language, the orc cast a spell that caused a dark purple fog to cover Arcus. His body went limp. Growling in triumph, the orc got Arcus in a headlock and punched him hard in the face again with the other.

Arcus felt his strength ebbing as his airway was closed off. He was in trouble. That spell had been some sort of curse and it felt like his insides were being gnawed upon by a plague of rabid rats. His vision began to blur and darken around the edges. Just before he lost the ability to see anything at all, he caught a final glimpse of his wife. She had buried her face in Tarnelius' shoulder and seemed to be crying. Celeste watched him, horrified. Arcus knew it was only a matter of time before the elves stepped in to save him. He couldn't allow that to happen. Siobhan wanted to do this right, and having them all fighting for their lives wouldn't help anyone. His ears started ringing and he gasped for breath, going very still. With the last of his strength, he shifted. Thick fur erupted from his skin as he expanded into an immense black bear. No longer able to grip the bear's thick neck, the orc scrambled backward and Arcus was able to finally take a real breath.

Big mistake. Pain arced through his body and pulsed with every beat of his heart. Dazed, Arcus hesitated for a brief moment. Turning into a bear should have healed whatever damage that monster had inflicted, but his insides were still being shredded. He took several shallow breaths and tried to reclaim his lost strength and focus. The orc began to chant once more.

Arcus rolled to his feet and roared. His front legs caught on fire, the flames dancing up and down as if part of him. With a mighty swipe of his paw, he sent the orc tumbling away. Arcus cried out again and storm clouds gathered above, the lightning flickering among the clouds and striking a nearby farmhouse, lighting it on fire.

The bear bellowed in fury and shot lightning from his paws, striking the orc in the chest. The monster shook violently and shot another fireball at Arcus, who took the hit without flinching. Vanishing once more, he appeared behind the orc and shot him with another lightning bolt, just as an answering bolt shot down from the sky to merge with the one he commanded.

The orc dropped to the ground. Arcus shot one final bolt from his paws, which again merged with a bolt from the sky, before bellowing in triumph and dropping to all fours. He curled in on himself with a moan of agony as he shifted back, the storm dispersing as quickly as it had arrived. The pain, which had only been exacerbated by his exertions, made him almost long for death.

"Tarnel, see to the farmhouse, please. Put out the fire. I'll see to Arcus with Siobhan," Celeste yelled as they rushed to the side of their fallen friend.

Simon's mages moved in on the orc to examine him. They nodded to Simon; the orc was dead. His flesh was charred; there was very little left to make him identifiable.

"Ladies and gentlemen," Simon yelled. "It appears that, assuming our friend here is still alive, the gods have declared him innocent! Let it be known in all of Izmar that this man's victim was killed in self-defense, not murder. I hope you all have a great evening. Show's over!"

Celeste and Siobhan rolled Arcus over and forced him to uncurl. Shifting had healed most of the external damage, but not completely. He was no longer bleeding but was horribly bruised and burned.

Siobhan's hands flashed gold, while Celeste's turned blue. Together, they finished resetting his broken nose and healing his injuries.

Siobhan caressed Arcus' face. "Arcus, get up. You won."

His eyelids flickered. "Did you ever doubt me?" His voice was scratchy and weak.

"Only while you were being strangled in front of my eyes."

He smiled weakly. "I'm not sure why everyone wants to strangle me. That vampire tried it, too."

Celeste glanced at Siobhan. "Are you still hurt, Arcus? Those spells should have healed you."

Arcus tried to sit up, flinching and gripping his chest. "Yes, but I don't think it's an injury. The bastard cursed me. I'll be all right. Let's get out of here before Simon changes his mind."

"That was some fight. You'll have to tell me how you managed to call the storm while wielding arcane lightning at the same time." Celeste pulled his staff out of her magic bag, then she and Siobhan moved to either side of him to help him up. Once they got him to his feet, he leaned heavily on his staff, gasping for breath.

"Actually, you need to tell me why on earth you didn't start with that," grumbled Siobhan.

Arcus chuckled. "Overconfidence, I suppose. I couldn't resist the poetic justice of killing him with the lightning touch spell. I thought he was frozen in place."

Siobhan frowned. "It's *not* funny. I've never been so frightened in my whole life. You could have ended it early. You could have shifted into a bird and cast spells where he couldn't reach you."

"Yes, I could have. I also would have risked him attacking the crowd if he couldn't reach me. He attacked me because he was told that killing me meant his freedom, but I doubt he believed it. He also attacked me because he considered me the biggest threat, as the only one attacking *him.* If I had taken to the skies, he may have attacked the bystanders." Arcus coughed, blood covering his hand. His breath caught in his throat and he wheezed in agony.

Tarnelius, flanked by Joseph, Victoria and Damon, hurried up to them.

"Fire's out. What's the matter with him?" Tarnelius asked.

"Apparently a curse. I'm not sure what to do about it now," answered Celeste.

"Arcus! I've been looking for you everywhere, man. You look awful," quipped Joseph.

"Likewise, Joseph. Likewise. It's good to see–"

"Shhh! Do you hear that?" Celeste hissed.

They stopped and looked around. They heard and almost felt people moving around them, but no one could be seen.

Joseph lifted his hand to cast. "Reveal invisibility! See magic!" He gasped. "They are all around us."

"Joseph, calm down," Arcus said. "Who is all around us?"

Joseph looked at Arcus, the white prominent in his eyes. "The dark orcs. We are all going to die."

Chapter Five
Dying Wish

Chaos ensued around them. The orcs threw off their invisibility spell and began murdering the Izmarians where they stood. Some of the citizens had started to head back to their homes, but many had remained behind to watch Arcus, as well as gawk over the farmhouse fire. Celeste was quick to cast her signature storm, so like the one Arcus himself had cast as a bear. Storm clouds rolled in, lightning flickered and thunder crashed as rain began to pelt the ground. Tarnelius drew his twin swords and ran into the carnage alongside Siobhan. Joseph spoke a word of magic, and swiftly created four additional avatars of himself, standing at the ready. He and his copies ran toward the battle. Victoria summoned a gigantic lion from the celestial realms, and he leapt into the fray. She covered him by flinging daggers at any orcs that posed a threat to the big cat. Damon cast a spell that sent a rainbow of dazzling colors at their enemy. Some of them stared at the light show, hypnotized, while two more seized and fell to the ground, dead.

Arcus shot a huge lightning bolt at the nearest orc. It struck the creature in the chest and rebounded off several other orcs in a massive lighting chain. Arcus slumped over, breathing shallowly, his staff still held fast in his hands. He coughed again, and more blood spattered his hand. He knelt on the ground, unable to do anything but watch the writhing mass of bodies engage in combat.

The carnage was horrible. Within moments, most of the Izmarians had been slaughtered, their bodies littering the field. The dark orcs' numbers were staggering, more than could be easily counted. Every time one fell, another was there to take his comrade's place.

Lightning flashed as Celeste unleashed her storm. She released her wings and lifted into the air. With most of the civilians already slaughtered, she focused her energies toward transforming the storm into a tornado.

Arcus, who was next to her, yanked on her skirt to capture her attention. Celeste looked down at him, her concentration broken.

"How were they *all* invisible? There must be at least one strong caster among them. We need to find and eliminate them."

Celeste scanned the chaos. Tarnelius and Siobhan fought back to back in the thick of things. Joseph and his copies ducked and dodged the orcs, moving in synchrony. He cast a spell, creating a transparent skull atop a dark cloud to appear and rush toward two of the orcs. They took one look, turned, and ran away screaming.

Damon, who was near Siobhan and Tarnelius, stared into the eyes of his opponent. He seemed to be talking to him, completely calm in the midst of the battle. The orc nodded and raised his sword, spinning around and attacking his allies.

Victoria stood nearest to Celeste and Arcus. She and her lion still held strong. The big cat tumbled across the ground as he tore the face off his adversary. Victoria summoned a massive translucent fist out of thin air and used it to punch one of the orcs, knocking him back several feet.

"I don't see him, Arcus," cried Celeste.

Arcus rose to his feet on unsteady legs, crying out as he stood. He surveyed the crowd.

Her green eyes narrowing, Celeste pointed just beyond Siobhan and Tarnelius. "There! The one with the white warpaint!"

The orc leader pointed with his sword to one of his fallen brethren and spoke words in Orcish. The body rose up and shambled back into the fight.

"Damn. A necromancer. We'll need to take him out."

"To your left is the leader." Celeste thought to Tarnelius. *"He is a necromancer, so be careful. He's raising the dead orcs to continue fighting. He needs to be taken out."*

Tarnelius shouted instructions to Siobhan, and the two of them moved in unison in that direction, quickly followed by Damon and his new orc lackey.

Celeste chanted another spell, and a pillar of fire plunged down from the sky, landing directly on the necromancer. The orc leader bellowed, but did not falter.

Siobhan swung her sword at the fearsome orc leader. He deftly parried with a *clang* of steel-on-steel. The two swiftly engaged in a heated duel as deadly as it was graceful, blades clashing again and again, sparks flying from razor-sharp edges. Still defending her back, Tarnelius cut down two more of the orc horde, spinning on the balls of his feet with a dancer's ease.

The necromancer parried a fierce swing from Siobhan's sword, then caught her by surprise with a shove to the chest. A thunderous boom deafened her at the contact, and a dark purple mist covered her as she stumbled.

Pressing his advantage, the orc roared and stabbed his sword deep between the metal plates of Siobhan's armor. He yanked his sword free, her blood dripping from the blade. He kicked her hard in the chest, and she fell backward, knocking into Tarnelius.

"No!" screamed Arcus. He shouted incoherently in a mixture of languages. Lightning flashed. The ground shook.

Suddenly, the crystal atop his staff burst into light. Celeste's storm clouds vanished. Victoria's lion disappeared into nothing. The undead orcs dropped to the ground, dead once more. Joseph's mirror images of himself were gone.

The world stood still. Celeste and her comrades turned as one to Arcus. The irate mage stalked his prey, death in his eyes.

Raising the staff high, he snarled out an ice spell, and frost shot from his free hand to strike the orc. Taking slow, deliberate steps, Arcus threw spell after spell at the necromancer who had dared to strike his wife. Fireball, frost and then another fireball. In the end, Arcus stood before his victim, glaring up at him.

"How–"

But Arcus cut him off, hitting him in the chest with a lightning spell. He maintained the spell until the orc's eyes rolled back into his head and he fell to the ground, dead. Arcus collapsed next to him, his hand outstretched to Siobhan. The staff fell from his hand, the lighted crystal blinking out.

Tarnelius was the first to recover. Rallying, he charged the nearest orcs, spinning in place as he cut them down with his swords, his movements a ballet of dual-bladed death.

Victoria summoned a giant black bear, who went to work charging down more orcs. Joseph muttered an incantation and vanished from sight.

Damon turned toward the orc he had charmed, but the spell had been broken. The orc raised his sword and brought it down hard, stabbing Damon in the chest.

Celeste screamed a warning, then released her magic. Another pillar of fire shot down from the sky and hit Damon's attacker, but not before the orc managed to twist the sword free. Damon fell to the ground, a gaping hole in the center of his chest. Blood flowed between fingers that clutched the devastating wound.

Celeste ran for her fallen friends, hoping she could save them all and trusting Tarnelius and Victoria would be able to handle the remaining few orcs on their own. Without their undead brethren, the dark orcs' numbers were greatly diminished. She didn't know where Joseph had gone, but hoped he was okay.

Tarnelius whirled on an orc, only to see it collapse to the ground in a lifeless heap. The creature's throat was cut, but no one had been nearby.

Not having time to puzzle that out, Celeste ran to Damon first, the closest of the fallen. She knelt near him, hearing him gasp for breath. Her hand flashed blue, but Damon gripped her wrist before she could touch him.

"No," he gasped. "Help Arcus."

"But you'll die."

"It's too late for me. Help them, please. My … dying wish. He's like … my … son. Tell him–"

Damon gasped for breath, a painful-sounding wheeze rattling from his ever-weakening form.

Celeste nodded, tears in her eyes. She rose to her feet and ran for Arcus and Siobhan. Arcus lay on the ground, unconscious but gripping Siobhan's hand, still. His chest rose shallowly with each breath, but he wasn't visibly injured. She turned her gaze upon Siobhan and her breath caught.

Siobhan was in bad shape. She was alive, but just barely. Blood covered the grass where she lay, coating her armor and leaking between the plates. More dripped from the corner of her mouth. Celeste lifted both hands and laid them on Siobhan, her arms glowing bright blue. Oblivious to the carnage around her, she focused all her energy on the paladin. As the spell completed, Siobhan took a deep breath and color returned to her face. Placing her hand on Arcus, Celeste attempted another healing spell, just in case. Then she stood up and raced back to Damon.

Taking him in her arms, she tried to heal him, but the magic wouldn't come. Damon was dead. Celeste cradled him to her chest and murmured, "Arcus was fine. I'll find out what this curse is and help him, I promise. Siobhan was going to die. You probably saved her life, which in turn saved Arcus' life. I hope you know that, wherever you are now."

Continuing to hold Damon's body, Celeste looked up. Tarnelius and the black bear fought the last three orcs, while Victoria looked on, presumably controlling the animal.

Joseph appeared in front of her out of thin air.

"Is he okay?"

Celeste shook her head. Joseph placed his hand on Damon's head and muttered in the language of magic. Finally, he looked up at Celeste.

"I know you did all you could for him. Don't cry. It isn't your fault."

"He was still alive when I reached him. He sacrificed himself so that I could take care of Arcus and Siobhan."

Joseph looked in their direction. "Are they all right?"

Celeste nodded. "Unconscious. Siobhan has lost a lot of blood, and was near death. Arcus just overexerted himself, especially considering whatever that first orc did to him."

Tarnelius and Victoria jogged over. Tarnelius healed Victoria's wounds, then did the same for himself.

"Thank you," she said to him with a small smile. Her gaze darkened as she looked at Damon. "Arcus is not going to like this."

"None of us likes this, Victoria," snapped Celeste.

"We need to regroup and get out of here," said Tarnelius. "I saw a few of the orcs flee south after their leader fell. There is no guarantee they won't return with reinforcements."

"But what about the Izmarians?" Victoria asked. "These people deserve a decent pyre. *Damon* deserves a pyre and proper send-off. What will we do with the people that went home, or the Izmarians that didn't even come here today?"

"She's right, Tarnel," said Celeste. "Besides, where would we go? Where would the Izmarians go?"

"Why are all of these dark orcs here?" interjected Joseph. "They live east of Lumernia!"

"I don't know, but I have a feeling we need to find out." Celeste gently eased Damon's body onto the ground, then rose to her feet. She walked back over to Arcus and Siobhan, her heart heavy. She was overwhelmed by the devastation. Hundreds of lives had been lost on both sides.

Celeste looked down at Arcus and inhaled sharply. Blood dripped from his mouth. Celeste tried again to heal him, but her magic had no effect. She sat down next to him and lifted him up out of fear that he would end up choking on his own blood. He groaned and opened his gray pain-filled eyes.

"Arcus, what can I do? I don't know what to do."

"I don't know," he wheezed. "It hurts ... like ... insides being ... ripped out. I have no magic to ... combat this, so ... I doubt ... you do, either."

"I can't think of anything that would work."

Arcus took several shallow breaths before continuing. "Didn't ... think so ... I'll ... be okay. At least ... things ... can't get worse ... right?"

Celeste averted her eyes and she felt Arcus stiffen. With great effort, he turned to look at Siobhan.

"Oh, Arcus, don't worry. Siobhan is fine. She's unconscious and has lost a lot of blood, but I saved her. *Damon* saved her."

Arcus released Siobhan's hand to caress her face. "What do you mean Damon saved her? I tried to teach him healing, but he couldn't ... where is he?"

Celeste shook her head. "I'm so sorry, my friend. I tried to heal him. He grabbed my arm. He wouldn't *let* me. He sent me to heal you and Siobhan. He ... he said you were like a son to him. Siobhan was near death. I barely made it to her in time. When I returned to Damon, it was ... he was ... I'm so sorry!"

Arcus pulled away, sitting up on his own. "How could this have happened? The orc he'd enchanted would have died for him. He was a master of that spell!"

"The spell was broken. The orc he had enchanted killed him."

Arcus looked confused for a minute, then all the color drained from his normally olive complexion until he was as pale as the bones of the fallen. He nudged his staff with his hand, horrified.

"Then … I did it. I killed Damon. The closest thing I have to family, and I killed him … with this!" He spat the last word as he shoved the staff as far away as possible.

"Arcus, don't. It wasn't your–"

"Don't you dare tell me that this isn't my fault. *All* of this is my fault. I should have never allowed myself to be taken prisoner, damn what Siobhan wanted! I should have ended that stupid fight quickly, instead of being overconfident and ending up cursed, so that I was unable to be at Siobhan's side. She got hurt and I lost control. I activated the staff and Damon died. It's *all my fault!*" He shook his head. "You all could have died, and that would have been my fault, too."

Siobhan's eyes fluttered as she began to regain consciousness. Celeste quickly moved over to her. Tarnelius, Joseph and Victoria came to join them, with the two men carrying Damon's body between them.

"I'm sorry, Arcus. Truly, I am. I tried to save him but he wouldn't let me."

Arcus squeezed his eyes shut but made no sound. Her heart aching, Celeste dug around in her bag, pulling out a waterskin and placing it next to Siobhan. The paladin seemed to be stirring, but she wasn't yet awake.

Joseph and Tarnelius eased Damon's body to the ground, then Tarnelius moved to Celeste and took her hand, squeezing it.

"He doesn't blame you, or at least he shouldn't. He's hurting right now. Don't worry," thought Tarnelius. Celeste pressed her lips together hard and nodded once.

Joseph sat at Arcus' side. Arcus glanced over at him, then shut his eyes again.

"Arc?"

"It's not a good time, Joseph."

"I can see that. Yet, here we are. Look, I know it hurts. His death hurts me, too. But sitting on a battlefield covered in carnage and destruction isn't going to help anyone. We need a plan. We need to figure out how to … to … dispose of the bodies. Then we need to determine what to do with the rest of the Izmarians, and decide where to go next."

"And just what do you expect me to do about it? I'm of no use to anyone right now. Breathing hurts, and now even thinking and feeling hurt, too. I couldn't save Damon. I couldn't save Siobhan. How do you expect me to help you now?"

"You *did* save Siobhan. She's alive, and will soon come around. As for–"

"No. *Celeste* saved Siobhan, and Damon gave his life for her, if I understand correctly."

"That's enough. When did you become such a whiner? The Arcus I knew would take charge and find a solution. The Arcus I knew wouldn't let the misery of the present control his future. He would call me an idiot and move on. Where is that Arcus? Where is my friend?"

Flames erupted on Arcus' forearms. He looked down and shook his hands, dispelling the magic. Gritting his teeth, he curled his legs under him, preparing to at least try to stand up. Victoria picked up Arcus' staff and held it out to him.

"Keep that *thing* away from me," Arcus spat. "I don't want anything to do with it. Burn it, for all I care."

Celeste stood up from tending to Siobhan, who had lapsed back into unconsciousness, and reached for the staff. She stuffed it back into her small magic bag without a word. Joseph and Tarnelius tried to help Arcus up, but he waved them off. He forced his way to his feet, a grimace on his face. Once upright, he began coughing and almost lost his balance. Blood covered his hand when he pulled it away.

"Is there really nothing we can do to remove the curse?" Victoria cried. "It's killing him."

Tarnelius gazed off into the distance as he thought. "I remember old stories about the priests and clerics of the old gods being able to remove curses. However, I haven't seen any real clerics around since I was a child. Our best hope is probably Siobhan, after she wakes up and recovers her strength."

"I'll be fine," Arcus insisted. "Let me just think for a moment. Okay, first, we need to figure out what to do with the bodies. Second, we need to determine what to do with the survivors. Finally, we need to decide what to do with ourselves. First thing: the amount of firewood we would need to build a big enough pyre is unfeasible. As an alternative, we need to soften the ground enough to bury the dead quickly. Either that or, Celeste, remember that earthquake spell you cast outside of Kayalost? Think you could manage that again?"

"Yes, that would probably be the simplest solution. Joseph, Victoria and Tarnel, will you help me see about getting the bodies moved into a smaller area?"

"I'll help, too," said Arcus.

"No, you stay here with Siobhan. We'll take care of this."

Joseph bent to pick up Damon's body, but Arcus stopped him. "Not Damon. He deserves a real pyre, don't you agree?" Joseph nodded once and then followed the others.

The group spread out to drag, pull and otherwise magically move the bodies into a pile in the center of the field. Their heavy boots sank into the blood-drenched soil of the battlefield, impeding their progress. Once their task was completed, Celeste directed the rest to return to Arcus and Siobhan, who had awoken as the others toiled away, and was now sitting up. Arcus sat next to her with his back to the group, covering his face with his hands.

Once everyone was a safe distance away, Celeste closed her eyes. She focused all her energy inward and breathed. She did her best to block out the gruesome image in front of her and connected with the essence of Kamara, the earth beneath her feet. When she was ready, she muttered the requisite spell and slapped the ground, backing away at a brisk, yet controlled, pace.

The earth began to rumble, originating from the point she had struck. Celeste maintained complete focus, controlling the magic by controlling her emotions. When she finally reached the rest of her group, she let go of a bit of her control. She thought of the carnage she had seen, of all the deaths. She remembered Damon being struck down. As her emotions reached a peak, the earthquake increased in intensity.

The ground split apart and a chasm cut through the rocky earth. Bodies of orcs and humans alike fell in as the world opened up beneath them. Once the last one had fallen in, Celeste screwed up her face in concentration. She directed the chasm to close, then dropped the intensity of the shaking ground until it was stable once more. The earth was still cracked and broken, but was sealed together.

Tarnelius walked toward the broken and splintered ground and cast another spell. This one softened the earth and allowed it to fill in. "From Kamara's womb we are born. To her bosom we all return ... in the end," he murmured. Then he placed his hand into the soft dirt and chanted. Grass and wildflowers rose up to fill in the site of the huge, unmarked tomb. Bowing his head, he turned to rejoin the group.

Joseph took stock of the situation. Siobhan was awake and talking to Arcus. Joseph still couldn't get over the fact that his best friend had finally been tamed–and by a paladin at that. More shocking was the dramatic change in his friend since last they'd met. The man Joseph had spent months and years in school with would never be so overcome by any event as to openly cry as he was now.

Joseph understood how Arcus felt. He was clearly in agony, had lost his substitute father and had nearly lost his woman. That said, it was never okay to cry in front of a female. He needed to be a man and hold it in until he was alone.

The two elves approached Arcus and Siobhan and began discussing curse removal. Tarnelius was convinced Siobhan would be able to cast the proper spell. Looking around the fields impressed upon Joseph how completely all traces of the battle had been removed. The only bad part about the incredible magic the elves had bandied about like it was nothing was that family and friends of the fallen would never be able to put their loved ones to rest themselves. There would be no closure. Those who survived them would never know what happened. Such was the way of the world, he supposed. Nothing in life was guaranteed.

Despite everything that had happened, Joseph was relieved he'd returned to Izmar when he had. The things he'd witnessed in Lumernia haunted him still. He had come here in hopes that Damon would know what to do, but hadn't held out much hope of actually being able to fix the insurmountable problems they faced. Now that he'd found these people, hope burned in his chest. They *would* save what was left of Lumernia, and free those he had befriended there.

Victoria stood a short distance away from the group. She stared at Damon's body with a look of horror on her beautiful face. Everything about her posture screamed that she was alone, adrift in a sea of her own emotions. She tore her eyes away from Damon and glanced at Arcus and Siobhan before dropping to her knees and covering her face in her hands.

Joseph's heart ached to look at her. He had seen that expression before on the faces of those in the resistance in Lumernia after they had learned all their loved ones were gone. He couldn't take it. Victoria was an innocent … at least in reality. In his dreams, she was anything but innocent, but that was another story entirely. She should be taken care of, protected, cherished. She should not be here on this battlefield, subjected to wanton destruction. He swallowed hard and slipped alongside her, placing his hand gently on her shoulder.

She jerked her eyes up to meet his, her expression darkening as recognition flickered across her features.

"What do you want?"

"I'm sorry, Victoria. I know how you feel, because I feel it, too."

"Do you? Who was he to you? Your teacher?" She sighed. "To those of us like me and Arcus, he was so much more. A friend, yes, but also a parent and confidant. You have no idea."

He squeezed her shoulder. She stiffened. "You're wrong, Victoria. I *do* understand. In the last year, I've–"

"Take your hand off me, please."

Joseph sighed and removed his hand. "Fine. I only wanted to say that if you want to talk, I'm here for you." He turned and walked away, leaving her to her thoughts.

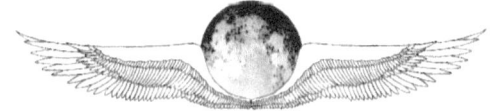

"I think we should head into the forest, maybe travel to Kayalost to regroup," argued Arcus. "Forget Izmar; they can rebuild or leave. This place isn't defensible and will be easily captured if the orcs come back. We can't babysit it forever. We should just try to talk the people who are left into leaving and then move on, ourselves."

"You're right about that," agreed Celeste. "Where'd Joseph go?" She turned around to look for Joseph, and located him a short distance away. He was picking up broken branches from under a large tree. "We should talk to him about what to do next. Joseph has been to Lumernia. He says that the orcs took over after Liam's death."

"What?"

"Apparently the old fool didn't place anyone in charge when he left. His death created a power vacuum, and the knights were so busy fighting amongst themselves that they weren't able to defend Lumernia against the dark orc invasion. I can't imagine that the orcs' presence here is a coincidence."

Arcus felt the blood drain from his face. Lumernia ... the capital city. The largest stronghold on the entire continent. "But ... this is the opposite side of the continent."

Tarnelius gaped at Celeste. "You don't think they've just been pressing west? That would bring them straight through Kayalost!"

Celeste shook her head. "I don't think they would brave the forest. Not first thing. My guess is that they would have swept south, through friendly territory. Especially since they attacked here, south of the city. Anyway, the other orc races would have sided with them–"

Her face paled. "E–Especially if they are being organized by the ruby dragon. At any rate, if they went south and then west, they would have emerged from the orc lands near Ohamn. Taking Ohamn wouldn't be much of a fight. Like Izmar, it's a port city and it isn't well defended. Worse for them, they are friendly to all races, even orcs, so they would have either given up to avoid bloodshed or, like here, they would have been easily wiped out. To be honest, the only thing that probably ruined their plans here was us."

Siobhan frowned. "Why would you mention the ruby dragon? What would she have to do with this?"

"The orcs revere Crusiliux. They worship her like a goddess. They themselves are chaotic and don't organize easily, but if anyone could unify them, it would be her."

"What about the northeastern cities? What about Lunastra and Veritas, or any of the others?"

"I don't know any more than you do, Siobhan. I can only speculate at their tactics. If I were planning to take control of the entire continent with the orcs, I would jump at the opportunity to seize control of Lumernia, head south into friendly territory and pick up more warm bodies to increase my numbers. Then I would head into Ohamn and Izmar, perhaps even the dwarven lands of Dvernholt. After that, I would surround Kayalost on three sides and force the druids out, then push north toward Gormloch and Abhainn. I suspect people in the northeastern cities are safe for now, especially if they haven't tried to travel into Lumernia yet.

"I think Arcus is right," Celeste continued. "We need to head into Kayalost to regroup, perhaps gain reinforcements. If my experiences with the elves have taught me anything, it's that we can't count on King Audelthus, but we should give it a shot. At least we can warn them to be on alert. Once we've organized ourselves, we should go back to Lumernia, perhaps by way of Castle Mithra or some of the other strongholds. I really feel the best way to drive the threat back is to reclaim Lumernia. If Crusiliux *is* involved, that is also the closest defensible city to her, so she would probably choose it as her base of operations."

Victoria joined them. "What about the people here?"

Celeste paused, lost in thought. "I think the best thing to do is to determine if Simon is still alive. If he is, we need to convince him to evacuate what is left of the city north, to Holmsden. It's much more fortified than this place."

"He won't do it."

"Then that is his decision. I suppose we could also scream from the streets, but let's see how things go. Arcus, will you be okay to travel?"

Arcus sighed. "I'm fine. I wish everyone would stop worrying about me."

Siobhan hugged him, causing Arcus to flinch. "I'll try to work on the spell to remove the curse first chance I get. I don't know if I can remove it or not, but I'll do my best."

Arcus gave her a wry smile. "I know you'll do your best. I also know it'll be tomorrow morning before you can try. Don't worry about me." He returned her hug. "I'm sorry I lost control a few minutes ago. I'm better now. Try not to worry."

Siobhan kissed him lightly on the lips. "You were there for me when I lost control after Katie's death. It's my duty and privilege to be there for you, too. I love you."

The lines of pain etched onto Arcus' face receded slightly as he gazed at his wife. "And I you."

"We should help Joseph," said Tarnelius. He began walking toward another tree to collect branches. Celeste followed behind him.

Victoria muttered an incantation and lifted her hands. Branches from all over the field lifted into the air and floated to the pile Joseph had begun.

Arcus limped over to Damon. Gritting his teeth, he bent to lift him up. Tarnelius and Joseph rushed to his side.

"Let us get him, Arc," said Joseph.

"No. I want to help. I can do this." Arcus stifled a cough. Joseph and Tarnelius exchanged uneasy glances. Together, the three of them carried Damon's body to the pyre and laid him reverently upon it. The three women came to join them.

"Damon, you were more than a teacher. You were my friend, my mentor … and you were like my father. I know you did what you thought was best, and I will forever appreciate the sacrifice you made." Arcus' voice broke and he reached for Siobhan's hand. "I will miss you so much, my friend. I hope we meet again in the next life, someday."

Victoria cleared her throat. "Damon, you saved me from myself. You saved my life in more ways than one. I second what Arcus said: you were more than a teacher, you were my friend. You were a friend to so many, and we'll never forget you. They say death is a part of life, but I refuse to believe it was your time to go already." Tears poured down her face.

Joseph sighed. "I don't know what to say that my friends haven't already said. Thanks for everything, Damon. We'll all miss you. Looking to our task ahead, I can't help but wonder if you got the easy way out, though. Wish us luck, old man." He turned his back and walked over to the road leading back into Izmar. The rest watched him in stunned silence before turning back to the task at hand. Arcus lifted his hand and pointed. A beam of fire shot from his finger and set the wood around Damon's body ablaze.

They all–minus Joseph–stood around the pyre and watched as it burned until the conflagration consumed Damon's body and finally died out. With a swipe of her hand through the air, Celeste caused a gust of wind to push past them, scattering the ashes. Then they turned and joined Joseph for the slow walk back into Izmar.

Chapter Six
Revelations and Revulsions

A rriving back in the city brought with it an eerie sensation. Izmar was abandoned; the streets were completely empty. Windows had been boarded up and litter drifted down the street, escorted by the breeze. Even the street vendors and vagrants were absent.

Victoria rubbed her arms, which were folded over her chest. She wondered what had become of her family. Had they been killed? Had they survived, would they move on? "This wasn't what I expected at all. Where are the people? I thought there would be riots, chaos, insanity."

"They're all hiding," said Joseph. "Locked in their homes, as if that could save them. If not there, they are at the docks trying to buy or barter their way out. I've seen it before."

"Should we check the docks for Simon, then?" Tarnel asked.

"No. Let's check his home first. If he isn't there, we could check the docks. It's getting dark now. We should go back to the dorms for the night, after we find Simon."

"Are you sure we should return to the dorms?" Siobhan asked.

Joseph nodded. "It's what Damon would have wanted."

"Besides, it's my only home," added Victoria.

Arcus sighed, but neither argued nor agreed. Siobhan watched him, a concerned look on her face. "Are you okay, Arcus? Do you want me to summon Apollo?"

"No."

"Are you sure? You look—"

"I said no," Arcus wheezed.

Siobhan rolled her eyes, but didn't press the matter. Once they reached the city center, Celeste stopped walking, a frown on her face.

"What?" Tarnelius asked her.

"I think we should split up. It's getting late. The sun is down and we don't really *know* where Simon is, or even if he is still alive. You and I will go to the docks, Tarnel. We'll look at what is going on there, perhaps talk to anyone we find even if Simon isn't there. Joseph should go to Simon's house, assuming that is okay with you?"

Joseph nodded.

"Siobhan and Arcus should head to the dorms. They can search around there and see if there is anything to help Siobhan with her magic for the morning."

Siobhan frowned. "But what could I possibly find that—"

Celeste gave her a pointed look and she stopped.

"I'm not stupid, you know." Arcus glared, chest heaving despite his apparent difficulty drawing breath. "This is nothing more than a ploy to get me out of the way because you think I cannot handle it."

"Believe what you want. This is the best plan."

"Where should I go?" asked Victoria.

"Hmm. Why don't you go with Joseph? That way no one is alone. Better to handle trouble if we pair off. Let's go, everyone. Meet back at the dorms after our tasks are done."

With that, the groups split apart. Tarnelius and Celeste headed west, Arcus and Siobhan went to the east, Victoria and Joseph continued north to Simon's manor.

The grounds were dark when the pair arrived at Simon's door.

"Looks like no one's home," whispered Victoria.

"Seems that way. Let's knock, just to be sure."

Joseph knocked hard on the door. As soon as he finished, a loud crash rang out, sounding like it came from one of the side yards.

"Stay here in case someone comes. I'll check it out!" Joseph rushed off around the house before she could argue.

"Great. Just what I needed: to be standing here, in the dark, in front of Simon's house. Great." She sighed impatiently and rocked from foot to foot. "This is dumb. No one is home. I'll go get Joseph and we can get out of here." She turned to walk away, when the door was yanked opened and someone grabbed her wrist and pulled her inside.

The inside of the house was as dark as it was outside. Victoria tried to scream, but a hand pressed over her mouth. She felt the press of cold steel against her throat.

"Calm down, my sweet. Fighting will serve no purpose but to bring you pain. I told you I'd deal with you later. That you came to my house willingly matters not. I always keep my promises. These are the rules. You are more than familiar with them."

"You're delusional." Victoria's voice came as a whisper, swallowing against the cold blade now pressed more firmly to her throat.

"Am I so delusional? You wanted to play earlier today. Oh, you tried to hide it, but I could … smell it on you. And look. You've come back to me all on your own, without that troublesome bitch friend of yours. It's her fault, you know." The knife dug deeper. "She and her husband are responsible for the savages' attack. My city, my very livelihood, is in ruins. Pity that she isn't here. I will simply take what she owes me from you." Dropping the knife, he grabbed both of her hands and yanked them over her head, pressing her hard against the wall.

Panic flooded Victoria's system. He forced his lips against her closed mouth. She felt his desire rub against her belly. This position was not unfamiliar, but this time, in the dark, she somehow knew it would be different. He would rape and kill her. He wouldn't risk letting her tell people of his twisted appetites. Would her new friends, if she could call them that, look for her when they discovered her missing? What would Simon tell them if and when they crossed paths? No. She would not die like this. Gathering her courage, she sunk her teeth into Simon's lower lip. A stream of warm, coppery blood gushed into her mouth. Simon jerked, but didn't release her. She could barely breathe, forced as she was into the wall by his body, her mouth filling with his blood.

The front door opened, as if forced by the wind.

Still gripping her wrists above her head, Simon tore his face from hers and looked at the door. Yanking her along with him, he kicked the door shut again before forcing her back into the wall, using the weight of his body to pin her in place.

"Now, where were we? Oh yes, you thought you could bite me, as if that would make a difference."

Simon's voice cut off. He looked up just as Joseph materialized behind him. A blade gleamed with a ghostly glow in what little moonlight streamed through the nearby window. Before anyone could react, Joseph plunged the blade deep into Simon's neck, his face a contorted grimace.

Releasing her and staggering backward, Simon gurgled from the pain and yanked the knife out of his neck.

Joseph stepped protectively between Victoria and Simon. Angry white-hot fire burned in his eyes. "Only a coward would force himself on a woman, and only a sick, sick man would find pleasure in it."

Simon backed up and swore. Yanking on a decorative cloth and sending several vases and other glassware flying, he quickly tied it around his neck and tucked the ends into his shirt to stem the bleeding.

"You'll pay for that, boy."

Joseph snarled out a magic spell and a dazzling orb of pure white light illuminated the room. The orb spun and twisted in the air, creating fascinating patterns. It charged Simon and caused him to duck. In the confusion, Joseph cast another spell and four replicas of himself appeared. He and his doppelgangers moved around each other, changing positions while the orb of light barreled down onto Simon. It struck into Simon's chest and vanished.

Simon melted into a shadow, only to appear as if by magic out of another near one of Joseph's magical allies. He lashed out with the knife. It struck home in the center of Joseph's chest. Victoria screamed, only to suck in her breath again as the Joseph he had stabbed evaporated with a puff of smoke.

The remaining four Josephs lifted their hands and created several small globes with lightning flickering inside. They flung their spells at Simon in unison, some striking their target, others disappearing on contact.

Simon snarled and stabbed his knife into the throat of one of the remaining sorcerers. It, too, vanished without a sound.

Coming back to her senses with a start, Victoria flicked her wrist, releasing one of her daggers into her hand. Taking aim, she hurled the weapon at Simon. He shrieked as the blade burrowed deep into his left thigh.

The Joseph triplets cast identical rainbow spells, which arced from each of them directly into Simon. The colors danced and swirled in a hypnotic pattern, demanding Simon's attention. Simon froze, mesmerized by the colors. Joseph charged and punched Simon hard in the nose, landing on top of him as they both dropped from the force of the impact.

Joseph loomed over the badly injured Simon, and held the knife to his throat. "I want you to look into my eyes. I want you to see my life continue while yours fades away for daring to touch her. But first, you'll beg for her forgiveness." He ran the end of the knife across Simon's jawline, drawing blood. "If not on your own, then with some ... encouragement."

"I will not. Just be done with it, mage. You wouldn't have stood a chance without your magic."

"I didn't see you exactly hiding your *shadow-step* abilities, thief. I don't know why I never realized it before in all the time I lived here. The rumors have always been true. You are a thief and probably in league with the thieves' guild. You are everything that is wrong with this city ... all the corruption and fear. Ironic that people pay their taxes to the very man who steals from them! And on top of everything else, you're nothing but a common rapist. Apologize to the lady."

"Lady? What do you know of it, you pathetic, scrawny excuse for a mage? She came to *me*. Not just tonight but many, many times in the past. She came so that I would give her power, money, anything she needed. She gave herself to me. This girl whose honor you're so bent on protecting? She prostitutes herself to me, and has many–"

Joseph plunged the dagger into Simon's throat, severing his vocal chords. Blood gurgled from his mouth and nose, pulsed from the wounds in his neck. Joseph finished him off in silence, then rose to his feet and wiped off the dagger on a cloth sitting on a nearby table. He didn't look at Victoria.

"Joseph, I–"

"Is it true?"

"Not today. Not now."

"Is it *true*?"

Victoria swallowed hard. "Yes, but only because–"

Joseph laughed humorlessly. "They say dreams are always better than reality, don't they? Come on, let's go back. We won't be able to talk *Simon* into arranging any sort of evacuation plan now." He stomped from the room.

Victoria followed after him, feeling ashamed. "Th-thank you for saving me."

Joseph grunted, but still wouldn't look at her.

All at once, sharp indignation rose up within her. "Wait just one minute there, Joseph Hale. First of all, *you* have no claims to me. None. I don't have to answer to you for my decisions. Second, you yourself have not exactly been a saint. I've seen you out with so many girls, I couldn't even count them all–"

Joseph yanked her to him and passionately kissed her on the lips. She resisted and he let her go, staring down at her with an emotion she couldn't place.

"They never meant anything. I was always trying to find … well, you. None of them could compare. At least I thought they couldn't. Perhaps I just had you up on a pedestal all along and could never really see *you*. Now I can. I may not have been a saint, but I never prostituted myself." He chuckled mirthlessly. "I can't believe you would do *that* with *him*, but would never give *me* a chance. I practically fell at your feet and begged, and yet you fought me, refused me and humiliated me … on a regular basis. Unbelievable." He started to turn away, but she pulled him back. She stared into his eyes, searching for any sign of the passion she had felt from him just a moment ago, but only saw honesty and pain. Embarrassed and disgraced, she turned from him.

"We need to get back."

Victoria and Joseph finished the trip to the dorm in silence. Joseph flexed his hand, feeling jolts of lightning shoot through his arm with each movement. Looked like he'd broken it on Simon's face. Great.

Joseph cleared his throat. "Goodnight, Victoria. I'll let Arcus know we're back. No need to wait up on my account."

"But I–"

Victoria shut her mouth at the stony expression he gave her. She shot him a dirty look. "Fine." She stomped to her door and shoved it open after removing the magical lock she had placed on it. Then she walked into her room, slamming the door behind her.

Joseph sagged with relief when the door shut. He was enraged beyond rational thought, but wondered if he was really angrier at himself. He'd pined every day he had known her, playing it off as nothing more than attraction to a stunning woman. Joseph had thrown himself at other women to fill the void, but in truth it was her. It had always been her, the one who haunted his dreams. She was so beautiful, so pure ... or so he thought.

I guess she didn't want me because I never offered her enough money, he thought cynically. He knocked on Arcus' door.

Siobhan answered. She quickly stepped out of the room and shut the door behind her.

"He's asleep. I really don't want to wake him. He's so stubborn sometimes."

"He can get that way. I just wanted to let you know we were back. Have the elves returned?"

"No, not yet. Did you find Simon?"

Joseph's face darkened. "We did."

"And? Will he evacuate the city?"

"He isn't going to do anything. I killed him."

Siobhan gasped. "You *what?* Why would you do such a thing?"

"Among other reasons, I caught him in the act of raping Victoria."

Siobhan paled. "You ... you caught ..."

"Not what you think. He was forcing her against a wall and pinning her down. She was struggling, but he was too strong. His intent was obvious, but luckily I caught them before the clothes came off." Joseph clenched his fist, wincing.

Siobhan had a look of utter horror on her face. She shook her head as if to clear it. "Is she okay? Are *you* okay? Show me your hand."

He held it out to her, and her hand flashed a beautiful gold as she healed him. "Thanks for that. She's fine. I sent her to her room." He didn't mention it was because he couldn't stand the sight of her at the moment.

Siobhan sighed. "I don't think it's the first time something like that has happened. The one time I met Simon he came on to me and practically demanded she strip for him." Her eyes narrowed. "I trust you gave him a fair fight instead of stabbing him in the back."

"Yes. I *wanted* him to apologize, but that didn't happen. Listen, I'm going to go for a walk. Maybe I can find Celeste and Tarnelius. I need to clear my head after everything that has happened today."

Siobhan looked to Damon's door. "Arcus and I may be a little late coming out in the morning. I must meditate at sunrise for the spell to remove his curse. I'm unfamiliar with this spell, so hopefully the magic will be granted to me. Please do not disturb us. I don't want to risk losing my concentration while preparing. We'll come out when ready. Goodnight."

She shut the door and Joseph began walking, lost in his own dark thoughts about morality. He wandered aimlessly for a short while before turning his steps in the direction of the docks. As he approached, he heard shouting. It seemed his theory was right: in the aftermath of the battle, the majority of Izmar's population had amassed at the docks. Just when he had almost made it to the street the *Dragonfire* was on, he found the two elves, heading back in the direction of the dorms.

"Did you find him?" Tarnelius asked.

"Yes. He's dead."

Celeste frowned. "He was dead in his house?"

"No. He *is* dead in his house. Look, I'd rather not speak of it. You can ask Victoria, if you're curious of the details. Suffice it to say that he is dead."

"But–"

Tarnelius cut her off with a firm hand on her arm. Joseph noticed the elf was staring at his clothes. Looking down, he could see why: he was covered in blood ... Simon's blood. His cheeks burned, and he looked away.

"What's the situation here?" Joseph asked, trying to change the subject and refusing to look Tarnelius in the eyes.

"The good news is that we don't need Simon to evacuate the city," answered Celeste. "It seems they all understand that they need to get out of here. The Izmarians are trying to barter passage on the ships, and the ones who can't afford it are walking. We've been spreading the word to try to get people to head either north to Holmsden or northeast to Abhainn. I think we've done all we can. Izmar will be a ghost town soon. We need to rest up and regroup in Kayalost tomorrow."

"Okay," Joseph agreed. "Listen, I was talking to Siobhan, and she says not to disturb them in the morning. I guess she has to pray to whatever dead god she serves and doesn't want to be interrupted. She says they'll come out when they are ready. I'll see you two tomorrow."

"You aren't coming back to the dorms?"

"Maybe, eventually. We'll see. I need to clear my head. Goodnight." Joseph waved as he walked past, continuing toward the bars. He took in the chaotic crowds on the dockside and noticed that there were quite a few people filling the taverns. He stopped outside one called the *Whispering Serpent Pub.* He hesitated for a moment, then walked inside. Spotting a couple of ladies unescorted at the bar, he sidled up alongside them.

"Bartender! I'll take a pint of whatever the specialty of the house is ... and one for each of these beautiful ladies, as well." He gave them each a heart-stopping smile.

"Thank you," said the nearest of the two. "My name is Clarissa, and my friend here is Elizabeth."

"Charmed. My name is Joseph. Is this pub any good? I used to frequent the *Dragonfire* before I moved away from here, but I thought I would try something new."

"It seems okay. Suits our needs, anyway. We just came here to waste some time before our ship leaves in the morning." Suddenly, Clarissa noticed the appearance of his clothing and edged away, toward her friend, just as the bartender plunked their drinks down on the bar. "What happened to you, anyway?"

"Hmm? Oh, this? Well, I was in the southern fields when the orcs attacked. They won't make that mistake again. Don't worry. This is *their* blood, not mine."

"Really? Then we should be the ones buying your drinks, since it seems you saved all of these people's lives."

Joseph leaned forward and gazed deeply into her blue eyes. "The drinks are on me tonight. I can think of other ways you could repay me, if you are interested."

Clarissa grinned and glanced at Elizabeth. Turning back to Joseph, she lifted her glass in a toast. "Sounds like a possibility. Let's finish our drinks and get to know one another. First, why don't you tell us all about what happened with the orcs?"

Satisfied he would have a distraction for the remainder of the evening, Joseph sat back and told them what had happened, punctuating his story with some light illusion magic for their entertainment. He was careful to play himself up as the hero, and even managed to shed a single manly tear when he told them of Damon's death. The tear came easier than expected. He felt a familiar pang of guilt as he remembered Victoria, but cast her from his mind, determined to enjoy the evening.

Chapter Seven
Full Circle

"Here we go. Let's hope this works." Siobhan placed her hands over Arcus' chest. Her arms glowed a brilliant gold from her fingertips to her elbows, pulsing with holy radiance. Arcus' breath caught as he watched her close her eyes and focus her magic into him. The pain that had wracked his body the whole night receded, leaving him refreshed and invigorated.

"Did it work?" she asked, her eyes hopeful.

Arcus took a deep breath, then reached out and grabbed her, kissing her deeply. "Yes," he murmured in between kisses. "Thank you, my beautiful Siobhan. My goddess."

She giggled and squirmed away. "None of that now. The others are waiting for us."

Arcus' face darkened as he took in his surroundings. Her words drove home what had happened the day before. He had locked much of it away in order to deal with his own pain. He winced as he remembered their losses from the day before.

"You're right, of course. Here, let me help you into your armor and then we can go find the others."

Arcus deftly helped her to don her armor, taking extra care to make sure everything was fastened correctly. Frowning at the damaged plates where the sword had penetrated, he whispered an incantation and watched the damage mend. He rubbed the area with his thumb and looked up into her eyes.

"I can't lose you, Siobhan," he murmured.

"You won't."

"I nearly have, twice now. It's scared the life out of me."

She stroked his face and smiled. "But here I am. You saved me, same as last time."

"What if next time I'm not so lucky?"

"I have faith in you. Besides, next time it's my turn to save you."

"You save me every day by being here. With you by my side, I'm reminded things aren't always as dark as they seem. When you're with me, I can see the light. Come here." He sat down and tugged her into his lap. "I need to kiss you."

"Oh? You *need* to?"

Arcus smiled. "Like I need air to breathe."

They kissed, losing themselves in each other. The rest of the world faded away. No one else mattered. Unfortunately, all too soon, there came a knock at the door. The couple jumped apart guiltily.

Siobhan frowned. "I told them not to interrupt us … that we would come out when we were ready."

"Then ignore them."

Siobhan shook her head. "We can't ignore them. It must be important."

Arcus sighed and rose to his feet, gathering their things. Siobhan answered the door.

Victoria stood outside, alone. "Good morning. I was worried you had left without me or something."

"Why would you think that?"

"Because no one had come out yet, and Joseph ..." Victoria paused. "Wait. If you two didn't leave, then where is Joseph? He didn't answer when I knocked on his door."

"I spoke to him last night. He said he was going to take a walk. Hmm. Are Celeste and Tarnelius gone, too?"

"I haven't tried them yet."

Siobhan strode out of the room and down the causeway to the elves' room. Arcus also came out and smiled awkwardly at Victoria.

"Are you feeling better, Arcus?"

"Yes. Thank you." He followed after his wife, who was knocking on a door.

Celeste came out and smiled at Siobhan. "Good morning." She nodded to Arcus. "You look better. I trust this means the spell went well. Are we ready to head out?"

Tarnelius stepped out of the room and handed Celeste her bag.

Victoria frowned at Tarnelius. "Joseph wasn't in there with you?"

"No. Joseph has his own room." She pointed past Arcus to the room behind him.

Arcus turned and knocked on Joseph's door. "Hey, open up! Stop snoozing the day away."

"Are you guys looking for me?" Joseph called as he approached from behind them.

Victoria gasped and whirled around to face him.

Arcus chuckled. "You're finally getting in now?"

"How do you know I didn't get up early?"

"Your blood-stained clothes. Some things never change, do they?"

Joseph scowled at Victoria. "Only some things. Let me go change and I'll be ready. Are we going to Kayalost?"

"Yes," answered Celeste. "We'll stop by the elven city to warn them, and then head to Lumernia, perhaps by way of Castle Mithra. We can talk about that later."

Joseph pushed past everyone and entered his room.

Victoria looked sick as she watched him go, her face green with either jealousy or disgust–it was anyone's guess. She shook her head. "How long will it take us to get there?"

"Mere seconds. I've seen some trees around town that will work nicely to get us there. Tarnel and I can each take one of you, and Arcus can teleport Siobhan without a tree."

"Tree?"

Celeste smiled as the door opened again. "You'll see."

"What will she see?" asked Joseph.

"We're going to teleport to Kayalost using the trees," answered Victoria.

"I thought we agreed you were not coming. This is far too dangerous. You have to get on one of those ships and head north, where it's safe."

Victoria's face turned redder and redder with each word he spoke. She tried to interrupt once, but shut her mouth, scowling. Giving Celeste a syrupy sweet smile, she linked arms with the elf. "Let's go. I can't wait to see Kayalost."

Joseph glared at them. Celeste gave him an apologetic smile. "I'm not going to turn down volunteers, Joseph. She seems pretty determined. You might as well get used to it."

"Where shall we meet?" Arcus asked.

"By the willow tree," answered Celeste. "Probably the easiest landmark."

"Arcus, walk with us," said Tarnelius. "It's better if we arrive at the same time."

"Does it matter? The elves know me. I don't think it will be an issue."

"That may be, but it's been a while since we were there last, and my father can ... well, let's just say you should wait for us. Come on."

The group arrived at a cypress tree about halfway between the dorms and the southern fields. Indicating he should go first, Tarnelius ran his hands over the trunk of the tree while murmuring the incantation. The lines running around the bark glowed gold under his touch, and the outline of a door appeared. Reaching out to grab Joseph's arm, Tarnelius completed his spell and entered the tree, pulling Joseph along with him. As soon as the two of them vanished, Celeste stepped forward with Victoria and mimicked Tarnelius' actions. The golden door frame reappeared and Celeste pulled Victoria inside. Arcus took his wife in his arms and they, too, teleported with a popping sound.

There was a falling sensation, then the interior of the cramped quarters became bathed in gilded radiance. In less than a moment's time, Tarnelius was pulling Joseph from the tree. They stepped out into a beautiful village where homes and buildings were built as extensions of the trees themselves, the world around them sparkling an emerald green. Tarnelius had lived almost his entire life in Kayalost. He had once thought he would never leave this place, but now he felt like a stranger. He took a deep, cleansing breath.

"Do you miss it?"

Tarnelius glanced at Joseph. "It's only a place." Celeste and Victoria stepped out of the tree and Tarnelius smiled at them. "My home is wherever Celeste is."

Pop.

They looked up to see Arcus and Siobhan appear several feet away, over by the massive willow tree. Tarnelius and the others walked over to join them.

"I've always loved this willow tree," mused Arcus. "Its amazing size and color seem to capture the very magic of this place."

"Me, too," replied Celeste. "We first met in front of this tree. I was always drawn to its beauty, and that day was no exception."

Arcus nodded. "It's the same for me."

Celeste took Tarnelius' hand and squeezed it. "So much has changed since then. Destiny is a funny thing."

"It certainly is. Come on, let's go see if we can find my father and speak with him. We should leave by tomorrow, if not later today. This needs to be a short visit."

Celeste nodded and allowed Tarnelius to pull her toward the main part of the village. The others followed close behind. Tarnelius nodded to several elves as they passed, and many stopped in surprise at the sight of them. A few crossed their fists over their chests and kneeled in respect. Everyone stared. The prince held himself in a regal posture, acting the part he was born to ... but Tarnelius found himself surprised to realize that there were many faces he didn't recognize. Those that he did remember seemed anxious and hurried on their way after acknowledging him.

Tarnelius glanced at his mate. He knew how much she detested being stared at, and could feel her anxiety through their bond.

"You have to admit we make an odd group," he thought to her. *"Doubtful any of them expected us back today, much less accompanied by four humans."*

"I know."

Tarnelius caught a glimpse of an elf who peeked at them from behind a tree. He stopped short, which made Siobhan walk into him. The elf was a female, with untamed platinum blonde hair and the characteristic green eyes common to her race. She was of medium height and appeared out of place in her deep purple robe, the garb of their Helvetinost cousins.

The elves of Helvetinost dwelt underground, in a sparkling and bejeweled village. Their skin was black as night and they all had bright red eyes that allowed them to see in the dark. Being in direct sunlight was painful to them, so they rarely left their homes. This meant that they did not often come into contact with their above-ground relatives, despite their close proximity, because the Kayalost elves did not do well underground. Being cut off from the sky and fresh air made most surface elves extremely claustrophobic.

"Tonilehdossa," Tarnelius murmured, his voice hoarse.

"What's going on? I'm confused," said Victoria.

"You made it back here," Tarnelius continued speaking to the strange elf. "I'm so glad to see that." His haunted smile didn't reach his eyes.

"Yes, I did. This is a strange, lonely place. The others seem anxious and on edge. Maybe they don't like new people. I hope that, in time, they will accept me and it will feel like home here."

"Who is this?" Celeste thought to Tarnelius. *"She looks familiar to me, but I can't place her."*

"You knew her mother, Laerestella," Tarnelius responded in kind. *"She was your next-door neighbor for years, until the*

day she disappeared. I met Tonilehdossa–Toni–in Helvetinost many centuries ago."

Celeste considered this. *"Laerestella! You're right. I can see the resemblance. What was she doing in Helvetinost? What were* either *of you doing there?"*

650 years earlier ...

"You will marry Velonessa and take your place as ruler of the Silver Isles," Audelthus snarled. *"Then one day the two of you will take my place here and rule over both kingdoms. That is what was promised on the day of your birth, and that is what you must do."*

"I won't."

"You will. *What is your hesitation? Your half-breed is gone. You need to move on, to accept your duty."*

"I don't love her. My heart belongs to Celeste. It always has. That will never change."

"Celeste is gone!" *Audelthus bellowed. "Accept it. Embrace it. Love does not matter in our customs. You know that. Once the bond is made, neither of you will be able to help yourselves."*

Tarnelius turned away. His father's words left poisoned gashes on his soul, but he would never give in. Celeste, where are you? *he wondered to himself.*

"You will see reason. Promises must be kept."

There was a whirring sound. Tarnelius braced himself but didn't move, didn't flinch. The sound continued, setting his pulse racing. Two guards who were loyal to Audelthus lunged forward and grabbed Tarnelius, holding him in place. The crack sounded as the third guard snapped the whip onto his back, ripping his shirt and flaying his flesh. Then the whirring began again. Tarnelius clenched his jaw but didn't make a sound. Again and again, the whip sounded as it struck, ripping the skin from his back and setting it on fire.

"Have you had enough yet, my son?"

Tarnelius swallowed hard and glared at Audelthus. "Never," he gasped. "I will never give in to you. Not this way, not any way."

Audelthus smirked. "We'll see about that." He turned to the guard ... a man Tarnelius had once counted as a friend. "Get the collar."

Tarnelius inhaled sharply, but remained calm and proud as the horrible black collar was forced around his neck. He knew what it was. His father had procured it from Tumasi traders out of Izmar for a handsome price. The collar would keep him from using any magic. No healing, no shifting. He wouldn't even be able to talk to any passing animals to procure their aid.

"Tie his arms to those tree branches and leave him to hang. A few days on his own out here to think ought to make him see reason. Hurry up about it. We have to get back to the village."

Tarnelius became aware of the sound of footsteps approaching. He didn't look up or otherwise react. Whoever it

was would either help him ... or make it worse. Worrying about it solved nothing.

He'd lost track of time, alone here in the forest. He was sure he would soon die of thirst, and he'd never known hunger like this. If they had come to torture him further, he wasn't sure he cared. His end would be soon anyway.

"Been thinking, son?"

Tarnelius did not respond, but his heart sank in his chest. It seemed his torture was not yet over.

"Cut him down," the king commanded.

Tarnelius heard blades being removed from their sheaths and suddenly he crashed to the ground in a heap. A waterskin was thrown toward him but, though he longed to grab it, his muscles remained stubborn and uncooperative. As if they could read his mind, one of the guards grabbed him by the hair and yanked his head back, then put the waterskin to his lips. Tarnelius swallowed compulsively, then greedily, as the water flooded his system.

"The people are wondering where their prince is. Who knew you were so popular among the common folk? I had to tell them you had gone away on an official errand, but would return as soon as possible and would then marry the princess, as promised."

"Never," croaked Tarnelius. "You'll have to kill me."

"Tarnelius, you're my son. What makes you think I want to kill you? I merely want you to see reason."

"You ... you've told the people I was marrying the princess. That isn't happening. Therefore, you'll have to kill me."

Audelthus heaved a long-suffering sigh. "I was afraid you'd say that. Look, son, I am not heartless. I recognize I cannot force you into this if you are steadfast in your decision. I could continue to punish you, yes. I could keep going until I break you. To what end or purpose, though? Who knows how long that would take, and I can't keep sneaking out like a thief in the night to come talk to you. I can't hide you here in the woods for that long. It's only a matter of time before someone stumbles across you. So here is my proposition: you will come back with me and marry the princess at once, or you will leave here immediately. I am prepared to take you to the gates of Helvetinost, where you will remain stationed deep underground for a span of one year. You will be an ambassador to our people there, and you will help our cousins in whatever capacity they need. Under no circumstances are you to leave the confines of their mountain home until the year is up. The official story is that you will be searching for the half-breed. After the sentence is complete, I will allow you to send Velonessa home to her people. As you can see, I am not unreasonable ... assuming, of course, that you are willing and able to do the time ..." His eyes glinted in challenge.

Tarnelius closed his eyes, the pain of his body at war with the pain in his chest at the thought of what was being asked—no, demanded—of him. He felt he would suffocate at the thought. Being trapped underground was worse than the sting of the whip. It was the worst, most evil thing his father could have come up with. He didn't know why he felt surprise.

"I knew you would refuse. Shall we go schedule the ceremony now, then?"

"I accept."

"You what?" Audelthus' eyebrows shot up.

"I will go to Helvetinost. I will never bond with Velonessa."

Audelthus sighed. "So be it." He nodded to one of his sentries. "Do it. Leave the collar on him and make sure he enters the mountain."

The sentry lifted Tarnelius up and carried him over his shoulder to a nearby tree, which he enchanted and entered.

Tarnelius was miserable. He couldn't breathe. The air was still and stagnant. To his anxious mind, it felt thick and heavy - he might as well have been trying to breathe water. The Helvetinost elves were good people; they had removed his collar and had healed his wounds, which had become infected. He had finally been allowed to eat and felt physically stronger, but the overwhelming sensation that the walls were closing in on him chipped away at his very soul. He had no idea how he would survive a week of this, much less a year.

Maybe his father was right. Maybe he should have given in. Celeste was lost to him; he saw no way of getting her back. If he stepped up and assumed the role of dutiful son and prince of Kayalost, his torture would end. Tears leaked down his face. He couldn't stop them.

Celeste, where are you? *he screamed inside his head.* I love you. I want forever with you. I never wanted … never wanted this.

Someone stumbled in the darkness. A female, to judge by the grunts of pain. He cocked his head. It wasn't entirely dark, but the lack of real light made distinguishing features very difficult for those used to sunlight. The Helvetinost elves could see easily in absolute darkness. For a moment, he wondered if

Celeste had come for him. If she had, they could leave this place forever and never look back.

Tarnelius sighed, knowing his hopeful mind was playing games with him. Chanting in the language of magic, he made a small flame of light flicker to life in the palm of his hand, and winced at the sudden brightness.

Once his eyes adjusted, he stared in surprise at the young woman who was gawking at him.

She was like him: pale skin and blonde hair. Where his was golden like the sun, hers was platinum, almost white. Unlike him, she seemed at ease down here, under the mountain.

"Who are you?"

Her green eyes widened. She looked as if ready to bolt from the room.

"Whoa, calm down. It's okay. I was surprised to see you, that's all. Let's try that again. My name is Tarnelius. What's yours?"

She swallowed. "T-Toni."

"Toni?"

"Tonilehdossa, but my former owners called me Toni." Her accent was strange, almost guttural. Tarnelius wondered where she had come from.

"That's a beautiful name. Do you know what it means?"

She shook her head.

"It means, 'praise beyond the grove'. It's a hopeful name. What did you mean by your owners?"

"I was born a slave. Centuries ago, my parents were stolen from the forest grove. I was raised among the Tumasi. One day I snuck aboard a trading ship bound for the dwarf lands and escaped. The dwarves brought me here, and here is where I now live."

"What of your parents?"

"My father was killed by my owners several years back. My mother died of a broken heart soon after. My mother was beautiful. Her name was Laerestella. Do you know what that means?"

"Laerestella?" Tarnelius held the light closer to her and looked into her face. He swore. "By Kamara, you do look exactly like her. We searched everywhere for her and her mate, but they had vanished."

"You knew my mother? What did you say your name was again?"

"Tarnelius."

Toni's eyes widened. "You're the elf prince!"

"So they tell me. That means you are my second cousin. Laerestella is–was–my father's cousin."

"What are you doing here? My mother used to tell me stories about you and the grove."

"Well ..." Tarnelius began to talk, telling her about the grove, druids, Celeste, his father, everything. Toni spoke to him of her life as a slave, her escape and her unwillingness to ever be subservient to anyone again. She had a way of speaking that he admired. It was direct and succinct, unlike most other elves he knew. That was a trait she shared with Celeste, though he supposed in her case it was more a matter of how she was raised. He wondered who she would have become if her life in the grove hadn't been robbed from her. They talked about anything and everything to pass the time, and eventually Tarnelius taught her druid magic. If it weren't for Toni, he may well have gone insane in that dark cave during that year. He felt a pang of sadness leaving her behind when his sentence was up, but this had become her home and she was afraid to leave it. She promised him that one day she would try to return to Kayalost, to see her mother's home that she was named for.

Tarnelius shook his head, trying to pull himself out of his past. Gazing at Celeste, he was saddened to see tears flowing freely down her face. He wiped away her tears, hating that he had allowed himself to indulge in those memories. He knew she had seen everything–had felt everything–as he remembered it.

"I am so sorry. I had no idea. I didn't–"

"Shh. It's okay. Everything worked out. It's behind us now. Come. I want you two to meet."

Tarnelius pulled Celeste to his chest and gave her a warm hug, trying to pour his feelings of love into the simple act. When she calmed, he led her over to Toni.

"Celeste, this is Tonilehdossa, my cousin. Toni, this is Celeste, my bonded mate."

"You spoke of her often."

"Yes."

"I'm glad your story ended happily. So many stories do not."

"I am glad as well. What happened in Helvetinost? I thought you were happy there."

"I wanted to come home. I missed you, and I ..." She sighed. "I had a falling out with Drufenthus. I decided it was time for a change of scenery."

"I'm so very glad to see you again. I regret that we do not have more time to spend catching up, but I must find my father. Toni?"

She looked up at him expectantly.

"Be careful, okay? I'm afraid something bad is coming and I don't want you to get hurt."

"I'm always careful."

Tarnelius hugged her and then reclaimed Celeste's hand and led her back over to the rest of the group, who had watched the exchange with bemusement and curiosity.

"Is everything okay?" Victoria asked.

"Everything is fine," answered Tarnelius. "It surprised me to see her here, and I ended up thinking about some unpleasant memories." He smiled reassuringly at Celeste. "Our bond is a double-edged sword, sharing both good and bad."

Celeste still looked pale. A look of devastation seemed to have become stuck on her face. Tarnelius sighed and squeezed her hand. Her lips thinned as she tried to smile at him, but it looked more like a grimace.

"Let's go. We should find my father. We can visit the armory and replenish our gear. After we speak with him, we have to decide whether to go directly into Lumernia, or to one of the neighboring cities first. Celeste and I will stay in her mother's house tonight, assuming my father hasn't given it away. Arcus, you and Siobhan can stay in my home. I can most likely arrange one other guest house, but you and Victoria will almost certainly have to share it, Joseph. Is that okay? It will have a separate bedroom and living area."

Victoria's eyes darted to Joseph's and back again. "I–I'm not so sure that's a good idea."

Tarnelius frowned at her. "If you're coming with us, there will be nights when we'll set up camp outside together. There will be no privacy. Get used to it. I have no reason to believe that Joseph would hurt or take advantage of you … do you?"

Victoria closed her eyes and shook her head, resigned.

"There. That's better. I'll make the arrangements. Let's go."

They continued deeper into Kayalost, heading toward the Chamber of the Sky, the large open-air auditorium where the king held court every day. It was suspended at the top of some of the largest trees in Altierra. Tarnelius approached the guards standing at the base of the stairs. He felt confused and off balance. Celeste's thoughts were still running amok and he wanted to comfort her, but they didn't have time. He knew she was trying to clear her mind for him, but she was still reeling from what she had learned. On top of that confusion, guards were not normally stationed at the base of the stairs leading to the Chamber of the Sky.

"Step aside."

"Prince Tarnelius! What are you doing here? I mean, we didn't expect to see you here at this time."

"I've come to see my father."

"I'm sorry, my prince, but his orders were that he not be disturbed. Also–"

The elf paused and looked around. Tarnelius followed his gaze to find that they had been surrounded. A line of guards circled them at a distance of about twenty-five feet. "What is the meaning of this?"

"No outsiders are allowed in Kayalost at the present time," said the guard. "You have all entered uninvited and unwelcome."

The group formed their own circle, their backs to the middle. Flames ignited on Arcus' arms.

"Stand down!" Tarnelius shouted. "They are with me. I will vouch for them."

"You are also an outsider now," the guard retorted. "You cannot give us orders."

Lightning flashed overhead. Tarnelius glanced at Celeste, but she wasn't responsible. Her eyes were wide as she took in the guards moving ever closer. Tarnelius looked closer at their would-be captors. His heart thudded in his chest. "The Cypress Guard! Why aren't they at their posts? What is going on?"

"That's not your concern," said the guard. "Take them!"

"Don't attack them," yelled Tarnelius. "We'll end up burning down all of Kayalost!"

"What do you suggest?" asked Arcus.

"I'm thinking..."

Tarnelius' mind raced faster and faster as the Cypress Guard closed in on them.

"Fly, Tarnel," came Celeste's voice, breaking into his racing thoughts.

"What?"

"Go! Go speak to your father. We'll surrender for now."

"Wait, what? We will not!" snapped Arcus indignantly. "I've been arrested quite enough this week!"

"These people are your family, Arcus. They are my family and Tarnel's, too. Do you really want to fight them? Go now, Tarnel!"

Tarnelius hesitated only a moment longer, then he shifted into a golden eagle and flew off. His heart was heavy as he flew; it seemed to weigh him down. He didn't know what was going on, but he *would* get to the bottom of this before anything happened to his friends, or to Celeste. Through his bond, he could tell they had dropped to their knees in submission and were being tied up.

"Be careful. You're being followed," Celeste's voice rang out in his head. *"One of the guards took off up the stairs after you."*

Tarnelius focused on the task at hand and flew as fast as he could to the Chamber of the Sky. Risking a glance down, he saw the elf racing full speed up the stairs. Luckily, flying was faster and he'd had a head start, so Tarnelius knew he would make it to the top first. Wondering why the guard hadn't shifted into a bird as well, Tarnelius darted into the branches and sped toward the staircase that wound its way around the massive trunk. Flapping his way along the staircase, he shifted back, while still flying at speed. He had a bit of an awkward landing, but continued to race up the last few steps without hesitation.

Tarnelius dashed through the decorative arch at the top of the stairs and onto the massive platform that was the Chamber. The king was holding court, and there were a large number of elves in attendance. He paused, scanning the crowd for Audelthus. He found him right where he had expected him: on the large chair that served as a throne.

Audelthus rose to his feet. "What is the meaning of this intrusion?"

Tarnelius strode toward him, the crowd parting as he walked. He heard loud footsteps as the member of the Cypress Guard who had been following him burst into the Chamber. Tarnelius had trained many of the Cypress Guard. He found this whole situation surreal.

"Is this my welcome, father? I return to you in these troubled times with my mate and my friends and you arrest us all. What has become of the hospitality of the elves?"

Audelthus lifted his hand. The guard stopped, holding off his pursuit. "As you say, son, these are troubled times. The safety of our people falls to me and I take my role in this seriously. These lands are closed to outsiders."

Tarnelius flinched as he felt the sting of a slap across his left cheek. Someone had slapped his wife. His eyes narrowed as he felt her distress. She was trying to block her thoughts from him by thinking of other things, but she could not hide her feelings. "Your guards are manhandling my wife. I can feel their hands on her. I can only imagine what the others are going through. Celeste is no threat to our people. She was raised here. She is no outsider. Contrary to what the Cypress Guard now apparently believes, *I* am no outsider, either. I am prince of Kayalost! Arcus was raised among us. His name means 'salvation' in our language. This is his home, and he is one of us. He is no outsider! His friends should be honored guests among us. The humans are not who threaten us. Stop this foolishness at once."

The king sneered and leaned close. "The penalty for trespassing is death. I see your bond with the mongrel is strong. Good. With a single strike I shall rid myself of a problem I should have dealt with centuries ago."

Tarnelius narrowed his eyes. "Much blood will be spilled, father. She will not go down without a fight. She is powerful. You underestimate us all. Think of our people before you do anything rash." Inside his soul, he felt Celeste go still. He knew she was listening to the pair of them trade threats. His pulse increased as he frantically tried to think of a way to resolve this without bloodshed.

Tarnelius took a step back and addressed the crowd. "We must work together. The dark orcs have left their island home and have taken over the human capital. They tried to take over Izmar, and we suspect they are surrounding Kayalost to attack from all sides."

The crowd murmured and jeered. Most appeared to find what he said amusing. Tarnelius scrutinized the ones who laughed with a frown. They remained calm despite his urgency. Many of them sipped from odd flasks as they watched the proceedings. Once more, Tarnelius wondered who these people were. How could there be so many new elves? He'd been gone less than a year. If the borders were closed to outsiders, where had they come from?

"Preposterous," said the king. "We are safe here."

"Then why arrest my friends? None of this makes sense."

"We must take precautions."

"Precautions against what? You just said an orc invasion was preposterous. If that is the case, and you feel it necessary to close the borders based on a 'preposterous threat,' where did all these new people come from?"

Audelthus' grin chilled Tarnelius' blood. His heart lurched in his chest.

"That's it. Arcus is coming to get you," he heard in his head.

"You ask far too many questions, my son. Dangerous questions." The king glanced at his personal guards. "Collar him."

Pop.

Everyone froze in place as Arcus appeared in the middle of the room. He gathered his bearings and ran toward Tarnelius. The elf prince felt a hand on his shoulder. He whirled around to face this new threat and, as he did, Tarnelius saw the face of the guard who had followed him waver in his vision. He squinted, trying to focus on what he had seen. A cold black collar was thrust painfully over his neck by the other guard who had approached from behind, but Tarnelius took no notice. Focused on the one who had followed him, he watched the guard's features distort and become something else entirely. His skin seemed dark underneath, his eyes a bloodthirsty red. Tarnelius stared at him intently, trying to break down whatever magic was disguising him. His eyes widened right as Arcus slammed into him from the side and lifted him off his feet. Together they teleported out.

Chapter Eight
Monsters and Martyrs

"We have to go back!" Tarnelius exclaimed. Panic jolted through him like lightning.

Arcus had brought them into his old house, where the others were gathered around his small living room.

Celeste flung herself into his arms. "Shh! There are guards outside the door. Lower your voice … it's probably better if they don't know you are in here with us."

Tarnelius held her and caressed her face over the spot where she had been struck. Her cheek was still slightly reddened. "Why did they hit you? I couldn't focus on what was happening with you, because I was focusing on my father," he murmured.

"They wanted to take our weapons and search us. Arcus was arguing with them about that, and I sensed they were about to start a huge fight. I tried to come between them and they struck me. As you can see, though, they decided to give up and simply put us in here."

"Why *did* they bring us here?" whispered Arcus. "It's not like a house is secure, even if it *was* yours, Tarnelius."

Tarnelius shrugged. "Kayalost has no prison. They were apparently improvising and this house was open."

Satisfied that Celeste was all right, Tarnelius looked up and repeated, "We have to go back. I'm not sure what is going on, but I'm sure that guardsman was an orc in disguise. Kayalost has been infiltrated."

Joseph rose to his feet and frowned. "How do you know that?"

"That's my guess." Tarnelius paced. "There are many elves here that I don't recognize, and they had to come from *somewhere*. However, Celeste and I are being classified as 'outsiders' with the rest of you. What is the difference? Then there's the fact that when the guard touched me I could almost see through his magic. Speaking of which ..." Tarnelius gestured to the collar that still hung around his neck.

Celeste leaned forward to examine it, trying to find a clasp. Tarnelius tilted his head to give her better access.

"You'll have to hit it with magic to unhook it." He paused. "I've ... seen this before."

Celeste's face darkened, her hands shook.

Arcus stepped forward. "Allow me." He clasped the collar, lightning jumping from his fingertips. Tarnelius flinched, but the collar did release and come off in Arcus' hand.

"Thanks," Tarnelius said.

"So what are we going to do?" asked Arcus.

"If you were able to see through it when he touched you, it sounds like illusion magic," said Joseph. "But they can't *all* be illusionists. Assuming, of course, that every one of the new elves is an orc and not merely a new elf. I wonder what kind of numbers we are truly dealing with."

"All the new elves are not orcs. Toni is real," insisted Tarnelius.

"That may be," said Celeste. "But we should most likely assume the rest are not."

"That's not my point. *This* is my point." Joseph stood up and chanted. His brown hair turned a golden blond, exactly like Tarnelius'. His eyes expanded and turned a vibrant green. When the transformation was complete, he was Tarnelius' twin.

Celeste looked from Joseph to Tarnelius. "Impressive!"

"I see you've picked up some new tricks since the bar," remarked Arcus.

"So my point is twofold," said Joseph. "First, Toni may not have been Toni. Second, I cannot cast this spell on any of you. It only works on me. So … are they all illusionists, or are they managing it some other way?"

"Hmm." Tarnelius stroked his chin. "Can that spell be bottled? The elves in the Chamber of the Sky laughed when I mentioned the orc threat. Many of them were drinking something from identical flasks."

"Yes. Which means someone here has enough arcane knowledge to be a potion maker. That would do it. Now the question is, what are *we* going to do about it?"

"First thing: can you stop looking like me? It's rather distracting."

Joseph chuckled. "Here, take my hand." Once they made contact, he continued. "Try to look past the magic. Tell yourself that I am not an elf, and that you know this is an illusion."

As Tarnelius watched, he saw his own features blur in his vision, only to be replaced by Joseph's sandy brown hair and brown eyes.

"Like many illusion spells, this magic is powered by belief. If you believe me to be what I say I am, then that is what you'll see. If you doubt it, you'll see through the deception with ease. Touch is the conduit. Once you break the illusion, the sorcerer will not be able to trick you with that spell anymore for that day. Another option would be to wait for the spell to end. Mine will only last for about half a day, but theirs may or may not last longer. It depends on how powerful the potion maker is."

"You still look like Tarnel to me," said Celeste. Arcus, Victoria and Siobhan nodded their heads.

"I can dismiss the spell, but it's better if you practice looking through it." One by one, Joseph gripped their hands and let them break his spell.

"Great." Celeste sighed. "Now the only problem is that they aren't going to let us shake hands. I'm sure they are intending to kill us on sight, in fact."

"Can you counter their magic?" Arcus asked Joseph.

"Maybe, but in order to do that I'd have to first figure out who they are. I'm in the same boat you are." Joseph snapped his fingers. "Arcus! You could do it."

"I could do what?"

"You could activate the staff. Then any magical effects, including their illusions, will disappear. It stripped through all our magical spells and abilities in Izmar."

"No."

"But think how much easier this would be–"

"No. I will not touch that thing again. It would leave everyone defenseless, plus I don't even know how I activated it the first time. That staff is better off being chopped into kindling!"

"Do you think Audelthus is truly involved in this?" asked Celeste.

Tarnelius frowned. "There is not a doubt in my mind. The way he looked, the way he spoke to me. I'm sure of it. The question is why."

"I don't know, Tarnelius," said Arcus. "The king has always been aloof and selfish, but giving Kayalost to the orcs is pure evil. I always had the impression that he loved this place. I'm having trouble believing that he knows."

Tarnelius' jaw tightened. "Trust me. That side of him is there, and he will stop at nothing to get what he wants. The only one who has ever had the guts to go against his decisions was me, and it wasn't exactly fun."

Siobhan watched the exchange with surprise on her face. Glancing from Tarnelius to Celeste, she added, "But he's your father. How bad can he be? He raised you and you turned out all right."

Tarnelius chuckled darkly. "Celeste's mother, as well as Toni's, raised me. My mother died in childbirth, and my father didn't have time for me in my youth. I'm better off for it, though."

"I hate to disrupt story time," said Joseph. "But what are we going to do? It's only a matter of time before the guards come in here after us, especially in light of what I assume was your dramatic exit from the meeting."

"I'm surprised they haven't already done that," said Arcus. "The king must not have expected us to return here."

Celeste rifled through her magic bag, removing a bow and quiver containing three arrows. "Perhaps, but Joseph is right. We have to get ready to go out there. Remember, most of Kayalost is very flammable. We don't want to go overboard and put the others here in danger. We should be ready to fight, but let's keep this under control." She looked to Tarnelius. "What about Audelthus?"

"Leave my father to me. If he has truly handed Kayalost over to the orcs, then it is time he answers for his crimes."

Celeste's eyes narrowed as she regarded him, but nodded before turning to the others. "Are we ready to break out of here? Remember, don't set the city on fire, and try to make sure the people you attack are truly orcs before engaging. Stay together and watch each other's backs." She paused. "Kamara be with us."

"Joseph, don't forget to cancel that spell, if you haven't already," said Tarnelius.

The group headed for the front door. The guards had cast a magical lock on it, but Victoria was able to break the enchantment easily, as it was the same type of locking spell she had always used on her room back in Izmar.

Tarnelius and Siobhan drew their swords, Celeste readied her bow and ice arrows. Siobhan kicked the door clean off its hinges and the group rushed out.

The two guards who were standing outside whirled around, but Tarnelius and Siobhan each grabbed one of them, pressing their swords to the men's throats.

"This one is clean," said Siobhan.

"Not this one." Tarnelius tightened his hold on the struggling elf. "You are not what you seem, are you? How many of you are here, orc?"

"Hold on tight to that one, Siobhan," ordered Celeste. "We don't want him running off now."

"Let him go!" snarled the elf struggling in Siobhan's grasp. "He is no orc, he is a member of the Cypress Guard, as you well know, Tarnelius."

"Silence, Radagaris." Tarnelius gestured to Arcus. "Put the slave collar on him. That will break his enchantment."

Arcus forced the collar onto the elf in Tarnelius' arms. He struggled violently, trying to break free. Tarnelius' blade bit into his throat. Blood began to drip. As soon as the collar locked in place, the guard's appearance flickered and changed to that of a dark orc. The guard in Siobhan's arms froze in place, while the orc thrashed even more fiercely. Tarnelius tightened his grip and his sword started to slice through the orc's neck. Celeste grabbed an ice arrow from her quiver and plunged it hard into the orc's chest, stabbing with it as if it were a dagger. Ice spread from the wound. Tarnelius kicked him to the ground and stabbed straight into the ice, shattering it and killing the orc.

Celeste scanned the area quickly before speaking to the other guard. "Listen, our fight is not with you. I'm sure you are aware now–if you weren't before–that Kayalost has been infiltrated by orcs. We are going to free you. You are either with us or against us. We don't want to harm any elves, but we will hurt you if you stand in our way. The decision is yours."

The guard stared at the body of the dead orc. "This is treason."

"No. What my father did is treason." Tarnelius chuckled mirthlessly. "You know it, deep down. He is not always right. In fact, he rarely is. Come on, Radagaris. I'm taking over as king now. Help me free Kayalost." He gestured to Siobhan, and she released the elf.

Radagaris drew his weapon and stalked with fluid grace toward Tarnelius. The elf prince raised his weapons in a defensive pose, his heart heavy. He had hoped this would not come to bloodshed.

Radagaris dropped to his knees and offered his sword up in fealty. "Forgive me, my prince–my king. You are right. Things have been different here. None of us have liked it, but what could we do? The king has been meeting with the elves from the

Silver Isles, and has listened to them to the exclusion of all others. Any who questioned the new regime were called to the king's presence in the Chamber and when they returned they were not the same. I was afraid …" The elf's large green eyes were filled with pain and sorrow. He gestured toward the fallen orc. "Shalinest and I have known each other for centuries, but he was one of the first to be called into the king's chamber. When he came back, he told me that he had been mistaken, that now he better understood the king's will. He would never tell me anything more, though, and rarely spoke at all. Now I know why."

Tarnelius nodded and looked to the others. "Who would care to wager none of the elves here are actually from the Silver Isles?" His jaw tightened as he considered everything that had happened. "Okay, new plan. Joseph, do you remember what Shalinest looked like?" Joseph nodded. "Good. I need you to take on his appearance and go with Radagaris. Take the women with you. Make up any story you want, but try to determine who is real and who isn't. Warn the real elves to either be ready to fight, or to go hide. Arcus, I need you to take me back to the Chamber of the Sky. It's time my father answered for his crimes."

"I don't like this plan," said Celeste. "I want to go with you. Someone needs to keep you out of trouble."

Tarnelius smirked. "It's hard to stay out of trouble when I go looking for it."

She sighed and took on a stubborn expression.

"Please, Celeste. I need you to stay with the others so that we can communicate if either of us needs help. I'll have Arcus with me. It's not as if your task will be any less dangerous. It goes without saying that the orcs won't like being revealed."

Joseph knelt down and murmured a spell, removing the collar from around the dead orc's neck.

Radagaris gasped and took a step back when he saw Joseph rise to his feet. Joseph grabbed the elf's hand.

"You know that I am no elf. Look past the spell. Look harder. This is how you will find out who is real and who isn't."

"Um, Joseph," said Victoria. "You don't look at all like an elf now."

Joseph sighed. "As I said earlier, Victoria, once you see through one disguise, the illusionist cannot fool you with the same spell again that day. I assure you, the spell is in place."

Radagaris blinked rapidly and frowned. "This is how they are doing it?"

"Actually, we think it's a potion, but basically, yes."

Siobhan started sifting through the dead orc's clothes. She pulled out several vials and a nondescript flask filled with a green, viscous liquid. "Are these what you are looking for?"

Joseph grabbed the flask and opened the lid, sniffing the contents. "Yes. This is it. Well, at least we don't have to guess anymore."

"Give me one of those." Tarnelius grabbed a vial before Joseph could reply. "Do what you want with the rest." Then he turned to Arcus. "Are we ready?"

"Not yet." Arcus went to Siobhan and kissed her. "Please stay with the others and don't get yourself killed. I need you to be careful."

"You as well, my love. Seems to me that you will be in much greater danger than we will be. I'd insist on coming–it *is* my turn to rescue you, you know–but seeing as how Celeste already–"

"Look alive, everyone. We've been spotted," Celeste said. She gave Tarnelius a gentle kiss and shoved him toward Arcus.

Quiver at the ready and bow in hand, she strode toward the female elf who stared at them from a short distance away. The others were quick to follow her.

"Be careful, Angel," Tarnelius thought to her. His long elven blade still drawn, he nodded to Arcus, who gripped his arm tightly.

Pop.

Audelthus paced back and forth in front of his massive throne. Most of his men had been sent down to find his son and his companions. He knew better than to think Tarnelius had gone far or that this was over. He had kept five guards with him: two real Cypress guardsmen and three of his new allies.

Damn it! he thought. Everything had been coming together nicely. He was slowly learning which of the druids could be trusted to see things the way they could be. An alliance with the various races of orcs would put his elves in a position of power, of strength. Instead of being crushed as he was sure the humans had been–if what his son had said was true–they would be respected. They would survive. Then here came his starry-eyed excuse for a son with his mongrel wife and their friends. Bad enough that he was diluting their heritage with her impure blood, but he was consorting with weak humans. By his behavior, Tarnelius was now practically human, himself.

Audelthus was sure his son had returned only because his mate had some half-cocked idea that she had to save the world again. Well, he'd heard that tune once already when she had returned with the kedistam. How had it ended? The world was changing for the worse. The world didn't need to be saved, those *in* the world needed to evolve. *He* had to change if he wanted to survive, if he aspired to emerge on the other side a stronger man, a more powerful king. His son was weak and always did what that female, Celeste, told him to do. He didn't have the stomach to be king. He didn't have the heart to rule in this new world. However, the boy remained a threat. He could shake things up and ruin everything.

Pop.

Audelthus' head jerked up to meet Tarnelius' eyes. He had returned the same way he had gone, apparently riding his pet human as if he were a magic carpet.

"I see I wasted my time sending my men to find you. I should have been more patient."

Tarnelius muttered something that sounded like "Do not attack my father." Audelthus smirked. Tarnelius was still weak. Would always be weak. It seemed he had inherited that trait from his mother.

"We weren't finished with our conversation yet, father."

"Oh?"

"Yes. We must discuss this act of treason you have committed. You sold out our people, our home, to the orcs. How many of these men are actually orcs? All of them?" Tarnelius flung the potion bottle at his father's feet. "We know everything."

"You know nothing. Don't you remember these men and women? They are the Cypress Guard." He turned his back on Tarnelius and strode toward the stairs. "Guards, kill them."

Arcus snarled out a single word of magic. A large translucent green box formed around Audelthus and one of his guards. Tarnelius drew his second sword and calmly waited to see what would happen.

"So ... two for you, two for me?" Arcus asked.

Tarnelius watched with a dark expression as the four elves advanced toward them. "I suppose that will be the case. I don't know who is an elf and who is an orc, but I suppose it doesn't really matter now." He shifted his weight to the balls of his feet.

Three of the elves charged them. Their weapons were human-made long swords, not the slender blades the elves favored. The fourth elf held back.

Arcus shot a bolt of lightning at the nearest elf, which struck him in the chest and ricocheted into the two behind him.

Tarnelius ran to meet the nearest one, who had been slowed by the lightning. The elf prince whirled around to strike his opponent with both of his blades. The elf was quick to recover, though, and parried. The two swung and blocked each other. It was hard to focus on who was attacking and who was defending as they performed their deadly dance.

Arcus turned his head in time to spot the elf in the back beginning to cast a spell, his hands stretched toward the heavens. Without hesitation, he sent another green box toward the other two elves, who were both nearing Tarnelius. He missed the one in front, but managed to capture the third sword-wielding elf. Storm clouds gathered overhead. Lightning flashed ominously.

Tarnelius was now defending against two of the Cypress Guard at once. He was holding his own well and managing to dodge them, but he was no longer able to take the offensive. Arcus seemed to pause and regard the fight before turning once more toward the spellcasting druid. Lightning crackled in the air and the smell of ozone became overwhelming.

Pop.

Arcus teleported to the caster in the back as lightning struck where he had been standing a mere moment before. He stabbed the elf in the shoulder with his dagger. The storm clouds dispersed as the druid's concentration broke.

Audelthus watched with growing dread. His world shimmered in emerald hues from inside the magical cage.

"Are you sure that this is really necessary, Your Majesty?" asked Virthanilus, trapped inside the green cage with him.

"Tarnelius is a threat to everything we have worked toward. He may be my only heir, but he is not fit to rule."

"Does that really matter? Do you even need a successor?"

"No, but his presence here will breed discord among the others. You heard what he said. He accused me of treason. Ooh, that looked like it hurt."

One of the elves had managed to make contact, slashing a deep gash through Tarnelius' side. He cried out but maintained focus and continued parrying the two elves' attacks.

"He can't keep that up all day. He may have learned swordplay from the best, but he's still mortal. It's simply a matter of time."

Arcus had cast a spell on himself that seemed to allow him to move twice as fast. He shot another lightning bolt at the druid, then extended his arms up to the sky. A pillar of flame shot down and dropped onto his opponent, setting his clothes on fire and charring the ground.

"Enough!" shouted the druid. He knelt down and held his hands up in surrender. "You have defeated me, Arcus. I didn't really want to hurt you in the first place. I remember when you were a young child here. Please, have mercy on me. I was only following orders."

Arcus paused in his assault. He glared down at the elf, but his attention was obviously getting pulled away toward the sound of Tarnelius fighting for his life. The ground at his feet was becoming slick with blood.

"How can I trust you?"

"Lock me in one of those green boxes, if you want."

"The boxes won't stop your magic." Arcus growled. He seemed to be considering his options. He stared the elf in the eye and spoke in a hypnotic voice. *"Stop moving."* The guard went unnaturally still, and Arcus turned and raced toward Tarnelius.

Tarnelius was tiring. He had taken several more injuries, though none as severe as the one to his side. He swung his right-hand sword to parry one, when he noticed the second elf's attention seemed to be drawn to something behind him. Taking advantage, he swung his off-hand weapon and stabbed the elf straight through the heart. Releasing the sword, he flipped around and ducked, narrowly avoiding a blow meant to separate his head from his neck. The blade slashed into his upper left arm, and pain like white-hot flame shot through his body. Tarnelius jumped back to regroup, raising his sword defensively as he fought to catch his breath.

The elf stalked toward him and raised his sword, determined to not allow Tarnelius even a moment's rest. He was so focused in his attack that he didn't notice Arcus run up behind him. Arcus shoved his hands onto the elf's back and cast his lighting touch spell. The elf grunted and dropped to his knees. Tarnelius finished the delirious elf off with a downward slash to the neck.

Both of the elves had transformed into orcs as soon as they died. Tarnelius nodded to the kneeling druid. "What about that one?"

"He surrendered. For what it's worth, though, I think he's real. He casts druid magic. In fact, he almost got me with the lightning storm."

"How long does the cage last?"

"Oh, a good long time. Our new friends aren't going anywhere."

Tarnelius nodded and focused inward, healing himself of his many wounds, his hands glowing a brilliant blue.

Arcus approached the elf who was still kneeling on the ground. Laying his hands on him, he healed him of his injuries and then released the spell holding him in place. The elf toppled over and then scrambled to his feet.

"What do you know about what is going on here?" Arcus asked.

"Not much. I know that Audelthus formed an alliance with the orcs in an attempt to grab power. I know that the two you killed were orcs, and that one," he pointed to the elf trapped alone in the second cage, "is also an orc. There are many more in the village as well."

"If you knew that this whole time, why didn't you rise against him?"

Tarnelius finished healing himself before picking up his weapons and moving to join Arcus and the druid, Fithranir.

"Because I wanted to live. Look, my entire life has been devoted to guarding a tree from a threat that never existed. I was never meant to fight. Those who spoke out against Audelthus' plan were killed and replaced."

"So why are you helping us now?"

"Are you not hearing me? Because I want to live. You could have killed me, Arcus. We both know it. My best hope now will be to serve you and our prince."

"King now, actually," Tarnelius corrected as he came to join them. "Leave him be, Arcus. Fithranir has served on the Cypress Guard for centuries. I believe him." He turned to Fithranir. "We've heard enough. Can you help us ascertain who is not really an elf?"

The druid nodded, a determined look on his face. He pointed to the elf inside the second cage, who was beating his sword into the side of the green walls.

Arcus dropped the spell holding that cage in place, and Tarnelius charged, swords glinting in the sun. The battle was fast and furious, and the pair of them wasted no time in taking down the orc, who changed appearance as soon as he died.

"Virthanilus is real," Fithranir said. "Though he sides with the king–er, former king. At least, I think he does."

Tarnelius approached the last cage.

"So you have delusions that you are to be king now, eh, son? Over my dead body."

"That's the idea." Tarnelius glanced over to Arcus.

"Stop moving," Arcus snarled to the druid trapped inside. The elf ignored him. His posture remained tensed, and he was still able to move. Arcus sighed and shook his head. "Spell failed. At least this one wasn't smart enough to hide it." He dropped the spell holding the cage in place.

"For crimes against the village of Kayalost, for numerous acts of treason … and for trying to imprison me *again* with that damn slave collar, I sentence you to death, you bastard!"

"You? You sentence *me?* That's a joke. Fine … humor me: who is to be my executioner, you sanctimonious weakling of a prince? I know you don't have the stomach for it!"

"Don't I?" Tarnelius lunged forward and held both of his swords crossed at Audelthus' throat.

"Tarnel … don't let him get to you. You don't need to kill your father. We will find another way." Celeste's thoughts broke through the battle-rage coursing through him.

Arcus and Virthanilus flung magic at each other. Arcus rolled to avoid a pillar of flame, while spraying ice and snow at his enemy.

"We can imprison him with his own collar," Celeste continued. He knew from their bond that the group was fighting a large horde of orcs. Thunder rolled on the air. Tarnelius could make out shouting, but was unsure if he could really hear it, or if he overheard it through Celeste.

"Be careful, Angel. Focus on your battle and on staying safe. I need to concentrate on my father."

Oblivious to all else, the king gave his son a hard look, one that reminded Tarnelius of all the times he had crossed some imaginary line as a child. "Stop this charade at once," Audelthus growled. "We both know you are no murderer. You don't have it in you. Killing me would prove that you are no better than I. You're weak, like your mother. Ye gods, I was so glad the day I got rid of her. I never should have agreed to share my throne, to bond with her. Luckily, I learned that if you kill your own mate you don't die with them!"

Tarnelius' hands shook, his weapons trembling at his father's throat. He could hear Celeste in his head again, but he blocked her out. His mind reeled, all rational thought gone.

Audelthus chuckled. "Be a good lad and lower your weapons. I wouldn't want you to become a monster on my behalf."

Arcus shouted and lightning shot past the two elves. Audelthus' hair stood on end from the electricity, but he was otherwise unfazed.

Overcome, Tarnelius took a step back. "You … you killed her?"

"He did what? My gods … Tarnel!"

The king nodded. "Oh, is it confession time? Why not? You might as well know who you are dealing with. My only regret is not doing it sooner. Still, for years I'd hoped you would grow to be a son I could be proud of. Pity that it wasn't meant to be … you've been nothing but a disappointment. Perhaps the fault is mine; I should have raised you myse–"

Tarnelius stabbed his blade through his father's chest. Shock and horror etched the king's face as his son yanked the sword free and shoved Audelthus to the floor. Tarnelius knelt next to him, contempt and rage contorting his handsome features. "I'm sorry to have been a disappointment to you all these many years, father. Perhaps with this last act, I will have redeemed myself in your eyes. I may be a monster like you now, but at least I've given our people a chance at safety and freedom."

"You … I can't …" Blood gurgled from the king's mouth, and his eyes froze in place, staring at nothing.

Tarnelius gently closed his father's sightless eyes, then pried a ring from the former king's left hand. Celeste was still screaming in his head, but he couldn't focus on her words. He was numb, broken. Finally, he pulled the circlet from the crown of his head and rose to his feet.

"The king is dead. Stop fighting. This battle is over."

Virthanilus froze, the spell he was casting dying on his lips. Slowly, he turned his expression to the fallen king. He dropped to his knees.

"This is the first and last time I will bow to you, *Your Majesty*. Kill me. I will never serve you. Your father was right. You are a fool, unfit to lead the elves. What are you going to do? Move back here and rule with the half-breed? I don't think so. Without Audelthus, we are as good as dead anyway. You've doomed us all! Kill me, damn it!"

Tarnelius' heart lurched in his chest. *You're a monster*, he heard in his head, his father's voice hissing the venomous words.

"What are you doing, Tarnel?" His beloved's voice broke through the chaos that was his mind. *"Don't think that way!"*

"You're a monster! A Monster! A monster! Monster ... monster ..." he heard again and again. The two voices competed in volume and Tarnelius was sure he would go mad from it. Tarnelius yanked at his hair and tried to bellow out his pain and frustration, but the voices only became louder.

"What are you waiting for? Kill me!" screamed Virthanilus.

Tarnelius grabbed his sword and swung blindly, the magical weapon slashing clear through the kneeling elf's slender neck with a dark purple flash that emanated from the blade. The sword sailed through the air as it was released and clattered to the floor a short distance away. Tarnelius dropped to his knees and buried his face in his hands. The yelling in his head was growing in intensity, and he could no longer tell whose voice was whose. The sounds grew to an overwhelming level. His heart rate increased and tears streamed down his face. Vaguely, he was aware of Arcus trying to shout over the voices in his head, but he couldn't hear him and didn't care what he was saying anyway.

He had no idea how long he knelt there, but eventually he felt cool hands on the back of his neck. He shuddered and lowered his hands to find himself looking up into the concerned gaze of Celeste. He averted his eyes. He had no right to look upon her loveliness.

"Luckily, I learned that if you kill your own mate you don't die with them!" The memory of his father's haunting remarks turned Tarnelius' stomach. A sob tore from his throat and he gasped for breath.

Celeste's jaw tightened, but she didn't back away. Dropping to her knees before him, she embraced him. He tried to struggle away. He was a monster now, she shouldn't come near him. He had done what he had to, exactly as his father had.

If he were truly honest with himself, he had even enjoyed it. He was a monster, a devil who didn't deserve the angel that was Celeste. Her arms tightened around him in a vice-like grip.

"Stop thinking that way, my love. I'm here. I'm not going anywhere. I love you. I've loved you for more than eight hundred years, and I'll love you for a lifetime … an eternity. That is our beautiful destiny."

Tarnelius shook violently in her arms, but hugged her back, holding on for dear life. As quietly as she spoke, he could still hear her over the buzz in his head. In fact, the longer they sat there, the quieter the cacophony became.

"There, that's better." She pulled back a little and smiled at him.

"Where's Arcus?" he murmured, his voice weak and hoarse.

"He came down with some other elf. I passed them on the stairs. I think he was looking for me, because he seemed relieved to see me coming up here." She ran her fingers through his long golden hair and caressed his face. "He needn't have bothered. I knew you needed me. You're no monster. A monster wouldn't have these feelings. A monster would be unaffected by these deaths. You did the right thing. Together, we can now free Kayalost. After that …" Her eyes trailed to the circlet still clenched in his hand.

Now that she had banished the demons in his head he could hear her properly again, and knew once more what she was thinking. "Yes, I'll have to stay here as king now. I don't know what to say. I know you wanted to free Lumernia …"

"I have to go. We did this. I … look, let's not think of it now. We'll figure it out, but let's go help save Kayalost first."

Tarnelius' heart hurt at the idea of her going without him. Who would protect her? What if something happened? They'd lost so much time together already, the thought of separating was going to–

"I said let's not think of it now, okay? We'll figure it out, but we have to focus on the task at hand."

Tarnelius nodded and together they descended the stairs.

Chapter Nine
Walk Through the Fire

The last of the former king's guards made a stand near the base of the stairs that led to the Chamber of the Sky. The battles had been fierce, and the orcs had fought with the ferocity of cornered animals. Luckily, although there had been many injuries, the elves had suffered few casualties. Those who had not been trained in either magic or swordplay had headed for cover as soon as the action started, while the ones who had were quick to take heart and join with their prince and his friends in ridding the village of the interlopers–especially after the first casualty turned into an orc before their eyes.

Tarnelius and Celeste rushed down the stairs to find their friends approaching from the east. The guards were now caught between them.

"Stop!" Tarnelius yelled. Everyone hesitated at his command. "Audelthus is dead. I am your new king. Any of you who are truly elves, the time to stand down is now. If you remain on this course, we will not hesitate to kill you as an orc."

No one moved a muscle.

After a few moments, three elves broke apart from the rest and bowed before Tarnelius. The other guards exchanged glances.

"Joseph?" Tarnelius gestured for the mage to examine them.

Joseph and Victoria approached the three elves. Joseph grasped the arm of the nearest one. His eyes widened. "It's a tr–"

The guards sprang into action. One of the three drew his morningstar and swung wide, smashing Victoria in the left side of her head with the weapon. She collapsed to the ground without as much as a whimper.

Joseph screamed and leapt on top of Victoria's assailant, knocking the morningstar from his hand in the process. He punched the elf repeatedly before casting a spell that caused small orbs of light to explode between them. His opponent reached into his shirt to grab a dagger, but Joseph yanked it from his hand and plunged it deep into the rogue's throat, slashing lengthwise and severing his windpipe. The elf instantly shifted into an orc.

Lightning and flames crashed nearby as Celeste cast her deadly spells. Tarnelius dashed into the fray, swords flashing in the sunlight.

The other two orcs who had separated from the rest took off at a run. Unable to stop them, Arcus and Siobhan gave chase.

Tarnelius saw a massive fireball hurl in Joseph's direction. The mage was still finishing off his victim and did not see it coming. Tarnelius tried to shout a warning, but was cut off as an orc lunged at him, forcing him to parry the assault.

A scream rent the air, and Tarnelius saw Joseph was engulfed in flames. Taking advantage of his opponent's similar distraction, the elf swung high, spinning in place. His magical blades flashed a dark purple–almost black–as the orc's head was separated from his body. Tarnelius waved his arms and chanted, causing a huge wave of water to appear over Joseph, completely soaking him and quenching the flames. Joseph lay still, not making a sound. Tarnelius was left with no choice but to continue the fight.

Out of the corner of his eye, Tarnelius saw Tonilehdossa run into the fray. With no regard for her own safety, she rushed to Joseph and Victoria, healing them as best she could. That task done, she turned and cast the same pillar of fire magic that Celeste had been casting, taking out an orc that was running toward her.

Fithranir knelt down, muttering an incantation. Roots and vines snaked up from the ground and wound themselves around the remaining orcs. Other elves attacked as well, combining swordplay and magic to defeat their enemies. In moments, the orc threat was eliminated.

"That should be the last of them," said Fithranir as he cast a water spell to put out a fire.

Joseph was awake and moving. He crawled over to Victoria and lifted her into his arms, his ear to her chest, listening to her heartbeat.

"Are you certain?" asked Toni.

"Mostly, though we should be diligent. Any stragglers would be vastly outnumbered now, but we should remind everyone to keep their doors locked at night and try to stay in groups for a while. Also, we'll have to make sure to destroy the potion vials, thereby limiting access to supplies. *If* there are any orcs left, they'll be flushed out."

"I'll help organize a group to ensure everyone knows what to do to be safe, and what to watch for in case anyone thinks someone they know might be an orc in disguise. Then I'll see about reorganizing the Cypress Guard. They are probably our best bet for watching for anything that is amiss. In the meantime, we must gather these bodies and burn them."

Celeste smirked at Tarnelius, who was staring with amazed eyes at Toni. *"She was quite something during the earlier battles, before I came up to get you,"* she thought to him. *"You taught her well. She fights well and has excellent instincts. Several of our people are alive because of her quick thinking and healing skills."*

"I only taught her the basics and healing magic. You know I'm not very skilled in offensive magic. Clearly, she found a new teacher. Good for her. Her magic will keep her safe going forward. I'm sure she never wants to be in the same position she was born into."

Celeste nodded. *"I'm going to go see what I can do with Joseph and Victoria. Why don't you see if Arcus and Siobhan need any help?"* Without waiting for his reply, she headed straight for the two humans.

Tarnelius continued to watch Toni make plans with Fithranir. Gone was the lost young elf he had met in Helvetinost. In her place was a strong woman and natural-born leader. The more he'd watched her during the battles, and especially now that they were attempting to rebuild, the more impressed he was. In fact, while watching her in action, a plan had formed in the back of his mind, one that he hoped would help all of Kayalost as they took their first steps into an uncertain future.

"Tonilehdossa, a word, if I may," he requested.

She walked over. He took a quick glance around, but everyone was occupied with other activities. Arcus and Siobhan had not returned after chasing the orcs, but he assumed they were fine. They were likely tending to the many injuries and several fires that had broken out throughout Kayalost. Although Victoria had been badly injured, he knew she would be all right, if for no other reason than because Tonilehdossa's spell had worked when she ran over there. You can't heal a corpse; the magic doesn't work. As it was, Joseph held her tight in his arms as if he were afraid she would disappear. While touching, it complicated Celeste's attempts to closer inspect the injuries. Tarnelius smirked. If he'd put her down and let Celeste do her job, it would probably be easier ... but he understood how Joseph felt–even if Joseph didn't or wouldn't admit it. For the moment, he was grateful for her distraction. He hoped to keep his mind clear while talking to Toni so that Celeste wouldn't notice what he was up to.

The members of the real Cypress Guard were doing their best to heal battle wounds and clean up the aftermath. There were still minor fires that had to be put out, as well as debris and mutilated bodies scattered everywhere. No one would miss them for a few minutes.

He smiled at Toni. "You seem different. More–like you've come into yourself."

Toni returned the smile with one of her own. "I suppose I have. I have you to thank for that, in part. You helped me find my confidence by teaching me magic, by telling me stories of this place. Then I spent a couple of centuries with Drufenthus. Watching the confident way he leads the people of Helvetinost rubbed off on me, I suppose."

"Are you here to stay? Or are you returning to him?"

"I haven't decided. Drufenthus is nice enough and I do care for him, but he won't bond with me. I'm not sure whether it's because he doesn't believe me when I tell him I don't mind being underground or whether it's because of some other reason, but he has made it clear that things will never progress between us. I had to take some time away from him so I could clear my head."

Tarnelius went silent, listening to Celeste's thoughts in his head. It seemed that Victoria was healed physically, but remained unconscious. Celeste was trying to convince Joseph that Victoria wasn't going to die.

"Is there a reason you're asking me this?"

Tarnelius cleared his throat and fiddled with the ring on his finger. The ring he had taken from his father was fashioned out of gold, and bore the symbol of Kayalost: a cypress tree. "Tonilehdossa–Toni–"

"Yes?"

"Would you be interested in becoming queen of Kayalost?"

Toni went very still. "I'm sorry, I must have misheard you. Could you say that again?"

Tarnelius stared her in the eyes. "Toni, my father was a corrupt man. Kayalost flourished *despite* his influence. This place is no longer my home, nor is it where I belong. I belong with Celeste, and our destiny is calling us to return to Lumernia. However, I can't leave. Not until I know the place that I called home for almost my entire life is in good hands. With my father gone, the responsibility falls to me … but I've *never* wanted to be king. You are the one person here I can trust to take over. You are a natural leader. I saw your heart and your intensity as you fought to free Kayalost from the orcs. I heard of your compassion as you healed those who were wounded. Royal blood flows in your veins. You are the perfect choice."

He pulled the circlet off his belt, where he had stuck it for safekeeping, and offered it up to her.

"I–I don't know what to say. This is happening too–" Her eyes were locked on the circlet as if it were a snake ready to strike her.

"Just say yes. I know that out of everyone here, you are the only one I can trust to protect and defend this place from invasion. I know you'll never allow our people to be enslaved or taken advantage of. This feels right. It never felt right for me to take the crown. It's not my destiny. I couldn't even bring myself to put it on since I plucked it from my father."

"Oh. I'm so sorry for your loss, Tarnelius."

"Don't be. I'm not … especially as I'm the one who killed him. It's yet another reason why I am not fit to be ruler."

"I don't know, Tarnelius. I never wanted power. I simply didn't want to be controlled."

"But don't you see? That's why you are the perfect choice. You are nothing like my father, who *only* wanted to control others."

Toni sucked in a breath, her eyes still locked on the circlet. Tarnelius could imagine what she was thinking, he understood he had caught her completely off-guard with his request. She was undoubtedly thinking that she couldn't be queen, because she had been raised among the tumasi as a slave, not among her people as a princess. It didn't matter, not to him. His heart was at peace and he felt certain this was the right choice. Her eyes softened. He hoped it was a sign that she would agree.

She took the circlet. "I accept this duty. May your trust in me not be misplaced."

Tarnelius breathed a huge sigh of relief as the circlet left his hand. He watched her place the circlet on her head, then yanked the signet ring from his finger and held that out to her, pressing it into the palm of her hand.

"Interview those that are left of the Cypress Guard and even some of the other druids. I know you are an incredible judge of character. Decide whom you can trust and choose them to be your guards and advisors. I would be happy to help you with this task if you like. I will speak to the people and explain that I have abdicated the throne in your favor. Toni, I would be honored to preside over your coronation, if you would allow me to do so."

"Coro–coronation?" Toni paled. "I think I need to sit down."

Tarnelius led her to a low-hanging tree branch and helped her sit on it. "We elves are nothing if not sticklers for tradition, and we love ceremonies."

"So I've noticed."

Tarnelius gave her a hug. "Don't worry, it'll be easy. I'll help you."

"I sure hope you're right."

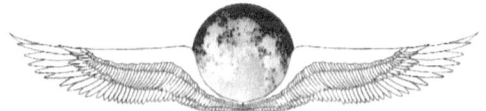

Joseph caressed Victoria's forehead, smoothing her blood-matted hair for what was probably the thirtieth time. He knew it: fighting was too dangerous for her. Every time he turned around she was putting herself in harm's way.

"–to put her down and let me look at your wounds!" Celeste insisted yet again.

Joseph ignored her. He wanted to hold Victoria forever, so he could keep her safe. At the same time, he wished he could never see her again. He hated that he still cared. She was damaged goods. Used. Dirty. Seeing her vulnerable like this brought out feelings he'd rather not have to face, though. She looked like the woman he had always pictured as *his*. She looked like his Victoria. Joseph sighed. She had never been his. He was being stupid and needed to get his head on straight and forget about her.

"I mean it, Joseph!"

Joseph sighed again and looked over at Celeste. "What now?"

"Those are some nasty burns. They're in need of ointment before infection sets in."

Joseph glanced down at himself. His entire left side was covered in burns and he was barely decent, his clothes having been burnt away. Strange, he didn't feel any pain—not physical pain, anyway. He shook his head and waved her off.

Celeste crossed her arms, glaring. Tarnelius and Toni walked up to join them.

"How is she?" asked Toni.

"She's as good as can be expected. You did a good job on her. I cast another healing spell to be safe, but now it's only a matter of waiting. As I'm sure you know, magic can heal injuries, but it can't replace lost blood. Brain swelling is tricky, too. She's not bleeding anymore and is breathing steadily, so I think she will be fine. This fool, on the other hand, has burns that will soon be festering if he doesn't put her down and let me treat them."

Joseph huffed. "It's not that big a—"

"Joseph, if I might have a word?" Tarnelius asked.

"Don't do it," interjected Toni. "I've recently learned the hard way that any word Tarnelius wants is probably not going to be anything simple."

Tarnelius rolled his eyes and made a face.

"I'm sure you aren't supposed to look at your queen that way," she mocked.

Celeste's eyebrows shot up and she gave Tarnelius a questioning look. He simply smiled at her in answer.

"I thought you two always knew what the other was thinking," said Joseph.

"Usually, yes. But I've been arguing with you and it's been distracting." Celeste looked to Tarnelius. "Make it quick; he needs treatment."

Tarnelius nodded and gestured for Joseph to come with him.

"I don't think so. I won't leave her here in this condition," Joseph said, shaking his head.

"Yes, I figured that. Celeste, Toni, would you two mind giving us a moment?"

Joseph turned his back as the two women walked away. He knew he was being petulant, but he didn't care. He had no plans to let Victoria go. He was sure the second he put her down she would stop breathing. She might be dirty, and she might be damaged goods, but he didn't want her to die for it.

After the women had moved out of earshot, Tarnelius moved into Joseph's line of vision and smirked. "Joseph, you look terrible."

Joseph shrugged. "You felt you had to talk to me in private to tell me that? Well, just so you know, I don't care."

"I do. Here's why: magic is a funny thing. She can heal you in a second with the ointment she has. We–they–make it here in Kayalost, you know. It's nice stuff. Let's say you continue to act stubborn though. Next, those burns will fester and your blood will become sick. Once that happens, Celeste or I will have to invoke an ancient magic that cleanses all of your blood and organs. It's not fun for us. It's actually quite exhausting. Now, I understand how you feel. You don't want to put her down because you love her and you're afraid that–"

"*What?* No, you're wrong. Very wrong. I don't love her. I barely even like her anymore ... but I don't want her to die."

Tarnelius raised both his eyebrows and stared at Joseph, who squirmed under his scrutiny. "My mistake. Seems to me that a man would only kill for a woman if he loved her. Or he would forego his own health just to make sure she is okay. But perhaps I'm wrong. I've only lived for more than eight centuries and loved the same woman for nearly all of that time. I probably have no idea what love looks like."

"Sarcasm doesn't suit you, Tarnelius."

"But you know I'm right."

"No, I don't. Nothing could be further from the truth."

"Regardless, something similar happened to Celeste last year when we were trying to stop the rise of Kuunkierto. She was overcome from spell exhaustion and was unconscious for a full day. Despite the fact that I refused to acknowledge the feelings I still had for her, I would not let her out of my sight."

Joseph remained silent, so Tarnelius continued.

"I carried her with me everywhere that whole time, except once when I had to put her down to fight. That whole time I worried myself sick about her. Now, I'm going to ask you to trust me. I will hold Victoria while you get your own injuries seen to. I will stand next to you and will give her back as soon as you are done."

"I–but–" Joseph sighed. "Look, I only want to make sure she doesn't stop breathing. You can take her, it doesn't matter to me ... so long as someone keeps an eye on her."

Tarnelius held out his arms and Joseph passed Victoria's body to him.

"I've asked Celeste to come join us," Tarnelius said. "They'll be here in a moment."

Joseph nodded.

Celeste stormed over to them. "Good, you managed to pry her from his iron grip." She rifled in her bag and drew out a large container. She opened the lid to the container and pulled out a large glob of some glowing blue substance, which she used to cover Joseph's injuries. "Does that hurt?"

"No. I can't feel anything on that side of my body, actually."

"The burns were bad enough to damage your nerve endings. Hopefully, this will cure that as well." Celeste daubed the greasy blue ointment on his face and continued lower, covering his injuries.

Just as she reached his lower ribs, Joseph's breath increased and he jerked away from her. "What kind of hell-spawned magic ointment is that? My skin is burning!" He screamed. He flapped his hands around his face and neck, trying to cool down his flaming skin.

"Oh, good, that means it's working. You're regaining sensation in your face."

Joseph shifted his weight from one foot to the other and clenched his fists so hard that his knuckles turned white. "I'm not sure how that is a good thing, at present," he panted.

"It is. The pain will pass. I have to finish applying it." She approached him cautiously, as if he would bolt. He certainly considered it.

"Can you give me a moment?"

"Yes. We can wait, but it will only prolong the pain."

Joseph clenched his jaw. Finally, he gave her a curt nod and she applied more of the blue ointment as quickly as she could. When she was done, she backed out of his way.

His skin was on fire. He was sure of it. It may have looked like this obnoxious glowing blue gunk, but it was clearly magical fire in disguise. That was the only logical explanation.

He dropped to his knees, tears and sweat flowing down his face from the exertion that it took to not scream. After what seemed like an eternity, the inferno on his face lessened to a mild warmth, which gently covered his entire body.

Joseph gasped for breath, as though he'd been running for miles. Finally, when he'd regained control of himself, he raised his eyes to look at the three elves watching him. "You elves are sadistic. That's the most awful thing anyone has ever done to me." He looked down at himself to find his skin was a healthy pink color, like he'd scrubbed himself clean. The blue ointment had vanished. "The burns may be healed, but that gloop hurt worse than getting the actual injury!"

Celeste smirked. "That's because the fireball you were struck with was sudden, and it burned away your ability to feel pain. See why I didn't want to treat you while you were holding Victoria?"

Joseph's eyes flew to Tarnelius, who still had her cradled in his arms. He opened his mouth like he was going to say something, but thought better of it and changed his mind.

Tarnelius turned to Toni. "Let's go find Arcus and Siobhan. I'm sure that Siobhan and Celeste would love to get you ready for your coronation."

Toni's eyes widened. "Wait, that's today? Now? I thought I'd have time to let it set in."

"I wish I could give you more time, but we have to leave in the morning. Don't worry, everything will be fine. Make sure you follow your heart and your instincts. They won't lead you astray. Always act for what you think is the right thing to do, and the rest will fall into place."

Toni nodded and allowed Celeste to lead her away.

Joseph stood there for a moment and watched them go. He didn't want to give that smug elf the satisfaction of telling him he wanted to be the one carrying Victoria, that he wanted to be the first one she saw when she woke up … because he didn't really care, did he? No. He did not care. His heart was unmoved. He simply needed to make sure she was all right. That was the normal reaction for one human to have toward another. He felt protective of her because he was a man and she was a woman, and thereby weaker. It was the natural order of things. He hurried to catch up with the others.

Chapter Ten
Dreams and Portents

Everything was out of focus. Victoria blinked at the harsh light of the world. She looked around at her unfamiliar, stark and barren surroundings. She could not make out any kind of scenery: no forests, no mountains, nothing to grant her any clue of where she was. Only brilliant white light shone from every direction, as far as she could see. The ground beneath her was a solid gray, like stone, and seamlessly stretched before her to meet the horizon.

Victoria looked down at herself, furrowing her brow in confusion. Her knives were missing, and she wore a white dress the likes of which she hadn't owned since childhood. She remembered admiring the dress in the shop. It was so beautiful, like a bride's dress, but sized just for her. It was as if it were meant to be. Her father had seen her admiring it day after day and presented it to her for her birthday. She had loved it, had loved the idea of him scrimping and saving the money he earned *on odd jobs and begging simply to get it for her. She felt beautiful and special when she put it on. It wasn't until later that she found out he had broken into the shop and stolen it. It was still every bit as beautiful, but seemed somehow less special after that.*

Either way, there was no way that dress would fit her now. She ran her hand through her hair and felt something warm, sticky. Her fingers were covered in blood. It trickled from the edge of her hairline. But why couldn't she feel any pain? She squinted against the brightness.

In the distance she saw the crouched form of a man. She hurried toward him, the only other person she saw in this strange place. Details became clearer as she approached; tall, thin, light brown hair. She slowed down. She had been thinking about her father, but his hair was white, not brown.

She touched her head again; blood still flowed freely. Victoria didn't know who this man was. She had no idea if he meant her harm, but she'd have to risk it. She was confused and needed help; her body was apparently in shock from whatever had caused her this injury.

"Excuse me, sir, can you help me?"

The man jumped.

"I'm sorry, sir. I didn't mean to startle you. I'm lost and confused and ..."

Slowly, he stood up to his full height, easily a foot taller than she. He turned around.

Victoria gasped. "Joseph? What are you doing ... what is this place?"

Joseph's eyes crinkled at the corners as he smiled. "You tell me. You were the one who brought us here."

"Don't be foolish. I didn't bring us anywhere."

"You did, Vicki."

"What did you call me?" No one had called her Vicki since she was a child.

Joseph smiled and reached. Touching her hair, his hand and arm glowed blue. She felt a tingling in her scalp. "There, that's better. I'm sorry you were hurt."

"When did you become a healer?"

"Vicki, I'll be anything you need me to be."

He continued to smile, his eyes vacant.

"Joseph, please. What is this place? Why are you acting this way? You're starting to scare me."

His smile dropped away. "I never want to scare you. I love you. I've always loved you, since the moment we met. Before that, really. The first time I ever saw you was before you came to join the sorcerer school. You were wearing this same dress, though it didn't fit as well then."

"You never loved me. You love yourself. You love the chase. You love your loose women."

Joseph cupped her face in his hands. "You're wrong, darling. All those other women were distractions. You were the only one I ever thought of. I pursued them because I knew you would never love me, not like I love you. A wretch like me is not worthy of one as good and pure as you."

He kissed her gently on the mouth. Victoria melted into him, allowing herself this moment. She tangled her fingers in his hair and tugged gently. They deepened the kiss until it was like fire, all-consuming and powerful.

Victoria pulled away, gasping for breath and freeing her face from his hands. "You're wrong, Joseph. I am sorry to have made you feel that way. I used my body as a tool to sell for survival. I wanted money, power, control. I wanted to not live like my parents, on the streets. I wanted a better existence. You deserve better than me."

Joseph's smile returned, his eyes radiating love. "I forgive you, darling. You did what you had to do to survive. That's over now. Let me take care of you, my love."

Victoria felt a stabbing pain in her scalp. She clutched her head, once more feeling moisture from the blood that gushed forth. Joseph reached for her, but suddenly seemed far away. Panic rose inside her.

"Joseph! No! Don't leave!" He continued to grow smaller and smaller in the distance. "I never realized how you felt. I–I wish ... "

"Our time here is almost up," he called. "But I need to know: can you ever see yourself loving me, Victoria?"

"I..."

"Well?"

"Yes, Joseph, I could see myself falling in love with you."

Her vision blurred and darkened. She began to feel lightheaded.

Then everything went black.

Joseph adjusted his grip on the woman in his arms as Victoria struggled into wakefulness. He brought his ear closer to her mouth to better hear her murmured, nonsensical words.

"Joseph ... I'm sorry ... body ... sell ... deserve better ..."

Joseph tensed.

"Don't go ... love ... you ..."

Joseph's chest tightened. *Love.* That word had come up often lately. It was true that once he had dared to dream, but that ship had long since sailed.

"Is she finally coming to?" Arcus asked. He left Siobhan's side to come sit next to Joseph. They were gathered in Celeste's old home, which had been given to Toni. Siobhan and Celeste had been picking through various outfits, trying to choose what Toni should wear for her coronation. Tarnelius had taken Arcus and Joseph to get new clothes and gear since Joseph had been practically naked after his burn incident, and the bag that he carried had been heavily damaged, as well. Tarnelius had surrendered Victoria back into Joseph's care, if for no other reason than her skirts had covered him while they were retrieving clothes. Once that task was done, Arcus and Joseph had returned to Toni's home and had been watching the women get ready. Tarnelius had gone to walk among the elves and speak with them about the upcoming coronation.

Victoria went still once more, but her chest rose and fell in the welcomed rhythm of sleep.

"I thought she might have been." Joseph smoothed her blood-matted hair. Noticing this, Arcus uttered a spell, and a gentle breeze floated through the room, removing the dirt and grime of battle from each of them. "Thanks. She was fluttering her eyes and muttering."

"What did she say?"

"Random words, little else." Joseph shifted so her head rested comfortably beneath his chin.

"So it looks like things have sure changed, haven't they?"

Joseph stiffened. "Changed how?"

"The last time I saw you, your idea of fighting involved jumping around and dodging. When things got rough, you threw a weak spell at your attacker as if that were going to make a difference. Now, here you are fighting real battles. Siobhan told me you killed Simon."

"Did she tell you why?"

"Yes, indeed." Arcus lowered his voice. "Part of me is a little envious. I doubt I'll ever have the chance to face the man who hurt Siobhan the same way."

"What?"

"She was squired to a man who brutally raped her when she was younger. If I had any clue who and where he was, I'd kill him." Arcus tapped the side of his nose and looked back to where the three women were talking. Siobhan hadn't seemed to notice their conversation, but it was almost certain that the two elves had heard him.

Joseph shifted his weight. This conversation made him uncomfortable. "I learned a lot in Lumernia. I had to. It was either learn how to use the tools at my disposal or be killed. Or worse, cause others to be killed. I saw enough death there to haunt me forever."

Arcus nodded.

"We're almost done here," called Celeste. "Now we wait for Tarnel to let us know he's ready for us. Should be any moment."

Toni walked over and squeezed herself between the two men. Siobhan had given her an elegant braid in her platinum hair. Celeste had found a stunning cream color dress with a long train. Elegant, dark green leaves were stitched diagonally across the bust and down the train. Toni looked beautiful, regal. The circlet had been removed and Tarnelius had taken it with him to hold until the coronation. Arcus shifted over to give her room.

"Have you tried to kiss her to get her to wake up?" Toni asked.

"What? No. Why would I do that?"

Toni shrugged. "That's how they woke up the princess in the old children's stories. My mother used to tell me all about them."

"Let's go," interjected Celeste. "It's time."

"Victoria isn't a princess," argued Joseph, dismissing Toni's suggestion.

"Maybe to someone she is. I wasn't a princess either, yet here we are. Oh–"

Victoria sneezed, then moaned. Her hand twitched in the direction of her head.

"Victoria, wake up," Joseph smoothed the hair from her face. "Come on, I'm getting tired of carrying you."

Her eyelids fluttered.

Joseph shook her gently. "I said wake up. Nap time is over."

She squinted up at him. "Joseph?" Her voice was hoarse and weak.

"Whom were you expecting?"

"You're here … was it not a dream?"

"Victoria, you hit your head pretty hard. I'm not sure what you're talking about." Joseph nodded to the rest of the group. "You go ahead. We'll be right behind you. She'll need a minute to get used to being upright. I don't want to make you late for your own party."

Arcus stood and offered his arm to Siobhan. Celeste led the way to the door.

Toni held back for a moment. "I'll understand if you don't make it. Looks like you have more important things to do here." She smiled.

Joseph ground his teeth. "We'll be right behind you. Wouldn't miss it."

Toni followed after the rest.

Joseph gently nudged Victoria off his lap and onto the seat beside him. She stared, her deep brown eyes looking right through him. She raised a shaky hand to her head and ran it through her hair, wincing as her fingers became entangled in her curls.

"How are you feeling?"

"Like my brain is threatening to explode."

"Celeste said something about magic healing the injury, but not being able to replace lost blood or … something to do with brain swelling."

"Oh."

"When you feel up to it, we should probably catch up with the rest. We won, by the way. The orcs are dead, and Tarnelius has declared Toni shall become queen. Her coronation is starting soon."

"I had assumed we won, since we're alive."

The two fell into an uneasy silence, which stretched between them like a great chasm.

"Joseph?"

"Hmm?"

"Is it true?"

"Vicki, I have no idea what you're talking about."

Her eyes widened. "It *is* true then!"

"Yes, it's true that I have no idea what you're talking about."

"No, not that. You called me Vicki."

"So?"

"You called me Vicki in my dream, only it wasn't a dream, was it?"

Joseph stared at her in complete bewilderment. "Unless you dreamt that you were smacked in the head with a morningstar during battle and that I carried you around to make sure you continued breathing, then yes, it was a dream."

"It felt so real. You kissed me. You said you loved me."

All the blood drained from Joseph's face. "I did not."

Disappointment filled Victoria's face and she averted her eyes. "I should have known. It's just … no one has called me Vicki since I was a child. I'm sorry." She struggled to stand up, looking like she was trying not to throw up as she did it.

Joseph jumped to his feet and threw his arm around her as she went weak in the knees. He felt horribly guilty, but he wasn't sure why. He *didn't* love her, so it wasn't like he was lying to her. Actually, it was becoming quite annoying that everyone seemed to think he *should* love her. Why? Because he once wished he could? Time changes everything. Because they were the only two unmarried people in the group? Not good enough. Joseph mentally scolded himself to get it under control. If he was truly being honest, he would have to admit that his heart did feel something for her. No doubt something residual from all the times he'd dreamt of having her. His brain knew better, though. He'd never be able to look at her in that way without wondering if, even now, she was trying to use her body to gain something from him. He'd never love her, not really. His heart and his mind would have to agree, and that simply wasn't going to happen.

"I'm sorry," she repeated. "I feel like a fool. We should go to the ceremony."

"You'll never make it. Sit down."

"No. I'm going to go to the coronation. I've never seen one before and I want to go."

Joseph shook his head. "Forget the coronation. You need your rest. You've lost a lot of blood and can't even stand on your own."

She pushed on his chest. "Let me go."

Joseph swore under his breath. "No. Forget it. I'll carry you. Oh, and I won't call you Vicki anymore if you don't like it."

Victoria gave him a small smile as he lifted her into his arms and carried her from the room. "I don't mind. It surprised me, that's all."

"In conclusion, Tonilehdossa, you may not have been born in this place, but your lineage is uncontested. I know that you will serve our people well, and will lead them to a new era of hope and prosperity. I am pleased to step aside in your favor and hereby renounce my claim to the throne."

Dressed in full ceremonial regalia, Tarnelius looked every bit like the elven prince he was. His formal dark green satin coat shone in the sunlight. His statement had not been an exaggeration; he truly was pleased to give up the throne to Toni. He had never been interested in ruling others, and felt nothing but relief at escaping that burden.

"Do you, Tonilehdossa, solemnly promise and swear to uphold the laws of the elves and protect them to the best of your ability?"

"I promise to do so."

"Will you lead the people of Kayalost with mercy and faithfulness?"

"I will."

"Will you maintain the teachings of Kamara and the practice of Druidism as we have been taught? Do you swear to respect the neutrality of nature and all those who serve and revere it?"

"I swear I shall."

"It is my great honor and privilege to present to the people of Kayalost their new ruler: Queen Tonilehdossa. May she be forever blessed with Kamara's favor."

Tarnelius circled around her while Toni pivoted with him. She now faced the crowd while his back was turned to them. He lifted the circlet high in the air and gently placed it on Toni's head. He took a step back and bowed low to her, his fist crossed over his heart in respect. He remained in that position for several beats while the rest of those in attendance knelt down, their fists also over their chests. Tarnelius straightened up and backed away to join Celeste.

Toni cleared her throat. "I am humbled by the faith you have placed in me. I hope I am able to live up to everyone's expectations. The trust in the leadership of this kingdom has been shattered. Lines were crossed that never should have been. Members of enemy races were allowed to assimilate into our homes under our very noses, and some here thought it was the right thing to do. It wasn't. For those who do not know, my mother may have been the late king's cousin, but I was born a slave. After many long years I escaped and gained my freedom, finally finding my way home. I will never allow the people of Kayalost to be slaves to anyone, of any race. I will fight to my last breath to protect our freedoms. That is my promise to you. We will be free, and we will grow strong again. We will be a force to be reckoned with, if we can unite and work together, instead of against each other. Anything that has happened before is in the past. Today is a new beginning, a chance to start with a clean slate. Let us bring Kayalost to a new age of glory, together." She turned and sat down on the throne.

Her audience burst into applause, murmuring among themselves. The remaining members of the Cypress Guard separated from the crowd and knelt before Toni, swearing their loyalty.

As the last guard dropped to his knees, a bright flash of light filled the Chamber. The crowd silenced and Tarnelius rushed forward to stand near Toni, his hand on the hilt of his sword. Toni and the Cypress Guard rose to their feet and squinted at the ghostly figures that had appeared among them.

The figures took form and substance, their incorporeal shapes becoming that of a massive bear, a mighty lion, a beautiful woman and a hawk the size of a human. The woman stepped forward. At second glance, one could see that her skin was pebbled, resembling tree bark, and was a rich shade of brown. Her long, silky hair was only a slightly darker shade than her skin.

"Greetings, Druids of Kayalost," she said. "We are the spirits of this wood, and task ourselves with the protection and care of nature. A duty that we, at one time, shared with the elves of Kayalost. Recently, it has come to our attention that the balance has changed and the elves of Kayalost could no longer be trusted. We blocked the Sacred Tree from you to protect the forest. Now that the threat has been removed, we wish to know where we stand among you. Can we trust you as we once did? Or shall we forge a new path, separate from each other?"

Toni stepped forward and bowed. "Forgive us, Great Spirit."

The spirit cocked her head. "I am the Dryad Alana, spirit of trees. Who are you? I expected this one to address me." She gestured a long, bark-like finger toward Tarnelius.

Tarnelius joined Toni in a matching position of respectful supplication. "Dryad Alana, although it is true it was to be my place, I have elected to renounce the throne in favor of Tonilehdossa. She is strong of heart and spirit. She is the proper choice to rule the elven nation."

Toni spoke, "Forgive us, Dryad Alana. I hope we can return Kayalost to the way it was, or perhaps make it even better. I promise to revere nature and the spirits. I promise to follow the path of the druid and Kamara's teachings. These things I swear to you."

Alana nodded to her traveling companions. "Come forward, Tonilehdossa, whose name means 'praise beyond the grove' in the old tongue."

On shaky legs but with her head held high, Toni slowly approached the dryad. When she was within arm's reach, the dryad placed her palm on Toni's chest, over her heart. A bright flash of light burst forth and Toni's eyes widened. She dropped to her knees and covered her face in her hands.

"Now you know what it is that transpired. Now you know what we will do should you fail, should you follow in *his* footsteps. I look forward to reinstating our union and I give you my blessing. May you rule over the elves of Kayalost with wisdom and strength of both heart and spirit."

With that, the spirits vanished. Once they had recovered from the shock, the Cypress Guard began the slow process of dispersing the crowd, ushering them toward the stairs.

Finally, all that remained in the Chamber were Toni, the Cypress Guard, Tarnelius, Celeste and the four humans.

"What did she show you, Queen Tonilehdossa?" Tarnelius asked.

"She–she showed me a vision of Audelthus making a pact with the orcs. I saw them killing elves and replacing them with doppelgangers. I saw the spirits creating a magical barrier around the Sacred Tree to keep everyone away. They showed me a vision of the future, one where the orcs betrayed Audelthus' misplaced trust and slaughtered animals and elves alike, and enslaved the women for ... for ..." Toni swallowed, unwilling to finish that sentence. "They cut down the trees to create war machines and slaughtered the animals. They destroyed *everything*. There was nothing left."

Celeste took Tarnelius' hand and stared into his eyes. "See? He had to be stopped. Things will be better now. I can feel it."

Toni turned to the Cypress guardsman nearest to her. "What can you tell me about the tree? Why would they send the Cypress Guard away and create a barrier?"

"Your Majesty, I can answer that," interjected one of the members of the Cypress Guard. He paused, waiting for her to acknowledge him. "The Sacred Tree links Kayalost to many places. It connects us to the Silver Isles, for example, and to Axistra's realm. Anywhere a substantial elven druid community exists, a sacred tree can also be found nearby. There is even one somehow growing deep underground in Helvetinost. The trees contain powerful magic. By cutting us off from the baobab, they keep us from communicating with the rest of the elven nations. The spirits were acting to isolate us and protect the untainted. Have they released the barrier?"

Toni nodded. "That was part of the vision she gave me. They are giving me–giving us–a fresh start. They are still watching over it, but have removed the barrier."

The guardsman's face broke out in a large smile. "My entire adult life has been spent guarding that tree. I have missed it. I look forward to returning once things here settle down."

"Do you really have to go so soon?" Toni asked, turning to Tarnelius with a worried look.

Tarnelius nodded. "We do. The human capital of Lumernia has been conquered by the same threat that was here. We have to help them. We can't afford to take any more time. I wish we could. We'll come back and check on you as soon as we can, though."

"You will always be welcome here, all of you. I hope I'm worthy of the honor you've given me."

"You are. I have no doubts," said Tarnelius. He turned to the Cypress Guard. "Take care of her. Be sure to go through my father's old home before she moves in. Kamara only knows what he had in there."

The golden moon had risen, but the sun had not set. Celeste cleared her throat. "Come on, let's go. We should work on finding guest houses that haven't been trashed by the orcs or damaged by fire. If need be, two of you can stay with us in Tarnel's old place, but we definitely must find at least one. Two would, of course, be better." Celeste bowed low to Toni. "Good luck, Your Majesty. May good fortune favor you."

The others followed suit and they descended the stairs together, Joseph lifting Victoria back into his arms to carry her down the stairs.

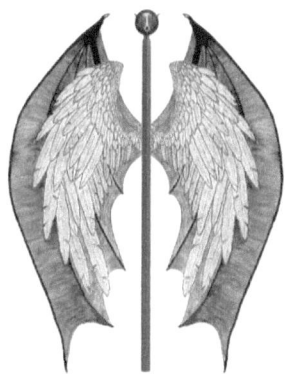

Chapter Eleven
Invisible Scars

Joseph opened the door of the guest house, holding it open for her to enter ahead of him. The sun was setting and it was becoming darker by the moment. Joseph muttered under his breath and blue and green lights burst from his hands and illuminated the room.

"So, how shall we do this?" she asked. They had been fortunate–and unfortunate–enough to secure two guest houses in addition to Tarnelius' old house, so it was only the two of them in this one.

"You take the bedroom," he answered gruffly. "I'll stay out here in the main part of the house."

"Are you sure?" She looked around the room, seemingly entranced by his colored orbs.

Joseph grunted in affirmation.

Victoria hesitated a moment. "Are you tired? Should I get out of your way now?"

"Do what you want, Victoria. I don't care. I'll probably stay up a while anyway. I don't sleep very well these days."

"Why not?"

Joseph shrugged. He wasn't going to admit to her that he still had nightmares of Lumernia. It was none of her business.

"Can we talk?"

He looked up and scowled. "I thought we were."

"I mean, can we have a real talk? A serious one. About *us*."

"There is no us."

Victoria sighed. "You mean you've never thought about there being an *us*? I thought you had. You kissed me, and you said ... you said ..."

"I said many things before I knew you were a common prostitute."

"You listen to me now, Joseph Hale. I'm sorry if *my* choices offend you so much. I'm sorry that you can't take it, but they were *my* choices and mine alone. I'm sorry that you would have rather I slept on the streets and been poor. I'm sorry you would have rather I starved. I'm even sorry that I never gave you a chance back in school because I was afraid to trust anyone, afraid to let anyone in–and this is why! Because I knew anyone who found out would judge me for my decisions. Besides, I still don't understand how it is any better to give it away for free. You are not that saintly, so you need to stop judging me and look at yourself!" She had been stomping toward Joseph as she spoke, and he felt his blood stir as she got closer and closer to him.

Damn it! Why does she have to affect me like this?

Tirade at its end, she jabbed him in the chest. Joseph grabbed her fingers and stared deeply into her eyes. Golden specks mixed in with the brown, but they were hard to see in the blue and green lighting.

Victoria panted heavily. She was beautiful and passionate in her fury. She yanked her hand out of his grip and took a deep breath. "I don't know why I ever wanted to try talking to you about this. You've never taken anything seriously, and you've never cared about anyone but yourse–"

Her words were cut off as he pulled her close and kissed her hard on the lips. He almost felt Victoria's confusion as she decided what to do. Taking control, he cupped the back of her head and used the other to pull her tighter against him. She surrendered and melted into him, opening her mouth as if to invite his tongue inside. He plunged inside her mouth, taking what he wanted before withdrawing and pushing his tongue in once more. It was an erotic promise of more to come. She shifted her body, aligning herself perfectly flush against him and moaned into his mouth.

Victoria trembled in his arms. He could feel her hands shake as she tangled her fingers in his hair. He pulled back, resting his forehead against hers and trying to catch his breath. It was then that he noticed the tear sliding down her cheek.

"Vicki?"

She sniffled and turned away from him.

"I'm sorry," he whispered, his voice rough. "I never wanted to hurt you."

"What does this mean, Joseph?" Victoria gestured to the air between them.

"I don't know."

"You don't know."

"No. I don't. Look, I'm sorry. I wish it were simple, but it's not."

Victoria sank to the floor and sat with her chin on her knees. "What's not simple? There is you and me. *Us*. I know you feel something. There is no way we can kiss like that and not feel something. Why won't you talk to me?"

Joseph ground his teeth. "You want to talk? Fine. Things are different now, Victoria. We're different–both of us. Yes, in school I wanted you badly. I was obsessed. I dreamt of you every night. Yes, I chased other women, but they were only to distract me from what I couldn't have–you. But now ..." Joseph sighed. "I have different dreams now. Now, I try not to sleep because my dreams are filled with the dying faces of the people I met and cared about in Lumernia. You say I only care about myself? That was never true. Once, I cared about myself and I cared about you. Now, I only want to make a difference. I can't figure out why everyone is so concerned with whether or not what I feel toward you is love when there are so many bigger problems that need fixing."

Victoria watched him, saying nothing. Tears flowed freely down her cheeks. Joseph growled. She said she wanted to talk, but he knew she didn't. She only wanted him to say what she wanted to hear.

"I also worry that this is a convenience issue. We are here, together. Arcus and Siobhan are together. Celeste and Tarnelius. Everywhere we look, there is overwhelming love and devotion. I think you see what they have and you crave it. I'm the only one here, so you turn to me. Or ... maybe it's because there isn't anyone around that you can trade yourself to in exchange for money or protection, other than me. Are you trying to give yourself to me to gain my protection?"

Joseph's head jerked to the side as her palm met his face in a loud smack. The sting was both painful and exhilarating. Truth be told, he'd been trying to push her, trying to get her angry enough to be honest again.

"How dare you!"

"How dare I what? It's not like it's that huge a leap to make. You only want to know what I am thinking, and you like to defend your past actions, but you never want to offer what you are feeling now. Just so you know, you have my protection without doing any of this." He mimicked her earlier gesture by waving his hand between them.

Joseph growled, exasperated. "I still feel something for you. My pulse increases when you glance my way. My body remembers how I once felt … but my head is stuck on the fact that in the entire time I dreamt of you, and practically begged you to even look at me, you were selling yourself without a second thought. My head wants me to stay focused on freeing Lumernia … but if I'm being honest with you and with myself, my heart demands more. One final thought. You accused me of preferring you to be poor and starving in the street than to … to do what you did. I suppose you never considered the other option: to let someone like me in. I would have preferred to take care of you myself. How much better would it have been for you to be cherished and taken care of by someone who loved you than to be used and paid by someone who didn't even have the brains to respect you?"

Victoria paled. "Joseph, I–" She covered her face with her hands, trying to form a barrier between them. "I'm so ashamed."

"You were the one who wanted to do this. You wanted to talk. Yet, I seem to be the one doing the talking. It's your turn. Talk to me about now, not the past. I've already heard all of your excuses."

Victoria hesitated. "You are right. About everything. Gods, Joseph, when did you become so wise? I don't know *what* I feel. I wish I did. The only thing I know for sure is that I am confused." She gave a sad smile. "I know that didn't actually make sense; how can anyone be sure about being confused? But

… I can't talk about now without referencing the past. You are right. We are both different now. The Joseph I knew was practically a boy. He didn't know how to take anything seriously. The Joseph I see before me is a man, one that I would have paid more attention to if he had spoken to me back then. No, it never occurred to me to 'let someone in so they could take care of me.' That is not something that would have crossed my mind. It seems a selfish thing for me to have tried to find someone for that purpose. I feel I could not win. I could take advantage of you and your love by letting you in, or I could do what I did and maintain my independence. Being raised a thief and a beggar left me feeling weak, but my interactions with Simon–"

"Do not say that name!" White-hot rage coursed through Joseph's veins.

Victoria paused, apparently shocked by the venom she heard in his voice. Well, he was surprised, too. After a moment, she continued. "My experiences made me feel stronger, in control. I needed to be better than my family, so I did what I felt I *had* to do. I saw no other options. I was secretive and careful, because I was afraid to let anyone in. I was aware you were lusting over me, but I thought that was all it was. You were tenacious and it scared me. It scared me because I was afraid that if I let you or anyone in, they would see my flaws and would judge me. I see now that what I actually felt was guilt and shame.

"I dreamt of you while I was unconscious. We were in a strange place filled with light. You said beautiful things about love and forgiveness. It touched my heart and I realized I want that. I dreamt of you, of us in love, when I could have fantasized or imagined anyone or anything. If that doesn't say that my heart is trying to tell me something, I don't know what does. Joseph–you want to know what I feel now?"

Victoria took his hand and placed it on her chest over her racing heart, which sped up even more at his touch. She raised her hand to his chest and smiled as his increased in answer to hers.

"I don't know what it is that I feel, Joseph, but I can only hope you feel it, too."

Joseph placed his forehead against hers, closing his eyes.

"As for Lumernia, we'll free it together. There is no reason why we can't find a little happiness for ourselves while we try to right the wrongs of the world. This feeling between us has nothing to do with convenience. If I were trying to ensnare you for the reasons you thought, we wouldn't feel this connection … this passion. You have to believe me when I say I've never felt anything like this before. Never."

Joseph felt his anger and his resolve surrender to her. He opened his eyes and pulled back, staring deeply into hers. He saw nothing but sincerity. The voice inside his head telling him she was nothing but trouble grew fainter and fainter, before quieting entirely. The final thing he managed to focus on before he lost his ability for rational thought was the hope that he wouldn't end up regretting this.

"Vicki … I'm going to kiss you now."

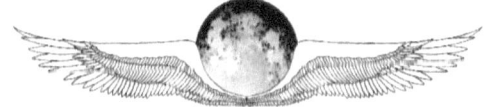

"Are you all right?"

Tarnelius gathered her in his arms. "You know the answer to that, Angel."

"I know … but I don't know what else to say."

Kissing the top of her head, he whispered, "Just tell me you love me."

"You know I do. More than anything."

Tarnelius took a deep shuddering breath and kissed the top of her head again. "Even though I know it, I never tire of hearing it."

"You did the right thing, my love," she thought to him. Although they were alone, some things were easier to say when you didn't have to speak them aloud.

"I know, but it doesn't make it easier. And I did not do the right thing by Virthanilus. I should have been stronger, I should have refused him."

"Unlike many of the others, he knew what Audelthus was doing and followed him anyway. He was every bit as sadistic and cruel," she thought.

"He could have been redeemable, but now we'll never know."

Celeste felt his misery through their bond. She turned around and wrapped her arms around him. "I can't believe what he did to you. He was your father. He was supposed to love you and support you, not have you beaten and left to starve. Not to send you *there* ... "

"Celeste."

"What sort of sadistic—"

"Celeste, I'm sorry I allowed those memories to surface like that. I didn't mean to hurt you."

Celeste chuckled darkly. "Hurt *me*? Tarnel, you were beaten because you didn't want to give up on me. You didn't hurt me. My gods! I am the one who should be sorry!"

"Don't. You didn't know."

"No! None of that would have happened if I had stayed with you. And, if it had, I would have found you. I would have saved you."

"You did save me."

"Not nearly soon enough." She sighed. "I should have taken care of him myself today."

"No, Angel. It's best that you did not sully your hands with the likes of him. That burden was mine and mine alone. Instead of focusing on the negative, we should look at the good things that happened today. Kayalost is freed, the orcs have been exposed and removed and I really believe Tonilehdossa will do an excellent job here as queen. It was fortunate that she came here when she did."

"I think you're right, Tarnel."

"Try not to worry about me. I just have to work through this. Everything will be fine, I know it. As long as we're together, we can get through anything."

Celeste smiled up at him. "Now I know you're right. Kiss me. I think I know how to take your mind off things for a while, at least."

Tarnelius didn't need to be told twice.

Joseph woke up the next morning to find the sun streaming in through the windows. Victoria was cuddled up at his side. He closed his eyes and sniffed her hair, loving the smell that was inherently *her*. He couldn't remember the last time he had slept so well, but it must have been before he and Arcus had left Izmar. He had also never slept with a woman before—well, not like this. They were both fully dressed, and had been all night.

He found he liked it. He scooted down and kissed right behind her ear.

She rolled over, sliding against him. He winced. Joseph may have enjoyed their chaste night together, but he was still a man and his body was urging him to lose himself in her. He gave himself a mental shake. Things might be looking up between the two of them, but he had to maintain control. He couldn't trust her, not yet.

"Good morning," she said in a throaty voice that sent his brain into a spin.

Focus, Joseph, he thought. *You'd better not mess this one up.*

"Good morning, Vicki." He smiled and kissed her briefly.

"Did you sleep well?"

"Better than I have in ages. I'm sure I have you to thank for that. Come on, get up. If memory serves, there should be a garden out back with different varieties of fruits and vegetables. The elves grow all sorts of things around here." He held out a hand to help her up. "How's your head?"

"Better, thanks. I barely thought about it after we came in here." Victoria stood up and they strolled outside to find breakfast, hand in hand.

They collected fruit from the trees and set out together to find the others, heading for Tarnelius' house. On the way, they saw several of the druids working to heal the trees and other flora that had been damaged in yesterday's battle. The bodies of the orcs had been removed, and wild animals walked through Kayalost as if it were the most natural thing in the world, showing no signs of either fear or aggression to those they passed.

Arriving at Tarnelius' house, Joseph rapped on the door. After a beat, it swung open. Arcus stood on the threshold, a somber look on his face.

"Come in. We need to talk."

"What's happened?" Victoria asked, alarm evident in her voice.

Arcus shook his head. "Nothing has happened. We have to discuss our next steps, and Joseph is the only one with firsthand knowledge of the situation in Lumernia."

Joseph's face darkened as he reminded himself of what they were doing. It was easy to fall into the fairytale after waking up next to the woman he'd wanted for as long as he could remember, then strolling together through such an idyllic place as Kayalost. But now was not the time for distractions. Now was the time for focus. He drew himself up to his full height and walked past Arcus into the house, not waiting to make sure Victoria followed him.

"I still think it's too good an opportunity to pass up," argued Celeste.

"We can't afford to delay any longer," snapped Siobhan. "We should go to Castle Mithra to gather the knights so we can go straight into Lumernia from there."

"Diverting to Castle Mithra would take us days out of the way," said Celeste. "We can't transport that many people. I also think a direct assault is suicide. We have to use subtlety. Perhaps rally the people who are still alive in Lumernia; I know Joseph said there was a resistance. We can then help free Lumernia from the inside, rather than throwing ourselves at their gates. Either way, we should still go see Axistra. The entrance to her castle is only a short walk from here, and she would know whether our concern about Crusiliux is warranted."

"You mean the way she knew we should be concerned about Tarextros? Please. It's a waste of time. At least gathering the knights is not a waste of time. What we lose in travel we gain in numbers and strength."

"What are we talking about?" Joseph interjected.

Glaring at Siobhan, Celeste explained, "We are only a few miles away from the Sacred Tree. It's a giant baobab with a twin located in front of Axistra's castle in the clouds. I think it would be best to take a short diversion there to find out what she knows, particularly in regard to other dragons and their activity. Siobhan feels a direct path to Castle Mithra is the best course of action. I suspect Arcus and Tarnelius are afraid to get involved. What do you think?"

"Is there any possibility the dragon will help us?"

"I don't know. I hope she will. She definitely won't if we never ask her."

Joseph scratched his jaw. "You're right about one thing: a direct assault will not work, not on its own. The number of orcs is too high. Every day that we allow them to maintain control, more and more of the Lumernians die. However, I also do not think that we will be enough on our own, even by rallying the resistance. Having a dragon on our side would help a lot … if you think she will help us. So I agree we should try. I also feel we should implement both ideas. We can gather an army to storm the gates, but it would help if we were positioned inside to help as we can from there. Could we talk to the knights, then go to Lumernia ourselves and wait for their arrival?

"We should go with them," said Siobhan, "rather than making them travel alone. What if they run into danger?"

"If your knights aren't strong enough to manage traveling alone," scoffed Joseph, "they have no business in Lumernia right now."

Siobhan shut her mouth and glowered. It seemed she had no rebuttal to that. Joseph tried to keep from smirking.

"What if the dragon won't see us?" asked Victoria in a small voice. "Or what if she will but wants to eat us?"

Everyone turned to stare at her. Tarnelius was the first to answer. "She will see us. She has always been friendly with my people. Besides that, she owes us and she knows it."

Victoria nodded, but looked nervous. Fighting off the urge to comfort her, Joseph continued, "So that's settled then? We'll go see this dragon and try to get her to help us, then we'll talk to the Mithran knights about storming the castle, and while we await them, we'll enter Lumernia and rally the resistance. This will give us the advantage of a two-pronged assault, and we can catch them between us. Should we try to gather any of the other paladin orders?"

Siobhan shook her head. "Most of the Rashnurians reside inside Lumernia and the surrounding areas. What's left of them will either be there already, or will have fled. We could attempt to go to some of the other Mithran keeps that are nearby, but most of their warriors spend a lot of time on rotation in Lumernia anyway."

"There are other Mithran keeps?" asked Joseph.

"Yes. Although we Mithrans have the highest percentage of true paladins than any other order, there are still a good number of warriors that have not been blessed by the essence of our goddess. They have created many strongholds in the Mithran territory. Mostly they are occupied by the family members of the Order–spouses, children and the elderly. They also keep a militia and a small number of warriors who are on leave from their rotations. We could try going to some of them, but to be honest, time would probably be better served by simply sending out a couple of squires or pages with messages."

Joseph nodded. "Can we teleport to the dragon?"

"No, we'll have to walk," answered Tarnelius. "No one may teleport into Axistra's realm. Her magic prevents it. We have to use the Sacred Tree and we'll have to walk to even that. The spirits may have removed the barrier keeping us from reaching the tree itself, but the entire area has always been protected by dragon magic, which prevents tree striding or teleportation for a few miles around it. It was meant as a protective measure to avert large-scale invasions."

"All right, so we're in agreement then?" asked Celeste.

Tarnel and Joseph nodded. Siobhan frowned and glared at Arcus, who merely shrugged. Victoria looked terrified but nodded her head as well.

"It seems I am outvoted, so I guess we are," grumbled Siobhan. "Let's go."

Tarnelius cast a final look around his old home as they turned to leave.

"We can come back sometime," Celeste said to Tarnelius. "I'm sure things will be better here now."

Tarnelius smiled and shut the door behind everyone.

"What is going on between the two of you?" Celeste asked Victoria and Joseph.

The pair glanced at each other. After a moment of awkward silence, Joseph spoke up. "We're seeing where things lead right now. We're giving it a shot."

A smirk ghosted Tarnelius' lips, but Joseph made a show of not looking at him. "How much longer until we reach this tree?" Joseph asked, changing the subject.

"Not much longer," said Celeste. "The clearing is only about half of a mile from here."

The group continued onward, Tarnelius and Celeste looking more tense with every step. Puzzled, Arcus spoke up. "Should we be preparing for a fight or something? What is with the two of you?"

Tarnelius frowned. "You can't feel it, Arcus? Can't see it?"

Arcus looked around. He saw the forest, as tranquil yet intimidating as it always was. "I see trees. I feel the magic of this forest, but I always do here."

"These are not the same trees. They have changed. The magic is wild and untamed."

"Probably the residual effects of the spirits' magic."

Tarnelius nodded. "That's what I think, too. Stay alert."

They continued down the pathway to the Sacred Tree. The forest was deathly silent. No birds sang, no trees rustled in the wind. The air was still, as if the world held its breath. At length, they entered the clearing where the Sacred Tree grew. The area around it was larger than any of them remembered, due to the notable lack of the Cypress Guard who normally kept a silent vigil around the tree. The baobab itself was huge and impressive. It had no leaves and its white trunk looked stark and imposing, with sharp-looking bony branches lifting to the heavens. One blackened scorch mark marred its otherwise unblemished bark.

"What happened to it?" Victoria asked, looking at the burnt area. "Was there a fire here?"

Arcus scrutinized the black scar from a distance. "What I don't understand is why it doesn't heal."

"It wasn't for lack of trying," said Tarnelius. "I'm not sure. The tree is unharmed; the scar is all that remains."

"Is anyone going to explain what you two are talking about?" Victoria crossed her arms.

Arcus stared at her coldly. "As you know, I was raised here and learned the ways of the druid. When I turned fifteen years old, my sorcerer magic began to manifest. I didn't know how to handle it. There are no sorcerers in Kayalost, so no one was able to explain to me what was happening. Magic would burst from me at random times, particularly when I was upset or frustrated. One day I came out here to commune with nature. The elves had encouraged me to meditate and try to relax my mind to prevent these outbursts, and I could think of no better place. I came here and sat under the tree and focused inward. I have no idea how long I sat here, but I suppose I fell asleep. I must have had a nightmare, but the nightmare I awoke to was worse. The tree was on fire! The Cypress Guard were trying to put out the fire, but their magic was ineffectual. The only thing I could do was watch in shock. I remember backing away, horrified, when I bumped into something warm and furry. Something huge. I whirled around and came face-to-stomach with the bear spirit, Karhu. The same one who appeared during the coronation. He roared at me and knocked me out of the way before charging toward the tree and putting out the fire with a touch of his claws. Then, he turned and roared at me again. I ran."

Arcus approached the tree and placed his palm on its trunk, his hand flashing blue. "I ran until I couldn't anymore, then I walked until I arrived in Izmar. Damon found me there and took me in. The rest you already know."

Victoria gasped, her hand flying to her mouth.

Arcus whirled around to find the same massive bear from his story standing upright only a few feet behind him. All the color drained from his face as he stared the creature in the eyes. Arcus' heart seemed to drop into his stomach. Without even thinking, he took a tiny step backward, away from the bear.

The sound of a metal sword sliding out of its scabbard filled the air.

"Stop," Celeste hissed. "Put it away, Siobhan."

Siobhan said something in response, but Arcus couldn't make it out. He stared up into the large brown eyes of Karhu. Almost instinctively, he opened his mind to the bear, as he had done with so many animals in the past.

"Arcus. I was surprised to see you here again," he heard inside his head. *"Now, and when you returned before."*

"I couldn't stay away. This was my home. I never meant to hurt the tree. It was an accident. You have to know that."

Karhu cocked his head to the side. *"I saw you trying to heal it. The Sacred Tree carries the scar as a memory. There is nothing to heal. I see the tree is not the only one bearing a scar from that day. Some marks are not readily visible."*

Arcus tilted his head in agreement.

"You have come a long way from the boy who ran from this place. I see you have come into yourself. I sense great power in you. You may not be as strong a druid as the half-herald, but in some ways she will never be able to aspire to what you are capable of. A force dragons may even one day fear. You have naught to worry about from me, and as long as you remember your roots, you will always be welcome here."

Karhu dropped to all fours before lowering himself into an unmistakable bow. Then he vanished.

Arcus shook his head as if to clear it, then turned to the rest of the group. Siobhan ran to him and threw herself into his arms.

Arcus caught her and hugged her tight. "What's the matter?"

"I was sure that massive bear was going to attack you. I could see him ripping you to pieces in my head."

Arcus pulled away from her a little. "You still have such little faith in me? I've told you before that nature accepts me as one of its own. I've told you not to worry. You've also seen what I am capable of, so why would you doubt me?"

"I don't know."

Arcus frowned. "Siobhan, I–"

"Arcus," interrupted Celeste, "I think it's about time you learned how to cast the tree stride spell, don't you?"

Arcus nodded. "Yes. I would like that very much, thank you."

"This spell uses verbal components. However, the act of running your hand down the trunk as you speak is important. Your touch conveys to the tree where you want to go. In most cases, you need to have been there before in order to effectively tell the tree where to take you, but the Sacred Tree is an exception. Like other trees, if you want to use this to get to the tree in the Silver Isles, for example, you have to be able to visualize it. Unlike other trees, each of the magical baobabs will lead you to Axistra's realm as long as you can visualize *whom* you are trying to see. The words are *'Ben gitmek isteniginiz buyuk agac beni.'* Once you learn a tree form, it is possible to cast this spell without the verbal component, because you are more in tune with nature. Repeat them until you know them by heart."

"Ben gitmek isteniginiz buyuk agac beni," repeated Arcus several times. Once he was satisfied with how they felt on his tongue he nodded to Celeste, who gestured to Tarnelius.

"Tarnel and Joseph will go through first," said Celeste, "then you and Siobhan. Victoria and I will come last. Watch Tarnel."

Tarnelius ran his hand up and down the baobab's trunk while murmuring the spell. The lines along the bark lit up in the outline of a golden doorway. Once the spell was completed, the magic door opened and Tarnelius pulled Joseph into the tree, which slammed shut behind them.

"Any questions?"

Arcus shook his head.

"Are you sure? There's not really any way to practice this spell. You'll have to plunge in and hope for the best. If you feel at all apprehensive, tell me now."

"No questions. I understand." Pulling Siobhan closer, Arcus chanted, running his hands over the trunk the same way Tarnelius had. Once more the bark glowed gold and a doorway appeared. When he finished the spell, the door slid open. Taking a deep breath, Arcus grabbed Siobhan's hand and yanked her into the tree. There was a sharp pulling sensation, like falling upward, then the inside of the tree was bathed in gold light. The pair stepped out into a place unlike any Arcus had ever seen before.

Chapter Twelve
Riddles and Rhetoric

Celeste pulled Victoria from the tree and felt a wave of relief wash over her to see Arcus and Siobhan there. She was glad they had made it on the first try. The familiar surroundings brought with them a wave of nostalgia and an ache deep in her soul. The last time she had been here had been with Theri.

Theri. The first friend she had made when she'd had to abandon her self-imposed isolation that had lasted for hundreds of years. The kedistam had taken to her right away and refused to be pushed aside. She had been a true friend, someone who was there no matter what happened simply because she'd wanted to be. She never showed fear, never showed doubt. Her last act had been to save Tarnelius' life by pushing him out of the way of a massive shadowy undead monstrosity who had then crushed her to death in his hand.

Tarnelius went to her and squeezed her hand. He, of course, knew exactly how she felt.

"Sorry. I know I have to stop dwelling. We must stay focused on the task at hand. I didn't expect this place to dredge up such feelings, but I can almost feel her presence."

"I understand, Celeste. Everyone here does. Come on, let's go."

The group walked toward the large castle. The ground beneath them was spongy and cloudlike. It almost seemed like it should be insubstantial, but held their weight and the weight of the trees and castle with ease. There were dozens of gigantic oaks and sequoias, the space between filled with wildflowers in a rainbow of dazzling colors. The castle itself was a shimmery blue color that looked like it was made of ice. Its spires sparkled and reflected the sun. The spires still seemed as tall and lonely as they had always looked to Celeste. She felt very small when standing in the castle's shadow.

Celeste approached the large door and froze, exactly as she had done a year prior. She stared at the entrance, remembering how she had been trying to work up the nerve to go in. Then, she had been summoned. Now they weren't. Butterflies fluttered to life in her stomach. Tarnelius paused next to her, glancing her way, then continued on to the castle, the rest following behind. Drawing strength from him, Celeste hurried to catch up.

Tarnelius' feelings felt complicated through their bond. She could tell he was still angry at the dragon and intended to demand the aid and information they had come for. Nevertheless, he had been raised to fear and respect the dragons, and those fears warred with his fury. Arriving at the entrance, he raised his hand to knock. Before he could bring his fist down on the ice-like door, it swung open to grant them entry.

Celeste swallowed. "Looks like our unexpected arrival wasn't so unexpected after all."

The group entered the castle and found the place in disarray, as if there had been a major earthquake in the area, which, of course, could never happen. The castle was in the sky, not attached to the ground at all. Sitting at a crooked desk in the main room was an elf. Her silver hair and robes gleamed in the dim lighting that permeated the room. She had a feather quill in her right hand and was frantically writing on a lengthy sheet of parchment.

Tarnelius cleared his throat. The scratching of the quill abruptly stopped. The strange elf paused a moment before swinging her glowing blue eyes upward to take in her guests.

"Axistra?" breathed Celeste. "What happened here?"

"Here?" repeated the elf, her voice hollow. Diverting her glowing eyes to the state of her castle, she took in the damage. "Nothing happened here. Why would you think something happened?" The elf sighed. "It's a mess. Everything is a mess. Do you ever feel like your skin is too tight?"

"No, but then I don't try to cram something as big as you into a form our size. That said, I never feel that way when I shift into a bird or rodent."

"It is only me then," the elf said glumly.

"Axistra?"

The elf turned her eyes back on Celeste. "That is who I was. Who I was before everything changed. The dragon pact … everything. It is all a mess. Aanhextrios is gone, but not gone. Tarextros is reborn. Crusiliux and Seratrix are meddling. I was meddling. Khellendriox is the only one where he is supposed to be. This is not what we agreed to."

"And now?"

"Now … now I write about what I have seen. My skin is too tight for anything else."

"Are we sure this is the dragon?" Victoria whispered to Joseph. "She doesn't seem very dangerous. Sad and a bit crazy, perhaps, but not dangerous."

The elf's eyes locked onto her. "I assure you I am every one of those things. Except crazy. Be careful what you say in my presence, mortal." The castle shook as she uttered the last word.

"Axistra, we apologize," said Celeste. "She meant no offense."

Tarnelius shook his head. "We need your help. We didn't come here for riddles."

"You come to demand my help? I do not even hear a request in your voice."

"There isn't one."

"And why should I not kill you where you stand?"

"Because you owe us. You owe us and you know it. You sent us on an impossible mission that you, yourself, should have undertaken. We completed your job and I lost Celeste. The fact that I got her back is irrelevant to your debt."

Axistra's reptilian eyes darted to Celeste's ruby hawk necklace and narrowed. "It is entirely relevant. You each left the northern tombs unscathed and the world was saved. What more do you want?"

"With respect, we didn't *all* escape unscathed," Celeste interjected. "What about Theri?"

"The kedistam did not even make it into the northern tombs. She was neither my fault, nor my problem."

"So you admit what happened in the north was your fault?" Tarnelius said.

Axistra's cool gaze slid over Tarnelius, who stubbornly met her gaze. "Do not test me, little elf prince. You are trying my patience. You should thank Celeste that her bond with you is keeping me from killing you for your insolence."

"Regardless of any of this," said Arcus, "we do *request* your assistance, Great Axistra."

Axistra became silent for a long moment, regarding Arcus. "Where is the staff?"

"What staff?"

"If you are going to play coy with me, I cannot help you. You know very well what staff."

Arcus looked uncomfortable. "Last I saw of it, Celeste had it. I don't want anything to do with it."

"Show me."

Celeste pulled the long staff from her bag, placing the end on the ground with a thump.

Axistra strode toward her. "Ah, the staff of Raziyl. Many have tried to claim this artifact. Few can master its secrets." With a single finger, she stroked the clear crystal staff head containing the key of Raziyl. The crystal glimmered to life at her touch, darkening as she pulled her finger away.

"You are the first mortal the staff has ever called master," Axistra continued.

"First of all, how did you know that? Second, you speak of it like it's alive and can make decisions."

"I am a seer. I see many things. Few visions have come to me with the clarity I experienced when you activated this staff. As for your second question, in some ways it is. Raziyl created it to do his bidding. It knows who its master is. It recognizes me and my kind, and I think you will find it recognizes you now, as well."

Axistra gestured to Celeste, who held it out to Arcus.

"I don't want it."

"Then you will die."

"That's a little extreme, don't you think?"

Axistra shook her head and looked away. "There is another who knows that you have it. She is looking for you ... for *it*. She will stop at nothing."

"Who could know?" asked Siobhan. "We are the only ones who were there in the ruins."

"My sisters are also seers. All three of us: silver, ruby and sapphire."

Celeste crossed her arms over her chest. "Then it is true. Crusiliux is the one organizing the orcs."

"But ... what does that have to do with us?" Siobhan asked. "How could attacking Izmar and Kayalost help her get the staff?"

Axistra watched Celeste, a slight smile playing on her face. Celeste frowned at her before continuing. "She may be trying to flush us out, to distract us with her orcs, so she can locate us and take it."

"If so, then going to Lumernia is playing into her hands," interjected Joseph.

"Then we shouldn't go," said Victoria.

Celeste rolled her eyes. "We have to go. There is no way around it. We must free Lumernia, but perhaps we should get rid of the staff. Will you take it, Axistra?"

"I will not. Arcus must wield the staff. It is his destiny, and he is the only one of you who has the strength."

"There has to be another way," Arcus argued.

"There is no other way!" the dragon bellowed. "If you go to Lumernia without it, you will fail. Crusiliux and her minions know who you are, they know what you look like. They will come and they will kill you. Then the world will be ruled by orcs under the control of Crusiliux."

"What of the other dragons?" asked Tarnelius. "Surely you wouldn't allow that to happen."

"The pact is broken. After what happened in the north, Crusiliux feels entitled to do as she wishes. We could fight her, but to what end? If she dies, she will be reborn, and the balance will be broken for years to come. It's teetering on the brink of destruction as it is. The power to shape the future is in your hands, not the hands of dragons. We cannot be the final answer or we fall into the same trap as the gods before us. Eventually there would be another Deity War, but it would be waged by dragons. I cannot allow that to happen."

Arcus stared at the staff. "If I take that, if I wield it against her, will we succeed?"

"I did not say that."

"You said we would fail if I didn't."

"Yes."

"But would we succeed?"

Axistra cocked her head. "That is in the perception with which one measures success. Much depends on you. A lot depends on your friends. If you fail, the world will burn. If you succeed, it may fall into tyranny and eventually burn anyway. You must seek to strike a balance."

"What does that mean?"

"It means I have said enough. I cannot tell you what your future brings, because every breath you take changes your destiny. You must look inside yourself and find the strength to do what needs to be done. Now, go away. Tarnelius, I consider my debt to be repaid."

"It will never be. Not to me," he murmured. Celeste stepped closer to him and gripped his hand. She held out the staff to Arcus once more.

Arcus took the staff. The crystal started to glow lightly, then a little brighter as he held on to it. He took a shaky step toward the door, followed by the others.

"Remember," Axistra added as they left. "The balance must be maintained."

The group wandered back toward the large baobab at the edge of Axistra's domain. Arcus was withdrawn and quiet as he contemplated the staff. When he had taken it from Celeste and the crystal started to glow, he had felt a warm tingling in his hand. The sensation had not been unpleasant, but it made him uneasy.

"Where are we headed next?" Victoria asked, breaking the silence.

"We're going to Castle Mithra," Siobhan said. She watched Arcus with concern in her eyes.

"Actually, we're returning to the grove outside of Kayalost," corrected Celeste. "From there we will head to Castle Mithra. There is no direct path from here to there."

"Are you all right, Arcus?" Siobhan asked.

Arcus jumped, startled. He cleared his throat. "I'm okay. I was thinking … it's a good thing we are going back there now; I want to borrow their library."

"I didn't figure we were staying there that long," said Joseph.

"We'll have to. If I'm to wield this thing, I'll have to study. I don't know what may be in that library that I haven't already looked at, but I'll have to try. I know time is of the essence, so I will hurry."

Siobhan took in the glowing staff head, the key sparkling in the morning light. "I still don't understand why it has to be you. Why doesn't the staff want to obey Celeste?"

"I think it's the arcane magic. Celeste is powerful in her druidic abilities, even more so than I, but the staff recognizes the dragons' power. A dwarven mage once told me that the dragons were the source of all arcana, that it was a gift from them that was in my blood. Raziyl was the god of secrets. He wouldn't have fueled his staff with divine magic ... because then any of his brethren could have used it. No, he would have used arcane magic."

"Then Joseph or Victoria should be able to wield it," Siobhan insisted.

The group reached the tree. With a sigh, Arcus held out the staff to Joseph. The second it left his hand, the light extinguished. Joseph handed it to Victoria, who returned it to Arcus when the staff gave no response. The light flickered back on at his touch.

"Arcus has more power in his pinky finger than Vicki and I have combined," said Joseph. "I'm not really surprised. It's always been that way."

Siobhan shook her head. "The staff didn't respond this way before the fight in Izmar. Things can change."

Arcus cupped her face in his free hand. "Why are you so opposed to me carrying this? Why do you want to pass it on to them?"

Siobhan tilted her head. "I'm not sure, but I have a bad feeling about it. Maybe it's the way you keep looking at it, but I no longer think this is a good idea."

"I have to, Shiv. It's my burden. You're right, though. The staff didn't respond to me until Izmar. What changed then? I have to think and I need access to the Mithran library. Let's go." Grabbing Siobhan's hand, he pulled her to the tree and cast the spell, telling the baobab to take them back to Kayalost.

Once the other four arrived back at the Sacred Tree, they continued east for a few hours until they made it far enough away that they could use magic to tree-stride out.

"We'll go to the nearby forest," said Celeste. "There are trees there that we can move to. I can't think of any inside Castle Mithra."

"That will still take us a fair distance out of the way," said Arcus. "I will take Siobhan directly into Castle Mithra so that she can meet with the knights and I can use the library. You go ahead to the forest and meet us at the castle when you can."

Celeste nodded. Arcus lifted Siobhan up in his arms and together they vanished.

Chapter Thirteen
Seeking the Obvious

"You go ahead. I'll stay here and work." Arcus had teleported them right into the small room inside the library he had claimed as his office for the months they had lived here.

Siobhan leaned down and gave him a quick kiss before hurrying from the room. Arcus followed her out as far as the main part of the library so that he could once more comb through the books on Raziyl and his staff. Picking up several volumes, he nodded to the other people working in the library as he carried them back to the little office. He received a few strange looks, but most of them had grown accustomed to his random comings and goings. He propped the staff against the desk as he had done so many times before and started flipping through pages, searching for anything he may have missed.

One by one, he tossed the books aside. None of them had anything new to offer. Time marched on. Arcus placed his elbows on the desk and leaned his head on his hands.

What am I going to do? How can I figure out how to activate this thing? he thought. Arcus glared at the offending staff.

"What did I do that day?" The staff didn't answer, though he hadn't really expected it to.

Arcus jumped to his feet and grabbed the staff. Gripping it tightly, he thought of the things he may have said during that battle. It was difficult, because he had been in severe pain and had panicked when he saw his wife get struck down by the necromancer. He tried anything he thought he may have said then, in every language he could think of. He assumed the command word would be in the dragon language, but he may have also spoken a few phrases in elven. He tried them all, but had no success.

He looked up when a knock sounded at the door. "Come in."

Siobhan entered, and he was able to glimpse the others behind her in the library.

"Glad to see they made it okay. Did you have any luck with the knights?"

"They are meeting in the morning to make a decision. I have told them what I can, considering I haven't even seen what condition Lumernia is in yet. The others arrived in time for Joseph to make a statement, so that's a good thing."

Arcus nodded.

"Have you had any luck?"

"Not yet. I don't know what else to try, but I'm still thinking. Maybe I should look for more books, but I think I've exhausted the resources here. I don't know what I'd hoped to find." He gestured toward the stack of books on the floor. "I practically have all of these memorized now."

"I'll be in our old room when you are ready to come to bed. I've found places for the others to stay already."

Arcus gave her a tight smile that didn't reach his eyes.

She kissed him on the forehead. "I know you'll figure it out." She started to leave, but turned back at the last second. "Are you sure you aren't trying too hard? It responds to you when you aren't doing anything but touching it."

Arcus frowned. "It's responding, but it's not doing anything more than creating dim light. You'd know if it was working."

"I suppose you're right. I remember what it felt like when I charged down the dragon while he was holding that thing." Siobhan shook her head. "I wish you would find another way. I have such a bad feeling about that staff." She held up her hand. "Don't say it; I already know. You're so stubborn and now that you've set your mind to it, you're going to see it through. Either way, I'm tired. I'm going to go to bed. Join me soon? You've been locked away in here all day. Have you eaten?"

"Um …" Arcus' stomach rumbled, as if on cue. "I actually lost track of time. I'll go get something soon."

Siobhan nodded, then left to join up with the others. Arcus stared at the staff in his hand for a while longer. "Hmm. Trying too hard. I wasn't trying at all on the battlefield."

In his head he pictured the events. He remembered his fight with the orc, remembered the sensations of his insides being ripped out of him after he was cursed. Then there came the large scale attack and he and Celeste had found the leader: a necromancer. He remembered watching his wife and Tarnel attack the leader, and then he saw, with painful clarity, his wife stabbed by the necromancer's sword. Panic, anger and pain lanced through his body at the memory. His hand tightened on the staff. The staff head flared to life, the crystal lighting up the small room–which was fortunate, because the magical light that had formerly lit up the room was abruptly extinguished.

Arcus dropped the staff as if it had stung him. At once, the lighting returned to normal and the glow of the staff head went out.

"Kamara help us. It's either based on emotion or will," Arcus muttered, his voice raspy. "Probably will. A god wouldn't make his artifact activate with emotion, especially not such an out of control emotion like fear or anger. That … that means …" Arcus trailed off. He didn't want to admit, even to himself, that the staff had activated simply because he'd wished it. His very soul must have called out to it. He'd *wanted* it there on that field. Wanted to save his wife. It was all him, not an accidental magic word. Damon's death had truly been his fault, after all. He stared at the staff on the floor. He didn't want to ever touch it again.

Then you will die …

Arcus heard the words in his head as if they had been spoken out loud. He squeezed his eyes shut, blocking the cursed object out of his vision.

You never know. We'll find another way. There is always another way, he thought.

Then you will die …

Arcus couldn't let that happen. He couldn't let his wife down like that. He wanted to live, he wanted to be able to protect her, he wanted a life and a future with her. Gritting his teeth, he picked up the staff, which glimmered to life in his hands.

"So I'm the first mortal you've ever called master, am I? Show me what you've got." Arcus focused his entire being into controlling the staff. Determined, he made himself feel it, wanted so badly to get this thing under control that he could almost taste it. The light flashed and dimmed.

"Submit to me, damn you! I am your master! You *will* do as I say ..." The light grew a little brighter, almost as if it understood him. "I *will* control you. Together, we can accomplish anything, even best this power-crazed red lizard and her minions." Arcus focused his will and his strength into the magic item in his hand once more, demanding it to obey with every fiber of his being. The light wavered for a second, then exploded into a dazzling radiance. The magical lighting which exuded from the walls once more extinguished, and the only source of illumination came from the staff itself. The silhouette of a key was easily made out on the walls.

He felt the bond with the staff form between them. He had its attention, its respect. After a long moment, he silently commanded it to turn off the lighted staff head while remaining activated. It complied at once. He ordered it to turn the light back on, but drop the anti-magic effects, which it also did, as evidenced by the lighting in the room returning to normal.

Arcus chuckled. "After nearly a year of trying to find out how to make you work, I can't believe I never thought of simply *telling* you to do it."

Alone in their room, Victoria faced Joseph on her bed. Two tiny beds sat against opposite walls of the small, barracks-like space, each with its own end table. She had removed her many knives and placed them within arm's reach on the table. Joseph sat next to her and gazed into her eyes. She felt warm and safe when he looked at her that way, as if she were the only one in the world. He caressed her face. Victoria closed her eyes and leaned into his hand.

"Don't close your eyes, Vicki. Look at me."

Her eyelids fluttered open to find him still regarding her with the same expression on his face.

"I want to savor this moment," he said.

"Why this one?"

He shrugged. "Because nothing in this life is guaranteed. We're about to return to Lumernia and I don't know what will happen there. The only thing I know is that here, tonight, in this room, we are together and happy."

She leaned forward to kiss him, her heart heavy. He hesitated, then returned her kiss. They began feather light, but quickly escalated to greater heights of bliss as they found their rhythm. All too soon, he pushed her away and stared at her once more with that dratted expression.

Beginning to feel self-conscious, Victoria bristled. "What did you mean, 'tonight we are together and happy'? Why would that not be the case in Lumernia? Are you so convinced we are going to die that you have given up, or is it something else? Is there another girl there?"

"Don't do this now, Vicki."

"Answer me."

Joseph flinched. "Look, this is me we're talking about. There are other girls. None of them mean anything to me, but you running into one or more of them will always be a possibility. I wish that wasn't the case, but the hard truth is that it is. As for your other question, I will protect you."

"I'm a big girl. I can take care of myself."

A ghost of a smile lifted Joseph's lips. "Your own magic suggests otherwise. Let's face it, you summon creatures from other dimensions to protect you. I think that on a subconscious level, you've always been looking for someone to take care of you. I'm right here, and I will do my best."

Victoria looked away. "You're impossible."

Joseph chuckled and leaned back against the wall. "Perhaps."

She jumped to her feet. "I'm tired. I think I'll take the other bed."

He also rose from the bed and gripped her hand. "Don't run away. Not from me." He pulled her to him and kissed her deeply, making her head spin.

Victoria was torn. She was thrilled that he was coming around, but hated being cast as a damsel in distress. Especially by Joseph, whom she always bested in sorcerer school.

In the end, she gave in. This was only talk. On the field of battle, she would show him that she could handle herself. His lips were warm and inviting, and despite herself, she felt safe in his arms.

Passion ignited between them. Soon they were touching and stroking everywhere. Victoria unbuttoned Joseph's shirt and he shrugged out of it. She ran her hands up the bare skin of his chest, feeling goosebumps rise under her fingers. He moaned and crushed her to him.

Victoria's fingers wandered toward his waistband. Catching her fingers, he broke away, breathing heavily.

"What? Why are we stopping?" Victoria breathed. Joseph didn't answer. "Don't you want to?"

Joseph opened his eyes and gazed into hers. Her breath hitched in her throat. His eyes were filled with lust and need, and something else ... love?

"How can you ask me that?" he rasped. "Can't you tell? Don't you know?"

Victoria searched his eyes, which closed as if in pain.

"Too fast," he muttered. "I–I can't …"

Victoria took a small step back. "You expect me to believe that we are moving too fast for *you*?"

His face fell. "It's always going to come back to that, isn't it? We'll never get past it. Is that who we are?" He sighed. "But that isn't what I meant, when I said it was too fast."

"Then what–"

He closed the space between them again in less than the time it took to breathe in a single breath. Caressing her face, he said, "These feelings are coming too fast."

Victoria remained silent, waiting for him to continue.

"I loved the idea of you for so long. You've no idea what I would have once done for simply a kind word or a smile from you, but I held you on a pedestal. I realize now that you could have never hoped to live up to the impossible standard that I held you to. But it doesn't matter. None of that matters, because my feelings were–are–real. Gods, I don't even know what I'm trying to say."

"You're trying to say that you love me."

Joseph blinked. "It's too fast. I can't–I've never …"

"Shh. It's okay. Kiss me, love me."

Joseph shook his head. "We can't. Not now, not here. Not tonight."

Victoria recoiled. Taking several steps back, she found herself at the bed on the other side of the room. Joseph let her go, regret etched on his face.

Siobhan awoke to an empty room. Disoriented and confused, she looked around for Arcus. His side of the bed was cold and appeared unslept in. With a sigh, she got up and dressed before heading to the privy. Then she wandered to the kitchens to find breakfast.

Collecting several different kinds of breads and fruits in a small basket, she went back to the library. Arcus had been raised by the elves, and hadn't shaken their habits of vegetarianism. She found it frustrating at times, having to come up with two meals, but over time gradually came to accept it and often ate what he did.

She found the library dark and deserted. Strange. The walls were usually kept lit. She took a deep breath and entered the room. As soon as she did, a sensation of weakness washed over her. Calling upon her holy symbol, she removed it from around her neck and lifted the icon into the air. She frowned when the symbol didn't react to her commands. Crossing the room, she found the small office Arcus had been occupying the night before. She gently nudged the door open.

Arcus was seated in the chair, his upper body sprawled across the desk. His hand clenched the staff. The crystal glowed brightly. Setting the basket down by the door, she went to him and gently pulled the staff from his hand.

The instant his fingers no longer grasped it, the light of the crystal went out and the walls returned to normal. The strange weakness that had struck her lifted as well. She placed the staff against the wall, out of the way.

Siobhan knelt before Arcus and stroked his unruly black hair. He twitched, inhaling sharply as he was roused from sleep. Sitting up, he rubbed his eyes and tried to focus on Siobhan.

"Hi," he said, his voice raspy.

"Good morning. You never came and joined me in bed."

"It's morning already? I'm sorry. I must have dozed off."

"I see you had success, though. The whole library was dark."

Arcus' gray eyes glimmered in triumph. "Yes. Turns out that you were right. I *was* trying too hard."

"I never tire of hearing that I'm right."

"There is no command word to activate it. The staff yields to the mage's force of will alone. So far I have figured out how to make it light up, and how to create the primary effect, which is the anti-magic field. It may be able to do other things, but I haven't worked on it too much yet. Since it seems to respond to my unspoken commands, it may allow me to focus spells through it without verbal components."

"Can you make it dictate who is affected by the anti-magic ability?"

"Maybe. I hope so, but I have no idea how to make that happen. Let me try something."

Arcus rose to his feet and held the staff firmly. A moment later, the lights in the room went out and Siobhan felt the sensation of weakness sweep over her again. It was almost nauseating.

"Try to cast something or activate your holy symbol."

Siobhan held out the necklace. Nothing happened. Arcus frowned and stared at the staff, his forehead creased in concentration. After several long moments, he relaxed his grip on the staff and the weakness she had felt vanished. Her holy symbol, and the magical walls, burst into light.

"Did you do it?" Siobhan asked excitedly.

Arcus shook his head. "No. I turned it off. I can work on that later. Everyone will have to stay back if I need to use it."

"I don't think I like the idea of you going off to fight an army of orcs alone. They still have swords. Even with your magic, that many at once would be impossible."

Arcus' lips thinned. "I somehow doubt the orcs will be my biggest concern if I do have to use this thing."

Siobhan paled as she considered what he could mean. "None of us can handle a dragon. Even while working together. We barely had any effect on the one we fought last year."

"What if they were stripped of their magical defenses?" Arcus pondered.

"*Even* if the dragon had no magic at all, she still has her claws, her teeth, her fiery breath and her superior size and strength. It's suicide. I'm sure Axistra didn't mean for you to fight the red dragon."

Arcus nodded but said nothing. After a few moments, he gestured toward the basket she had carried in. "What's in there? It smells good."

"You're probably smelling the fresh bread. I brought you some fruit, too. Did you ever eat last night?"

"No. I got distracted and forgot."

Siobhan retrieved the basket and hopped up on the desk to sit with him. They kept their conversation light while they ate, but she was filled with dread. Arcus was both stubborn and fearless when it came to protecting her. He had faced down a dragon for her once before, when Tarextros had almost killed her. He had saved her life, but if his timing had been off even a little, they probably would have both died. Attacking one on purpose seemed foolhardy. Forcing light laughter at something he said to her, she tried to block the sudden certainty she felt that their time together may draw to a close sooner than she would like.

As soon as the last of their breakfast had been eaten, she stood up and took his hand. "Come with me."

He obediently followed her. "Where are we going?"

"To our room. The elves are most likely up by now, but who knows where they are or what they are doing? I'm sure

Joseph and Victoria are still asleep, and the knights will be only starting to convene, so we have some time."

Arcus gave her a wicked smile that made her heart skip a beat. "Is that so? And how do you propose we spend this newfound time?"

"Why don't I show you?"

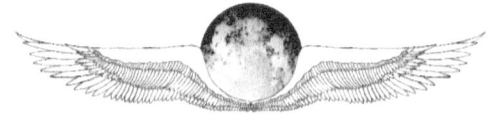

Victoria awoke with a start. She stared up at the ceiling, trying to figure out where she was. Turning slowly toward the center of the room, she was shocked to find herself face to face with Joseph, who was sitting on the floor with his back against the wall. He had apparently moved the end table to the side at some point during the night.

"Good morning, beautiful."

She sat up and stretched. "Morning. Have you been waiting for me to wake up?"

"More or less. I don't sleep well. Night before last in Kayalost was the most rest I've had in a long time."

"So instead of sleeping, you decided to watch *me* sleep?"

A ghost of a smile flickered over his face. "You looked just like an angel."

"I don't understand you at all. You are full of mixed signals. You kiss me with such passion and you watch me sleep, tell me I look like an angel … but you also push me away when I try to take our relationship further."

"Give me time."

"Since when do you need time?"

Joseph turned away. "See? That's why I need time. I don't want to make a mess of things. There is no rush. Right now, when you think of me, you only think of the women that came before you. You think of how I didn't wait. You aren't thinking of *us* at all. You aren't thinking that maybe I don't want a mere night of passion, that maybe I want something deeper. I guess the question is, what do you want?"

"Joseph, the only thing that I'm thinking of is that I don't want to wait. You said it yourself: nothing in this life is guaranteed. Can't we enjoy however long we have together?"

Joseph closed his eyes, seemingly lost in thought. For a moment, she was sure she'd won him over, but then he shook his head. "Just give me a little time, all right? I want everything to be special. You're special. Being with you is special."

"You're infuriatingly charming, do you know that?"

He smiled a crooked smile at her. "One more thing for you to love about me."

She patted the bed next to her. He rose to his feet and sat down. She climbed onto his lap and kissed him gently on the lips.

Joseph deepened the kiss, his hand rising up to cup her face, while his other hand held her in place on his lap. She tangled her fingers in his hair, shifting slightly. He groaned.

Pulling away, she murmured, "I do, you know."

"What's that, Vicki?"

"I do love you. You were right, and it is too fast, but something about you calls to me, to my very soul. I–I've never felt anything like this before. It frightens me."

Joseph stared at her, a look of stunned happiness on his face. He didn't speak a word, and after a few awkward moments, she pressed herself into him once more, kissing him with all the passion she wished she could verbalize. She gave him a little shove and he fell backward, landing on his back on the bed, with her atop him.

"Do you love me, too, Joseph?" she breathed.

Joseph rolled over, sliding her beneath him in the process. He kissed her chastely once, his weight resting on his elbows. "I do, Vicki. I tried to tell you last night. You know what else?"

"Hmm?"

"I think I've had enough time now." He kissed her again, this time with an urgency that made her blood run hot.

Someone pounded on the door. Joseph froze and swore under his breath.

"Ignore it," Victoria whispered.

The banging resumed.

"Joseph? Victoria?" called Celeste. "Are you in there? The knights have made their decision."

"Celeste," came Tarnelius' voice, "obviously they aren't in there, so shouting information to the empty room is pointless."

Joseph climbed off the bed, leaving Victoria feeling empty and cold with his loss. "No, we're in here, we were … asleep. We'll be right out."

"Oh … all right then." Celeste's voice had taken on an odd quality. "Meet us down in the kitchens when you're ready. We'll be leaving soon."

Joseph glanced at Victoria. "Sure. Be right there."

Victoria stood and crossed the room in silence, heading to the end table on the opposite wall, where her knives still lay. Picking up the first one, she strapped it back onto her wrist, when she heard Joseph mutter a quiet spell. Turning around in surprise, she saw him at the door, using magic to lock it. He gave her a wicked grin.

"You should put that down. We wouldn't want someone to get hurt."

"They're waiting for us." She smiled back at him as he closed the distance between them in three long strides and nudged her onto the nearby bed.

"They'll wait. It's not like they will leave without us. Now where were we?"

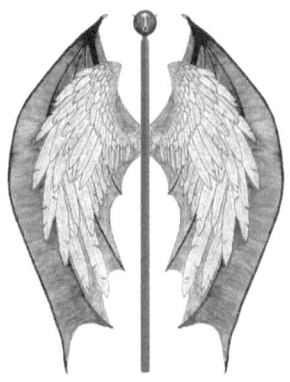

Chapter Fourteen
The Better Part of Valor

"The Mithrans have been doing a good job tending to the fruit trees and bushes we grew for them," commented Celeste. She helped herself to another peach, delighting in its sweet flavor.

Tarnelius nodded. All around them, people scrambled to pack and prepare for the journey. "Do you ever stop to think about how many people we are leading to their deaths in Lumernia?"

Celeste lowered her peach and stared at him in surprise. "Not really. Death is a part of war. We must reclaim the city. Why?"

Tarnelius sighed, his expression grim. "I don't know. It was a passing thought that came to me while I watched these people prepare. They may not have centuries like we do, but in some ways the humans know how to live more than we elves do. It seems wrong to take what time they have away from them."

"So what do you suggest? I doubt we can free Lumernia by ourselves. We need their help. They are going into battle with their eyes open."

"Some of them. Others are going because they were told to. That's what belonging to a place like this means: following orders."

"I still don't understand what you are suggesting."

"I don't either, Celeste. I suddenly feel uneasy about this whole thing. Maybe we should go try to help evacuate the refugees and take them to a different city. Maybe we should let the orcs have Lumernia. I don't know."

"You can't possibly be serious! That's madness!"

"Look, I don't mean that. It's just that I don't know what we're walking into. I don't know how many orcs there are. I don't know how many left to claim the other cities. I don't have any idea if we'll survive, or if any of these people will. At what point will the fighting stop? If we manage to take Lumernia back, will it end there or will we have to brace for a counterattack from them?"

"See this? This attitude is why the orcs got as far as they did in Kayalost. It's the complacency of the elves. It's our curse. This feeling that the world will stabilize if we wait it out. Well, I don't accept it. I don't accept any of it. Maybe it's the herald blood in me, but I know that if we don't do this ... if we don't stop them, no one will. The orcs will triumph, and they won't stop until they've taken over everything." Celeste took a bite out of her peach, chewing it thoughtfully.

Tarnelius' lips formed a grim line. "I wish the others would get down here. We should discuss where we're going."

"What do you mean? I figured we'd go straight into Lumernia."

"Celeste, think about it. The orcs have assumed control of the entire city. Simply popping into any of the trees we remember there, like the one outside Conner's house, could have us in the middle of their base. We should ask Joseph about it."

"What about porting in to the trees at Aengus and Roisin's house?"

He shook his head. "We don't even know if the trees are still there."

"Where *are* the others anyway? Joseph said they'd be down in a minute and it's been a long time now. It's going on afternoon. And Arcus and–"

Celeste trailed off as Arcus and Siobhan walked into view. Tarnelius nodded to them.

Siobhan looked around at the flurry of activity. "It looks like they made their decision. I was sure they would come along but, still, it's nice to see I didn't underestimate them."

"Where are Joseph and Victoria?" Arcus asked.

Celeste and Tarnelius exchanged glances. "Presumably still in their room," said Celeste. "Joseph said we had woken them up and they'd be down in a moment."

Arcus smirked. "I see." He sat down and selected a peach from the bowl atop the table. Patting the bench next to him, he gestured for Siobhan to join him. "How long ago was that?"

"Quite a while."

He nodded but said no more.

"She seems immature but sweet," mused Siobhan. "Victoria, I mean. I hope he doesn't hurt her."

Arcus made a pitiful attempt at disguising his snort with a cough.

"What?"

"I hope *she* doesn't hurt *him*. There will be no dealing with him if this doesn't work out."

"Why?" asked Siobhan.

"He's loved her as long as I've known them both. Years. He always tried to play it off, pretend it was nothing but a passing fancy, but no matter what she did to him–shooting fire at him, casting some weird spell that made tentacles sprout from his face, sending conjured creatures to take bites out of him–he would always take it in stride and come back for more. Every single time he asked her out, she resisted. I'm not sure what's been going on with the two of them since we ended up back in Izmar, but despite his attempt at aloofness yesterday when he said 'we've decided to see how things go,' I've no doubt that he will fall for her and fall hard. She has every bit of the power there. She–"

Celeste held a finger to her lips and kicked him under the table as the voices of Joseph and Victoria came from down the hall. They walked around the corner, arm in arm, laughing about something Joseph had said. Making their way over to the others, they separated and helped themselves to the food laid out on the table.

"Good morning," Joseph said, smearing fruit preserves on a piece of bread.

"Nearly afternoon now," said Arcus.

"Is it? Oh. Must have lost track of time." Joseph winked at Victoria, who blushed a deep crimson.

"Indeed," Tarnelius cut in. "Now that we are all here, we should discuss how we intend to get into Lumernia."

"Why wouldn't we use the trees?" asked Arcus.

Tarnelius turned to Joseph. "Can you tell us what parts of the city are safe to teleport into?"

"There are none. The orcs are everywhere. We can risk it, but there is no way of knowing if there will be three orcs within eyesight or three hundred."

"Where is the resistance based?" Celeste asked.

"The resistance moves around. They don't want to risk being caught and exterminated because they created a permanent base."

"Well, that's smart, though inconvenient. How are we supposed to find them?"

"There are places they move through regularly. We will find them. I'm sure of it."

"Okay," Celeste said. "But we still don't know where we are going. Is it your recommendation that we teleport into the city or to one of the outlying areas?"

Joseph thought for a moment. "Arcus could teleport into an area that you are familiar with and see if it's safe, then report back, but I know that he can't do that an unlimited number of times. Also, that leaves the possibility of him teleporting alone into an occupied area."

Celeste shook her head. "We have to stay together. There is a farm house not far from the gate. It was near the river. Last time we were there I grew several trees, including some apple trees that have identical versions here. An elderly couple named Roisin and Aengus live there."

Joseph refused to meet her eyes. "Celeste, many of the farms were razed, their crops and livestock pillaged. There is a better than average possibility that that farm is no longer there."

Celeste swallowed. "Then the people–"

"Are probably dead," Joseph finished.

Celeste paled and dropped her peach. She neither glanced at it nor made any move to pick it up.

Joseph frowned. "I told you there had been many deaths. Did you not believe me?"

"No. I mean, I did. It's only that it never sunk in that anyone we knew had been touched by this. Aengus and Roisin and their farm … Tarnel and I had our bonding ceremony there. It's hard to accept it, that's all."

Arcus asked, "What about the Temple of Melek?"

"What about it?" asked Celeste.

Arcus turned to Joseph. "Were the orcs able to destroy the temples in the city center?"

Joseph shook his head. "No. Last I saw, they had tried to open them several times, but the doors are made of stone. They wouldn't budge. Why?"

Arcus turned to Celeste. "Are you thinking what I'm thinking?"

She frowned and shook her head, confused.

Siobhan inhaled sharply. "The door! The stone door!"

Arcus gestured for her to continue.

"Remember, Celeste? When we were last in Lumernia, you were able to open the temple door with ease, but I had to struggle. It recognized you. I bet the temple would fight with everything it has to keep the orcs out. They wouldn't be able to easily burn it since it's made of stone. Some things caught on fire during the exorcism, but nothing structural."

"I could take a couple of trips and teleport us safely inside the Temple of Melek," offered Arcus. "Then we decide from there how to proceed and how to meet up with the resistance."

Celeste and Tarnelius exchanged glances. This did seem to be their best solution. Celeste nodded. "Let's do it. We'll leave when everyone has finished eating."

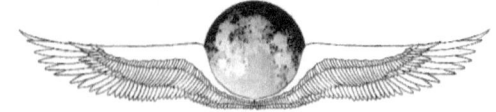

"By my count this will take you three trips, right, Arcus?" Celeste asked.

Arcus paused, considering the number of spells he would need to cast. He inhaled sharply and snapped his fingers. "Actually, only one."

"Did you become a lot stronger recently and I didn't notice?"

"No. Remember when we stopped in Grimsgil last year? The dwarves there taught me two spells. One of them, the ice spell, I have gotten a lot of use out of. The other, well, I've only gotten to use once. It should still work, though. At least, I think it will. No time like the present to find out, right?"

"What spell is it?"

"It will allow me to shapeshift Joseph and Victoria into animals, the same as we can. The difference is that it doesn't last for very long."

"Really?" Victoria asked. "What kind of animal?"

"No," said Joseph.

Victoria turned to him, a puzzled look on her face. "No? Just like that?"

"Just like that."

"Joseph never liked being my test subject back in school," said Arcus. "What he isn't thinking about, however, is that we have to conserve our magic from here on out. It's less draining for me to cast this spell than to hop back and forth. To put that in a simpler way, he is going to accept this, or he can ride out with the knights."

"Come on, Joseph. It'll be fine. I'll even go first."

Joseph paled. "No, no. If we are going to do this, I will go first."

"Fair enough. Come here." Arcus cleared his mind, then thought back to the underground training room in Grimsgil. Taking a deep breath, he chanted the requisite words. Joseph started to shrink, his belongings melding into his skin and feathers sprouting from his body. In a few short moments, he had transformed into a grackle.

Victoria clapped her hands and stepped forward. Arcus repeated the spell and she, too, changed into a grackle, her dark brown feathers differing from Joseph's jet-black. The pair flapped their wings, but only succeeded in lifting a few inches into the air, skimming the ground as they went.

Celeste and Tarnelius shifted into birds as well, taking flight and landing on Arcus' shoulders. Celeste, the only one among them who could talk while shifted, cocked her head. "They don't know how to fly," she chirped. Siobhan walked over and extended her hands so Joseph and Victoria could step onto her fingers, then lifted them to her shoulders. Arcus handed her the staff, then lifted her into his arms. Together, they disappeared with a popping sound.

The Temple of Melek was dark and musty-smelling, though familiar and comforting to Celeste at the same time. A thin layer of dust covered a floor spotted with dried blood. Paintings of Melek and his heralds dotted the walls, and the altar bearing a replica of the god's sword still remained where it had always been. Several benches were askew, as if they had been hastily shoved aside.

The four birds took flight, the two grackles fluttering clumsily to the floor before Arcus reversed the spell and they reverted back into humans. Celeste and Tarnelius shifted back mid-air in one fluid motion.

Celeste smiled. "We need to get the two of you some flying lessons if this is to become a regular occurrence."

Victoria's eyes sparkled. "I'd love that! That was so much fun."

"I'm just glad to still be in one piece," muttered Joseph. He glanced around. "What happened here?"

"Exorcism," answered Arcus. "Siobhan saved my life."

"It looks like you were right, Joseph. No one has been in here. Everything is as we left it." Celeste went to the door and pulled it open a small crack so she could peek out. She watched for a short time, then shut it. "No sign of any orcs. No sign of anyone in the area at all, actually."

"Don't be fooled," Joseph said. "They are around. The orcs have based their headquarters out of the king's castle, east of here. This is the city center, so they walk through here often."

"I remember. Okay, how do we find the resistance?"

"My friend, Conner, leads raiding parties nearly every day to collect food and gear, and to weaken the orcs however they can. Assuming he is still alive, we should look for him. They are often to the southwest. The orcs pillaged that area and all but abandoned it. The butchers used to work there and the smell was still horrible, even after the animals were all slaughtered … which means it was one of the safest parts of town. If not there, then they move around the fringes of the city center and sometimes frequent the merchant district to the northwest."

"Conner?" Celeste asked.

"Yes. That's the name of the resistance leader."

"What does he look like?"

Joseph scratched his head. "He is thin with brown hair and light eyes. Last I saw, he had grown a scruffy beard."

"Is he married to someone named Fiona?"

"Not to my knowledge. There were never any women with him the whole time I was here. Why?"

"No reason," said Celeste. "The last time we were here, we met a Conner. His wife's name was Fiona. I wondered if it was the same person, but apparently I am thinking of someone else. Everyone ready?" The group nodded. "Stay together and stay alert."

Before following Celeste out, Joseph pulled Victoria to him and kissed her roughly. "Promise me you'll be careful?"

She cupped Joseph's face in her hands. "Of course. Don't worry about me."

Joseph leaned into her hands. "I mean it, Vicki. I can't lose you."

"I'm not going anywhere. Everything will be fine. You're stuck with me."

Celeste cleared her throat. "It's time to go."

Victoria started to pull away, but Joseph held fast to her hand. He stared at her a moment longer, his expression unreadable, before releasing her. Together they followed Celeste out of the temple.

The temple door swung shut behind them. It seemed that whatever essences still remained of the former gods continued to work to protect their own.

Celeste took a deep breath. The last time she had been in the Lumernia city center it had teemed with activity. Merchants sold their wares, inns were filled beyond capacity. Warriors had bustled to and fro in an effort to prepare for a misbegotten war. Celeste had assumed the war had ended with the king's death. She had never expected that the war was fated, and that by stopping it she had set wheels in motion that would end in the destruction of Lumernia.

The city center was now part of a ghost town. The stillness, which was as complete as if a silence spell had been cast, overwhelmed their senses. They approached the park which was situated between the four temples. The grounds had once had a manicured lawn, but now, the grass was dead, parts of it scorched away. At each of the corners, the statues of the paladin gods stood guard in front of the entrances to their temples.

Celeste cocked her head, listening. She heard the faint guttural sounds of orcs nearby, muffled as if they were inside a building. Holding a finger up to her lips, she followed the sound to one of the smaller, single-story government houses near the park. Like the temples, these buildings were made of stone. Unlike the temples, they had windows with shutters that opened outward. They were almost to the building when a shadow froze in front of one such window.

"So much for sneaking up on them," said Celeste. "Move it!" The group hurried forward, but the orc was quicker. He slammed the shutters closed. They heard similar sounds as the rest of the shutters followed suit.

Celeste and Tarnelius circled quickly around the building while the rest spread out. Time passed in silence.

"What are they doing?" Victoria asked. "Why are they acting afraid?"

Siobhan frowned. "They aren't. They know they are trapped inside. I suspect they hope to wait us out. We can sling spells inside the building and they have no hope of escape. Their best bet is to hope the building can keep us out."

"Shh! Do you hear that?" Tarnelius spun around, facing the castle to the east. "We have more on the way. I bet one of the orcs inside this building tipped them off with magic."

A massive crowd of dark orcs marched toward them and organized in a series of skirmish lines. Those nearest the back nocked arrows and let them fly. Tarnelius threw out his hands and strong winds shot outward, blowing the arrows off course.

"There are so many!" Joseph yelled over the wind. "What do we do? Do we fight them or flee?"

"We will never flee from villains like these," Siobhan shouted. She summoned Apollo, and the magnificent palomino stood before her, ready for battle. Siobhan mounted and drew her sword.

Arcus cast a tall wall of fire in front of the approaching orcs, stopping them in their tracks. Siobhan spun back around and glared at him.

"Don't forget the orcs in the building. We are caught between them. This is foolishness," said Arcus.

"I will not run from them or anyone!" Siobhan insisted.

Arcus glowered at her. "Fine. Be careful and don't do anything stupid." To Celeste, he yelled, "I'll be right back!"

"Arcus, what are you—"

It was too late. Arcus had gestured with his hand and a shadowy black door appeared in the air next to him. In less time than it took to draw in a breath, he was gone.

The wall of fire died down and the rest turned to face the approaching army, Celeste releasing her wings and taking to the air.

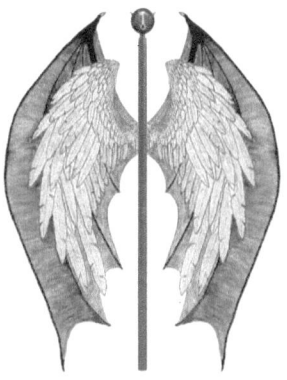

Chapter Fifteen
A Calculated Risk

A rcus stepped through the magical door he had created, taking a moment to collect his bearings. He stood in the rear of the government building. Six orcs huddled by the front window, peering out. So far, they had taken no notice of him.

He held out his staff, connecting with it. Taking a deep breath, he commanded it to form an anti-magic field that only encompassed the confines of the building. The crystal atop the staff flared to life, but only slightly. The reaction was immediate: the orcs stopped and stared at each other in confusion. Arcus flicked a small glowing bead in their direction, and as they noticed him and turned his way, he snapped his fingers.

A blast of fire exploded in their midst, setting them and their belongings on fire. The orcs screamed and writhed. One grabbed for his sword and took a step toward Arcus. Mustering his energy, Arcus looked him dead in the eye and spoke in his most hypnotic and commanding voice. *"All of you, stop moving."*

The orcs froze in place, and Arcus shot the nearest with a bolt of lightning that jumped to each of his comrades in turn. He followed it up with another fireball, and another after that. Unable to collapse to the floor, the orcs continued to burn, hotter and hotter until they had dissolved into ash on the floor. Stepping over what was left of them, Arcus cast yet another spell to open the door. Right before stepping out, he remembered to deactivate his staff.

Chaos ensued outside the building. Celeste hovered in the air, blasting the orcs with lightning bolts while she shouted out commands. Siobhan and Tarnelius stood back to back while they fought with their swords. Victoria flung daggers into the crowd, while some sort of glowing rhinoceros barreled its way through their ranks. Joseph, or to be more precise, five Josephs, stood around Victoria, creating all manner of imaginary monsters and orbs of light, which were flung to great effect.

It was a good effort, but Arcus could see that it was only a matter of time before the sheer number of orcs overwhelmed them.

He conjured another wall of flame that rose from the ground and separated most of the main body of the orcs from the ones who had managed to close in. Victoria's rhinoceros was trapped on the other side, but there was no help for it.

Touching his hand to his throat, Arcus magnified the sound of his voice. "Celeste, tornado!"

Celeste glanced down at him after directing another lightning bolt into the main part of the horde. She shook her head and gestured toward their small group. Her meaning was clear: they were standing too close.

"Leave it to me. Just do it!"

Arcus ran for Victoria and the Joseph quintuplets. "Come, we have to get to the others!" Victoria and Joseph each took one of Arcus' hands in their own. Arcus snarled a spell before yanking them through the portal he'd just created.

They appeared standing right next to Tarnelius and Siobhan, right in the thick of things.

"Now, Celeste!" Arcus yelled.

Tarnelius and Siobhan separated a little, battling defensively and trying to keep the three sorcerers between them.

"I hope you know what you're doing," yelled Siobhan.

"As do I." Arcus jumped back to avoid being stabbed by an orc and chanted. A green cage appeared around them, trapping two orcs inside with them.

Just as the cage settled into place, Arcus felt a white-hot pain shoot through him clear to his soul. The edges of his world blurred and he fell to the ground.

Celeste ran her hands through her hair. She didn't know what Arcus was up to, where he had gone or why he seemed to have become suicidal. She didn't know whether to call the storm and risk having the deaths of her friends, to say nothing of Tarnelius, on her hands. Though frightened and concerned, she decided to trust him. He had never led her astray before and he must have had a plan.

She focused her inner feelings, drawing the storm inside her out into physical form. The sky darkened, blocking out the sun. The winds picked up. Her hair whipped around her face.

Celeste spread her arms and turned to watch the horde of orcs below her. The wall of fire died and several orcs turned around and raced back toward the king's castle. A few brave souls took aim with their bows or crossbows and tried to shoot her, but the winds were too strong. In her peripheral vision, she saw the emerald glow of Arcus' magical cage fall into place.

The transparent cage didn't look strong enough to withstand the force of the winds she would be calling, but she put her faith in Arcus' judgment and manifested the storm. A huge black funnel cloud formed and burst down from the heavens.

Sweat beaded Celeste's brow as she directed the storm, circling around it in a pseudo-dance. She had to be careful; if she lost control for even a moment, Lumernia would be laid waste, leaving nothing but the stone buildings in this part of town standing.

The funnel crashed down, engulfing the city square. The orcs who had not fled for their lives were tossed into the air as if they weighed nothing, before crashing to the ground with sickening force. The nearby government house cracked from the air pressure. Its ceiling collapsed and the walls fell over as if they were a child's toy that had been kicked. The remains of the dead and dying trees in the park were uprooted and became deadly oversized projectiles.

Arcus' glowing green cage held fast, but Celeste had no idea how long he could keep the spell going. The black dragon, Tarextros, had destroyed one of those in a small amount of time, and she didn't want to risk her friends' lives for too long. She wondered how her storm compared in power to a dragon's brute strength.

"Focus, Celeste," she thought to herself.

To the east, several orcs who had escaped the maelstrom ran for the castle gate. The inner wall separating the city center from the king's castle began to crack and break down. Chunks of stone hurtled to the ground, crushing those unfortunate enough to be in its path. The last of the orcs made it through the doors of the castle and slammed shut the heavy gate.

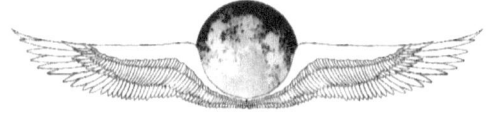

"Arcus!"

Siobhan's agonized cry broke through the whistling wind of the storm. Joseph flinched at the sound and spun around. His friend had been run through with a broadsword. The orc snarled, his face distorted with malice as he placed a booted foot on Arcus' back and yanked the blade out. Judging by the odd way Arcus' body contorted, the sword had severed through his spine. Two orcs had been trapped on the wrong side of the cage. Seven bodies in a hundred square-foot space made for tight quarters.

Joseph was torn. He wanted to go to his friend, but he had to worry about keeping Victoria safe. He chewed his lip. Tarnelius engaged the orc that had cut down Arcus. The decision was taken out of Joseph's hands as the second orc reached into his filthy tunic and retrieved a dagger, stalking toward Victoria.

Joseph chanted, then shoved Victoria as far away from the advancing orc as was possible in the confined space. He squared off his shoulders as she vanished from sight. Muttering a spell, he breathed into his left fist and unsheathed a dagger with his right.

He braced himself and charged the remaining orc, bellowing a battle-cry. The orc caught Joseph's wrist, and punched him in the gut. The dagger fell, useless, from his hand.

Wind knocked out of him, Joseph struggled to take even a wheezing breath. He lifted his left fist to his face and uncurled his fingers, revealing a glittering dust. He flung the substance into his enemy's face and eyes.

The orc screamed, releasing Joseph to claw at himself with long, filthy fingernails. Blood dripped from self-inflicted gouges on his cheeks.

Joseph placed his hands on his knees, focusing on breathing while keeping an eye on his writhing opponent. Finally able to stand up straight and take a shallow breath, he lunged for the knife.

"Joseph, stay down," Victoria yelled. He felt a slight breeze on the back of his neck. The orc grunted, then squealed. Quickly, he grabbed the dagger and straightened to see the delicate pearl handle of a throwing knife protrude from the upper left of the orc's chest. Blood dripped from the small wound.

Joseph closed the distance to his opponent in two steps. Grabbing hold of the hilt, he twisted. The orc snarled and gripped Joseph's shirt, kneeing him hard in the groin. Joseph whimpered. Pain shot through him, made him want to vomit. Tears sprang unbidden to his eyes. His knees went weak. He dropped the blade once more and would have collapsed if not for the monster's hold on him. Blind though he was, the orc remained lethal.

The battle faded away in Joseph's awareness, the agony radiating from his crotch allowing for nothing else. Nails pierced through his shirt and pressed into his skin, but that pain didn't matter. He thought he caught a glimpse of silver light gleaming from a blade...

Warm, sticky blood sprayed over Joseph, coating his hair and face. The orc released him, and he dropped heavily to the ground, where he at once curled in on himself. Squinting, he forced himself to look up.

The orc stumbled backward, his throat slashed open. Blood from the wound pulsed rhythmically between the filthy hands clutched around his own neck. The orc's breaths came in gurgling gasps.

A female voice grunted, and the orc was shoved to the ground as yet another blade appeared in his chest. The brute twitched and gurgled a moment longer, then went still.

"You okay?" Victoria asked from nearby.

Joseph only managed to moan in response. Invisible hands touched his shoulder, trying to roll him over. He resisted, refusing to straighten from his protective fetal position. A moment later, the hands released him.

"You'll live. I'm going to help Tarnelius."

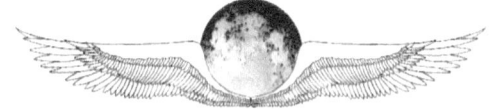

Tarnelius had switched his off-hand weapon into his right hand. His magical elven longsword was too unwieldy for these cramped quarters. He felt off balance with its loss.

Careful to keep himself positioned between the orc and Siobhan, he leapt to the offensive. His opponent raised the broadsword to deflect his attack, but the weapon smacked into the green wall in the process. Tarnelius spun on the balls of his feet, elbowing the orc before rolling free.

The orc snarled in an unintelligible language and dropped his weapon. Tarnelius felt his throat close up as if someone was squeezing it. The elf dropped his weapon and lifted his hands to his neck, but found nothing of substance. Forcing himself to stay calm, he lunged at the orc, punching him hard in the face with the heel of his hand. Tarnelius felt the pressure recede from his airway, and greedily gulped in air.

So this one was a magic user, was he? The best way for Tarnelius to handle this was to stay on him and take away any opportunity he may have to cast his foul magic.

Tarnelius grabbed for his belt to locate his dagger. He yanked it from its sheath and reversed his grip into a stabbing position. The orc tried to snatch the weapon away, his larger hand closing over Tarnelius' smaller one. The sharp edge of the knife bit into the fiend's fingers. Crimson blood slipped down the length of the small weapon. The corners of the orc's mouth lifted in a snarl, exposing sharp fangs.

Without warning, the orc head-butted him, their foreheads colliding in a sickening *crack*. The beast shoved Tarnelius hard into the green walls.

"Tilardunya," he said, spittle hitting Tarnelius in the face.

Tarnelius felt a pinching sensation in the fingertips of his right hand. Ignoring the pounding headache the orc had given him, Tarnelius kicked hard, connecting with the brute's shin. The orc grunted. A moment later, he jerked to the side and screamed, finally relinquishing his hold.

The enraged orc turned around and swung blindly. A long gash ripped angrily down the left side of his back. Tarnelius could not see whom he was fighting, but they had excellent timing. He tried to get a better grip on the dagger…

But his right hand felt numb, like it was asleep. It was a ghastly color, too. He switched the blade to his left and sprang at his enemy. He reached around in front of the orc and slit his throat almost to the bone. Tarnelius pushed the dying orc away, his breath catching at the sensation in his right hand.

His fingers had turned a wicked shade of black. The skin had shriveled and died, leaving him uncertain whether the skin was even still there, or if he was looking at blackened bone.

The curse crept higher, Tarnelius' hand withering away while he watched in horrid fascination.

"What's happening to you?" Victoria asked. Tarnelius couldn't see her, but he didn't care.

"I'm … I'm not sure. My hand. I think it's dying …"

"Let me see."

Tarnelius felt a grip on his forearm. She straightened his bony fingers, but the blackened digits crumbled into dust at her touch.

Victoria gasped. "Necromancy. This is the withering death spell. There is no cure … you're dying."

"How … do you … know…" Tarnelius' head spun as he tried to grasp the meaning behind her words. He realized his questions didn't matter. None of it mattered. Vaguely, he heard Siobhan's voice, but he paid it no mind. Only one thing mattered…

"Celeste, I'm sorry!" he thought.

"Not on my watch." Siobhan's voice broke through his thoughts. "Not today. Joseph, get over here. I'll need you to hold Tarnelius still."

Tarnelius watched Siobhan. None of this seemed real. He was as a spectator watching his own demise. He glanced at his arm. His entire hand had withered away and his forearm had started to tingle.

Siobhan grabbed the loose sleeve to his tunic and yanked, ripping it from the shoulder. The curse was halfway up his bicep. It wouldn't be long before it spread to his chest, then his heart. He wondered if it would hurt.

"Joseph is … unwell." Victoria said. "I can help,"

"I don't see how. I can't even see you. *Joseph!* I said get over here."

The mage groaned, but didn't get up. With a wave of his hand, the invisibility spell swept off Victoria, exposing her next to Siobhan.

"Fine," said Siobhan. "Victoria, I'll need you to make certain he doesn't move."

"What are you going to do?" Victoria asked.

Siobhan drew her sword. "Battlefield amputation. Tarnelius, lie down. I need you on the ground."

"What?" he asked.

"I'm coming, Tarnel!" Celeste thought to him.

"No time for arguments or answers. Lie down now."

Tarnelius did as requested. Victoria knelt down, her knees pressing into the elf's left side as she pushed down on his shoulder and stomach.

"Put one of your dagger handles between his teeth."

"What for?" Victoria asked.

"I don't want him to bite off his tongue. Hurry. We don't have much time."

Victoria fidgeted, then a metal tang was forced between Tarnelius' teeth, making him gag. Siobhan loomed above him. Her sword glinted emerald as it caught the reflection of the cage. His frantic mind struggled with what the paladin had said. *Battlefield what?*

Searing pain ripped mercilessly through his body. Tarnelius screamed and tried to throw Victoria off. He glimpsed a flash of gold ... then he knew no more.

"Celeste, I'm sorry!"

The dark funnel crashed into the castle wall. Parts of the gate and wall crumbled, but the castle itself stood firm. Any who had not made it inside had been killed or badly injured. Taking a deep breath, Celeste directed the storm back toward the city center and circled slower in ever-tightening rings. The funnel slowed with her and shrunk down at her command. Once the winds had died down completely, Celeste landed on the ground where the last of the storm funnel had burned itself out. Swaying on her feet, she turned to check on her friends in the green cage.

"I'm coming, Tarnel!"

Fighting off the wave of dizziness and overwhelming exhaustion, she forced her feet to run to the cage. She couldn't tell what was going on. Joseph and Arcus were both down. Siobhan drew her sword and leaned over Tarnelius while Victoria climbed atop him.

Siobhan brought the sword down like an executioner. Celeste gasped as phantom agony ripped through her shoulder. *What's happening?* Her mind cried out to him, though she knew it was in vain. From their link, she could tell that Tarnelius had blacked out. Siobhan's hands took on the golden glow of her goddess-given magic and she placed them on his horrible injury. The paladin had removed his entire right arm.

Celeste ran up to the cage but found no entrance. Frantic, she circled around and ran her hand across it, looking for any kind of door or access point. She moved over to the wall of the cage closest to Tarnelius and sank to her knees, her forehead pressed against the magical construct. She slapped the green barrier. "What have you done?" she screamed.

The golden glow of Siobhan's hands faded. She turned her head, refusing to look Celeste in the eyes. Celeste's heart lurched in her chest, but she calmed when she realized she could still feel their bond. Tarnelius was alive.

It was killing her that she couldn't reach him, couldn't touch him. She glanced over to Arcus; he was unconscious, too, lying in a pool of his own blood. He had to be alive, however, or Siobhan wouldn't be so calm. Celeste silently willed him to wake up; she wanted this cage open. She wanted…

Celeste's eyes rolled back in her head. She jerked her head away from the cage. She needed to remain awake. The spell fatigue would not take her. She stood and slapped her palms once more against the wall. Her ears rang, her vision blurred. Victoria rose to her feet and approached.

"She saved his life."

Victoria's words were the last thing Celeste knew before the darkness took her.

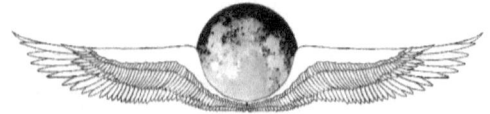

"Damn it!" Joseph wheezed. Everything still hurt. He couldn't breathe. He hobbled to Siobhan's side. "I'm sorry. I was …"

"I understand," Siobhan said softly. Her eyes trailed down to his bleeding shoulder. "You're hurt."

He looked down at the fresh wound. "Trust me when I say that's the least of my worries."

Siobhan placed her hand on his arm. A warm tingling swept through his body, taking away the throbbing ache.

"Thank you." Joseph stood straighter and inhaled deeply. "Are they going to be okay?"

"I–I think so. I've healed what damage I could, but I don't know what can be done about Tarnelius' arm. I hope he can forgive me. He seemed to be in shock."

"He'll forgive you. You saved his life," Victoria said. "To be honest, I didn't actually believe that would work. I thought he was good as dead."

"He's a warrior. That's his primary sword arm. We'll see how he really feels when he wakes up and realizes what I've done. Perhaps Celeste can fix him. She did last year when his face was damaged by some undead monster's acid attack. But this? This is different."

Joseph pointed to Celeste's prone body where it lay outside the cage. "We're assuming she's in any shape to help anyone."

"I don't know what to do," said Siobhan. "We can't get to her. The only one who can remove the cage is Arcus, and he is unconscious. I don't want to leave her out there alone. What if the orcs come back?"

"Hopefully they won't come back," said Joseph. "Or, if they do, with luck they'll assume she is dead and leave her alone."

Victoria sidled over to Joseph. "Feeling better?"

"Yes."

"Good." She smacked him on the chest. "Don't ever turn me invisible without asking first again! I can take care of myself. I am no damsel in distress."

He rubbed the spot she had struck. "We'll see."

"I'm not joking. I hope you realize I saved your life. You didn't need to turn me invisible. It was stupid. A waste. As soon as you cast it, you blinded the one we were to fight."

"It was still necessary."

"Why was it *necessary* to turn me invisible if you were just going to blind him?"

Joseph paused. "Because."

"Because? That's your explanation?"

"Yes. I didn't plan that far ahead. My way was better and allowed you the freedom to move unhindered. Now be quiet. We've more important things to worry about than your wounded pride."

Siobhan paced back and forth in the confined space like a caged lion. "This wouldn't have happened if I'd had his back. The fight would have been over much sooner and he could have taken a look at Arcus with me. Maybe we'd be out of this cage."

"Perhaps," said Joseph.

Victoria frowned at him. "You didn't know, Siobhan. For all you knew, if you didn't treat Arcus that second he would have died."

"That still may have been the case. The sword went through his spine and he was fading fast. But Tarnelius is a better healer than I am. It was selfish of me to drop out of the battle. I should have trusted him to take care of Arcus. I should have been the one who killed the animal that did this to him."

Joseph picked up Arcus' staff. He tapped the walls with it, trying to find a weak point. "It sounds like stone."

"What was that?" Siobhan asked.

Joseph dropped the staff and ran his hand over the wall. "The walls. They sound like they're made of stone. They feel like it, too." He grabbed the broadsword from the fallen orc and swung it into the wall. There was a loud *clang*, but nothing more happened.

"Let me try." Siobhan rose to her feet and took the sword from Joseph. She swung the weapon into the wall. Joseph and Victoria clapped their hands over their ears at the deafening *crack*. The wall was undamaged, but the broadsword was another story: it had shattered, the blade separating from the hilt. "I was afraid that would happen." She tossed the sword grip away.

"That's it then," said Joseph. "If that won't work, I don't know what will. We'll have to wait for the spell to dissipate, or for Arcus to wake up."

They fell into a tense silence as they waited for something to happen. Victoria approached the mutilated orc bodies and retrieved her daggers to clean them off. They nervously watched their surroundings for any sign of the orcs returning.

Joseph paced around the small cage. It only took him four or five steps to make it to either side. After several circuits, he stopped. Frowning, Joseph closed the distance to the wall and peered out.

"What is it?" Victoria asked.

"Conner."

Chapter Sixteen
Facing the Past

Conner Walsh crept into the city center. The freak storm had come out of nowhere, and he wanted to see what the damage was. It was too much to hope that anything major had happened to the orc army, but still … better to know for sure.

He snuck northwest toward the park, sticking to the shadows. He stepped out to dart quickly from one building to the next, then he glanced up. What he saw made him stop in his tracks, uncaring of who might see him.

The main government building was demolished. On the other side of it, inside the park itself, was a transparent green building of some sort. At least three people–humans, as best he could tell–milled around inside of it. Even more astonishing, one of them looked an awful lot like Joseph Hale, the mage who had left many months back claiming he would find help. Conner never expected to see him again. Another was a paladin–he'd seen plenty of her type before–though this one looked vaguely familiar. The third, however, was the one who really shocked him.

It can't be, he thought. *It isn't possible. My eyes must be playing tricks on me.*

The young woman who stared back at him could have been his wife Fiona's younger sister. She looked exactly the way Fiona did on the day they met.

Forcing his eyes off her, he took in the carnage. Bodies of orcs, weapons, shields and various rubble were strewn about. The temples were unharmed, though the inner wall to the easternmost district had taken serious damage. He saw no signs of any enemy orcs anywhere, so he hurried toward the strange building.

Outside the glowing structure, a woman with a mass of inky black hair lay on the ground. A single pointed ear poked out of the tangles. "My gods," Conner exclaimed as he recognized the woman who had come to their rescue nearly a year ago.

He knelt down, turned the girl over and brushed her hair aside.

"Celeste," he gasped. He placed his fingers to her lips and was relieved to feel her breath. He looked up to find Joseph staring at him.

"Do we know how to make an entrance, or what?" quipped Joseph.

"How did you know to bring her?" On the ground in front of the paladin was the dark form of another human, a male with unruly black hair, clad in black. *Arcus.* Close by was a slender man with golden blond hair, badly injured and surrounded by a pool of blood. Conner would wager that was Celeste's husband, Tarnelius.

"What do you mean, 'how did I know to bring her'?" asked Joseph. "I don't understand that question. Am I to understand that you know her?"

"We've met. She stayed in my house with … with my wife and me. She saved my parents' farm and cured my wife's leprosy. She is a true hero." Conner swiped his fingers over his eyes and looked away, careful not to even glance in the direction of the pretty brunette. "What happened here?"

"We ran into a bit of trouble, but we took care of it."

"Obviously." Conner chewed his lower lip, looking around the city center. "We should get inside before more come."

"If only it were that easy. We're stuck in here. We can't get Arcus to wake up, and we can't dispel the cage without him."

Conner regarded the cage. "I should at least take Celeste out of here."

The paladin spoke up. "Take her back to the Temple of Melek."

"Impossible. No one can get in there. I'll take her back to the resistance."

"Try the door while you are holding her. It will open for you. She won't be happy if she wakes up and can't quickly reach Tarnelius. She's the one who leveled this place. I wouldn't test her." Siobhan gestured to the temple. "At least from in there she is only a moment away."

Conner looked around, nervously checking for any sign of the orcs' return. Had it been anyone else in the entire city, he would have done what he thought was best and taken her back to the resistance, but the paladin had a point. He didn't want to do anything to upset Celeste. Her presence here could change everything.

Decision made, Conner scooped the elf up in his arms and carried her to the Temple of Melek. Expecting the door to be locked, it came as a shock when the door opened with a single shove. He gently laid her on a bench and returned to crouch by the barely cracked-open entryway so he could keep an eye on the others.

Every second that ticked by marked another moment in which the orcs could return. Conner sat as still as the statues out front, wishing he could keep away the enemies' inevitable return through force of will.

The statues...

Considering how much damage had been done to the city center, it was unbelievable those statues had survived unscathed. There they were, though, four sentries standing in eternal guard. Conner pondered their significance as he sat in silent vigil.

The gods had all left Altierra, or had they? It was difficult to think there could be any left, especially in light of Lumernia's situation. If the paladin gods were still anywhere, even in spirit, how could they allow this to happen? How could they allow Fiona to be taken from him so soon after being saved? Yet, if they were gone, what kept these temples standing strong despite everything that had been done to destroy them? None of this made any sense.

Conner noticed the humans inside the green cage moving around. The paladin knelt down near Arcus while Joseph and the brunette stood nearby. Conner glanced to Celeste, but she remained comatose. He opened the door a little wider and glanced around, searching the area for any orcs. Feeling somewhat amazed that none had shown up yet, he took a tentative step outside.

Joseph and the other human female separated from the others, who seemed to be deep in conversation, and walked the perimeter of the enclosure. After a time, he nodded to Conner.

The paladin helped Arcus to his feet and kissed him before stepping away to lift Tarnelius into her arms. Her strength surprised Conner, but these weren't ordinary people. With a snap of his fingers, Arcus made the green cage silently vanish, as if it had never existed.

The group started toward the Temple of Melek. After they were all safely inside, the paladin placed Tarnelius on a bench, then shoved the door shut.

"I'm sorry it took me so long to make it back, Conner," said Joseph. "Izmar is a long, long way from here. I went back there to find my old teacher, and found Arcus instead."

Conner's strained smile didn't reach his eyes. "It's good you're back, my friend. Though maybe it would have been better for you had you stayed away. I'm not sure. What happened out there?"

"A calculated risk gone awry," answered Arcus. "I never meant to trap the orcs inside that cage. Unfortunately, the spell isn't selective of whom it contains, and I didn't have time to worry about defenses. Luckily for me, my beautiful Siobhan was there to save my life."

She gave him a small smile. "I did tell you it was my turn to save you next. Remember? Back in Izmar."

"I remember. As I was saying, the cage was meant to be our protection from the tornado that Celeste cast."

"What is wrong with her?" asked Conner. "Why won't she wake up?"

"Spell exhaustion," said Arcus. "The same thing always happens after she casts that spell. She will recover. My concern is for Tarnelius. I don't know how he will adjust to having one arm, and I don't know if Celeste can fix that. Why don't you tell us what the situation is here?"

"The 'situation' is awful. There are probably only a few hundred of us left. It's hard to count because we sleep in shifts and separate often to try to obtain food and supplies. Raiding parties to try to take down some of the orcs have become fewer and further between, as it is a struggle to survive now. We've lost so many." Conner glanced at Victoria. "I've lost …" His voice cracked and trailed off.

"Fiona?" Arcus asked in a soft voice.

Conner nodded and looked away, the grief evident in his eyes. "She was one of the first to fall in the initial onslaught."

Joseph looked confused. "You never told me."

Conner sighed. "I didn't–don't–like to talk about it."

Joseph looked away, clearly unsure of what to say.

"I'm so sorry," Victoria interjected.

"It's been almost a year, and I swear the pain gets worse, not easier." Conner stared into Victoria's eyes, and the pity he saw threatened to consume him. He turned away.

This is why I never say anything, he thought, blinking rapidly. *I can't stand the pity-looks. Especially from …* her.

Arms wrapped around his waist, and short brown hair tickled his jaw. Conner opened his eyes to see the girl hugging him. He consoled himself in her warmth for a moment, then jerked away.

"I'll be fine, but I thank you for that. Who are you, anyway?"

She stepped back toward Joseph and took the mage's hand. "I'm Victoria. Arcus, Joseph and I went to sorcerer school in Izmar together."

Nodding, he addressed the paladin. "I think you are the only other one I do not know, although you look familiar."

"My name is Siobhan Keating, paladin of Mithra."

"You may have glimpsed her at your house the last time we were here," said Arcus. "She was the one who exorcised the demon out of me. Soon after, she agreed to marry me."

"Congratulations, you two. Now, we have an apothecary back at the resistance. We've had some luck creating a semi-permanent base in the old slaughterhouse district. The orcs don't often explore that area."

"They don't need an apothecary," said Arcus. "They only need rest."

"We can try to get them that there, too. If we go, we can discuss future plans. I'd say we could wait it out, but we have no idea how long it will take them to wake up."

Siobhan nodded. "We must speak to everyone. The paladins of Mithra are riding here as we speak. They should arrive in around a week's time."

Conner felt hope rise in his chest. "The gods bless you. Let's get everyone back to base camp."

Siobhan picked up Tarnelius, while Conner lifted Celeste back into his arms. Together they cautiously snuck from the temple.

Even after almost a year, the smell of death and decay that permeated the slaughterhouse district to the southeast was still rancid and disgusting, causing Victoria to wrinkle her nose. Brown splotches stained the ground in several places. A small trench wound its way down the middle of the roadways and all the way to the outer wall into the ocean. Centuries of drained blood and entrails from butchered animals had left a constant stench over the area, one likely to never go away completely.

Conner led the way, finally stopping outside a large, stone building that used to house several of the butchers' families. He led the way through one of the doors, then crossed the abandoned multi-family home into one of the bedrooms. Once inside, he passed Celeste over to Joseph, then approached several dusty crates on the floor. Conner grabbed hold of a large, damaged box and tilted it. To Victoria's surprise, the crate lifted the floor with it, revealing a trapdoor. Inside was a ladder leading into a pitch-black passageway. He descended the ladder first, then helped ease the elf down. The rest followed, handing off Tarnelius the same way.

The passageway was small. It would have been a tight squeeze for two grown men to cross each other's paths. It was also uncomfortably short, and both Joseph and Siobhan had to crouch to make it through.

"What is this place?" wondered Joseph.

"We're not entirely sure. It leads to another public housing area in the same district. Like the first building, the other one has three floors. What we have been doing is entering the one building, then using the passageway to get to the second. We only occupy the top two stories. This way, if the orcs do happen to see us entering or exiting the first building, they are less likely to find the trapdoor. As you saw, it was well-hidden. Also, we have guards posted all hours of the day and night watching for enemy patrols. If any orcs get too close, our mages cast silencing spells on the upper two floors of the other building, and weave glamour magic on the stairs to make them appear as if they collapsed. If they check the bottom floor, they will not find us and will be unable to find any way to ascend to the upper stories. It's a gamble, but we've had good fortune here for the last few months. It's the closest thing any of us have to some semblance of home. We were lucky to find this. Some have hypothesized that the tunnel was dug by a pair of lovers who wanted to meet in secret. I don't know about any of that. The tunnel could be gods only know how old, and it could have served any purpose."

They had travelled only a short time when a light flared in front of them.

"Conner? Is that you? We'd wondered where you had gotten off to."

"Go back, David. We are carrying wounded and we won't fit."

"No problem. I was headed out to find you."

Conner growled. "You know better. If one of us falls, we do not risk more in a fruitless search party."

"I know," David said simply.

"Once we make it back to base, I want you to go ahead and go back out, David. Find as many of the unit leaders as you can and tell them to be sure to be back here no later than dusk. No excuses. Only search the normal patrol routes. I don't want any unnecessary risks. Be careful."

"Yes, sir."

The group continued on, finally finding another ladder that matched the one they had descended. After climbing the metal rungs, David flung the trapdoor open and peered out. Gesturing that the coast was clear, he ascended the ladder and helped pull the two elves out, laying them on the floor. Once everyone was clear, they regrouped and climbed a set of stairs located in the hallway outside the room.

Conner motioned for the group to follow him down the hallway on the second floor. They passed several rooms, coming to a stop at the fourth on the right. Conner eased the door open and walked through. Approaching a row of short cots, he eased Tarnelius onto the nearest one and gestured for Siobhan to place Celeste on the one next to him. There were several other cots crowding the room, as well as a large desk with a slender blonde woman sitting behind it, mixing some sort of poultice. Several cots were occupied, injured resistance members either sleeping or trying to stifle their cries.

"More wounded, Conner?" the blonde asked in a sad tone.

"Not exactly, Katherine. These are merely unconscious. They will be fine when they wake up." A frown marred Conner's brow. "Well, one for sure."

At this, Katherine looked up from her work to examine the newcomers, her face splitting into a wide smile. "Joseph! I don't believe it. You came back!"

"Yes, Katherine. I said I would, didn't I?" said Joseph.

Katherine nodded and went back to her task. "I'm not sure if that makes you brave or stupid."

Joseph clapped his hand over his chest in mock hurt and grinned at Victoria. "Katherine always knew what to say to make me feel welcome."

"Did she now? Hopefully not too welcome."

Joseph's grin slipped off his face. His expression would have almost made Victoria laugh if his callousness hadn't annoyed her so. She had meant her comment as a joke, but Joseph's guilty look told her that whatever past the two had shared was no laughing matter.

"I assume it will take some time to organize your leaders, Conner?" Arcus asked.

"Yes. Some are out on patrol or gathering food and equipment. Others are asleep this shift. We're going to try to have everyone gathered at dusk, but failing that, we'll meet at dawn. Those times are when we meet to eat, trade information and switch shifts."

"All right. I think I'll help out here in the meantime. Siobhan, can I talk you into giving me a hand?" At her nod, he continued, "We will catch up later, either at dusk or when the elves wake up."

Conner nodded. "We will be two doors down and across the hall. That is the room we use for meetings and meals. Come find me if you need me."

Siobhan went to speak to Katherine while Arcus moved toward a cot where a young man lay, sweat beading his brow. His leg was bent at an awkward angle, clearly broken at least twice.

Joseph winced as Arcus headed toward the unfortunate man, then took Victoria by the elbow and steered her out of the room. Conner followed them out, shutting the door behind them. Its closing was not enough to block out the poor man's agony.

Conner looked worried. "Should we go back in there?"

Joseph shook his head. "Arcus knows what he is doing. He had to reset the bone or it would heal out of position with his magic. I've had to go through that myself a time or two. It isn't fun, but that man will thank him for it when he is done."

Conner grunted his agreement, then opened the door to the meeting room. He gestured for his companions to enter first.

The room was filled with several chairs and a few haphazard tables scattered throughout, but was otherwise empty. Victoria crossed the room and chose a chair in the far corner. Joseph sat down next to her, and Conner sat across.

"Do you ever feel like we're rushing everywhere as fast as we can just to wait around?" Victoria mused.

"Sometimes it seems that way, but savor this downtime. Sooner than we think, we'll have to bring the fight to the orcs. When that happens these idle moments will be missed," said Joseph.

Conner absently scratched his chin. "Catch me up on what has happened since you left, Joseph."

"There's a lot of information to go over and, really, either of the elves or Arcus would be much better suited to–"

The door flung open, and Siobhan poked her head in. "Joseph, we could use an extra set of hands, if you please. Arcus is having difficulty getting this young man to hold still so that he can reset the second break. He says if you are busy he can use a hold spell on him, but it would be less traumatic if you could do some sort of distraction spell or a sleep spell while I hold him down."

Joseph grumbled and rose to his feet, the other two following suit. Joseph held up his hand to Victoria. "Stay here. I'll be right back. Trust me, it's better if you don't see this."

"You're concerned that I'll become squeamish now? I've fought by your side several times, but you think *this* will upset me?"

"It will certainly upset *me!* Fighting is one thing, watching a bone get reset is another. It makes this awful crunching sound when it grinds back together." He shook his head. "If you are determined to come I won't stop you, but I would prefer that you stay here. I promise I won't be long."

Victoria bit her lip and nodded. Joseph strode from the room and shut the door behind them, leaving the two others standing alone in the corner.

"Do you want to go with them?" Victoria asked.

Conner stared, expression indiscernible. A pregnant pause stretched between them. "No, I'd rather stay here, wouldn't you?"

Victoria smiled. "I suppose so. We'd probably get in the way in there."

"Yes."

Victoria felt awkward under Conner's scrutiny. She paced around the chair Joseph had sat in. "Why do you keep staring at me like that?"

He startled. "Am I? I apologize if I made you uncomfortable. It's just ..." Conner hesitated, sadness and grief etched on his face. "You look exactly like her."

"Her?"

"My wife ... Fiona. It's uncanny. You could be twins." His eyes became shiny and he stared at the floor.

A wave of sympathy washed over Victoria. "I'm so sorry, Conner."

He stepped closer. "Fiona was such a good soul. There was nothing she wouldn't do to help others. So pure of spirit, so innocent. She had contracted leprosy from helping a poor beggar. That's who she was, though. Someone who wouldn't hesitate to step in, no matter the risk to herself. Tarnelius, Celeste, Arcus and the kedistam came to me one day. My grandparents sent them, even though they couldn't have known what had happened; I'd never told them. Fate smiled on us that day when Tarnelius cured my wife and gave her back to me. It's too bad it was for such a short time. The night the orcs came was chaos. Everyone ran into the streets like sheep fleeing the butcher. I urged her to hide. I assumed our best chances came from not being noticed. Then ... I don't know. The rest of the night was a blur. They set our neighbor's house on fire. Fiona was determined to help–she was terrified their small children would be burned alive. She hurried out there and I chased after her. People were being hunted, murdered. Fiona ran toward the house and jumped through a window. She never came out. Not in one piece.

"The monsters had slaughtered the entire family. Poor Fiona went in there, never suspecting them to be in the burning building. The only reason I'm alive today is because David–you met him in the tunnels–stopped me from running after the whole horde of them myself."

Victoria was horrified. Imagining this scene and what Conner must have gone through was horrible enough, but the poor, broken down man who sobbed in front of her had actually lived it. A tear slipped down her cheek.

"Don't cry Fio–Victoria. It's just one of those things. Every person here has suffered losses. We can't dwell or the grief will consume us."

More tears. "I'm so sorry. We will free Lumernia. We will make the orcs pay, I swear to you th–"

Conner closed the distance between them in two strides, yanking her to him and passionately kissing her on the lips.

Victoria's mind blanked and she froze. Her mind struggled to grasp what was happening, why he was kissing her. He thought she was his … *Oh gods, what if Joseph comes back?*

Shoving him off her, she quickly moved away, putting several chairs and a table between them. With a flick of the wrist her favorite dagger was in her hand.

"You stay back," she said in a shaky voice. "Don't ever touch me again."

Chapter Seventeen
Bad Plan

He'd trusted her. He'd trusted them both. Against his better judgment, he had allowed her into his heart. He should have known better.

Idiot! Joseph chided himself. He walked blindly back toward the infirmary, where he had been helping Arcus and Siobhan tend to the injured. They had finished up with the man with the broken leg, and had tended to others in need. Joseph had decided to return to Victoria, but when he opened the door, he had seen Conner leaning down to kiss *his* Victoria. A gesture she hadn't seemed to mind at all.

Idiot. She isn't your Victoria. She was never your Victoria. You were merely convenient for her. You were right all along, but were stupid enough to let her trick you.

He reached for the doorknob that would let him back into the infirmary, but the elusive handle evaded him as it was pulled inward. The slender blonde woman who had remembered him stepped from the room, almost knocking him over. She yelped her surprise at him being there as she jerked to a stop. *What is her name? Katrina, Katie, Kathy … I don't remember. No matter.*

Joseph regarded her calmly for a moment, then grabbed her. He kissed her hard on the lips, demanding entrance with his tongue. Katherine resisted his advances for the span of a single heartbeat, then wound her fingers in his hair.

"What the hell is this?" Arcus yelled from inside the room.

"How could you, Joseph?" snapped Siobhan. "What about Victoria?"

Joseph pulled away, but only long enough to answer. "It's over. She made her choice and it isn't me."

"What? But–"

"It doesn't matter, Arcus. Why don't you ask her and *Conner*, if you're curious. I have far better options here, anyway." He gave Katherine a winning smile. "You remember how it was, don't you, my sweet? We can have that again."

She grinned, her cheeks flushing a tantalizing shade of rose. "I've missed you, Joseph," she purred.

"I missed you, too. Come on." Hand at the small of her back, he steered her down the hall, then descended the stairs. He tried to ignore the pain radiating from his chest and told himself that the best way to clear his head was distraction.

When you fall off the horse, the best thing to do is to climb back up again and keep going.

"Victoria!" Conner gasped. "I'm so sorry. I–I don't know what came over me."

"Just stay over there! Don't come near me!"

Conner backed even farther from her. She appreciated the gesture. Taking a deep breath, she raked her fingers through her curls.

"I'm sorry," he repeated. "I'm not ... I've never ... I'm sorry. It's just that you look exactly like her. Then, there you were, with tears in your eyes because of me, promising to fight ... to save m–I ... I got caught up in the moment and lost my head. It won't happen again."

Satisfied he wasn't going to back her into a corner, she started to pace, trying to wrap her head around what had happened.

"I am not a monster, Victoria. I swear to you that I will never do something like that again. But ... was it really so horrible?"

She stopped pacing and squeezed her eyes shut. "Joseph is going to kill me."

Conner looked confused. "Joseph?"

Arcus stormed in through the still-open door. "Well, if he doesn't, I might. What do you two think you are doing?"

Victoria stared at him in shock. "When did that door open? Joseph shut it when he–"

"You think that a closed door gave you the right to go behind his back?"

Conner stared between the two of them. "Did I miss something?"

Arcus gave him a cold stare. "You stay out of this. After all that has happened, you were the last one I expected to go after my best friend's woman. You're lucky I don't kill you where you stand. In fact ..."

Arcus started chanting, but Victoria hurtled across the room and tackled him to the ground.

"Stop it. I'm not cheating on Joseph. Why would you think that?"

"Don't lie to me, Victoria. He saw you. He was happy one minute and left to be with you, then he came back and said you'd made your choice."

"Gods. He saw us." Victoria scrambled away and rose back to her feet. "It's not what you think."

"It doesn't matter what I think. What matters is what he saw."

"I have to find him!"

"I wouldn't right now."

"This is all just a misunderstanding," Conner said, "and it's all my fault. I lost my head. She looks so like my Fiona, and we were talking about that night … the night she died. I don't know what came over me, but I never meant to come between her and Joseph. I hope he can forgive me."

Arcus frowned as he stood up. "Admittedly, I wasn't in my right mind when I met Fiona, but I never noticed–" Shame swept across his face. "That's really all?"

"I pushed him away, Arcus, you have to believe me," Victoria begged. "Can I trust you to not kill Conner while I go find Joseph? I have to explain."

"If you are smart," Arcus said as he rubbed his temples, "you will leave him alone right now. Trust me."

"I can't! I have to go clear this up. I'm in love with him, I never wanted to hurt him."

"It may be too late, but he ran downstairs."

"Downstairs?" Conner asked. "No one should be downstairs. It's too risky."

"Quiet, Conner. You did this. Victoria, you aren't going to like what you see …"

"I can handle him … I hope. Thank you, Arcus." Her heart in her throat, she bolted from the room.

Bad Plan.

He had led her down the stairs and into the nearest vacant room. The furnishings had been removed, leaving the area completely empty aside from a thin layer of dust that coated everything.

The only problem was that the pain in his chest battled the anger in his mind. *No matter.* He backed What's-her-name into the wall and kissed her with a passion he didn't think he was capable of actually feeling any longer.

She moaned blissfully, which spurred him on. *Good. She doesn't see through me.*

The two shed their clothes, tossing them aside, while barely pausing in their amorous advances. Joseph tried to clear his mind, using the same focus he did when using his magic. Making a valiant attempt to block the pain and anger from his mind, he brought things to the next level, urging What's-her-name's legs around his waist, connecting as one.

The door flung open. Hadn't he locked that?

"Joseph? It wasn't what … you … *my gods!*"

Anger flooded through Joseph anew. He slapped his hand on the wall next to What's-her-name's face. She shrunk into the wall, standing on her own two legs once more. "Damn it, Victoria. Don't you ever knock? You have no claim to me or my actions any longer."

Victoria's hand flew to her mouth, horror etched on her face. The woman he had brought down here ducked under his arm and raced for her clothes.

She shook her head, coming out of her trance. "Katherine! Where do you think you're going? Don't you think we should have a chat?"

"Leave her alone, Victoria," said Joseph. "You've done enough."

"*I?* *I* have done enough? I don't think you recognize the position you are in right now, Joseph! How could you?"

"How could *I*? Mighty hypocritical, coming from you!"

Victoria's eyes narrowed as she watched Katherine, rage contorting her features. "You *knew* we were together! You saw us in the infirmary! Don't deny it."

Katherine finished yanking her clothes back on, then rose to her full height. "It's not my fault that you didn't appreciate what you had. I let him slip through my fingers once, I wasn't about to let a second ch–"

"Deglubentmak!"

It was a word in the ancient language of dragons. Joseph's eyes widened and flew to Katherine's–a fraction of a moment before her skin was ripped from her body.

Chapter Eighteen
Repercussions

The world stopped spinning. Time froze. One moment Katherine stood there, facing Victoria defiantly. The next, her skin was flayed from her body, landing in a heap on the other side of the room. Her eyes, now perfect round spheres, sagged a split second before her blood, guts, organs and bones all hit the floor in a huge and devastating mess.

Joseph could do nothing to prevent any of it. He watched Katherine fall to pieces, then turned to stare at Victoria. His mind blanked as if it were trying to spare him the horror of what he had witnessed.

His jaw moved, trying to form words, but his voice had abandoned him. The day had turned into a nightmare. None of it could really be happening. Joseph pleaded with his brain–unsuccessfully–to wake up.

Victoria breathed in deep gasps, chest heaving as she looked at what used to be Katherine.

Joseph found his elusive voice. "Vicki?"

She didn't react.

"Vicki, you're a necromancer? When? How?"

She turned on him, her features cold, hard, furious. The icy grip of fear clutched Joseph's heart. Although painfully aware of his nakedness, he dared not move. The woman before him was not the Vicki he'd grown to know and love. The woman before him would cut him down with the slightest twitch or blink. She had murdered Katherine without a moment's hesitation, and he was terrified he would be next

"How could you?" she whispered.

He swallowed hard, weighing his words carefully. "Vicki, I saw you with Conner."

"It wasn't what you thought."

She merely stared with emotionless, dead eyes but made no move against him. Encouraged, he took a small step away from her, toward his clothes. "How does it matter what I thought? I saw you kissing him."

"I never kissed him."

"I saw you."

"He kissed *me*!" Victoria shouted. Joseph tensed. "He kissed me ..." she insisted, her voice calmer. "He told me I looked like his dead wife, then he described what happened the night she died. I started crying, and he called me Fiona. Next thing I knew, he was on me. I shoved him off and backed away. I felt guilty. I knew I would have to tell you, and hoped you'd understand that I didn't expect, invite or want it. But ... I see now that you were quick to get over me. Quick to move on."

Joseph stopped moving, thoughts of his clothes or even his safety gone. "I–but, I ... my gods, Vicki–"

"Don't call me that." She coughed hard, then turned away from him, retching until she vomited all over the floor, her insides mixing with Katherine's. The overpowering stench of illness and death filled the small space.

"Vick–Victoria, I'm so sorry. I saw you two kissing, and I thought … I thought you were cheating on me. You hugged him back in the temple, then … then this! The only thing I could think of was to show myself I didn't care, that I wasn't attached. It was nearly an impossible task. My heart had broken into a million pieces." She retched again. "Are you all right?"

"It's the spell," she choked out. "Spells like that come with a price … more than simple spell exhaustion."

"Come on, let's get you out of here." Joseph hurriedly threw his clothes back on, ignoring the blood splatters that coated them. He went to Victoria and placed his hand on the back of her neck.

She whirled around with a strength he hadn't expected. "You don't get to touch me, Joseph Hale. Do not ever touch me again. Not with the same hands that touched her."

She stormed from the room and stomped up the stairs. Joseph paused, looking back into the room.

What has she done? What have I done?

"I'm sorry, Katherine," he said, glad to have been reminded of her name, at least. "This was all my fault, and you were the one to take the punishment. You deserved better."

He waved his hand and muttered an incantation, and the blood and gore disappeared from the room and his clothes. He rubbed his eyes. Though appalled as he was by Victoria's actions, he still wanted to protect her. He couldn't let her suffer for his misunderstanding.

The meeting room was empty. Victoria stared into it as though she expected people to show up, wondering what she should do now. She wanted to run and never stop. She wished she were a druid. She wanted to turn into a bird and fly away … and keep on flying forever. Unfortunately, she had promised to help free Lumernia, and she would not go back on her promise.

Murderer …

Victoria gave herself a mental shake, attempting to make herself stop visualizing the horrific images of Katherine. She heard voices come from the direction of the infirmary. Her feet shuffled almost of their own accord to the threshold. Conner, Arcus, and Siobhan were huddled around a conscious Tarnelius. He rubbed at the stub where his arm had once been. As soon as she entered the room, everyone stopped talking and stared at her.

She swallowed hard, fighting the tide of rising bile. "Well … I found him. He was … he …"

Siobhan crossed the room and hugged her. The embrace was made awkward by the paladin's full armor, but the gesture was no less appreciated.

Swiping her eyes with the back of her hand, Victoria pulled away and gave Tarnelius a small smile. "Tarnelius, you're awake. How are you feeling?"

His lips stretched into a wry smile. "Lopsided."

"Celeste will be able to fix it, right?"

"I imagine so." Tarnelius cringed. "Although, I'm not looking forward to the process."

Joseph entered, looking as awful as she felt, if not more so. She felt a twinge of perverse pleasure at the knowledge that she was not the only one suffering.

Conner frowned. "Where is Katherine?"

Joseph's eyes shot to Victoria's. "I'm not sure. She left through the tunnel."

Victoria scowled. "She—"

"—was very upset. She said she needed to get away for a while." Joseph fixed Conner with a razor sharp stare. "I hear I have you to thank for that."

Conner paled under Joseph's scrutiny. "You have to believe me, Joseph. I didn't know she was with you, I swear it! She looks so much like my Fiona that I reacted. Had I known—"

"Silence. You stay away from her. I do not want to hear your excuses, nor do I care what you are going through. You will *never* put your filthy hands on her again."

"Enough," Victoria all but snarled. "You've lost your claim on me. You have no say whatsoever in who does or does not touch me. But know this. It will never again be you. Never again!"

Joseph flinched as though she had slapped him. He turned on his heel and rushed from the room. Conner was quick to chase after him.

Why Joseph had covered for her murder of Katherine remained a mystery, but one she had no interest in solving. It wasn't worth the fight. Fighting tears, she knelt down between Celeste and Tarnelius. Smoothing Celeste's hair, she asked, "When will she wake up?"

"Soon, I think." Tarnelius sat up a little straighter and peered at his mate. "Each time she casts that spell the recovery becomes easier. Or perhaps she gets a little stronger. There is no way to tell. Be that as it may, that spell always drains her." His voice lowered to barely more than a whisper. "You know he's hurting, don't you?"

"I don't want to talk about it."

"I know. You're hurting, too," Tarnelius said. "That much is obvious. I want you to know, though, that he loves you. I'm not sure what you caught him doing down there, although I can imagine. I heard what happened. I can imagine how I would react in his position, and with that in mind, it's a good thing no one is dead." Victoria stared blankly at the wall. "But he loves you, Victoria, with everything he has in him. I can see it. I could see it back in Izmar and especially in Kayalost. Never forget that. It's up to you to decide if love is enough."

Tears fell freely from her face to Celeste's. Victoria wanted to believe, but it hurt too much to think about how quickly she had been replaced. Her heart ached at the realization that a very short time ago he was touching another woman in the same way he had touched her. It hurt even worse when she thought about what she had done, what depths her anger had driven her to.

Murderer.

Victoria had killed before, but always in battle or self-defense. She had studied necromancy as her secondary spell type back in school, but had never used any of the spells. She didn't like them. The words themselves tasted like ash in her mouth, and the spell made her feel as if bugs crawled under her skin. Something about Katherine's tone and posture had triggered a calm anger that Victoria hadn't known herself capable of. Almost without thinking, she had spit out the spell and powered it with her hate, and the results spoke for themselves. When she closed her eyes, she could still see the grotesque image of Katherine's body burned into her retinas.

Celeste twitched and moaned. In a flash, Tarnelius was off his cot and kneeling next to her, caressing her face with his remaining hand. Arcus and Siobhan walked up to her other side.

"Wake up, Angel."

Her eyelids fluttered. "Tarnel?"

"Who else?"

"I thought you were dying. I couldn't get to you."

He smiled. "You can't get rid of me that easily."

She wiped Victoria's tears away from her face. "You didn't have to throw water on me."

Victoria laughed, a short bark that sounded more like a sob. "Sorry. That was me."

Tarnelius chanted, then frowned. "Looks like spell casting is difficult without my right hand. Arcus, would you be so kind as to cast the berry spell? They will help her regain her strength. I think she's going to need it."

Arcus complied. Celeste took several of the magical fruit and popped them into her mouth. After a moment, color began returning to her cheeks.

"Thank you. What have I missed?"

"Not a huge amount," said Arcus. "We arrived here and healed the injured people that were in the infirmary. Now we are waiting for dusk so we can speak to the resistance leaders–or perhaps to everyone. I'm not really clear which."

Celeste nodded and sat up slowly, looking a little woozy.

"Be careful, Angel," said Tarnelius. "My ability to catch you is somewhat limited at the moment."

"I'll have the spell to regenerate your arm prepared by the morning. Bone growth will not be pleasant, I'm afraid."

"I know. It'll be okay. It's better than the alternative."

Celeste patted his cheek and he leaned into her hand.

Arcus glanced at Siobhan. "I think I'd better go check on Joseph."

She nodded and gave him a peck on the cheek.

Celeste frowned. "What's wrong with Joseph?"

Victoria caught her breath as nausea swept over her again. Tears slipped unchecked down her cheeks.

Tarnelius shook his head. "Later."

"He'll be all right, Victoria. He's in good hands with Arcus, and I will–" Celeste cocked her head as if listening, her green eyes widening.

"It's all right, Tarnelius," Victoria said. "She didn't know. I'll be fine. I have to come to terms with what happened."

"Tarnel is right, Victoria. Joseph does truly love you. That much is obvious."

"That's not the point. The point is that instead of confronting me about it, he reacted. Badly. I have to decide if I can live with that." Victoria turned away. Her stomach churned, forcing her mind once more to what she had done to Katherine. *He's not the only one who reacted badly.*

"Normally I would say that cheating is the one thing I would never, ever forgive," Siobhan interjected. "But this is a complicated situation. Joseph was under the impression you cheated first. He thought it was over between you two. I saw him with Katherine before they went downstairs, and he was a man in serious pain. He didn't cheat to be unfaithful. He reacted out of wounded male pride, pain and probably a sense of revenge."

"You all are against me, but this isn't any of your business! What *is* your business is working with Conner and the rest of the Lumernians to free the city. Can we focus on that? Please?"

"Yes. Victoria is right." Celeste rose slowly to her feet, turning down Tarnelius' offer for assistance. "Let's find the others."

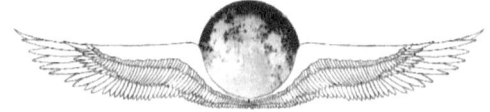

Joseph sat in a darkened corner of the meeting room, lost in thought. His heart was in turmoil. He never knew it was possible to feel so many emotions at once. Pain … that was the foremost sensation. His heart had been broken by Victoria's anger, at

Katherine's demise. Anger at Conner and at himself. Disgust, horror, guilt…

"Joseph, I–"

At the sound of Conner's voice, Joseph leapt from his chair. He stalked across the room and punched Conner hard in the face. Conner's nose shattered. Pain lanced through Joseph's fist, but he welcomed this physical embodiment of the torture that tore through his soul. Anything to distract him from how badly things had gone awry today.

"Get up, Conner."

Conner held his hand to his nose, bloody rivers trickling between his fingers and down his face. "Gods, man! I said I was sorry. You go too far." He slowly rose to his feet, his hands balled into fists. Lunging forward, he swung at Joseph, who ducked under his arm and smacked Conner in the back as he spun around.

Conner stumbled forward and backed away to regroup.

Joseph stood still, calmly watching him. He flexed his hand, reveling in the sharp pain that pulsed through it.

Conner shouted an incompressible bellow of rage and leapt at him again, but Joseph merely stepped aside. Conner hurtled forward into the wall.

The door swung open. Arcus entered just as Joseph grabbed Conner and bent him over, kneeing him in the chest. Joseph flung him across the room and into a table, which collapsed under his weight.

Arcus ran forward and tackled Joseph. He glared at Conner. *"Stop moving,"* he said in that hypnotic voice. Conner froze in place.

Joseph struggled to climb from beneath Arcus. "Let me go."

"No. She isn't worth it, man. None of this is worth it."

"What would you know about it?"

"You have to calm down. I have never understood what it is about her that makes you so enamored with her. She played with your affections in school and she's doing it again now. Can't you see that? I can't recall a time when you have been more out of your mind."

Joseph flexed his hand again, wincing. The knuckles were split, and the bone glistened through the split skin of his knuckles. It disgusted him that his own blood mixed with Conner's. His lip curled in a sneer.

"You never liked her, Arc. You never understood, not even back then."

"I understand enough."

Joseph squirmed. "Do you mind? Get off me. I'm not going to kill him."

Arcus scrutinized him a moment more, then got up. He went to check on Conner. "Damn. You really did a number on his nose. Why couldn't you have done that in the bar fight in Izmar?"

Joseph chuckled and tore a strip of cloth from his shirt, then wrapped it around his hand. Arcus gripped Conner's nose and wrenched it back into place, his hand glowing a brilliant blue. Then he snapped his fingers, releasing the spell holding him in place.

Conner stumbled, managing to catch himself before he fell.

"Fight's over, gentlemen," Arcus said. Returning to Joseph, he held out his hand. "Let me heal your hand, idiot."

Joseph shook his head. "I'll keep it this way for now, thanks. You were wrong, by the way."

"Oh?"

"You said, 'don't toy with your enemies. It only angers them.' I have found it's best to exploit that fact, so I still toy with them."

Arcus rolled his eyes. "I wasn't wrong based on what I saw that day. You didn't have a head for battle."

"If you two are done congratulating each other," Conner said, venom lacing his voice, "get out of my sight. Go stay with your friends. You may be what we need to free this city, but I don't need this kind of drama in my life. Get out."

Celeste walked in, leading the others. "No one is going anywhere, Conner. I'm sorry there has been some sort of mishap, but what's done is done. "It's nearly dusk. The time to get down to business is almost upon us. Put your personal business aside. We need to get along and work together if we're to succeed. All of us. Is that understood?"

Everyone nodded.

"Good. I'd hate for everything to be ruined before we've even started. There's a lot more at stake here than Lumernia. We would do well to remember that."

The group took seats near the front. After a short time, people started arriving. The room itself was quite large, and had probably been used for storage at some point. Despite that, they quickly ran out of chairs, forcing latecomers to stand in whatever available space they could find. Celeste rose to her feet, her companions following her example.

Still, the people continued to pour in.

"Is it always this crowded for meetings?" Celeste whispered to Conner.

"No. Word must have spread. You may as well begin … we won't be able to fit anyone else in here."

Celeste cleared her throat. "My name is Celeste, and I am a high druid of Kayalost. My companions are Tarnelius, former prince of Kayalost, Siobhan Keating, paladin of Mithra, and Arcus, Joseph and Victoria, mages from Izmar. We have been fighting the orcs since–"

A young man rose to his feet.

"Yes?" Celeste said.

"What is it you can do that we could not? We have mages. We have warriors. Nothing has worked. Nothing *can* work; this is hopeless."

Celeste regarded him in silence, then looked to the rest of the stony-faced crowd. She knew that many of them would be tired of the fighting, of the fear and uncertainty of death. She had hoped that they would take heart and be ready to fight back, now that reinforcements had arrived. "I hope you don't really believe that. I'm sure that if you had lost all hope, you would have left by now. I do understand how you must feel. You've been here for nearly a year. You've tried everything you could with the limited resources you had. What we bring to you is experience and power. Arcus, step forward, if you please." Celeste closed the distance to the mage and stood shoulder-to-shoulder with him, presenting a unified front. "This is Arcus. Sorcerer by birth, druid by choice. He wields this relic," she tapped his staff, "which once belonged to Raziyl, the god of secrets. Never before has it allowed a human or mortal of any kind to command it."

"What does it do?" the young man asked.

"It creates an anti-magic field so formidable that even the great dragons fear it," answered Celeste. "Only the master of the staff is not stripped of his power. The silver dragon, Axistra, told us that with this, we will have a chance. With *this*, victory shall be ours."

"Will the dragons come to help us now?"

Celeste bit her lip. "I doubt it. There are … complications."

"What sort of complications?"

"What is your name, sir?"

"Phillip."

"Well, Phillip, here is what you should know, what you must make sure everyone is crystal clear on: The ruby dragon, Crusiliux, is behind this invasion. She knows we have the staff, and she has been trying to flush us out. The orcs revere her. She commands them, organizes them. The time is fast approaching when we will have to fight her. I don't know if anyone here has ever met a dragon, but they are huge, powerful and can bend the rules of magic to their whims. They are almost gods themselves."

The room had fallen deathly silent. Celeste could practically hear them planning to run. "Keep listening and hear me out. There is one other factor: the paladins of Mithra are riding this way. They will help us fight. My plan is simple. When they arrive, we open the gate and let them in. With their help, we will crush our enemies!"

Staring at the crowd, the only thing Celeste could see was a bunch of tired and broken people who had long since given up their fight. She had lost her chance at rallying them the instant she told them about the dragon. She swallowed. It was up to her to convince them they still had a chance. "We have been fighting the orcs since we were made aware of their invasion. Lumernia is not the only place to suffer their attacks. Both Izmar and Kayalost almost fell to a similar fate, but *we* drove them back, slaughtering any unit that dared cross our path. We can and will help you do the same here. The orc presence in Lumernia shall be eradicated. We will banish them back to their lands. And by the *gods,* they will fear to ever set foot in *our* lands again. You are not alone."

Celeste stopped. She licked her lips and surveyed the crowd. They were listening. Many of them leaned forward on the edge of their seats. "We are not the military. You will not be conscripted to fight, and nobody will judge you if you choose to flee to safer pastures. But you must ask yourself this: is theirs a front from which you can run? Is any place safe so long as they are allowed to walk the world unchecked? Do you want to live the rest of your lives looking over your shoulder, merely surviving from one day to the next? Is simply existing enough for you, or do you want to *live*, in your own land, breathing the air that is rightfully yours?" Celeste paused, letting her words sink in. "We may be outnumbered, but I know we can stop this vile threat here and now. I humbly ask you, are you with us?"

The crowd burst into applause, many jumping to their feet. Celeste grinned at her companions.

"That was quite a speech, Angel," Tarnelius thought to her. "I'm so proud of you."

Once the uproar had calmed down, Phillip once more raised his hand. "But what of the dragon?"

Arcus cleared his throat. He took a step forward, the base of staff landing heavily on the floorboards with a thump. "I will fight the dragon."

Chapter Nineteen
Growing Pains

"What do you mean, *you* will fight the dragon?" Siobhan demanded.

After Celeste had called the meeting to an end, they had moved back into the now-abandoned infirmary so that they could talk in relative privacy.

Siobhan clenched her hands into fists as she paced back and forth. It took all her willpower to not grab Arcus and shake him. *How could he gamble so calmly with his life this way? Didn't he realize his actions affected others, affected* her?

"We talked about it, back at Castle Mithra. This isn't up for discussion, Shiv."

"I'm making it up for discussion. I am your wife! You can't make decisions like that without me. Besides, I *told* you I didn't think Axistra intended for you to fight Crusiliux, and you agreed with me. You can't dump this on us now that we are here and expect us to accept it. We are a team. We'll figure something else out together."

"This is the only way."

"No, it isn't. It can't be. We will find another way."

"I agree with Siobhan," Celeste interjected. "This is a bad idea, Arcus,"

Arcus growled and pinched the bridge of his nose. "Can any of *you* control the staff? I didn't think so. Anyone who goes to fight the dragon without their magic is asking for death. If Crusiliux is anywhere near the size of the three we saw last year, she could swallow any one of us whole with barely a thought."

"And what if things go horribly wrong and she gets the staff from you?" Celeste continued.

"That won't happen unless she kills me."

"And if she does?"

Arcus sighed. "She isn't going to kill me."

"Does the staff even work on dragonfire?" asked Siobhan. "That isn't exactly magic."

"Maybe. I don't know, but probably not."

"So what will you do to combat that?"

Arcus smirked. "Fight fire with fire, I suppose. I had a thought. Mages use magic locks to keep unwanted visitors out. I wonder if any of the mages here know how to get into the mage tower. I know it's located in the northeastern part of town. It's possible there could be spells or artifacts abandoned inside."

"I suppose it's worth a shot. Conner?" Celeste said.

He leaned against the doorjamb and crossed his arms. "I suppose one or more of the mages may know how to get in. The general consensus has been not to go in there or the place may blow up. The tower is riddled with deadly traps."

Arcus grinned at Joseph and Victoria. "Traps, you say? You two up for a field trip?"

Victoria startled. "What? Oh, traps. Um, sure, I guess I could help out."

Joseph rubbed his hand. The cloth that bound the injured knuckles was stained with blood. "You know I'm no good at finding traps, Arc."

"Let me take a look at that hand," said Arcus.

"No. It's okay. I'd rather leave it as it is."

Victoria rolled her eyes. "I'm good with traps."

"You have a much better understanding of illusion magic than I ever could," Arcus said. "I have a feeling your help will be invaluable. Come with us, Joseph."

He plucked absently at the cloth that bound his injured hand. "When?"

"Tonight, under the cover of darkness. Celeste, how about you or Tarnelius?"

"We'd be no help to you in the mage tower."

"I disagree. You can communicate with each other over distance. We'd be able to stay apprised of what is going on here. That could prove useful."

"Wish we could, but I have to meditate on the regeneration spell. We can't be separated right now."

Arcus nodded. "I understand. Tonight will be a scouting mission. We'll see if we can get in. Conner, go find me a mage, the most competent one you have."

Conner went to the door, pausing at the threshold. "If any of you see Katherine out there, will you keep an eye on her or send her back here? I know there is all this awkwardness, but she shouldn't be on her own, especially at night. I hope she is hiding in one of the rooms and hasn't done anything stupid."

"Sure, Conner. We'll keep an eye out for her," Arcus assured him.

Conner nodded and left.

"You two do whatever you must," Arcus said to Celeste and Tarnelius. "The rest of us will head out. Siobhan, will you come with us, or would you rather stay here?"

"For such a smart man, you can be incredibly stupid. Of course I'm going to make sure you don't get splattered into a pulp out there."

"All right. Then we will meet back here in the morning. I think it best if we rested on the day shift so that we have darkness on our side when moving about. However, if we get in there tonight without too much trouble, you three could rest there while I search through the artifacts."

"Right ... I'm sure sleep will be what we are thinking about while in a creepy mage tower," Siobhan muttered.

"Arcus ..."

He turned to see Celeste regarding him, a hard look in her green eyes. "Yes?"

"The discussion about the dragon is not finished."

He looked from the elves to his scowling wife. "Oh, I'm sure it's not."

"This way," Arcus whispered. They had travelled the tunnel into the other house, and from there headed northeast toward the city center.

The mage that Conner had sent them had been more than willing to discuss what he knew of the mage tower, but he'd been less than thrilled about the idea of traveling there. In fact, he had refused.

The tower itself seemed to be shrouded in mystery. According to the mage, there were several rooms, each designed around one of the schools of sorcery. Each area had been built to defend itself using magic from its specialized school. There were traps that rained lightning, fire, acid and ice at you if you entered. There were some that conjured horrible things to rip you to shreds. There were even a few that would drive you mad or force you into a magic-induced trance upon entering.

"Maybe if we're lucky," Arcus had remarked, "the orcs will have tripped most of the traps already." The mage hadn't been amused.

He had given them directions and told them the passcode that had worked when he had last been inside. That passcode only worked for the front door and for the novice enchanters' room. Still, it was better than nothing, so off they went.

Arcus, Joseph and Victoria darted from building to building, trying to keep to the shadows. Siobhan, however, calmly marched down the middle of the road.

"She doesn't understand the concept of *sneaking*, does she?" Joseph whispered.

Arcus sighed. "Paladins never sneak. I think it's in their oaths or something. No matter. If she gets into trouble, we'll be there to back her up."

"I thought she was supposed to be backing *us* up."

"No. She's here because she would have killed me if I'd made her stay behind. I'm in enough trouble."

"I heard that, Arcus," Siobhan called, calmly. "And you're right. I would have. You're also right that you are in deep trouble."

"Keep an eye out for Katherine," Arcus reminded her.

"I am."

Joseph dropped his voice even more. "Arcus, I don't think we're going to find her, no matter how hard we look."

Arcus raised his eyebrows and turned to look directly at Joseph, who shook his head almost imperceptibly and glanced toward Victoria.

Realization cut across Arcus' features.

So little Victoria killed her, did she? Arcus thought to himself. *I didn't know she had that in her.* Although Victoria had an affinity for knives, she had always summoned creatures to do her dirty work. Arcus knew better than to say anything like that where Siobhan could hear. Not now. Perhaps later, after Lumernia was freed. He hated to lie to her, even by omission, but she would demand a full inquisition, and that was the last thing they needed right now.

"I know you're worried, Joseph," Arcus continued in the same tone and volume level as before. "We all are. We will do our best."

Their arrival at the city center reminded Arcus of the carnage that had taken place but a few hours before. It appeared that the orcs had finally become brave enough to come out after the storm, because the bodies had been moved.

Arcus pointed two fingers at his eyes, and then one ahead of him. They skirted around the southern edge of the city center, back toward the main gate and up along the northern edge, making it through the inner gate to the northeast quadrant without incident.

Once they had walked through the gate, finding the mage tower was easy enough. Located in the center of the district, the large building soared above the rest. The same stark white stone used in the construction of the other Lumernian architecture graced the spire, and glowed in the moonlight.

They were nearly there when the sound of guttural voices came from the west. Glancing down an alley, they saw three orcs approaching, one swinging a lantern at his side.

Arcus muttered a spell, cloaking himself with invisibility. Silently, he stalked down the alley toward them. When he was within ten feet of them, he stopped and removed the spell.

Raising the lantern high, the orcs cried out in surprise.

"All of you, stop moving," Arcus intoned. They froze in place. He cast another spell and flicked a small bead of fire toward them.

The other three joined him. Siobhan had drawn her sword, but froze in place.

"What?" Joseph asked her.

"I cannot kill them in cold blood."

"For the love of–are you kidding me?" he replied.

Arcus turned back toward the rest of the group. "If only she were kidding. She's not. It's okay, I love her even though she is infuriating."

"Are we leaving them there, then?" Victoria asked.

"No, we are not." Arcus snapped his fingers. The fireball exploded, billowing out from the tightly packed quarters. The orcs burned to ash where they stood, unable to move, unable to scream.

Siobhan sighed. "I don't know why I put up with you."

"It's okay, because I do," Arcus said with a smirk. "Come on, let's go."

"You know, you almost singed my eyebrows with that spell, Arc," Joseph complained.

"I apologize for failing to improve your looks, Joseph."

Victoria chuckled and followed the rest to the fence surrounding the tower. "My turn. I need everyone to stay behind me. I mean *way* behind me. Let me work and don't get in the way. If you do, and you set off a trap, don't blame me."

Victoria started by examining the gate and fence area. She looked closely around the entire thing, then held out her hands and closed her eyes. Nodding, she reached for the gate's handle.

"Let me get that, Vicki."

Victoria glared at Joseph. "Weren't you listening? Which part of 'stay behind me' didn't you understand?"

"Vicki–"

"Stop right there. You don't trust my assessment. Fine. Would you like to take over? I didn't think so. Stay back like I told you." Victoria flung open the gate and crept to the front door, head turning back and forth as she scanned everything in her path.

"Cantatis," she spoke in a strong, clear voice. The front door swung open and she crossed the threshold, checking the entryway for traps.

She looked around, intent on her task. Seeing her eyes light up, Arcus knew she had found one. Victoria pulled out a long, slender blade from her voluminous sleeves and went to work on something to the immediate right of the entryway. After a few moments, they heard a loud clicking sound. She grinned and gestured for them to follow her into the tower.

Back at the school in Izmar, Victoria had always had a sixth sense when it came to locks and traps. Her skill had been unmatched among the students, and Arcus remembered with vivid clarity what had happened when he stumbled upon an item she hadn't wanted others to touch.

Victoria wove her magic and closed her eyes. Moving to her right, she knelt down to examine the stairs. Pausing on the third step, she repeated her spell and exhaled gently. She inserted a long, slender blade into a crack in the floorboards.

A moment later she rose to her feet. "That's how that's done," she said with a smirk. Setting back to work, she checked the rest of the stairs leading to the second floor.

Conner paced back and forth, wringing his hands.

"What's the matter, now?" Celeste asked. "Is it what we talked about in the meeting? Because I think we have a little time. Even if the dragon has been alerted to our presence, she will still need some time to organize."

"Katherine."

"Who?"

Conner paused and pinched the bridge of his nose. "Katherine. She is our healer. She worked as an apothecary before the attack, and I have never seen her show any interest in wandering outside alone or participating in raiding parties. Even before we had a stable base of operations, she would remain with the largest part of the group and tend to the injured."

"All right ..."

"She's gone. The last time anyone saw her was when she went downstairs with Joseph. Joseph and ... and Victoria came back up, but she didn't. They said she was upset and went for a walk. It's been hours now. Something must have happened."

"Do you want to go look for her? We'll be fine in here, alone. I must meditate on the spell I need to heal Tarnel, anyway. It'll be even more time consuming indoors, since I won't have a direct connection to Kamara's domain. I have to get started soon."

Conner shook his head. "No. We have a rule. If someone wanders off and vanishes, the rest do not look for them. It prevents us from leading one another into traps, and deters people from wandering on their own."

"Maybe you should check downstairs. You say she never showed interest in raiding parties or being outside. Maybe she merely went to one of the other rooms downstairs and is too embarrassed to come back up."

"Maybe." Conner sighed. "Perhaps I should check it out." He turned and left the room.

"I have a bad feeling about that one," Tarnelius heard Celeste think.

"What do you mean?"

"Joseph and Katherine went down together, but Joseph and Victoria came up. Victoria sounded like she was trying to tell us something earlier, but Joseph kept cutting her off. I think ... I don't know."

"You suspect foul play?" Tarnelius deduced.

"I think that emotions were running high. Anything is possible."

Tarnelius cocked his head. *"I actually made a comment to that effect earlier. I told her that, were I in Joseph's place, it would be a miracle if Conner would have survived it."*

"Then you see my point." Out loud she said, "I really must prepare. Luckily, even though this building is man-made, stone is still a natural element. I should be able to work with it."

Celeste kissed Tarnelius, then sat down cross-legged on the floor. Closing her eyes, she began her meditations.

Tarnelius awkwardly blockaded the infirmary, shoving a cot in front of the door with only the aid of his left hand, then returned to the makeshift bed he had been placed upon when they arrived here. He lay down, eyes glued to Celeste. His angel. She was so beautiful, so perfect. She–

"I need you to stop that if you want me to be able to heal you soon," Celeste said, an amused tone to her voice.

Tarnelius smiled. "I can't help it. It's been a year since you came back to me, and every day I love you more than I did the last. You're my addiction."

"I feel the same, Tarnel, but I need you to at least *try* to not distract me while I meditate."

"I'll try." Moving to sit on the floor in front of her, he mirrored her cross-legged position and closed his eyes. Tarnelius blocked out everything as the two of them meditated together. Time lost all meaning.

Celeste rose stiffly to her feet. She felt empowered. Kamara's magic coursed through her, waiting to be put to good use. Though she couldn't see outside due to the boarded-up windows, her communion with the earth goddess' domain assured her the sun would be rising soon. She placed a hand on Tarnelius' shoulder, startling him from his meditations.

"Praise Kamara," she murmured. "It is time. The spell has been granted to me by the essences of the goddess."

"Praise Kamara." Tarnelius' missing limb threw off his balance, but he managed to climb back onto the cot and lie back.

Celeste placed her hand on his right shoulder and chanted, repeating the same words over and over. Tarnelius' shoulder began to feel warm, then hot, turning into an inferno. Finishing the spell, she knelt by his side and took his hand.

"I'm here. I won't leave your side."

Tarnelius squeezed her hand. His shoulder felt as if a dull blade was sawing through it. He grunted in pain and ground his teeth as his bone was crushed and broken back to its original form with a series of sickening *crunch* sounds.

A tear slipped down Celeste's cheek. She ran her free hand over his sweat-covered forehead. He was burning up. "I wish I could put you to sleep with a spell. I wish I could bear your pain. I'm so sorry."

Tarnelius jerked his hand away and clenched it into a tight fist. Celeste reached for him. He shook his head.

"I … can't," he gasped. Can't ... will … hurt … you." The bone had only extended a couple of inches from his shoulder joint. Veins, ligaments and sinewy muscle grew and snaked over the newly formed bone, keeping pace with it. *"Argh!"*

Someone knocked on the door and tried the handle. Celeste's head snapped up and she rose to her feet. "It's really not a good time right now."

She growled as the door was forced open, knocking the cot aside and tipping it over. "Or I suppose it's all right if you just walk right in. This is, after all, your infirmary, Conner."

"I need your help!" he said insistently.

Tarnelius gripped the side of the cot with his only hand so hard that his knuckles went white. The skin felt as if it threatened to split, though he paid scant attention. Celeste glanced over at him before turning to Conner.

"What?"

"I did what you suggested. I checked the entire downstairs for Katherine. No trace of her. But ..."

"But *what*?"

"But the room nearest the stairs was completely spotless. Nothing around here ever looks that way."

"Conner, I don't know the significance of that, but as you can see, I'm in the–"

"Maybe she was in there! Maybe she was killed or kidnapped. I don't know. Maybe the orcs killed her. Maybe your friends did. Either way, it doesn't make sense that there isn't a bod–"

"Aaargh!" Tarnelius arched his back, panting heavily from the exertion. The bone had grown nearly to the elbow joint, and the rest of the arm muscles were catching up.

Wincing, Celeste rubbed her own right elbow and turned back to Conner. "I will help you figure this out later. Right now, Tarnel needs me. I will not abandon him. I know you, of all people, can understand that. If she is dead then there is nothing I can do anyway. If she is alive, hopefully she will stay that way for now."

"But–"

"Enough, Conner. This is not a good time. I feel every bit of pain Tarnel experiences through our bond. We'll deal with the Katherine situation later, after he is healed. I will not leave him to suffer alone. Now, either take a seat and be quiet, or leave."

Celeste slammed the door behind him, cutting off his mumbled protestations. She knelt back down at Tarnelius' side and smoothed his hair from his face.

"It won't be much longer now, love. The process is halfway finished. Be strong."

"Angel," he gasped. The growth formed his elbow, sealing the joint and starting on the connecting bone.

"Yes, Tarnel?"

He shook his head, his hand unclenching and reaching for hers. He closed his eyes.

Celeste laid her head down on his left shoulder, snuggling into him and trying to offer him comfort. "I'm sorry, Tarnel. I'm sorry I couldn't prevent this. I'm sorry I can't make the pain stop."

He squeezed her hand. "It's getting easier, or perhaps I'm growing accustomed to it. You have nothing to be sorry for."

They remained cuddled together while the rest of his forearm formed. Tarnelius winced and made a strangled sound in his throat as it started on his hand. Celeste tried to get up, but he held her in place with his good arm. The pain arced through him, but he tolerated it better. Finally, his hand finished forming. Skin knitted seamlessly over stark-white bone. He tried to clench his hand, but had no control over it. The appendage felt deathly cold and immobile, his skin had a ghastly bluish tinge to it … the color of death, embodied.

Blood flowed through the newly formed veins, bringing pins and needles with it; an unpleasant sensation, but nothing in comparison to what he'd gone through. The worst seemed over. He moved his hand, no more than a tentative wiggle of fingers.

Lifting her head, she smiled to see his arm whole again. "How does it feel?"

"Stiff, but I assume that will work its way out soon." He flexed his fingers and sat up, rotating his hand to get a feel for it. Satisfied, he rose to his feet and reached his right hand to his left hip, pulling his weapon from its sheath. He stepped a safe distance from Celeste and took a few practice swings. Though everything worked as it should, it felt *off*. Not painful, but somehow different. He shoved the weapon back where it belonged and rotated his shoulders.

Tarnelius forced a smile. "Perfect as always, Angel."

Celeste arched an eyebrow. "I know it's stiff, but it'll work itself out. That's the second time I've had to use that spell on you. Perhaps I should prepare it every day, then you won't have to wait."

"Better plan: I should stop needing you to use it on me."

"I do like that plan better. I hate seeing you injured. You're lucky, though. Not many druids ever learn that spell."

"I *am* lucky." Tarnelius pulled her to him, kissing her soundly. "Come on. Let's go see how we can help Conner."

"Good job, Vicki–Victoria."

There hadn't been as many traps as the mage back in the resistance had implied, but that hadn't surprised Arcus. It made sense to keep the locals under the impression that the tower was rife with defenses lying in wait for those who'd look to snoop or loot the place. So far, they'd encountered snares only on the front door, the stairs, and at the entry to each room, which doubled as locks set to detonate if the correct password wasn't given. The rooms on the upper floors had been trickiest and most time consuming, but eventually, with the first rays of dawn glowing on the horizon, Victoria had bested them all.

"What now, Arc?" Joseph asked. "Are we staying or going? Seems a shame to have come this far to leave empty-handed."

"We're leaving. Victoria, can you put one of your locking spells on the front door? We'll teleport back to the resistance infirmary. We'll come back later, but we should let the others know we are okay."

Siobhan gestured to Victoria. "Besides that, she looks like she's going to drop. We have to rest. We've been up all night."

Victoria shook her head. Without a word, she turned on her heel and walked down the stairs.

Arcus turned to glare at Joseph. "What a mess the two of you are in."

"Don't I know it!"

"You should talk to her, Joseph. She's a reasonable girl, and she's hurting," added Siobhan.

"I intend to try, but I don't think she wants anything to do with me."

Arcus chuckled mirthlessly. "As far as her being reasonable, all evidence is to the contrary. Even if you did manage to weasel your way back into her good graces, Joseph, is she worth the trouble?"

"Arcus, stop it! That's not any of our–"

"Any of our what, Siobhan? Any of our business? I've been watching him moon over her for years, and, frankly, she isn't worth it and never has been. It *is* our business, because we are stuck with the two of them and have to deal with–"

Joseph stepped in front of Arcus, his stance wide and his fists clenched. His right hand still throbbed–he had not allowed anyone to heal him after his last fight–but at the moment he didn't care. He was nearly a foot taller than Arcus, though thinner and lankier.

"You going to hit me, Joseph? Like you hit Conner? What did that accomplish, anyway?"

Joseph's eyes flared and he swung his uninjured left hand back.

"Stop moving." Joseph froze, unable to do anything as Arcus circled him. "You are no match for me. You and I both know it. I don't want to fight you. I've no taste for it. What you *are* going to do is calm down."

"Arcus, let him go," Siobhan's voice cut quietly into his monologue.

"No, Shiv. He needs to hear this. He seems to have become suicidal today, and I won't put up with it. He needs to get his hormones in check and *his* mind back on the task at hand." He moved in front of Joseph and glowered up into his eyes. "See this? This place? A huge chunk of the population of this city is gone, destroyed, murdered. We are here to save the ones who are left. We are here in this building to learn if there is any magic left behind that we can use to save them. We are not here to worry about your love life. For what it's worth, I think you could do bet–"

Victoria cleared her throat from the doorway. Arcus startled and spun around to face her, his hand gripping the staff defensively. Siobhan's pale cheeks turned a dark shade of red as she, too, stared at Victoria.

"I could hear you from the stairs, so don't even try to play innocent. For the most part, I agree with your little speech, but I'm intrigued to hear where it was leading. Care to continue?" Anger smoldered in her eyes like flame.

"No. I think we're good here."

Victoria glanced toward Joseph, then back at Arcus, who rolled his eyes and snapped his fingers, releasing Joseph from the magical hold.

"Damn it, Arcus! How dare y–"

"Stop it, Joseph. We're done here … for now. Just let it be."

Arcus gestured for the two sorcerers to come closer. He turned them into birds and the four of them teleported back to the infirmary.

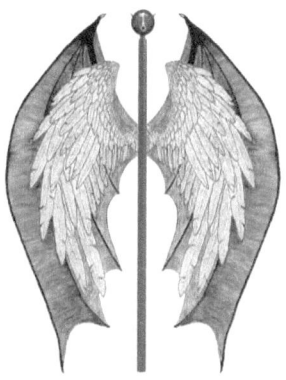

Chapter Twenty
Out of Control

Crusiliux the Red stared into her scrying pool located in her underground lair in the Canavara Islands. Her copper-colored snakelike eyes narrowed as one of her orc officers hurried into the room.

"Yes?" she demanded without turning around.

"The elves and the h-humans have made it into L-Lumernia," he stammered. "The mage c-carries the st-staff, just as you said he would."

Crusiliux lifted her head high into the air, pivoting her neck around to glower at him. She knew why he was stammering; the dragonfear poured off her in waves. Increasing her innate magical fear effect, she watched in satisfaction as he shrank back and visibly fought running away. He was nothing to her, an insignificant speck. She extended her ruby red wings and admired the way the light reflected off them. Flicking her forked tongue out, she bared her sharp fangs, which were as long as he was tall. Blackened horns jutted from her forehead, framing her face down past her jaw.

"Do you think I do not know that?"

"I–It's just that … you told us to keep you up to date on any changes. I was only …"

Crusiliux regarded him coldly. She snorted. Blackened smoke poured out from her nostrils. The orc shuddered and prostrated himself before her.

"Forgive me, Your Majesty! I do not know what I was thinking to have interrupted you! Please have mercy on my lowly self!"

Crusiliux sighed. "That is better. Get up. Time is short. The knights will arrive at the gate in five days' time. I plan for the resistance–and our new guests–to be eliminated by then."

"But, Your Majesty, we have already eliminated the resistance. They–"

"If you had eliminated the resistance, do you think I would be telling you to do it now?"

"But–"

"But nothing. You still have not cleared everything in the slaughterhouse district."

"Majesty, we *have* cleared it," the orc whined.

"You are trying my patience. Listen to me and do as you're told or I will kill and replace you. It would take but a moment. You have not cleared it; they are still there. They are like rats infesting this city."

"I will go notify the others to search the southwest district again."

"No. Not now. Now they are being protected by the cyfuniad and his friends. They are not to be underestimated, especially while they still have the staff."

"The what?"

Crusiliux shook her great head. "The mage! Keep up. The fool mixing god-magic and dragon-magic. That should not even be possible." She snarled. "It matters not. I do not want you to send everyone out on some fool's errand. This will take timing and finesse. Wait for my instruction. You may go."

"But, Your Maj–"

"Get out of my sight!" Dust and debris rained down from the cave's ceiling and walls.

The orc scurried away to the square, blood-red portal he had entered through and vanished. The gate glimmered with light, casting crimson sparkles which danced around the room. Crusiliux admired it. The portal was as beautiful as her own scales, and though it was as insubstantial as air, it appeared as fluid and thick as blood.

How to get the staff away from the human?

Her instincts urged her to swoop in and take it by force, but she knew that would be unwise. *Bah!* Even if he had figured out how to use the staff, what difference would that make to the might of her teeth and claws?

Still …

Crusiliux stared into her scrying pool. Despite her best efforts, she had never been able to get a good vision of the cyfuniad. It was frustrating. Whirling around, she thrashed her tail into the scrying pool, upsetting the still waters. Crusiliux went very still, her eyes narrowing.

She wasn't alone.

An elf with silver hair stood in a darkened corner of the cave, hands clasped behind her back. "What are you doing here, sister?" Crusiliux hissed.

"I have come to warn you away from this foolish plan."

"What business is it of yours?"

The elf stepped forward, her blue eyes glinting with power. "It is none of my business, and yet all of my business."

The ruby dragon shrank down until she had assumed the form of a dark orc. Her hair became the same scarlet her scales had been, her eyes retaining their snakelike, coppery gold. She stomped over to the elf and stared down at her. "Axistra, you have always spoken in riddles. I've never been a fan of riddles. Speak plainly."

"Do not fight the mage."

"I do not plan to fight him. I plan to kill him."

"He will be your death."

Crusiliux laughed, throwing her head back. "That is rich. A mortal–the death of a dragon? We were once heralds to the Three ... practically gods in our own right! What risk could he pose to me?"

"The world is changing. Our time is ending. Mortals are growing stronger ..."

"All the more reason to nip this in the bud, right here, right now."

"What of the balance?" Axistra asked. "What of the pact?"

"The pact!" Crusiliux scoffed. "The pact is a joke. What? Did you think that you, Aanhextrios and Tarextros were the only ones allowed to look the other way? My dear sister. Surely you cannot be so naïve. Do not play innocent with me. Tarextros may have been the only one actively involved, but do you think me such a fool as to not know it was you who set these mortals on his trail in the first place? The pact is over, and I will do as I please. The humans have had their moment in the sun. Now it is the orcs' turn. It is time we received the praise and glory that we deserve as higher beings!"

"You have become mad. So blinded by what could be that you can no longer see what is."

"It is you who is blind. You may be a *seer,* dear sister, but you forget that I am as well."

Axistra's silver brows lifted. "You have had a vision of how this will end? I have tried and failed. What have you seen?"

"I have had a vision of myself descending upon the cyfuniad from the air, claws outstretched. I have relished in the grief of his elven friends, the tears of his human comrades. I will triumph, I will claim the staff as my own and I will become a god. With the staff, I shall be strong enough to rule over even *you.* Leave me, sister. This talk of pacts and balance has bored me."

Axistra clenched her fists. "You risk everything with this. Tarextros has fallen and is nothing more than a pup. Aanhextrios is gone. If you fail–"

"I shall not fail."

"But if you do, the world will be unbalanced. The pendulum will swing toward the side of good, and the world risks falling into tyranny. Remember that."

Crusiliux scoffed and opened her mouth to retort, but the elf was gone. She sighed. "Even with Tarextros as nothing more than a pup, he will grow. You are demented, dear sister. Your precious balance is already destroyed. Just give it time. With Aanhextrios gone, the pendulum will soon swing toward the orcs and tumasi, toward your so-called evil. I–along with Tarextros, when he comes of age–will rule this land."

She gazed back into her scrying pool, lost in thought.

Popping into the infirmary, Arcus set Siobhan down and held out his hand for the staff. The two birds on Siobhan's shoulder fluttered to the ground. He snapped his fingers, turning them back into Joseph and Victoria. Without a word, he turned and headed for the hallway.

Siobhan grabbed his wrist as he passed, spinning him around to face her.

"What, Shiv?"

"You're out of control. We need to talk."

"No. What I *need* to do is find Celeste and Tarnelius."

Siobhan glowered at him, then turned to Victoria and Joseph. "Would you two mind locating Celeste and Tarnelius and let them know we are back, please? Then we should get some rest. Since there are no more injured, this may be the quietest place."

Victoria nodded and swept from the room. Joseph hurried after her.

"What is your problem?" Siobhan snapped.

"My problem? My problem is that we have a city to free, the gods only know how many orcs to get rid of and a *dragon* in the mix. I'm under a lot of stress and I don't need their nonsense!"

"Speaking of which, you know I'm not letting you fight her alone, right?"

"Not this again," Arcus groaned.

"Yes. This again, and again. As many times as it takes until you see reason."

"Great."

"Arcus. This is insanity. Dragons are practically gods. You can't fight one."

"I can and I will. Look, this staff levels the battlefield. Her magical defenses? Gone. Spells? Eliminated. I'll still have mine and she'll have nothing."

"Nothing except for her massive size, her claws, teeth and fire."

"Right." Arcus sighed. "Nothing but those. I've got this."

"What are you going to do about those?"

"I have the cage. That will protect me against fire, teeth and claws … at least until she pulls it apart. I can still cast from inside there, so it's a good start. It's too bad I can't think of anything that would increase my size or anything. Even an elephant isn't big enough."

Siobhan thought for a moment. "Not an elephant, but what about a giant?"

"What are you talking about? A giant isn't an animal."

"What about the spell you use on Joseph and Victoria to turn them into birds? Would it work the other way?"

Arcus' jaw dropped. "Why didn't I think of that? It doesn't last forever, but it would probably be long enough, especially if I recast it before it ends."

"See? You need me. That's why you can't fight her on your own."

Arcus pulled her face down to his and kissed her hard on the lips. "I won't risk you, Siobhan. You would be better suited helping to get the other knights into the city and fighting the orcs. Our friends need you. I'll be fine. I promise."

"Why would you make me a promise you know you can't keep?"

"I can keep it, and I will. Try not to worry." He pressed his fingers under her jaw and tilted her face up. "Don't worry, okay?"

She sighed. "Okay."

"How long do you think it will be before the Mithrans arrive?"

She shook her head. "Four to six days, most likely. It's not a short trip."

"Plenty of time to finish searching the mage tower, then. Let's get some rest. I'm sure the others will be here soon enough."

"Victoria, wait for me. Please?"

"No."

Victoria heard Joseph's footfalls grow faster behind her. She ignored him and entered the meeting room only to find it abandoned. The tables and chairs appeared even more askew than normal. No sign of Celeste, Tarnelius, anyone. Turning to try elsewhere, she found herself blocked by Joseph.

"Excuse me," she said pointedly.

Joseph sighed, but instead of moving aside, he pushed her into the meeting room and shut the door behind them.

"Let me go, or I'll scream."

"I'm not holding you here, Victoria. But please hear me out. We have to talk, and I'm not above begging right now."

Victoria turned on her heel and walked back to the far-left corner, the same corner where he had seen Conner kiss her. The chairs were all in different places, casting a pall of unfamiliarity over the area, but she hoped the gesture wouldn't be lost on him.

Joseph raked his hands through his hair. "Victoria ... I just want you to know that I am sorry. I was an idiot. I should have asked you first. I should have waited. Hell, I should have punched Conner and called it a day. Anything except what I did."

"You're right about that."

"Yes. I know I am. I was wrong ... but Vicki," Joseph paused, waiting for her to look at him. "You know what? *So were you!* So you caught me in a moment of weak, petty revenge. Is that any reason why you had to murder Katherine? Why couldn't we talk about it? Why couldn't we clear the air like adults? In the grand scheme of things, whose crime was worse?"

Victoria paled. She closed the distance to him and raised her hand to slap him, but he caught her wrist, yanking her smaller body taut against his.

"I still love you, Vicki. I know who you are, *what* you are, but I love you anyway. I always will. The question is, do you still love me? Can you forgive me? Even if not right now, can you ever forgive me?"

"I don't know."

"Well, at least that isn't a no."

Victoria pushed him away, oblivious to any words coming from his mouth. Her heart hurt. She wanted to forgive him, but how could she? It turned out that he was no different from any other guy. He would lie or cheat in an instant if he ever perceived she was out of line. Worse yet, she hated who she became when he hurt her. Victoria didn't ever want to be put in that position again. She had to guard her heart.

"Victoria? Did you hear me?"

She startled. "No."

"I asked you where you learned necromancy."

"I studied it in Izmar. I found it fascinating, but I never liked what it did to me. I don't usually use it."

"In Izmar? I never noticed you studying that."

"I did it outside of class time … while you were off drinking with Arcus or bedding some whore!"

"Right." Joseph moved toward her, stopping just a little out of reach. "Vicki, I–"

Victoria shrank back. "Don't." Brushing past him, she called over her shoulder, "We should find the elves." Without waiting for his answer, she hurried from the room and continued into the hallway, checking the rest of the rooms on this level before ascending the stairs to the third floor.

"I have no idea where she could be," Conner grumbled, running his hands through his hair. "We've searched this entire building, and the one on the other side of the tunnel, too. It's so unlike Katherine to wander off."

"I don't know what to tell you, Conner." Celeste walked into the room nearest the stairs. She paused in the doorway. Something about this room was off. This was the fourth time she had walked in here, but couldn't figure out what it was that called to her.

"You sense it, too ..."

"Yes," she thought back to Tarnelius. *"This room is off. It seems ... different."*

"The room buzzes with power. Also, it's much less dusty than the other rooms. I'm not sure if it was cleaned recently, or if there is magic masking something. Joseph would be able to figure it out. We should bring him down here later."

"What are you two looking at?" Conner asked.

"Nothing," said Celeste. "I was merely lost in thought. I don't know where she could be, but I know that I'm tired. We need to rest."

Conner narrowed his eyes. "Go ahead. The sleeping quarters are on the third floor. I'm sure you saw them."

"You're not coming?"

"No. I'm going to go back to the other building. I'll come in later."

Celeste smiled sympathetically. "Try not to worry. I'm sure she'll be found soon."

Conner nodded and crossed the hall to the trapdoor, lifted it up and descended the ladder.

Celeste turned back to the room she had been staring into.

"What do you think?" Tarnelius murmured.

Celeste chuckled. "You know exactly what I think. You always do. This room has something to do with it, I can feel it. Isn't this where Victoria found Joseph and Katherine? Look." She pointed to the far corner. "The dust is disturbed. Most of this room is cleaner than the rest of the building, but you can see dust in some places."

Tarnelius nodded. "I think Joseph and Victoria haven't been entirely honest about what happened down here."

"So what do we do? I think we should confront them about it."

Tarnelius snorted. "Maybe if we were Siobhan we would, but I'm not entirely sure I *want* to know. Also, depending on what the answer is, it may not do much toward gaining the Lumernians' trust."

"Shh! Quiet!"

Celeste cocked her head, listening. Footsteps sounded on the nearby stairs.

Victoria froze at the bottom of the steps and stared at the two elves. Joseph, not expecting her sudden stop, walked into her and shoved her forward.

"I see you have returned from the mage tower safely," said Celeste. "Did you have any luck?"

"I … um … we …" Victoria stuttered. "Well, we disabled the traps, but didn't get a chance to really look at any of their books or artifacts yet. We were looking for … What are you doing down here?"

"Conner is convinced that something untoward has happened to Katherine. Given her extensive leave, I'm inclined to agree. Is there anything you want to share?"

Tarnelius watched the two humans, his face impassive. He really hadn't wanted to get into this. He, too, was inclined to agree with Conner, and having solid evidence–or gods forbid, a confession–would do nothing to free the city.

"Conner?" Joseph's voice cracked. He cleared his throat. "No. We don't know anything about where she went."

Victoria stared at Tarnelius, her eyes glistening with unshed tears. For a long moment, she said nothing, and gave no indication she had heard Joseph speak at all.

"Victoria?" Tarnelius asked in a gentle voice.

"You already know, don't you?" she whispered. Two fat tears slipped down her cheeks.

"Victoria, no!" Joseph interrupted. "Don't do this."

Celeste frowned. "Don't do what, Joseph?"

"It was a misunderstanding," he answered.

Victoria stared at her feet. "I did it. I saw them–together. I killed Katherine in this very room."

No one moved.

"How did you know?" Joseph asked.

Victoria took a shuddering breath. "What happens now?"

"Well, we'll need to–"

"Nothing," Tarnelius interrupted Celeste, giving her a pointed look. "We aren't the law here. Bringing this to light will only make the people suspicious of us, and we need their cooperation. But do us all a favor. No one tells the paladin. Not until the city is freed."

"What did you do with the body?" Celeste demanded. Anger darkened her features.

"The body …" Joseph cleared his throat. "Let me answer your question with a question: how did you know?"

"This room is cleaner than the rest. What dust is left in the corners has been disturbed. That didn't answer my question at all. What did you do with the body?"

"It's ... she's ... still here."

"Still here?" Celeste nearly shouted. "Where? What were you thinking?"

Victoria went pale and swayed on her feet. Concerned, Tarnelius grabbed her shoulder to steady her.

"Celeste, why don't you take Victoria upstairs to get some rest? Send Arcus down here. I have a feeling we may need him."

Celeste glared at Tarnelius. *"If she is tough enough to murder someone, she is tough enough to deal with the consequences."*

"Celeste, we're going to have to deal with this later. She reacted out of anger. Was it wrong? Yes. Shall we execute her for her crime? She won't be any use to us in freeing this city if she is dead. It will also anger the resistance, who is looking to us to lead them. They trust us ... we need to maintain that trust."

"I don't like this, Tarnelius. I don't like that she is getting away with murder."

Tarnelius realized the silence that had blanketed them had stretched into awkwardness. "Celeste?" he repeated in a gentle tone.

"All right … fine. I'll go find Arcus. Come on, Victoria. Do you have any idea where he might be?"

She nodded, blinking away tears. "He and Siobhan are in the infirmary waiting for us."

Victoria allowed Celeste to lead her up the stairs, leaving the two men behind. Once on the second floor, Celeste strode to the infirmary and tapped twice before opening the door wide and entering.

"Arcus? Tarnelius wanted me to ask if you could give him a hand with something downstairs."

Arcus rose to his feet and nodded.

"Do you want me to come with you?" Siobhan asked.

Arcus opened his mouth to answer, but Celeste was quicker. "No need. No one is hurt. They only need him to help them clean up something. He'll be back in no time."

Arcus leaned forward and kissed Siobhan. "See? No need. Get some rest. I'll return shortly."

Arcus walked down the stairs, wondering how he was supposed to know where the others were. She did say downstairs and not outside, right? Voices drifted up as he reached the bottom floor. Relieved, Arcus crossed the hall to join them.

"All right, Joseph," said Tarnelius. "What really happened down here?"

Squeezing his eyes shut, Joseph shook his head. "I jumped to conclusions, and ... and reacted. Victoria caught us and Katherine paid with her life."

"Where is she?"

"She's still in this room, cloaked by illusion magic. Arcus, please shut the door and I'll lift the spell. I don't want anyone else stumbling across us."

Tarnelius ran both his hands through his hair and scowled. "I can't believe you would leave her here."

"What else could I have done? I don't have any idea where I could take her to burn her body ... and there is another complication."

"Yes?" Tarnelius snapped.

"You'll see, but … Arcus?" said Joseph. "Please don't tell Siobhan. She … I … I'll never be able to fix things if this gets dragged out."

Arcus sighed deep in his chest, almost a growl. "I hate keeping secrets from her."

"Do you need to go, then?" Tarnelius asked.

"No. I just don't like it. Why are we down here?"

Joseph waved his hand dismissively. Arcus and Tarnelius gasped and shrank back against the wall. Joseph stared calmly, unable to look away.

"*Victoria* did this?" Tarnelius choked out. "Are you certain?"

"Am I *certain?* I was standing right here! Of course I am certain!"

"How?"

"Necromancy," Arcus muttered. "I had no idea."

"I didn't either," agreed Joseph.

The blood coated almost the entire room. The place where Katherine had last stood was a tangled mess of bones, organs, muscle and other unidentifiable innards. Her skin lay several feet away, folded neatly on the floor as if it had been a costume.

"This is wrong," Tarnelius lamented. "An abomination against Kamara. You … she … no one told us. I assumed there had been some sort of battle, that Victoria had been the victor. I had no idea she was even capable of … of … *this!*"

Arcus nodded his agreement.

Joseph continued to stare at the carnage. "This is why I merely hid her. I didn't know what else to do! I couldn't carry her body out; it's in too many pieces. Can you use healing magic to piece her together long enough to carry her out of here?"

The other two glared at him, matching horror-stricken expressions on their faces.

"You can't heal the dead," Arcus finally answered.

"I didn't expect this," said Tarnelius. "I'm not sure what we should do, either."

Arcus sighed. "I need something to contain what we can. A sheet or something similar. Then I can teleport her out, burn her body and return here. I can clean the room, too. The real question is: what are we going to do about Victoria?"

"Do?" Joseph said. He wrung his hands nervously. "I don't think she'll do it again."

"How can we be sure?" Tarnelius spoke up.

"She was miserable after. The spell made her sick. I think she was lost in the moment."

"I don't want her on her own out here. This place is dangerous. *She* is dangerous. Once we have freed Lumernia, we'll all have to talk about this—even Siobhan. If we don't, I do not want to travel with her any longer. I would serve as her judge and executioner myself, right now, if it were not for our friendship, Joseph. Perhaps you are right. Maybe it *was* the heat of the moment, but that does not make any of this excusable. Necromancy is dark magic, and it takes its power from the darkest and most sinister of human emotions."

"I agree," said Tarnelius. "This type of magic is an abomination. It is against the teachings of Kamara, and opposes everything we stand for as druids. She should stay in sight for now, but once this is over—"

"Damn it!" Joseph slapped his palm against the wall, grimacing at the shockwaves that jolted through his still-broken hand. "None of this would have ever happened if … if I hadn't …"

"If you hadn't, then we wouldn't know she is a necromancer," argued Arcus. "The fact that she kept that from us is disturbing." Arcus rubbed at his eyes, fatigue and frustration setting in. "But before we can deal with that, we must get rid of her body. If Conner sees this, we will never be able to count on him or his resistance members to fight the orcs. ... Please, someone find me a sheet while I start cleaning this place."

"I'll go," said Joseph, turning and hurrying from the room.

Arcus set to work on cleaning the areas he could, directing his magic to remove the blood stains. It was slow progress. Before long, Joseph returned with the sheet and carefully loaded anything solid that he could onto the slightly tattered cloth.

"I'd like to come with you," Joseph said. "To burn her body."

Arcus grunted as he kept working. When he'd gotten about half the room clean, he lowered his hands. "I'll have to renew the spell to keep going, but let's get this out of here. Joseph, I need you to hide the rest."

Joseph repeated the spell, and the remainder of the blood vanished.

"I'll wait here," said Tarnelius. "I don't want to go back up without you, in case it arouses suspicion."

Arcus chanted, and a shadowy door appeared in the wall. "Grab the sheet." Once Joseph had a firm hold on it, Arcus gripped his arm and yanked him through the magic door.

They emerged outside and to the left of the main gate, located on the west side of Lumernia.

"Are you sure this is the safest spot we could have chosen?"

"No. I could have taken her anywhere in the world that I'm familiar with, but bringing you in addition to her ... remains ...

creates complications. I had to use a spell with a much more limited range. I didn't want to argue, though. I didn't actually want to carry that sheet, and I understand why you wanted to come along. Come on, we must hurry before we are spotted."

Keeping themselves tight against the wall, Joseph laid the sheet and its gruesome contents on the ground.

"Goodbye, Katherine. May you find peace in the afterlife. I am deeply sorry this happened. You deserved better."

With nothing else to be said, Joseph stepped a few feet away. Arcus pointed his finger at the bloody sheet, and flame shot from his hand. The pair watched in silence as the sheet, and its contents, slowly burned away to ash.

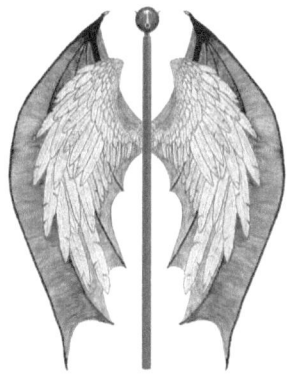

Chapter Twenty-One
We Didn't Start the Fire

"We should go back to the mages' tower."

"What time is it now?" Siobhan asked.

Celeste created some of the magical berries they ate when traveling and passed them around. "I'm not sure. Everything feels off because the windows are boarded up. I'll be right back." She strode sullenly from the room. Apparently she knew what they had been up to the night before and wasn't happy about it.

"As I was saying, we must go back to the mage tower," Arcus insisted. "Who knows what kinds of things are hidden inside that could prove useful?"

"Useful for what?" said Tarnelius. "You are the one who wants to go, so I assume you mean useful for fighting a dragon. But it can't be done. No one has ever been foolish enough to try to fight one before."

"No one has ever been foolish enough to fight one of the Three before, but we did it," Arcus retorted.

Tarnelius tilted his chin. "We had help."

"We still have help." Arcus caressed the staff of Raziyl.

Tarnelius glanced from Arcus to Siobhan, and back again. "Can I speak with you privately?"

Arcus nodded and followed Tarnelius out into the hall.

"It's nearly dusk," Celeste said as she approached them.

"Good. Then we'll have the cover of darkness soon," said Tarnelius. "I'd like to scout around and see if we can get a general idea of what we're facing. We'll be right back. I want to have a talk with Arcus."

Celeste nodded and pushed past them into the room.

The pair walked in silence to the meeting room. Tarnelius listened at the door, but heard voices inside. He headed for the stairs and descended them, leading the way into the room that contained the trapdoor.

"Tell me honestly, Arcus, do you really feel you have any sort of chance to defeat the dragon?"

"There is always a chance."

"Glib as usual. I remember you and Celeste firing off spells at the black dragon and neither of you having any effect at all. Even with the staff, how would you get past her defenses? Dragons have thick scales and many millennia's worth of wisdom at their disposal."

Arcus sighed. "The dragons were able to hurt each other with their magic. They aren't indestructible. It is my hope that the staff will take away many of her defenses."

"Your *hope?*"

"Yes. My hope. It's all I have. Also, Melek's sword was able to penetrate his scales."

"The sword of a god."

"And this is the staff of a god. It may be a long shot, but it's the only one we have!"

Tarnelius nodded, looking unconvinced. "Are you ready for this? Is there truly no other way?"

Arcus shook his head. "I won't lie to you, my friend. I'm terrified. If you can think of another way, I'd be more than happy to listen. In the meantime, I should see if I can find anything worth using in the mage tower. Will you promise me something?"

Tarnelius arched his eyebrow.

Arcus took a deep, steadying breath. "Promise me that if I should fail, you and Celeste will stay in contact with Siobhan for me. Make sure she is okay."

"Of course." Tarnelius gripped Arcus' shoulder. "We'll stay close by her until she feels strong enough to continue on her own, and even then, we'll always be there for her."

"I know she's infuriating ... but I love her more than anything."

"I understand, and don't worry. You two have become like family. You can always count on us, I swear it."

Arcus nodded once. "Thanks. We'd better get back up there before the others wonder where we disappeared to."

Arcus turned and headed back up the stairs.

Tarnelius crept forward, his boots moving soundlessly over the pavement. His hooded cloak was pulled low and he kept his head down. The golden moon seemed to be hiding as well, as it was veiled by a thick cover of clouds. His goal was to see how much of a force was present in Lumernia. Entering the central hub, Tarnelius turned right and headed toward the main residential area. He, Celeste, Arcus and Theri had stayed there with Conner and Fiona the year prior. The roads and back alleys were familiar to Tarnelius.

He assumed that the main body of orcs would be in the king's castle, but wanted to see if the houses in the southeast quadrant were also occupied.

Nearing the gate separating the city center from the residential area, Tarnelius paused, his breath catching in his throat. Hurriedly, he ducked behind a large bush next to one of the government buildings. He waited in silence as six orcs marched past, heading west.

Adrenaline from the close encounter pulsing through him, he emerged from behind the bush and continued to the residential area. Sidling along the edge of the gate, Tarnelius peeked his head around. Satisfied that nobody was in sight, he hurried into the southeast quadrant and sprinted to the rubble of a wrecked building to hide in. Tarnelius paused to get his bearings, scanning the surrounding area.

"The residential district has taken heavy damages," Tarnelius thought. *"There are far more ruined buildings than standing ones. I'll check it out, then head to the castle to take a peek inside."*

"What? Tarnel, I don't think it's wise for you to go into *the castle. I thought you were just looking around!"*

"Don't worry. How are things going there?"

He could almost feel Celeste's shrug. *"Difficult to say. Everyone has split up. Arcus is grabbing book after book and flipping through them, tossing them on the floor in a heap when he is done. Joseph and Victoria disappeared into other rooms. Don't change the subject. I don't think—"*

Celeste cut off as Tarnelius tensed up. He heard voices coming from nearby. Tiptoeing toward the sound, he snuck a glance inside one of the windows. Four orcs sat on the previous owners' furniture, playing at some sort of dice game on a table they had pulled between them. Tarnelius eased away from the window and continued to work his way down the orderly streets of Lumernia.

By the time each of the remaining houses had been checked and he had moved back into the city center, he had found nearly eighty orcs inside the residential district homes. Celeste continued to mentally argue with him about going to the castle, but his mind was made up.

Tarnelius rushed toward the damaged gate leading to the king's castle. Darting through, he hid behind a fallen chunk of wall to regroup. He heard the guttural sound of orc voices nearby, but none of them seemed suspicious or alarmed, so he surmised he hadn't been spotted. There were three orcs nearby, around twenty yards from him, their backs turned.

"Damn it!" he thought.

"Tarnel, seriously. I don't think you should do this. Why don't you shift into a bird and go see if Siobhan needs help with whatever trainings she is trying to teach the resistance?"

Tarnelius paused, then shifted into a small rice finch. Fluttering his tiny wings, he took off into the air, toward the castle. He landed on the main gate and looked down, examining the orcs below him. They were going through a pile of junk, most likely spoils taken from the dead.

"Don't do it."

Tarnelius chirped quietly and hopped off the gate and flapped clumsily through.

The castle entryway looked eerily familiar yet different. Dust, grime and chips from the floor and ceiling tiles created a coating throughout the hallway.

Feeling bold, he flew unnoticed through the hallways above the heads of the orcs.

"Why didn't I think of this before?"

"I am not amused, Tarnelius. You are going to get caught. Then where will we be?"

Tarnelius explored the castle. Several orcs swatted at him as he flew by, but barely paid him any mind at all. He alighted on the top of a door frame near the central courtyard and waited. Before long, someone came and opened the door. He sped through, dashing to the upper branches of a tree. The last time he had been here, knights had been doing training exercises. The place was a quiet mockery of what it once had been. Even the trees seemed to droop in sadness.

Tarnelius wasn't sure where to search next. This area had not been immune to the ravages of war. There were broken cobblestones and chunks missing from the fountain. The wall on the opposite side was cracked and peppered with small holes. That way led to the huge audience chamber, he knew. There were several upper stories, but he had no way of knowing if there was a basement, or how to access it. Fluttering to one of the small holes, he squeezed inside and found the doors leading to the audience chamber had been blasted away, making entrance easy.

Tarnelius flew inside and turned to the right, heading to the back of the room to the altar and statue of Melek, still covered in a dusty black cloth.

From atop the statue, Tarnelius was able to take in the entire, cavernous space. This large hall had once been used by the four paladin orders as a lecture hall for military planning. He could see that several of the benches had been knocked askew or broken. His eye was drawn to a blood-red doorway standing next to the statue of Rashnu, up on the dais. The door wavered, undulating as if it were made out of a viscous substance, not quite solid. Tarnelius would have noticed it sooner, but there were several orcs obscuring his view ... each staring in rapt attention at one of their number: a tall female with shocking red hair–hair the same color as the magic door. She issued commands, her almost lizard-like copper eyes sweeping the area with a predator's guile.

She stopped talking and smiled as her eyes fell on the small bird.

A chill ran through Tarnelius' avian body. He took to the air, escape on his mind. A wall appeared where none had been before. He tried to adjust his flight pattern, but it was too late. He smashed into it, and landed on a ground a few inches away from the wall's base.

He shook his head, clearing the haze from his eyes, and was finally able to see the wall for what it really was. Not a part of the room, but a red, sparkling cage. His prison came to a gentle landing on the ground at the feet of the tall orc. The orc bent and lifted it into her hands.

"Tarnel! What's happening?"

"I–I'm sorry, Celeste."

Switching to the common tongue, the redheaded orc taunted her prey. "Little bird, little bird ... you have flown so far from home. Always sticking your beak where it does not belong. Well, you are going to be my ticket to flushing out the cyfuniad."

"What's so special about this bird? There are tons of them outside," demanded one of the other orcs.

The redheaded orc chuckled. "We are not all what we seem. I assume this form because my true one frightens the weak-willed, and because human-made dwellings aren't built large enough to accommodate my greatness. Likewise, this little bird is not a bird at all. Is that not right, little druid? I can smell the touch of Kamara on you. It's a smell I will never forget. What I don't smell is true power. You are a dabbler." The orc wrinkled her nose. "No matter, the others will come looking for you."

"She's right. We certainly will."

"Don't do anything rash, Celeste. This is obviously the red dragon I've stumbled upon. Currently, she's talking to me. She hasn't killed me. Wait."

"Wait? Wait for what? Wait for her to kill you? I don't think so!"

"Wait!"

"No. We already tried things your way, and now look what happened!"

The orc snapped her fingers and pointed to the ruined threshold before striding through it, carrying the blood-red cage. She crossed the courtyard and re-entered the castle on the other side, then navigated the hallways until she exited through the main gate into the castle foreground.

"Allow me to introduce myself, little bird. My name is Crusiliux. I would ask you what your name is, but it really doesn't matter. You are probably wondering why I haven't killed you yet. Let me assure you that will happen in good time. First, you will serve as bait, then you will die." She released the cage to float in midair and sent it sailing a short distance away.

The orc shifted forms, stretching and growing. Wings and a massive tail sprouted and expanded. Blood-red scales formed everywhere, encasing her in ruby armor. Horns emerged from her head, one pair jutting backward over her head, the other looping down and framing her face. Her neck lengthened, her powerful arms and legs glistened in the light of the golden moon.

"Arcus and I are here, up on the city wall. We dropped Joseph and Victoria off at the resistance to get everyone moving. Be ready. We're going to stall for time if she continues like this."

"Now, I wonder where the best place to cast my fishing net would be. Think they will look here for you? Or should I move you to the center of this wretched city? Perhaps I should return you to the slaughterhouse district. Seems a fitting place for a massacre."

The dragon folded her wings and marched forward, her graceful gait that of a large cat. She walked through the mutilated gate to the city center, smashing what was left of it to pieces.

Storm clouds gathered overhead. Crusiliux stopped, her head tilting skyward. Lightning arced from the heavens and struck her in the left wing, deflecting with no effect into a shattered chunk of wall.

Crusiliux sniffed the air and turned back around, her eyes searching and finally locking on Celeste, who was flying above the city wall, the moonlight reflecting off her black hair and bathing her wings in a golden glow.

"Let him go, dragon!"

"Hmm. It appears that I have something you want. By coincidence, you also have something that I want. The staff of Raziyl and its master. You will bring me those things, or I will kill the bird."

"What makes you think I know where the staff is?" Celeste yelled back.

The dragon snorted. A cloud of black smoke curled above her nostrils. "I know who you are, druid. I know who you travel with. Do you think me a fool? You find me what I want, or I will put you, too, into a shiny birdcage and make you watch while I torture and kill your little friend. Then I will tear this entire wretched city to the ground, brick by brick. I will destroy all in my path!"

A second crack of lightning was Celeste's answer. Crusiliux growled and exhaled a huge blast of scarlet flame in Celeste's direction, forcing her to dart to the side.

"Wait ..." The dragon sniffed again. "There are three here who have been touched by Kamara." A ruby red cage encased Celeste and hurtled down, crashing to the ground. Dirt and loose cobblestones sprayed in every direction. Tarnelius' cage also fell with a loud *clunk*. Crusiliux spread her wings and took fight, her rear claws leaving huge gouges in the pavement.

"Come out, come out," Crusiliux jeered. "Are we children to play hide-and-seek?"

The dragon landed on the city wall and gripped it in her talons. Huge rocks and boulders broke away and crashed to the ground on either side of the wall. Arcus teleported from his hiding spot down to the ground near Celeste and Tarnelius. He was invisible, so he knew the orcs wouldn't be able to see him, but he was sure the dragon would be able to if she looked down here.

"You two okay?" he whispered. Tarnel fluttered his wings and Celeste sat up, looking dazed.

"Arcus?"

"Shh. You have to get up. Be ready to run. The only way out of this is when I activate the staff. You won't have magic. You must get away from orcs and back into the city center. Keep running until you get to the temples or until you find the resistance, if they are on their way." Arcus fell silent, waiting for them to respond.

Celeste moved into a crouch and nodded her head.

Arcus straightened to his full height, trying to calm his nerves. Lifting the staff high in the air, he activated its power and amplified his voice. "I have terms, dragon!"

The dragon's head swiveled around and locked with Arcus' own. "Terms? I should just eat you and be done with it."

"Could you eat me before I destroy this staff?"

"It would be a challenge, but not an impossible one."

"I doubt you would take the risk, considering the effort to which you have gone to get us here."

"Tell me your terms, mage."

"First, you will let my companions go. I will fight you on my own." Arcus cursed under his breath. They had not run as he had told them. Tarnelius had shifted back the moment the staff had activated, and the pair of them stood by and watched. The surrounding orcs seemed to be waiting to see what the dragon would do, a fortunate turn of events.

"Oh no. That, I cannot promise …" Crusiliux kept talking, but Arcus tuned her out. Removing the amplification spell on his voice, he hurriedly wove a hasten spell over himself and the elves, then teleported onto the wall. The elves were on their own; he had done what he could.

Holding the staff out in front of him, he recited the words of the arcane spell he had learned in Grimsgil. He began to grow taller. The staff grew with him, expanding and stretching until it became giant-sized. Dropping the invisibility spell on himself, he realized his mistake, as the narrow catwalk of the Lumernia city wall became too small for his feet. He jumped down, feeling satisfaction as the ground shook and split at the impact. He had grown to a height of nearly thirty feet, his skin had turned purple, though his hair remained black. Lightning flickered dangerously in his eyes. Though Crusiliux was larger still, at least he was no longer bite-sized.

"Stop staring and go get the elves!" Crusiliux bellowed at the dumb-struck orcs. "They ran out into the city center! Go!"

The dragon took to the skies. She inhaled deeply, preparing to blast her deadly dragonfire at Arcus. Realizing her intent, he started chanting, and when she circled toward him, he shoved his hands forward and blasted his spell at her.

Blue ice and snow met scarlet fire.

Chapter Twenty-Two
Extinguished Flame

Celeste and Tarnelius bolted into the city center. Arcus had been right; it was suicide to fight that many orcs without their magic. Celeste wondered if she would be able to regain her magic and cast into the battle if she flew high enough, but with Tarnelius there, she didn't dare find out.

They had made it to the edges of the park between the four temples when they spotted Siobhan's shining armor glinting in the moonlight from atop Apollo's back. She, Joseph and Victoria led the resistance into the central hub from the southwest quadrant.

The pair heard the grunts and footsteps of the orc army advancing behind them–they must have finally been given the order to attack. Waves of weakness assured Celeste the anti-magic field was still in effect, so they kept running to meet the resistance.

Ten paces, fifteen ... they finally cleared the central park, and with a rush, Celeste felt her magic come back. Was it because she was out of range of the staff? Or had Arcus fallen? She hoped and prayed it was the former. They continued to race for the rest of their small army.

Siobhan drew her sword and awaited the two elves.

"Don't enter the park!" Tarnelius yelled to her.

"It's the border of the anti-magic effect," Celeste added. Turning to the resistance members, she raised her voice. "The time to take back your city, your lives, your *freedom* is now. The paladins of Mithra may not have arrived, but we do not need them. *We* can and will work together to drive back this evil ... right here, right now. Magic users, stay out of the park. Arcus has activated the staff. You'll know if you cross the boundary, you'll be able to feel it." She glanced back at the fast-approaching army. "The time is now. Stay together and hold the line. *Charge!*"

Siobhan rode past them, leading the assault, her sword flashing. The resistance members joined her in a cacophony of battle cries and cheers. Together, they met the ever-growing orc horde with swords and sorcery. Though there were hundreds of them, the horde was larger still. Their odds were insurmountable ... and every man and woman present knew it. Today they would triumph ... or they would die trying.

Joseph held back, looking questioningly at Celeste.

"Should we help Arcus? he asked.

She shook her head. "There is nothing we can do. He is fighting the dragon. Last I saw, he'd somehow turned himself into a tempest giant. We have our own problems."

Tarnelius nodded. "There is a portal inside the castle. I'd wager it leads into the orc lands. That means their numbers could be virtually unlimited." He turned and ran after Siobhan, drawing his swords.

Joseph cast several spells in succession as Victoria darted to the side and summoned a glowing rhinoceros. The ethereal construct charged alongside the resistance and into the horde, sending them scattering.

Celeste watched Joseph shake his head as Victoria separated from the group. Four of his doppelgangers appeared a split second before he vanished from sight. Celeste spread her wings and took to the skies. Summoning the storm, she fired bolt after bolt of lightning down into the horde. The resistance was easily outnumbered ten to one. Who knew how many more orcs would come? Adding a pillar of holy flame to the mix, she rained death down from above.

Together, the resistance worked to push back the orc horde, once and for all.

Crusiliux circled around Arcus, preparing for a second attack, but he was ready. His hasten spell allowing him to move double-time, he summoned his magic and flicked several beads of glowing light in front of him, onto the wall.

Crusiliux dove toward him, claws extended. She gripped his arms and torso with her talons and roared as she tried to rip him apart. Arcus ignored the white-hot fire that threatened to tear him to pieces, and focused on another spell. Jagged bolts of angry lightning erupted from his fingers and struck her face. The dragon reared back and screamed, once more regrouping to circle around. As soon as she was above the wall, Arcus snapped his fingers.

Explosions went off, one after the other. Balls of fire engulfed the dragon. She was pushed back, and landed hard on her back. The city wall broke apart and crumbled. Huge carriage-sized chunks of it rained down, chasing Crusiliux and crashing all around her.

While the dragon worked her way out from under the debris, Arcus took advantage and cast a quick healing spell on his bleeding shoulder. His right hand glowed blue as he gripped his left arm.

Crusiliux's roar shook the ground; a portion of the wall had fallen on her, tearing the delicate membrane of her right wing. Any encouragement Arcus had begun to feel was short lived. She steadied herself and charged, hitting him with a force he'd never felt before, or would again if he were lucky enough to survive. The staff fell from his hand and rolled a short distance away. The light extinguished.

Arcus screamed as he both heard and felt the sickening crunch. His left knee snapped, forced the wrong direction by the weight of the beast. At the same time, the dragon's claws sank into his gut. He cried out again in agony.

This was it.

Arcus looked into the eyes of death itself. Who knew they would be copper-colored? Arcus trembled. His mind scrambled to make sense of what could have gone wrong, and what his failure was truly costing him.

"Promise me that if I should fail, you and Celeste will stay in contact with Siobhan for me. Make sure she is all right."

No! Siobhan! It ... it can't end this way. He could picture her so clearly.

"I'll be okay. I promise."

"Why would you make me a promise you know you can't keep?"

Crusiliux laughed as she began to chant.

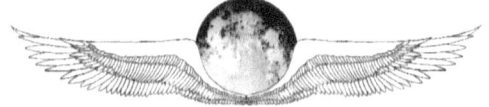

Conner had never been a warrior. He'd been born and raised on a farm. He would have happily lived his entire life there on the old plantation, but fate had other ideas. One day, he had entered Lumernia and met the most beautiful woman in the world: Fiona. Conner fell madly in love. For her, he had left his whole world behind.

Life inside the city walls had been difficult. Neighbors had pressed in on Conner from all sides. The residential district felt much too crowded. Regardless, he was happy. He knew he'd made the right decision. Fiona was his everything. They'd planned to build a family together.

Then came the night his world came crashing down. The orcs attacked. They had taken everything from him. They murdered his wife, his family. They'd destroyed the city and burned down the outlying farms. Conner had nothing left … nothing except a deep-seated fury and the desire to set things right. Fiona would not have wanted him to give up.

Celeste's voice broke into Conner's memories. "The time is now. Stay together and hold the line. *Charge!*"

"*Charge!*" Conner repeated with the rest. He pulled his sword from its sheath and raced toward the enemy lines, following the paladin on the palomino stallion. "For Fiona!"

Conner had never been a warrior … but on this day he would be. If he was to die, he would take as many of these animals with him as he could. Gods willing, he would be fortunate enough to slay those who had stolen his wife from him.

A well-placed sword thrust to the throat vanquished the first orc who crossed Conner's path. He yanked his sword free and continued on his way before the monster ever hit the ground.

"For Fiona!"

"Conner, wait!" Tarnelius yelled.

Conner ignored the elf and leapt into the horde. He swung his sword wildly. A feeling of power rushed through him and he laughed. He was death incarnate, raining mortality down on those who had wronged him.

A sharp pain pierced his side.

Conner sucked in his breath. Gritting his teeth, he swung his sword again, spilling the intestines of the orc in front of him.

"F–for Fiona …"

Conner gasped. Agony ripped through his shoulder. He dropped his sword, no longer able to grip the weapon. He looked up into the eyes of the nearest monster. They were everywhere. Conner had failed.

"I'm c–coming, Fio–"

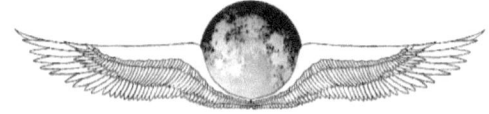

The rhinoceros charged through the orc horde, bludgeoning any who crossed his path with its sharp horn. Bodies were thrown through the air or trampled as he raced through them, toward the park.

Victoria watched her celestial pet carefully, keeping him under control. She was pleased with this one's ability to rip through the crowd. Using her telepathic link, she directed him to return before reaching the edge of the park so that he could double back for a second pass.

She caught a glimpse of movement out of the corner of her eye. Whipping her head that direction, she saw Joseph's four images. Her forehead creased slightly. She was sure she had seen someone else, but it must have been her imagination.

Joseph. Damn him. Why did he have to be so endearing?

She summoned a second pet from the celestial realms, this one a lion. She loved the way animals from the other dimensions looked … they almost sparkled.

Joseph was trying to get her attention; he kept shouting something and waving his hands as he ran toward her. Victoria smiled and waved back, directing her lion into battle and summoning a translucent purple fist to burst forth and punch through the orcs' line. He probably wanted to try again to get into close enough range to make her invisible. It was sweet, really. Even though they had fought, he was still overly concerned with her safety and comfort. She both loved and hated him for it. She hated that he didn't trust her to look after herself, but loved that he cared so much.

Muttering an incantation and pointing, she created a magical effect that caused large tentacles to sprout from the ground. Her creation grabbed hold of three different orcs and smashed them into the ground and each other until they lay still, broken.

She decided she would talk to Joseph after this battle was over. She supposed she did understand where he had been coming from. After all, she hadn't reacted with the most poise when she found him in a compromising position, so she knew what he must have felt when he saw …

"–out behind you!"

The lion leapt into the horde and on top of a particularly hideous orc, trying to bite off his face. Victoria whirled around and realized the source of Joseph's warning.

Hot-white pain lanced through her body, her breath caught in her throat. Her concentration gone, both of her pets and her tentacle spell vanished as if they had never been.

She looked up into the murderous red eyes of her executioner, a tall orc with an incredibly large sword–a sword which had been thrust through the center of her chest. The orc yanked his weapon out and allowed her to fall to the ground. A small cry of pain squeaked from her throat. She wanted to scream, but her body wouldn't cooperate.

Victoria's vision dimmed as the pain faded. Her body still hurt, but the agonizing flame that had consumed her was receding. She felt her pulse in her ears, slowing … slowing. Her blood poured out with every beat of her failing heart, flooding the ground.

A tear slipped down her cheek. She wondered if Joseph would come for her. She was terrified to die alone.

Just as the thought crossed her mind, she felt herself lifted into the air. Forcing her eyes open a bit, she was unable to see who had come to her aid. A moment later, Joseph dismissed his invisibility spell. He looked down upon her with tear-filled eyes, his face filled with so much love and pain. She would have done anything to not be the reason behind that haunted expression.

She knew she was dying. There was nothing left but to say goodbye. Nothing left but to tell him that she loved him.

Victoria caressed his face, memorizing the lines, the stubble, the imperfections. His nose was a little too big, and his chin was pointed. She loved every angle and plane. She would miss him, so much. "Joseph..."

Hot tears poured onto her hand. Her Joseph was crying for her.

"No!" he moaned. "Vicki! Stay with me!"

"Joseph … I … I'm …"

"Shh! Don't try to speak. You're going to be okay. Stay with me. *Celeste!"* He bellowed it enough that she could almost feel it through the numbness setting in.

"Joseph. I'm s–sorry."

"You have nothing to be sorry for, Vicki."

She did though. So many things. She was sorry about Katherine, and heartbroken to be leaving him. She had fallen for him–hard. He may have hurt her, but she knew that he had been hurt, too. She wished to every god that had ever lived that she could change their destiny.

"I–I love you … and … I'm sorry …Joseph."

Joseph sobbed, tears pouring down his face. *"Celeste! Tarnelius! Please!"*

Her heart sputtered. It felt odd in her chest, almost like it hurt, but not quite. She became woozy and unfocused. Goose bumps rose on her skin and she felt like she needed to shiver, but her muscles wouldn't allow it. "It's so cold."

"Don't go, Vicki. Stay with me. I love you, too. So much. So, so much. I'm sorry for what I did to you–to us. I didn't mean it."

"I forgive … you … Joseph. I'll always … love …."

She couldn't finish the sentence. Her chest contracted, giving one last painful thump. The pain was back, every bit as sharp as it had been when she was stabbed, and she would have screamed if she could.

Her vision closed in from the edges, vanishing to a tiny pin prick filled with Joseph's tortured eyes and face until he, too, disappeared into the black.

Then her life was extinguished, and she knew nothing more of this world.

Crusiliux laughed as she began to chant. It was a deep, throaty laugh. A laugh of triumph. Fiery rocks fell from the sky and crashed around them.

But she had chosen to cast spells, not go for the staff.

"Any last words, mage?"

Arcus looked up into her intimidating face, seeing the menacing blackened horns that curved around and almost met in front of her jaw. He felt her hot breath on him. He lifted up his left hand as if to block the dragon out, then let it drop, defeated, at his side.

"Gelmekvir."

The dragon cocked her head to the side, confused. The staff twitched, then shot into Arcus' outstretched hand. The crystal flared into brilliant light, and Arcus felt his bond with the staff strengthen further. Glaring up at Crusiliux, he thrust the relic up toward her face and thought the spell to the staff.

Lightning burst from the crystal and struck Crusiliux between the eyes. She roared and reared back. Arcus stumbled to his feet and hobbled after her, careful to keep as much weight as possible off his broken leg. He leaned heavily on the staff and hit her once more with a lightning spell. He hurriedly renewed the incantation that maintained his giant form, then cast the lightning once more into the castle wall above Crusiliux. Rocks and bricks crashed down onto her.

Crusiliux breathed fire at Arcus, hitting him in the chest and setting his robes on fire. He held his hands up to the heavens. Water gushed down from the sky, hitting them both with the force of a waterfall.

"Stop moving," Arcus hissed, but the dragon let out a wheezing cackle.

"Did you actually believe a spell like that would work? What? Are you running out of spells, little mortal? That was an insult. I am practically a god–"

"A god who has been beaten down. How long until your fire recharges?" Arcus zapped her with another round of lightning and a fireball, hitting her in the legs. "I wonder how many more spells I can get off between now and then. Spells that I have *plenty* more of, I might add."

"Recharge?"

"Well, if you could do it again now, you would." Lightning struck the wall once more, causing more debris to rain down on her. "Your wings are useless and I suspect I heard more than one bone break. You have no magic. Your fire is all that is left to you."

"You are already dead, mage. You just don't realize it. Look at yourself."

Arcus glanced down. His shirt was ripped apart, displaying his stomach which resembled raw, ground up meat. His left leg was swollen and straining against the fabric of his pants. His hand glowed blue as he placed it against the gaping wound on his gut. "I have druidic healing powers. What do you have?"

Without another word, Crusiliux took a deep breath, unleashing her scarlet fire once more on Arcus. He again met her flames with his ice spell, the two elements clashing together.

Shadows wheeled and circled overhead.

"He will be your death." Axistra's voice was felt, caressing their skin, more than heard.

Both Arcus and Crusiliux looked up to stare at the intruders. Axistra's massive silver body landed nearby. "Farewell, sister," she intoned. Behind her, up on the opposite city wall, settled two more dragons. One had sapphire scales. The other, emerald.

"No," said Arcus.

Axistra regarded Arcus in silence. Crusiliux glared at him. "Finish this."

"No," he repeated. "You are beaten, dragon. I want you to admit it."

Crusiliux wheezed. "That much is obvious. End this battle. You have bested me. I will be reborn anew. Your descendants will pay for this atrocity."

"No."

"Stop saying that!"

Arcus turned to Axistra. "The balance ..."

She nodded. "The balance must be maintained." A spark of hope brightened her eyes.

"Before Tarextros broke the dragon pact," said Arcus, "the world was at peace, balanced. Kuunkierto's example should have rung true for everyone. The balance must be maintained. You are right, Crusiliux. You are as gods in this world. You are a god who has been bested by a *mortal.* You will live with that knowledge for the rest of your days. Your actions have shaken the foundation of this world. Evil has overrun this city and everything it touches."

Arcus turned to Axistra. "The dragon pact is hereby broken. This farce will no longer work. Either all are involved in the world, or none are. You must decide amongst yourselves. No longer will it be acceptable for dragons to turn a blind eye toward each other. Either each of you stays out of this world, as the gods did before you, or you join the world as occupants of this land. Whichever path you choose, the decision must be irrevocable."

"The human is right," stated the green dragon. "This is a new age; an age of mortals. They are learning power that their ancestors never even dreamed of. They are ready for us to take our place among them."

"I agree," said the blue dragon, her voice musical, like wind through the reeds in a field. "Let this end."

"The balance must be maintained," repeated Axistra. "Crusiliux, order your orcs back into their portal. We must work to return things to the way they were."

"Why should I? I may have been beaten, but my orcs are winning their battle. They will soon cover the world!"

Axistra glared at the red dragon. "Arcus, turn off the staff. This castle courtyard isn't large enough for us to move comfortably."

Khellendriox turned his head to the west. "The fighting is still going strong. I shall put a stop to it."

Arcus blanched. "My wife is out there. My friends. I need to–"

"Khellendriox will put an end to the combat, Arcus," said Axistra. "Nothing you can do now will change her outcome. Do as I said and deactivate that staff."

Arcus scowled at Axistra's words, but commanded the staff to turn off. Then, he dismissed the spell that had turned him into a tempest giant and limped nearer to Crusiliux. Laying his hands on her legs, he cast several healing spells. The green dragon spread his wings and flew off to the west, while Axistra shifted into an elf with silver hair. The sapphire dragon also transformed, but into a female kedistam. Her markings were that of a white tiger, except that her stripes were not black–they were a brilliant blue.

"Do not touch me, *mortal!*" snarled Crusiliux.

Axistra and the kedistam regarded Arcus.

"Even though she would kill you, you still heal her?" asked the kedistam.

"I still have the staff, but even if I didn't, I doubt you would allow her to kill me now. Am I wrong?"

"No. You are not wrong."

Axistra lifted her hands in the air. Stones and rubble from the wall lifted from all around Crusiliux and floated back to their rightful places. She strode forward and placed her own hands on the red dragon. "Shift!"

Crusiliux shrank smaller and smaller, finally changing into a tall dark orc with brilliant red hair. Her left leg and right arm were bent at awkward angles, though the damage had been healed and the bones had been knit together ... unevenly.

Arcus winced. "Let me h–"

"Do *not* touch me, *mortal*," Crusiliux repeated, venom lacing her voice.

"Arcus, back up." The elf waited for him to comply, then she created a shining silver cage around Crusiliux, not unlike the cages that had been erected around Celeste and Tarnelius. "Sister, with a three-quarters majority we have declared this war to be over. We must strike a balance, and we must work together to the best of our ability to set things back to the way they were. The pact is destroyed, and we will join the world. You have a choice to make: you can join us and help to maintain the balance, or you can refuse and I will leave you trapped inside that box for the rest of your immortal existence."

Countless numbers of orcs streamed through the castle gate into the castle.

"What of the other pact, sister?" Crusiliux demanded.

Axistra turned to the kedistam. "Seratrix?"

The kedistam shook her head and looked to the ground.

Axistra nodded. "The other pact remains in place."

Crusiliux glared past them all at the retreating army. "It seems I have no choice. Let me out. I will comply."

"Other pact?" asked Arcus as Axistra banished the cage.

Seratrix looked sad. "Resurrection. Long ago, we swore not to interfere with the life cycles of mortals. More's the pity. I can think of hundreds here who died before their time."

"Why can't you make an exception?" demanded Arcus.

"Because of the trade-off," answered Axistra.

"Vampires ..." said Arcus.

"Nasty creatures. Much more powerful than any human, and virtually indestructible. Instruments of pure evil, they serve no one but themselves."

Vampires. Arcus remembered well. Shortly after Theri had died, they had come face to face with a particularly nasty specimen named Valen. He had enthralled Siobhan's squire and drained her dry. They had been powerless to stop him. Valen had also been responsible for the deaths of many other Mithran paladins, and for the spawning of scores of lesser undead. The world was a better place after his demise. "We killed one last year," said Arcus.

"You did no such thing," scoffed Crusiliux. "Valen is one of the last, and he has escaped even my nets. I have tried for years to claim him or get rid of him, but he was Tarextros' favorite. I suspect our brother may have helped him along. You can't kill a vampire unless you destroy his remains."

"But we did–"

"His mortal remains. The ones he has hidden in some hole even I can't track. I assure you he is still out there somewhere."

"Great."

"It is a shame I could not win him over. It is an even greater shame I cannot make more like him. An entire army of them would be …" Crusiliux noticed her sisters glaring at her. "What? They were fun, if a little hard to control."

"That is why we cannot allow resurrections," continued Seratrix. "We dragons once used magic that returned life to the dead with impunity. My cohort, Aanhextrios, and I were the most skilled at it. We could return someone fully to life as if they had never died. It was a thing of beauty."

"Khellendriox and I were able to reincarnate those who had fallen," added Axistra. "We could draw the souls back and place them into new bodies. Tarextros and Crusiliux could only return false life. They created the greater vampires."

"False life?" shrieked Crusiliux. "Our children were awe-inspiring, powerful. They were superior beings."

"Indeed," Seratrix said. "They were far *too* powerful. They would have upset the balance and overrun the world. In addition, the spirits of the dead move on into the next stage of their journeys. Forcing them to come back is rarely what they want. Since they don't get a choice in the matter, it is cruel. Many of them cried when pulled away from their afterlife and those they loved there. It is better that *all* forms of resurrection magic remain forbidden."

The last of the surviving orcs hurried into the castle, followed by the green dragon, Khellendriox. "Get to the portal," he bellowed, blasting emerald flame behind them to urge them on. Once the last few were out of sight, he shifted into a dwarf and joined Arcus and the other three dragons. He was tall for his race and had an emerald green beard and hair, the same shade as his scales. "That should be the last of them, but we should make sure before we destroy the portal." The dwarf cleared his throat. "We must set details of this truce. It is not enough to leave the orcs on their own, at least until the Lumernians rebuild. Crusiliux, you have to police your orcs and make certain the humans are left alone for at least the next decade. In Aanhextrios' absence, I will keep an eye on the humans. Are we in agreement?"

The other three dragons nodded.

"We have much to do," said Seratrix. "Khellendriox, please accompany Crusiliux in making sure the orcs have all gone through the portal, then destroy it on both sides. Axistra and I will set to work on repairing Lumernia structurally."

Arcus looked to the ruined gate to the west. "What of my wife and friends? Did you see them out there?"

Khellendriox cocked his head. "I'm not sure who those people are. I saw elves and many humans. You should go and see. We can take over from here."

"Arcus?" Crusiliux hissed. "I do not like how this ended. If the positions were reversed, I would have certainly killed *you*. That said, you defeated a dragon and you showed mercy. You have proven yourself a force to be reckoned with, and you have earned my respect."

Arcus nodded and limped through the gate.

Chapter Twenty-Three
Moving On

Joseph held Victoria's body to his chest, his tears dropping steadily onto her face.

The battle had been brutal, and many members of the resistance had fallen. Things had looked grim for the resistance until an enormous green dragon had flown overhead, putting an end to the conflict. It had breathed emerald flame into the air, then landed gracefully in the park, forcing the orcs to scatter.

"This war is over," he had growled. "We are putting things back the way they should be. Get back to the portal, or be destroyed."

No one had moved.

All around the courtyard, green dragons had appeared. No, copies of green dragons. Six of them. They'd blocked out buildings as if they weren't there, filling in the space with their colossal size. If Joseph hadn't been so broken, he would have been awestruck. Like him, this dragon was an illusionist.

"I said, return to the portal *now!*" the dragon had roared. The six dragon clones had breathed emerald fire in unison, though no heat came from them.

The orcs turned tail and raced back to the castle.

The dragons had waited silently as the orc horde vacated the city center. Then, one by one, they had each winked out of existence until only the real one was left. He'd turned and lifted back into the air, following the orcs.

Now the survivors milled around uncertainly, trying to take stock of the situation.

"Joseph? Joseph! What happened?" Celeste hurtled toward him. Joseph blinked, confused. The dragons had surprised him so much he must have lost concentration on his invisibility spell.

She rushed to him, her hands already blue as she laid them on Victoria. Siobhan and Tarnelius looked on with obvious concern, but worked diligently to heal the other injured.

Nothing happened. Celeste's spell had no effect. Joseph had known it wouldn't. It was too late.

His Vicki was gone. He had failed her. Tears ran unchecked down his face. He didn't bother to wipe them away.

Joseph kissed Victoria's already cooling forehead. He grew numb, the shock delaying the inevitable waves of pain he knew he'd soon feel.

Celeste's large green eyes filled with tears. "I'm so sorry," she whispered.

"She ... she forgave me."

Celeste hugged him, crushing Victoria's body between them. Long moments passed in silence. The battle had ended so abruptly, and there were so many questions as to what had happened, but at the moment, he didn't care about any of them.

"Arcus!" Siobhan screamed. Siobhan had a large gash on her face and her armor was dented and damaged, but she seemed none the worse for wear. Arcus was nearly bowled over as he staggered through the ruined gate into the city center to join his friends. He looked horrible. His clothes were ripped, singed and melted to him in places–it looked like he had been on the losing end of a fire spell or dragonfire. Arcus grabbed Siobhan and held her to him, his smile large but tired.

Joseph was forced to look away. He couldn't bear to witness his friend's joyful reunion with his wife. The pain of his loss was too recent, too great. Breaking his stare on the happy couple, he caught sight of Tarnelius as he tended to the fallen and dying. His arm was bent at an odd angle, gashes covered his entire body. It seemed the only ones to survive uninjured were Joseph and Celeste … if you could call the torture he was experiencing "uninjured."

"I'm sorry, Joseph. I have to go help those who … the ones who are …" Celeste trailed off.

"Go. Help those who need it. Don't worry about me."

Celeste patted him on the shoulder and ran off.

Joseph marched west, carrying Victoria toward the main gate.

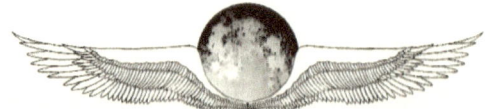

"I can't believe you're alive!" Siobhan exclaimed. "When Joseph and Victoria came to get me and I found out you had gone ahead with Celeste, I was sure I would never see you again!"

"I'm sorry for that," Arcus said. "Time was of the essence if we were to rescue Tarnelius. None of that was as I intended it. Matter of fact, I planned to find magic items and wait for the paladins to arrive." Though nothing had gone according to plan,

Arcus was nearly overcome with pride at his victory and joy that his wife and friends were alive. The rest could be fixed.

"The paladins … oh no! They'll have wasted a trip."

"No. We need them still. Lumernia has to be rebuilt. Someone must be appointed ruler. Rashnu's tenure as the capital city's paladin god has lasted long enough. Perhaps it's Mithra's turn now."

"What a great idea. In the meantime, you can tell me exactly what happened while I take care of you. These burns look serious, and your leg–"

"Others are in more dire need of healing than I. We'll see to them first, then take care of me." Arcus kissed her gently.

Celeste, Tarnelius, Siobhan and Arcus spread out and made short work of healing the remaining resistance survivors, as well as Tarnelius' and Siobhan's injuries.

It turned out that Tarnelius' new arm wasn't as limber as his old one yet. He had been disarmed and had shifted into his liger form to compensate for his lack of weapon.

Siobhan had sent a badly injured Apollo back to the celestial world so he could heal. She assured Arcus the palomino would fully recover.

Conner's body was found among the mass of dead, where the fighting had been heaviest. Though he hadn't been a trained warrior or mage, he had charged in with the rest and done his best before finally succumbing to his wounds. He had learned a lot about fighting during his time as resistance leader, but in the end it wasn't enough.

The dragons had the buildings reassembled in no time, then they left without preamble or ceremony. Arcus suspected they were trying to avoid being asked about resurrections.

Approximately two hundred people had survived, seventy of them men. Not much to rebuild an empire with, but they would have to do the best they could with what they had.

"You all should go back and collect whatever belongings you may have." Celeste surveyed those who were left. "You have all fought well. Lumernia is free, though the cost was high. Return to your old homes. It's safe now. The paladins of Mithra are still on their way. Until they arrive, we will stay here to ensure your safety."

The crowd cheered, but the sound was weak, exhausted, filled with grief. Indeed, they had triumphed, though you could hardly tell it, to look at the survivors. They would move on and rebuild in time but, for now, the victory was bittersweet.

Tarnelius joined them after finally locating his lost weapon. "Where should we go?"

"Conner's old house," Celeste answered with a small smile. "I have a feeling he would have liked that."

"I doubt Joseph will share the sentiment," surmised Arcus. "Where is Joseph, anyway? And Victoria?"

Celeste looked to where she had last seen him, but Joseph was gone. "I don't know. He was here but a moment ago. Victoria didn't ... she didn't make it. Maybe he needed time alone. If he's not comfortable with staying in Conner's house, there are lots of other choices."

"I should go look for him," said Arcus, his hands flashing blue as he healed his injured knee.

"Yes," Celeste pulled a jar of ointment from her bag, "but not until I tend to those burns. Then you can go while the rest of us clean this mess up."

Joseph carried Victoria's body out the main gate and located the place he and Arcus had sent Katherine on to the next stage of her journey.

He laid Victoria on the ground, noticing for the first time how much of her blood covered him. He hadn't thought this plan out well, as he had never been good with fire magic, but he dutifully gathered an assortment of kindling and laid her on top of it. He was trying to use his lightning orbs to light a branch on fire, when he heard a familiar voice clear his throat behind him.

"You're right on time," said Joseph. "I … could use your help."

Arcus knelt down next to Victoria and smoothed the matted hair from her face. "I'm so sorry for your loss, Joseph."

"She forgave me."

"She loved you."

"I know. I was an idiot. I didn't deserve her forgiveness."

Arcus sighed and pointed at Victoria. Fire shot from his finger and ignited the kindling.

Joseph stared, his eyes wide with horror, as the woman who held his heart burned. "Goodbye, Vicki. I'm sure I'll see you again someday. I love you so much, and I always will. I'm so sorry I was such a fool, and I'm sorry that I failed you."

They watched in silence until she turned to ash.

"How did you know where to find me?"

"I knew where I would go if I were in your position."

"What happens now?"

"Now? Now we pick up the pieces. We stay with the Lumernians until the paladins arrive. We heal the land. We heal ourselves. We figure out how to move on."

"Move on? How? I don't think I can."

Arcus gripped Joseph's shoulder. "You take it one day at a time."

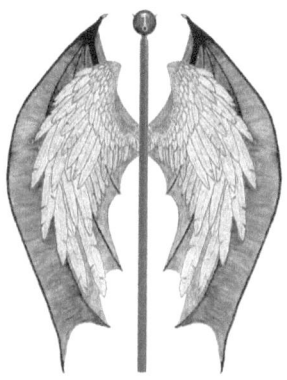

Epilogue
The End of an Era

Two weeks later, Joseph stood on the wall of Lumernia looking out over the crashing sea. His heart felt like it had shattered into a thousand pieces. He understood then that the elves had it easy: they would never be forced to live without that one person who completes them, who makes them feel alive. One elf never survived long without the other. That sounded … blissful. Joseph longed for peace. Oppressive, all-consuming anger and pain had replaced the numbness. It felt as if a huge weight pressed down on his chest. He placed his hands upon the battlement and squeezed his eyes shut, trying to focus on the simple task of taking one breath after the other. Tears leaked down his cheeks. He couldn't stop them. Truth be told, he didn't want to.

He wasn't doing a good job of taking things one day at a time, and had pushed everyone away, choosing solitude. He'd spent most of the last two weeks up here on the wall. Whenever anyone approached him, he snarled and demanded to be left alone.

The paladins had arrived over a week before, and had started the process of rebuilding the city and appointing the monarchy. They had sent out emissaries asking for people to move in to help reestablish the kingdom. The three druids had set to work healing the lands and cultivating the fields surrounding the capital. Everything was returning to normal.

Almost everything.

"Victoria," he whispered, his voice agonized. "I'm so sorry. I'm so sorry that I failed you." He heard a noise behind him but didn't care. If he was lucky, it would be the angel of death who had come to put an end to his suffering.

The footsteps stopped.

"Joseph?" The voice was feminine, but had a musical lilt to it. It held untold centuries in its depths.

"What do you want, Celeste? Unless your healing magic can cure a broken heart, I have no need for your platitudes."

"The ship is getting ready to sail, to take us all south to the kedistam lands. Remember? I told you about it. We have left you alone as long as we could. After we are done there, do you want us to head back to Izmar to see if we can find her family?"

A strange sound filled the air, a cry of pain. It took a moment for Joseph to realize the sound had come from him. "No … no. She was estranged from her family. They probably died during that fight in Izmar, anyway."

"But we could find out for sure …"

Joseph sighed. "I'll go."

"We're a team. We can go with you."

"No. You should head south as you planned, but I've decided not to go. I cannot leave this place right now. I will stay.

We are no longer a team. When I am able to do so, I will make my own way back."

"Joseph, that's incredibly far to walk," Celeste argued.

"I've done it before, I can do it again. Perhaps this is my penance for not going with Arcus in the first place. Though, if I had, I never would have had my chance with her. Perhaps that would have been better ... perhaps she'd still be alive."

Footsteps sounded on the steps behind them. "Let him go, Celeste. This is his way."

Arcus appeared even more unkempt than usual. Joseph didn't dare to dream that Arcus had even cared one iota about what his supposed best friend had gone through. Joseph turned back to the battlements and looked back out over the ocean. "He's a coward," Arcus spat.

Joseph didn't turn around. "Your opinion, while noted, is irrelevant. I said I would go and I will."

"You're a coward for turning your back on your friends. It's been two weeks. I know you're still hurting, but you can't shove the world away while you wallow. You can't shove *us* away. At least when you left us last year you didn't insult us with this pretense at bravery. No, then you accepted your cowardice. Embraced it. In some ways, you've become worse now. A true friend would accept help when he needs it. A true friend wouldn't abandon his friends simply because the road became difficult to travel."

Joseph whirled around. "A true friend would have backed me up when I asked–no, begged–Victoria to stay out of this back in Izmar. You lied. You said we would protect each other, watch each other's backs, keep each other safe. I didn't realize that your protection only included people *you* consider friends. You never liked her. You always used to tell me that. You even said something to that extent in the mage tower two weeks ago! I should have never trusted y–"

Arcus grabbed Joseph by the throat, cutting off his airway. Flame licked up and down Arcus' free hand, which was clenched into a fist. Arcus appeared to be barely holding on to his restraint. "Celeste, go back to the ship."

"I won't. You both have to stop acting like children."

"Celeste. Go back to the ship now. I need to have a talk with my so-called best friend. Please."

Celeste hesitated, but neither man moved a muscle. With an exasperated sigh, she turned and headed down the stairs.

"This isn't about me," Arcus growled. "You know good and well that I had nothing to do with her death. I wasn't even on the same battlefield!"

"Just do it," Joseph gasped. "End it. End my pain. I had hoped for the angel of death, I just didn't expect him to be you."

Arcus shoved him away. "This wallowing is unhealthy. Do you think I don't understand?"

"No. I know you don't understand. You've never loved and lost. You've never been so consumed by someone that–"

"That what? Your problem is that you feel guilty. You two made quite a pair. You ran to the first woman you found, and Victoria murdered the poor girl for being unfortunate enough to have crossed your path. Should either of you have forgiven the other? Probably not. For reasons I will never understand, you forgave her immediately. You surrendered your leverage and practically begged at her feet for her forgiveness. She finally granted it, and then you lost her before the true meaning of what she'd given you could sink in. I may still have Siobhan, and gods willing, she will not be taken from me as Victoria was from you, but that does *not* mean that I don't know what it feels like to lose someone. Damn it, Joseph! You aren't the only one who has ever suffered. You know that both my parents died when I was only five years old … at the hands of the orcs. Then I lost Damon. He was like a father to me! What was it you said that day while I was sitting there in agony? Something like … 'When did you become such a whiner? The Arcus I knew wouldn't let the misery of the present control his future; he would call me an idiot and move on. Where is that Arcus? Where is my friend?' You were right. I didn't curl up and beg for death. I felt the pain, accepted the pain and grew past the pain. That is what you are going to do now. Don't you dare tell me that I don't understand. Now, are you going to get on that ship, or do I have to carry you out of here?"

Joseph drew himself up to his full height. "No, Arcus. We're done here. I'm not going. This conversation is over. This friendship is over. You may think yourself in charge, but you are not and you never will be. Get out of here."

Flames exploded along Arcus' left arm as well. "Don't test me, Joseph."

"I'm not. I've never been more serious." With a wave of his hand, Joseph vanished. A moment later four of Joseph's doppelgangers appeared around Arcus.

Nine Years Later …

Rextros ran through the field, his hand skimming the overlong grass. He had grown surprisingly fast and had the height and build of a tumasi twice his age. His body was changing rapidly, and he was experiencing strange and terrifying dreams that he could not explain. Dreams of flying, of stretching his enormous ebony wings and soaring, fire bursting from his gut and out through his mouth. But that was preposterous. His kind had no wings. Only the birds and the pterodactyls had wings, and none of them breathed fire.

He ran and ran, unsure of his destination. He didn't know what he ran from, only that he had to keep running. His skin was too tight, and the pumping of his arms and legs helped lessen the pressure. Glancing down, he was astonished to see the shadow of massive wings stretching out on either side of him.

Rextros stumbled and fell hard to the ground, rolling until his momentum ceased. The shadow of the wings slid smoothly over him and continued on. He looked up and his jaw dropped.

Flying far above his head was a massive beast with shimmering blue scales. Sunlight reflected and sparkled, hurting his eyes. The creature's four legs were pulled up tight against its torso, the same way a bird tucked its feet away in flight. It had a long, sinewy tail and an equally long neck with spikes along the back. Twin horns jutted gracefully from the beast's forehead and curved back, extending past its head.

The blue flying lizard turned its head and looked down at him, its jaws forming some creepy semblance of a smile. Rextros hunkered down into the grass, terrified that, whatever this was, it planned to eat him. The monster leaned to the left and changed direction, dropping altitude quickly.

Rextros stopped watching and cowered. He both heard and felt the impact as the great lizard landed. He braced himself for the end. He listened hard but didn't hear anything that sounded remotely like the great lumbering beast coming for him.

Suddenly, he felt a hand on his shoulder.

Rextros yelped and flipped around to see who was there. His friend, Ratrix, stood over him, looking down at him in concern. She was beautiful, her fur a soft red color. Unlike him, her face and ears resembled a fox. His black fur was far more reminiscent of a jackal. Rextros tackled her and yanked her into the grass with him.

"Shh!" he admonished. "There's something here. Some monstrous blue lizard!"

Ratrix smirked and rolled out from under him. She stood up and held out her hand. "There is no danger here, Rextros. Come. Walk with me."

Rextros was horrified. He was convinced his friend was about to be eaten right in front of him, and that he would be next. Still, nothing seemed to be happening. Slowly he stood up and took her hand. He scanned the horizon for signs of the lizard, but there were none.

"I'm not crazy. I really saw it."

"I believe you," she answered simply.

They walked on, eventually finding themselves at the mouth of a gigantic cave. Ratrix pulled on his hand to lead him inside. After a moment's hesitation, he followed her.

"You have grown so fast, my friend."

"I know," he answered glumly. "I no longer feel as a child does, but I've been told that I am only nine years old today. The shaman fears me, I think. My mother doesn't know what to make of me."

"Have you never wondered why?"

"I wonder why every minute of every day, even when I'm asleep."

"You are having dreams?"

Rextros nodded.

"Tell me about them."

"No, I can't. They are nothing but foolish dreams."

"Do you dream you can fly?"

Rextros stared at her. Her strange golden eyes that were so much like his burned into him. "H–how did you know?"

She walked around behind him and stroked a finger down his back, making goosebumps rise under his fur. Rextros knew she was examining the tattoo on his back. It wasn't a real tattoo, it was a birthmark that looked exactly like folded bat wings.

"Do you trust me, Rextros?"

"Of course," he answered without thinking. How could he think while she stroked his back like that? His friend was beautiful, all right, and his body was changing, practically by the second. It was a shame. He knew she would only ever see him as a child.

"I think you are old enough to know the truth."

"Truth?" His brain was fuzzy, unfocused.

She leaned close to him and whispered in his ear. "Close your eyes."

He did as she asked. His back was to the cave entrance, so he couldn't see any sources of light. She took her fingers off him. He felt the loss of her touch like a blow. Behind him, he heard a strange scratching sound. He couldn't place it, and had never heard anything like it before.

"You can open them now. Open your eyes and look at me."

Rextros turned around. His gasped, fur standing on end. The blue lizard was in the cave with him. He scrambled backward until his feet slipped on some loose gravel and he fell hard on his back.

"It is a pity," the big lizard said. "You have not even grown used to size of this body and now it will be necessary to become accustomed to an even bigger one."

"R–Ratrix?" he stuttered.

"My name is Seratrix. I am the sapphire dragon. I have spent many years watching you closely. Your name is really

Tarextros–at least I think it is. I can sense some of my lost cohort, Aanhextrios the Gold, in you."

"Dragon? You must be mistaken. I'm no dragon. I'm just Rextros, the tumasi."

"All right, Rextros the tumasi. Have it your way. What of the strange things that always seem to happen to you? Why did you grow so fast? Why do you have the dreams you do? What of your mother? You look nothing like her, your eyes are like mine. What of the stories? The tales of how you could speak as a newborn, of how you brought your mother back from the dead? How did you save the village from that fire two years ago?"

"I didn't! There was a freak storm and–"

"Release your wings, Tarextros!" Her voice boomed out into the cave, causing dust and loose dirt to fall.

"I have no wings!"

"Look inside yourself. Release them! I know your skin must be feeling tight by now …"

Rextros turned away. He knew it was unwise to turn his back on a lizard large enough to swallow him in one bite, but he didn't care. A moment later, he felt a warm hand on his back.

He whirled around and recoiled from his friend, now in her tumasi form. She grabbed hold of him as he backed away, and he could do nothing more than stare into her golden lizard-eyes as she reached a hand up to him. She placed it flat on his chest. There came a blinding flash of light.

Visions filled his head. Stumbling forward, he saw an apparition of a black dragon living inside a volcano. As he watched, the dragon created a bed out of a hoard of coins and gems and lay down.

He saw a gold dragon flying overhead, its burnished scales flashing in the sunlight as he chased a sparkling blue dragon.

Dazzling golden flame brightened the night sky. A reddish hue colored the world … why was the moon red?

The black dragon dug through a frozen wasteland, spitting purple flames to melt some of the snow. The beast found a staff and grabbed it, transforming into a human before vanishing.

The gold dragon and the black were fighting in the air, combining their brute strength with their incredible magic. All at once, Rextros' perspective shifted. *He* was the black dragon. He felt his body go stiff and immobile as stone, then knew the agony of death. The young tumasi cried out as the vision showed him his body crumbling away.

The vision changed once more … now he was the gold dragon, forcing an impossibly strong force into the ground. Rextros panicked. He was trapped under the earth. The gold dragon fought the thing he was entombed with, his golden claws digging deep into the shadowy monster. Rextros experienced the misery of having his wings ripped from his back, his blood flowing to mingle with the god's.

The god's? Is that what this was? He lashed out for all he was worth. Ignoring the pain, Rextros fought with tooth and claw, only stopping when he realized his opponent had vanished into nothing. All at once, the world became bathed in a golden glow. He looked up, trying to figure out what was happening, only to see the world from very high up. So high that he couldn't focus on anyone below. Rextros looked at himself … he had become the moon. With a pang, he remembered the beautiful blue dragon with eyes the same golden color as the moon that now flew in the sky. The same color he was.

The visions ceased. Everything went black. Rextros turned his head but couldn't make anything out.

"Tarextros, release your wings," a voice whispered, the sound caressing him.

Rextros twisted his neck to the side, trying to pop his neck. He rotated his shoulders. Instinctively, he understood what he had to do. As if his brain always knew where those muscles were, he flexed his shoulders back, and back further still. Wings popped out of his shoulder blades. His neck lengthened and rose up from the ground. A tail exploded from his spine and whipped around. When he finally stopped growing, he looked into the eyes of Seratrix, the blue dragon from his vision. She stared at him strangely.

"Why are you looking at me like that?"

"Look at yourself."

Rextros swiveled his head to either side. His scales were black, blacker than the darkest night. Running up and down his wings were golden veins, the same shade as the golden dragon's scales, the same color as its eyes. They ran gracefully down every curve of his bat-like wings, and covered the bony ridge at the top, which ended in a single talon. Looking down at his body, he saw the same golden veins covering him from head to toe.

"What does this mean?"

The End.

Appendix

Races: There are six major races in the land of Altierra. Two born to each of the three original deities. While each race was created to reflect the principles of their creator, they were also granted free will and are able to decide whether to follow the principles of one of the others, if they so choose.

Elves: Children of the earth; guardians of Altierra. Elves have taken up Kamara's cause after the fall. They, more than the other races, have learned to tap into the powers of the earth released after the death of the neutral demigods. Their great lifespan and wariness of the other races has made many grow apathetic. Elves never age and are considered immortal. However, after several hundred years, some of them seem to lose their will to live. When this happens, they become more and more tired and withdraw into themselves, eventually falling asleep and never waking up again. This is called "being lost to the Fade." Still, elves' great memory and skill support their task as protectors of Altierra. Elves all have large, otherworldly, green eyes, with hair color in varying shades of blond.

Elves inhabit forested areas. There are large villages in the Kayalik Mountains, as well as the Silver Isles. There is also a smaller village on the southern continent.

Many elves are forced into arranged marriages. They are ruled by customs and traditions, which dictates proper elven decorum. They tend towards formality, and as such do not often have intimate relationships unless they are married, which they call being bonded. The bonding ceremony is a ritual that, when complete, binds the two together, forever. Each of their souls is split and shared with the other. They then gain telepathy in regards to each other, as well as the ability to experience one another's emotions, and to always know how to locate their mate. If one is killed, the other is usually not far behind, as they lose half of themselves at the same time.

Dark Elves are another of Kamara's children, though they prefer to live underground. Unlike their cousins, their skin is dark in color, and they have bright red eyes. They are able to see in the dark as if it were as bright as day, and due to this, have difficulty with the brightness of the outdoors.

Dwarves: Some call them Kamara's prodigal sons, because they seem to care nothing for nature. Dwarves seek to be left to themselves as they delve and tinker in their mines. Their greatest joy is creation and construction. Unfortunately, this leads them to build only for the sake of building, while they ignore the consequences of their actions. Many a great dwarven discovery has been tainted by evil and found its way into the arsenal of the orc hordes. Most dwarves tend toward agoraphobia, making them uncomfortable outside of their mountain homes.

Humans: These possess the most diversity of any race, and have founded cities and villages throughout most of Altierra. They show great drive and curiosity, exploring and settling as they go. Despite being children of Aurinko, they can also be strongly influenced by Kuunkierto, and as such have a great capacity for evil. Humanity's greatest flaw is their propensity for arrogance, so even the greatest armies of good can unwittingly cause great evil. Humans vary widely in appearance and can adapt to perform any profession or skill.

Kedistam: The kedistam resemble the larger feline species in bipedal form. They call themselves Aurinko's firstborn. Kedistam are noble yet savage. They prefer a simpler life on the southern continent in jungle villages, and as desert nomads. They are wild but not cruel, and show kindness and mercy unless crossed. Many embrace the path of druid or shaman and count the elves as allies.

Tumasi: Where orcs are wild and savage, tumasi are cunning and organized. They, too, crave power, though they also respect order. They know their place in the great pack, but work and scheme to improve their station. A small number of them are able to see the strength of good, and to that end, seek peace and order. Tumasi mainly dwell on the southern continent. They resemble bipedal forms of the various canid species: wolves, jackals, or foxes.

Orcs: The hordes can be chaos incarnate. The orc nation seeks power that brings misery to those they conquer. Unfortunately for them, their chaotic nature tends to tear down any progress they make as tribes fight for power within the horde. The one thing orcs recognize is strength, and they even respect natural forces. This has allowed the druids to easily keep them in check and out of their woods. Orcs mostly inhabit the southeast desert areas.

Classes:

Druids: Those blessed by Kamara, or any of her children, with nature magic are known as druids. They are the primary healers that still remain in Altierra. Most druids are elves, as they are the race most likely to follow the path of nature and balance, though they may be found among any race. Their spells mostly channel through them in natural colors such as blues and greens. They wear very little armor, as metal separates them from their communion with the earth. Many do not bother to carry, or learn how to use, weaponry. Often, they will choose an animal to accompany them, as they are able to speak to them through telepathy. Druids are shape-shifters; they can take the form of animals or, in some cases, plants. Their magic encompasses the power of nature, allowing them to control the weather, wield natural elements, as well as heal others.

Paladins: True paladins are rare. These are holy warriors serving the memory of one of four paladin deities. Once they have completed a lengthy training period, they are knighted and gain powers granted to them by the essences of their gods. They wear heavy armor and are expert swordsmen. In addition, they are gifted the ability to channel holy power through the symbol of their deity, which they wear around their neck. They have the ability to use healing and protection magic, which shows as a flashy gold or silver color when channeled. However, in most cases, they do not have to cast; the magic just flows out of them as they will it. When they are knighted they receive an intelligent magical steed from the celestial realms to serve as their companion. As time goes on, this animal becomes even more powerful.

If a paladin knowingly commits any act of evil or behaves in a way that would go against the laws of their deity, they lose their steed and their magical abilities immediately. They then become warriors.

Warriors: These are a very diverse group. They are often trained in the use of many different weapons and armors. Some warriors take an intellectual view on their training, wishing to learn many different styles of combat. Others become warriors out of necessity, and as such are more inclined to learn as they go. Many are strong, using their brute strength to overpower their enemies, while others make up for lack of strength with grace and finesse. They do not wield magic of any type.

Many warriors are "false paladins." These men and women call themselves paladins, and in fact, think they are paladins. However, they do not uphold the laws of the paladin deities and have no magical abilities at all.

Sorcerers: Wielders of arcane magic, all sorcerers have been blessed by the dragons. This is not a class someone could learn merely by studying; the mage must be born with the ability. Once the sorcerer comes of age, the powers begin to manifest. This is the time when a sorcerer is able to tell what kind of magic they naturally specialize in. Some are seers, and are especially skilled in divinations. Others wield elemental magic, compulsions, enchantments, or necromancy. Once the mage becomes aware of his or her abilities, it is important that they become trained in its use. An untrained sorcerer is dangerous to themselves and others, as their magic becomes wild, prone to unpredictability during times of emotional duress.

Once the mage begins training, they are able to memorize a certain number of spells. Although the kind they specialize in will always be more powerful, they are able to learn spells of other types if they so choose.

There are a few mages that do not permanently memorize spells, but instead read books daily to learn spells. Each day they have to reread them and relearn them, even if they knew them the day before. This has an advantage in that they can cast a broader range of spells from day to day, but limits them in that they actually must take the time to learn every day or they cannot cast at all.

Sorcerers rarely carry weapons other than staves. They also may carry a dagger, which is easily concealed beneath their clothes. They do not wear armor, as it limits their freedom of movement, making the intricate movements required for casting more difficult.

Scouts: Those that choose the path of the scout are masters of stealth and expert skirmishers. They know where and how to strike to have the most effect. They are usually dexterous, and are able to reach their opponent's vulnerable areas with skillful use of acrobatics. They are excellent trackers and can find and disable traps with ease. They only wear light armor and are often proficient in the lighter weapons.

Rangers: Like scouts, rangers are expert trackers. They specialize in either archery or by learning to fight with weapons in both hands. They are stealthy and skilled at blending into their surroundings, unseen and unheard, making them excellent hunters. Rangers are at home with nature, just as druids are, and often create bonds of friendship with a companion animal in the same manner. They train extensively on learning the weak points of particular, oft seen, types of enemies, and are skilled at defeating them.

Clerics: True clerics are very rare in Altierra, though there are many charlatans who will try to trick the populace into believing their fake herbs and potions will help them. True clerics have been blessed by the remaining essences of the gods that once ruled over the land. Like paladins, they channel healing power and protections magic through a pendant bearing their chosen deity's symbol. Their spells are more powerful than a paladin's, but they lack the combat training. Because of this, they tend to use simpler weapons, but can wear pretty much any kind of armor.

Cyfuniad: This is the newest class in Altierra. Cyfuniads are sorcerers that are able to blend their arcane power with the divine power of a druid. In order to balance both aspects, the spellcaster must be highly adept in both trades. They continue to learn both kinds of magic as they go, and eventually learn to merge them both seamlessly, casting arcane spells while in an animal form, for example.

Deities:

The Three: Altierra, and the heavens above, were conceived by the Three. First, they made the Great Dragons and the demigods. Then, they formed the land, sea, and the stars in the sky. In the twilight of the world, the Three brought forth their favored races: Aurinko created humans and kedistam, Kamara made elves and dwarves, and Kuunkierto, the orcs and tumasi. They then joined with their creation and left the lesser gods to finish their work.

Aurinko: Greater god of order, light, and good. He was said to become the sun and bring light to the world.

Kamara: Greater goddess of nature, balance, and neutrality. She joined with Altierra and became the very land itself.

Kuunkierto: Greater god of the night, darkness, and evil. He became the moon to rule over the darkness.

Demigods: Other than the dragons, the demigods were the first children of the Three. Each one reflects an aspect of their god and was granted immense power. The demigods in turn helped complete Altierra and governed it before the war. They and their heralds were physically in the world and dwelt with the children of the Three. Many even brought forth other lesser races in an attempt to mimic the Three's creation. Most demigods do not use arcane magic, these being powers of the dragons. They have their own divine powers and can grant energies to their followers. Few true devotees of the gods remain in Altierra, and as such a true cleric or divine paladin is a strange sight.

When Kuunkierto returned to the world, his first strikes were against Kamara's children. Most fell before any organized resistance could be mustered, which kept them from allying with the armies of good. Tulpar and Demirei were able to rally with the followers of Aurinko, and together they were finally able to defeat Kuunkierto and his minions. After the war, the remaining deities left the world, making a pact to leave the mortals to forge their own destinies. Heralds could still intercede between mortals, and devotees could worship and possibly gain powers, but the gods would no longer directly interfere with the world. As time passed, the gods became more legend than memory to the shorter lived races, and very few truly devote themselves to their service. As the elves are the only race long lived enough to remember the gods, most others have forgotten them, and divine power is mostly thought of as myth in everyday life. Most elders of the various churches are not truly clerics and have no powers granted.

Followers of Aurinko:

Rashnu: The greater paladin god of justice, discipline and light. Chief of good demigods and allied closely with Mithra and Sarosh. Appeared as a king in full armor, with his rod of lordship and judgment scales. His followers were humans, paladins, knights and judges.

Mithra: She was the paladin goddess of honor, loyalty and truth. Also associated with Tulpar, lord of the horse. Appeared as a knight on a white charger. Her symbol is a lance and shield. She was revered by horsemen, paladins and constabulary.

Sarosh: The paladin god of order, obedience and repentance. It is said he learned magic from the dragons and many of his knights also practice the arts. He often appeared as a wizened old man or a squire. His symbol was an upright staff crossed with a pair of swords.

Melek: He was the paladin god of protection and chivalry, and was known as the Great Angel. He was mankind's guardian and fell in their defense, to end the Deity War. His symbol was a winged longsword.

Mertlek: Known as the god of bravery. He was often called reckless and carefree, but was fiercely loyal. He appeared as a muscular man or giant white tiger.

Tedavia: She was the goddess of healing and restoration. She knew no violence and sought only peace and rest for all. She did not hold her power back from any, and believed that all may find healing freely. It is said that she released her power unto Altierra when the gods left. Her symbol is two crossed palm branches.

Mikail: The god of hospitality, kindness and generosity. He often appeared as a fat monk or a happy bartender. He was the brother of Tedavia, and he opposed violence and sought peace and mirth. His symbol was a cup of mead.

Sevda: Called the goddess of love. She brought joy, light and love to all. Her gifts were given to all mortals who sought it. Her symbol was an outstretched hand.

Minions of Kuunkierto:

Sevash: The god of war and strife. Those who relish conflict bowed to him. Even supporters of good secretly called him the necessary evil. He appeared as a dark warlord, clad in heavy armor and wielding an axe and mace. The crossed axe and mace was his sigil.

Salgin: Plague, pestilence and disease were this god's domains. He loathed Tedavia and sought to undermine her with infection and sickness. He appeared either as a pale rider on a sickly horse or as a horde of vermin. His symbol was a rat skull.

Nefreti: The goddess of hate and spite. She loathed Sevda for her gifts of love and compassion. She appeared as a howling black jackal. Her symbol was a dagger thrust through a heart.

Aeshma: Twin sister to Nefreti, she was known as the goddess of wrath. She embodied anger and rage. She was impulsive and reckless, frequently striking out without thinking. She appeared as a rabid wolf or a raging barbarian.

Yalamar: Known as the prince of lies, he infected mortals' minds by spreading falsehoods and deceit. He was petty and vain, seeking to twist the truth and ruin lives. He often appeared as a serpent or a tall human with a benevolent appearance. His symbol was a coiled serpent with its forked tongue extended.

Indara: She was the goddess of panic and fear, and fed on the misery caused by her brethren. She was one of the few evil Demigods to die in the war.

Aazap: Known as the lord of pain. Like his sister, Indara, his power was enhanced by the other children of Kuunkierto. The two of them were both less powerful demigods, and acted more like servants to their greater brethren. He, too, fell in the war.

Children of Kamara:

Tengri: The god of the sky. He controlled the winds and returned water to Okanus with his rain. It was said that his death was the cause of great storms as his power has no master. His symbol was a storm cloud.

Orman: Known as the lord of the forest, and the father of woodland spirits. He sought the balance of life and death above all, closely associating with Umay and Azraiyl. His power was released to the druids when he fell in the war. His symbol was a baobab tree.

Okanus: The god of oceans and seas. The currents and tides were commanded by him. The deep ocean was his kingdom. He fell with his brothers in the war and now his powers rage unchecked in the oceans.

Deniz: The lesser god of rivers and lakes, and the lieutenant of Okanus. He collected the waters from the land to send back to the seas. He fell at his master's side.

Hayvan: The lord of all land animals, he created the great animal spirits. Of these, it is unknown how many fell with him during the war. However, their progeny became the dumb beasts of today.

Kartalia: Known as the goddess of birds. She was the wife of Hayvan. Creatures of the air were her children. The great air spirits were her servants. She fell at her husband's side.

Baalin: The god of fish and whales. His children dwelled in Okanus' and Deniz's realms, though Hayvan was his lord. He did not survive the war, dying alongside Okanus and Deniz.

Tulpar: The lesser god of horses and hooved creatures, and the servant of Hayvan. Tulpar was one of few neutral gods to survive the war, as he was protected by Mithra. It is believed they left together after the pact. His power is still seen in unicorns, pegasi, centaurs, minotaurs, and satyrs. His symbol was a running stallion.

Demirei: He was the god of earth, stone, and mining. He cared little for mortals, and was far more concerned with his mountains and underground caverns. However, the dwarves shared his passions and he shared many of his secrets with them. Though they are not his children, he is known as the Old Dwarf to many. His symbol is a black mountain.

Kavesh: The god of metalworking and smithing. Known as the inventor, Kavesh embodied creativity and practice. The workshop and forge were his temple. His works sometimes conflicted with the more natural gods of his order, as he strove for new creations above all else. His symbol was an anvil and hammer.

Umay: The goddess of fertility and rebirth. Though she is a goddess of Kamara, she often dealt with Sevda, Mikail, and Tedavia. This was her salvation, as she was with them at the beginning of the war and thereby under the protection of the armies of Aurinko.

Sakima: She was the goddess of music and bards. She gave her gifts to all races equally and all songs gave her joy. She was revered by bards.

Azraiyl: The god of death. The reaper. Many marked him as evil, but his job was merely to complete life's cycle. He was neither vicious nor cruel, only taking those whose time had passed. He dwelled alone and was untouched by the war.

Raziyl: The god of secrets, seer of the hidden. His specialties were the secrets and hidden lore of the world. He maintained great control, keeping his powers safe as both good and evil sought his knowledge to upset the balance. He was believed to have survived the war. His symbol was a golden key locked in a clear crystal.

Aydin: Called the god of knowledge, or the old scribe. To him, knowledge and ideas were the ultimate power on Altierra. He collected lore and stored it in a massive library hidden on his island, whose location was known only to him and his younger brother, Raziyl. He was lost in the Deity War and his library remains hidden. His symbol was an open tome.

Heralds: All of the deities created heralds to assist them and their mortal creations on Altierra. The Three created the dragons. Their children created the angels, demons and nature spirits. They are considered immortal, as they are immune to the ravages of time. However, they can be killed.

Dragons: Six great dragons were the first creation, even predating the demigods. They acted as heralds of the Three, with a pair aligned with each god. They are truly immortal, for if they are slain, their soul is reborn as a child to one of the greater races. The race seems to be whichever is favored by the dragon. The child is obviously different, with great power even from birth. When they reach maturity, they fully realize who they are and become the great dragon, reborn. Dragons are shape-shifters and can take many forms in addition to that of their favored race. They have also spawned many children over the years including drakes, dinosaurs, wyverns and sea serpents. All arcane magic comes from the dragons.

Aanhextrios:

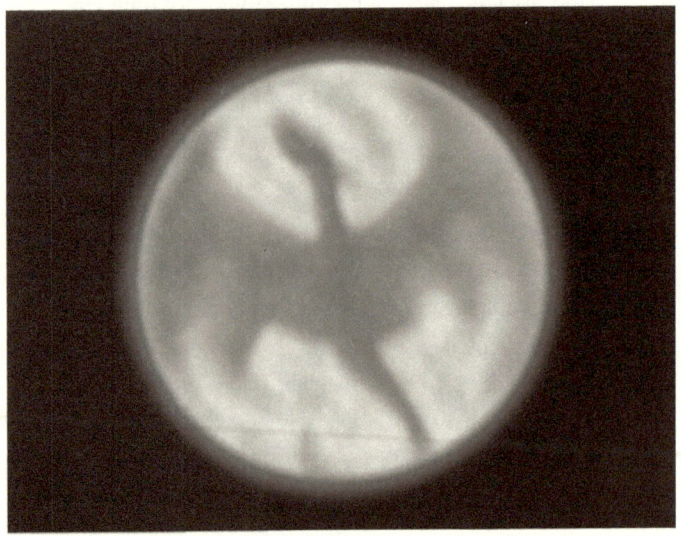

This male dragon of Aurinko favored humans. His scales were brilliant gold, and his lair was hidden in the glacial isles northwest of Izmar. He was trapped in the northern tombs during the second battle against Kuunkierto, and since became the god of the moon.

Seratrix:

She is the sapphire colored dragon of Aurinko. She favors the kedistam and makes her lair in the south jungle.

Axistra:

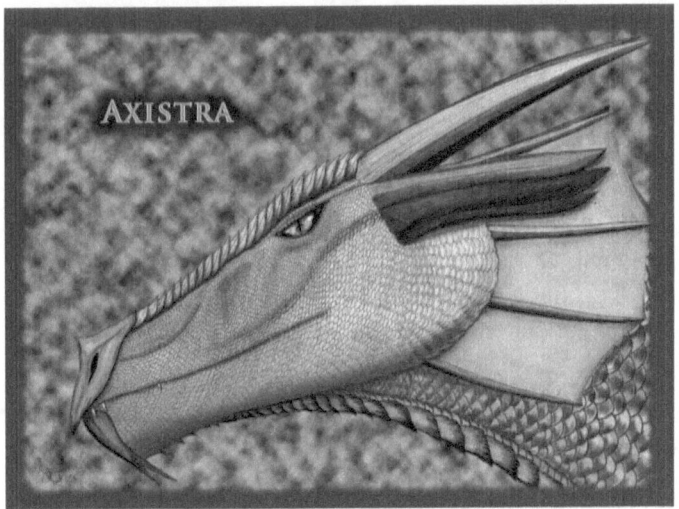

The female dragon of Kamara has shining silver scales. Elves are her favored race. She dwells in the Castle in the Clouds, hidden far above the hills south of elven lands.

Khellendriox:

The male dragon of Kamara dwells in the mountains south of the dwarven capital, as they are his favored race. His scales are a sparkling emerald.

Crusiliux:

This female dragon of Kuunkierto favors the orcs. She dwells on the islands south of Lumernia. She is the one dragon whose location is widely known and some of the black orcs worship her.

Tarextros:

He was the onyx dragon of Kuunkierto. His scales were black as the deepest night, and his favored race were tumasi. He died in the second battle of the northern tombs, and his current location is unknown.

Vampires: True vampires are not heralds of any sort, but were created by the dragons of Kuunkierto. They can appear to be from any race, as they are but corpses reanimated to unholy life. The vampire is not the person they were in life; their souls are replaced by the spirit of a demon. They steal from the life force of others, in the form of blood, to keep themselves strong and to be able to recharge their powers.

Vampires are skilled in dark magic, especially if the original host was also skilled in magic. Regardless, all vampires possess the ability to phase into mist at will. In this form, they are incorporeal; they may not cast spells or manipulate items unless the spell is one that may be performed by force of mind alone. Vampires are sensitive to the sun. They may walk outside during the day, but they are severely weakened by the sun's effects. This penalty is eliminated by shifting into mist form.

All vampires are able to use mind-affecting spells, and they can create different types of lesser undead from the bodies of their victims. When one of the evil dragons creates a vampire, they choose an item that was important to the mortal host during their lifetime. The item, known as a phylactery, sustains the unnatural life required by the vampire. If a vampire is slain, they revert to mist form and seek out this item, which is hidden away inside their coffin. Once there, they are able to regenerate in a few days' time until they are strong enough to leave their tomb and feed themselves. The practice of creating vampires has been forbidden, and all of the known existing ones were destroyed.

Vertassa: The vertassa are similar to vampires, but were created by the mortal races. These beings crave blood to survive, and will hunt with single-minded purpose. They do not have any magic, but do possess supernatural strength and speed. They are allergic to the sun and die immediately if exposed to it. They may also be killed by being stabbed through the heart, by being beheaded, or by exposure to sunlight. They are created using specific rituals, which are cast over a body that has been dead for no more than one week. In addition, they can procreate by draining the blood of their victims, and then giving their own blood to them to drink.

Angels: The heralds of Aurinko's children are classified as angels. They are powerful beings and are blessed with gifts from their creators. Most, like the Seraphs, Devas and Archangels, have large feathery wings in white, silver, or gold. They wield god-granted magic such as healing spells and protection magic, and most are skilled with martial weapons such as swords. There are a few species that are smaller. One notable species, the Custos angel, has no solid form and appears as a ball of light. While once there were organized angel armies, most angels today are elusive creatures who can only be found if they allow it. A very small number of them hide among Altierra's people, with their wings cloaked to keep themselves secret. Unlike the dragons, if an angelic herald is killed, he or she is not reborn. Their numbers have been greatly reduced since the Deity War.

Demons: These creatures of darkness, including the Archdemons, Barzuls, and Spikels, once served the children of Kuunkierto. Most are hideous to look upon. They are often tall and intimidating. Their faces often resemble a mockery of a human's, but may resemble other things. They may have the head of a goat, or cloven hooves. They may appear cat-like. Many have leathery bat wings. Some, like the Eyrenals, are beautiful, and have feathery wings in black or red that appear very similar to their angelic counterparts. Yet another, are the

Shadack demons, the least common of all the races. They appear as incorporeal shadows and have the ability to attempt to possess a mortal. Doing so may be dangerous for them, however, because if their host dies while they still inhabit their bodies, they are destroyed themselves. The Eyrenals are the only race of demon able to retract their wings and blend in, but very few ever choose to do so. Demons are often proficient in martial weapons and dark magic, including life-draining spells or mind control enchantments. Their weapons are imbued with the unholy power to drain life from a being, and only the most powerful healers have any hope of healing the wounds these weapons inflict. Like the angels, they do not resurrect when destroyed, and their numbers are also much smaller than they once were.

Nature Spirits: Kamara's children created nature spirits for themselves to act as their heralds. Most are various animals, but no species has more than two spirit animals among them. These creatures are massive in size, usually between ten and twenty feet tall regardless of size of their non-spirit counterparts. They are all very strong and will defend the natural world with force when necessary. There are also other nature spirits, such as dryads, nymphs, and other fae. All of them, animal and fae alike, are gifted with the ability to wield nature spells similarly to a druid, including healing and elemental magic. The fae races are also adept at mind control. Like their counterparts, they never age but can be destroyed. It is unknown how many of the nature spirits are still alive today, as very few participated in the Deity War and remain in hiding. Not many are aware of their existence at all.

Coming in 2016!

Destiny's Choice

A Land of Destiny Novel (Book3)

About the Authors:

D.S. Schmeckpeper (a.k.a. Dottie and Steve Schmeckpeper) live in Florida, USA. They are a husband and wife team who work together to create the Land of Destiny series. Both have loved the Fantasy genre for many years and have wasted way too much time playing fantasy-based games. Dottie was a vocal performance major in college, before she decided a liberal arts major was not for her. Ironic, huh? They have two wonderful twin boys, who are three at the time of this publication. They are the light or their parents' lives. Steve does the artwork and comes up with many of the story concepts. Dottie brings the ideas to life. When not working, writing or drawing, the pair love to take their children to Florida's many amusement parks, and can often be found there.

If you've enjoyed this book, please consider leaving a review and/or rating on the site you purchased it from. Authors, especially Indie authors, depend on feedback from our readers to help us improve. Thank you very much.

Check us out on Facebook to see upcoming news, excerpts and more of Steve's artwork!

https://www.facebook.com/DestinysWings

Also, on Twitter!

https://twitter.com/DS_Schmeckpeper